BLAZE

BLAZE

JOAN SWAN

BRAVA

KENSINGTON PUBLISHING CORP.
www.kensingtonbooks.com

BRAVA BOOKS are published by

Kensington Publishing Corp.
119 West 40th Street
New York, NY 10018

ISBN-13: 978-0-7582-6640-8
ISBN-10: 0-7582-6640-5

First Kensington Trade Paperback Printing: October 2012

10 9 8 7 6 5 4 3 2 1

Printed in the United States of America

ONE

Keira O'Shay flexed and released her fingers around the grip of her Colt AR-15 assault rifle, her mind on the little boy inside the religious-cult compound. The boy she'd been tracking for over a year now.

She squinted through the hundred-and-twelve-degree heat rippling off the hard, dry Nevada landscape. The ranch house and barns of the property danced in watery distortion, shifting like reflections in a house of mirrors.

Fitting. From the very beginning this situation had taunted Keira with reflections of her own twisted past.

Her commander, FBI Senior Special Agent Angus West, leaned his hip against the bed of an agency pickup ten feet away, arguing logistics with the incident commander from ATF while she and her team steamed like vegetables in their SWAT fatigues.

Fucking departmental posturing. Fucking egos. Fucking waste of time.

So much precious time already depleted in briefing, staging, arming, negotiating.

Gunfire cracked through the air, followed by the *clang, clang, clang* of bullets against metal. The sting of anxiety burned across Keira's ribs. The half-empty bottle of Gatorade exploded beneath the crush of her fingers, orange liquid drenching her hand. She chucked the shattered plastic at the dirt.

Crack. Crack-crack-crack.

"Don't return fire, you idiots." She clenched her teeth to keep her voice low so the team, hovering beneath the shade of a single pathetic Joshua tree nearby, wouldn't hear. "My boy's in there."

Her stomach coiled tighter, something she hadn't believed possible. She already felt like a bottle of champagne—shaken and still corked.

Enough of this bullshit.

She pushed off the SWAT van that acted as a barrier to the hostilities. The men supposedly in charge had ceased their dispute to watch FBI and ATF agents scuttle among pickups and outbuildings for cover.

"Excuse me, sir." From beneath the brim of her uniform ball cap, she trained her eyes on Angus. "What are we waiting for? A neon sign flashing 'Armageddon this way'?"

The ATF leader standing across from Angus sliced her with a critical sneer. One that indicated he had a dick the size of a peanut and had to compensate by making everyone else's life a living hell.

Angus's gaze remained locked on the other man, his demeanor controlled as he raised his index finger to Keira.

Don't push it.

Yeah, she got it. Didn't even need her clairaudient abilities to get that message as loud as the gunshots across the compound and as clear as the growing risk she faced with every passing moment.

But, dammit, this waiting was killing her. She wanted that little boy. Wanted to see him. Wanted to touch him. Wanted to prove that the kid was real, and that she hadn't spent the last year of her life chasing a ghost only to end up in the same haunted, hopeless, helpless place she'd started.

She didn't understand the gravity of her needs. Only that they'd driven her from the moment she'd first seen his photograph. He was important to her. She just didn't know why. Just as she didn't know why another vague anxiety gnawed low in her belly. One she'd cued into as soon as she'd stepped onto the scene.

She scanned the landscape again, searching for the source of her discomfort. Clusters of FBI, ATF, local deputies, military personnel, support staff, and vehicles cluttered the staging area. Nothing stood out.

She reached into the front pocket of her jumpsuit for the child's photo, a talisman of sorts now after all this time. The moment she touched it, a young voice loped through her head.

Thia, edo eeme. Edo eeme. Thia.

Whatever that meant. She couldn't exactly ask the missing boy's father why the kid was speaking another language without exposing her clairaudient abilities. And if that happened, she faced an ugly path of workplace inquisitions, governmental psychological testing, probable suspension, and possible termination. If her powers, or more important, the source of her powers, caught the wind, her life and the lives of those she loved would hit the fan.

Keira studied the boy's face for what had to be the thousandth time over the past year. And wondered, for what had to be the hundredth time in the last few hours, whether she'd recognize him now, three years older than he was in the picture. Would his eyes still be warm and trusting? Would his face still be round and full of color? Would he even still be alive?

Crack-crack-crack. Clang-clang-pfffft.

Keira looked up just as one of her fellow agents, crouched behind a metal storage shed for cover, bucked and pitched backward. She sucked an audible gulp of air. "Oh, shit." Her stomach clenched and burned. Two backup agents swept in, hooked their hands under the armpits of her academy buddy, and dragged him to safety.

"Was that . . . Connor Royal?" she asked.

"Yes." Angus pressed his fingers to the earpiece feeding him information over the airwaves as he spoke to her. Sweat glistened on skin the color of fresh ground coffee beans. "It was Royal. Not a fatal hit. They're bringing him out."

Nerves split her professional shell. She couldn't stand it anymore. Screw all this testosterone. "Are you going to send us in or wait for him to kill our whole squad?"

She'd catch hell for the attitude later, in private. Now, Angus focused on Keira with his customary intensity. "Yes. You're going in."

The other leader threw his shoulders back. "Now, wait just a—"

Yes! She tuned out the argumentative ATF ass and swung back to signal her team.

Finally. She could get her hands on this kid, turn him over to his father, and get the hell on with her life. And even save a few other lives in the process. Win-win.

"Wait." Angus put a hand on her arm and signaled the team to hold tight. "This isn't a rescue mission. Not yet."

"Sir, you can't be serious." She glanced back to make sure the ATF asshole wasn't within earshot. "There are women and children—"

"I'm dead serious, Keira. At this point, the best way to salvage the lives of those women and children is to take out the shooter. Either by capture or elimination." He pulled the Colt from her hand and slapped a Remington sniper rifle in its place, then released a five-by-seven photograph from his clipboard and held it out. "This is your target: Andre Rostov. And lose the attitude, would you?"

Her new mission came into sharp focus. Sweat slid between her shoulder blades.

She studied the photo, but didn't take it. She wasn't ready.

The man in the image was in his late fifties with nearly white hair and a clean-shaven jaw exposing a fair share of wrinkles and age spots over a plain, expressionless face. Light eyes, a color she couldn't determine, beamed with intelligence and defiance.

"Rostov's got another one of our teams isolated at the west end of the main house." Angus drew her attention. "Pinned between a silo and an outbuilding."

"Once we pull the kids out—"

"No, Keira." He had his boss face on. Hard. Demanding. Unyielding. "You are going to take him out of the equation before he starts handing weapons to those kids."

A shiver tracked her spine. She stepped closer, forced her voice lower. "But, Angus—"

"No buts. This is what you were trained for. You are our best chance of getting this guy before he hurts anyone else." He pushed the photo toward her. "Do it for Royal."

She peered toward the ranch house—the lower level windows boarded with shutters, the charcoal gray roof and stark white siding wafting in the inhumane heat.

Yes, she'd been trained. Yes, she could kill in self-defense. But, elimination? Assassination? Murder?

The department picnic two months prior flickered in her head with images of Royal's young wife and their two toddler daughters.

The fingers of her empty hand curled into her palm and squeezed hard before she reached for the picture. At the first touch, a tangle of sounds and voices snarled in her head. She let them murmur in the background until she was ready to unravel and apply.

That other, unrelated unease resurfaced, chewing at her belly. And it definitely wasn't coming from the photo. She glanced over the various groups again. Looking for . . . what? What the hell was bugging her on this subversive level?

"We'll get Tony's kid out, Keira," Angus reassured. "But to get him out alive, you're going to have to remove the threat, and we both know this maniac won't let you take him alive."

Yes, she did know. Which was why she wanted to get to the boy so badly. "I understand, sir."

Keira tuned out the background voices of her colleagues, the rumble of vehicles, the murmur of generators. One by one, she sorted through the sounds: the clink of glass, bubbling liquid, a ringing timer. When none of those made sense, she focused on the disjointed voices. *Control group . . . placebo . . . quantitative results . . .*

The skin over the back of her neck tingled. "Angus, are you sure about the intel on this? A religious group?"

He pulled his attention from a map spread over the hood of a pickup. "Why?"

One more check of Rostov's picture, just to make sure . . . *Absolute measure . . . controlled environment . . . clinical trials . . .*

"I just . . ." *Hear voices that tell me it's wrong.* How fast did she want to lose her job and land in a pink padded room wearing a straitjacket? "Look at him. Not much of a Koresh look-alike. I mean, come on, he's no cult leader."

"It was your research that led us here."

"To find the kid. I knew it was a commune of some sort, but I never said it was a religious compound."

"Well, others have, and it's a moot point anyway. He's now shooting and holding hostages."

And she'd been entrusted with this boy's safety. Angus was right. The underlying purpose of this ranch didn't matter anymore. What mattered was rescuing a child from a nut job. Reuniting a loving father with a stolen son. She'd seen the court custody papers, the ex-wife's psych evaluations. Now, she'd all but proven the abuse allegations.

Angus yelled at the ATF commander, huddled among other bigwigs, "My sniper's ready. Get me your best agent to guide her in."

Sniper. Keira's lip lifted toward a grimace.

"Ransom, suit up." The man's growl stilted the conversation of several agents loitering around the back of an ATF van. "You're going in."

Keira's brain was still pushing around *sniper,* searching for a comfortable fit in some unused crevice when the name registered.

"What?" she asked Angus. "Who?"

"I don't know. Someone named—"

"Ransom," the asshole yelled again. "Get moving. You're babysitting the Feebs' prima donna."

Ransom? Her stomach jumped and went icy hot.

The hostage she'd vowed to rescue and the cult leader she'd agreed to kill faded in her mind, replaced by memories of a man she hadn't heard from in three years. A man who shared her complex past and still secretly held far too much of her heart.

Lord, she could not afford to think about Luke right now. Besides the name had to be a coincidence, because Luke *was not* an ATF agent. He was a fire captain in northern California. He wouldn't be at a government-run siege in the Nevada desert.

Surely there were thousands of men by the last name of Ransom in the western United States. She scanned the ATF camp, focused on one group of swarming men, and swallowed hard. Okay, maybe hundreds named Ransom who were also tall, well-built, and blond like the one suiting up, his back toward her.

There have to be, because Luke is not ATF. Shit, he's not.

The man dropped a black bulletproof vest over his navy uniform T-shirt. He leaned down to tighten the holster securing a semiautomatic at his jean-covered thigh and grabbed a Ruger submachine gun handed to him by a colleague.

Keira's stomach jumped. Jesus, the fluid movements, the tilt of his head . . . they created a delicious, familiar pressure in her chest. Which terrified her. *Please, no. Please, no.* Keira held her breath as the man pivoted toward his commander.

Before he'd fully turned, her stomach bottomed out. She knew the slant of that cheekbone. Knew the angle of that chin. Knew the slope of those lips. In fact, every inch of her body knew that mouth.

No! Dammit. Luke is not *ATF.*

But denial couldn't erase the fact that he stood yards away, just as striking as the day she'd left him for the academy. Same intense blue eyes. Same long legs. Same wide shoulders. Same commanding presence.

Same Luke.

"Screwed. I'm *so* screwed." Keira turned her back before Luke spotted her. Not to hide—far too late for that. Just to regroup. Just to get herself together before she faced him.

Angus looked up from his map. "What?"

"This vest is screwed." She yanked at the canvas-covered Kevlar as her heart scrambled for a dark corner. "Who last wore this thing, a two-year-old? It's choking me."

He turned from the truck and took hold of the straps, tugging to test the fit. "It's fine. Fits perfect."

"Then why the hell can't I breathe?"

"It's called anxiety and it's totally normal. Relax, O'Shay." The hint of a pride-filled smile turned his dark lips. "You're the best in the nation."

"Don't start bragging." The thought made her cringe. "You know how guys go all weird when they hear that."

Angus's attention locked on someone behind Keira. Luke. She knew. Her guts knew. She could *feel* him, as if his presence physically compressed her lungs until she could drag in only a wisp of air on each breath.

Angus sidestepped her with his hand out in greeting. "Agent Ransom, you're going to be taking care of our sharpshooter. And I promise you, she does not have an ounce of prima donna in her blood."

She?

The word popped into her head from nowhere, vibrating like an echo. The same way thoughts from images played beneath her skull. God, it was happening already. She hadn't even spoken to him, hadn't even looked him in the eye, and her powers were rising like a kite in high wind.

Keira's eyes closed. She allowed herself a split second of dread, of doubt, of pain, before she drew all her strength into her core. Then she envisioned a metal door shutting out every agonizing memory and secured the shield before facing the men.

Luke's clear blue eyes dropped from Angus's face to Keira's. Her stomach sizzled as his gaze held hers. His flat, impersonal expression lasted two full seconds before shock set in. The reaction would have been comical if it hadn't been so quickly followed by a look of heated, almost sickening, contempt.

Her psychic armor took a heavy hit.

"Don't let that sweet face fool you, Agent Ransom," Angus said. "Mobile targets, mobile platforms, extreme distance, night shots, you name it, O'Shay will hit it. She's a pit bull."

For an extended second, his eyes remained steady and unblinking on her face. A deep vertical line pulled between his brows, as if someone had smacked him upside the head and he hadn't quite recovered.

He hadn't had a haircut in months, hadn't shaved in at least two days, hadn't been using enough sunscreen. And he looked . . . amazing. Absolutely mind-numbingly amazing.

Asshole.

"Yyyyyeah. You could say that." His tone suggested an unsavory subject. He squinted at Angus. "Sir, can I have a word?"

Goddamned sonofabitch. Keira's millisecond of admiration splintered, and the hurt and anger from their past boiled to the surface. "If you have something to say, *Agent* Ransom, say it to my face."

Luke's eyes reconnected to hers with a cold snap. He shifted his weight and cocked his hip, a move she'd once found sexy but which now struck her as arrogant.

"Okay, *Agent* O'Shay." He put the same venom on her title as she had on his. "Are you qualified to do this job, or are you just a pretty face for the news cameras? 'Cause I'm risking my ass here, and I'm sure as hell not doing it for you."

Air siphoned into her throat with the sucking sound of a gut-punch. Her stomach responded with a painful hitch. After so much time, he could still stab her right in the heart.

That came out really fucking wrong.

The thought drifted from Luke, but his expression remained unchanged. And after that greeting, he didn't deserve the benefit of the doubt.

She forced the imprisoned air out of her lungs. Refused to wince at the pain centered beneath her ribs. And faced Angus.

"I'm not going to recite my résumé for this . . ." *Pissant.* "If he doesn't trust me, get someone else to take me in."

The ATF commander invaded the group. "Problem here?"

"No." Luke's chin went up. Stubborn sonofabitch never changed. "No problem."

"Then get on with this before that fucker starts throwing bodies out windows."

Luke's boss stomped toward their camp, wiping the sweat from his bald head with a handkerchief.

Keira pulled off her ball cap, tossed it on the hood of the truck, smoothed her hair into a ponytail, and pulled on her helmet.

"Keira," Angus said, "*is* there a problem here?"

Hell, yes. "Nope." Two could play this game. "I don't give a flying fuck whether he goes or not. I can handle this on my own."

You always could. Never needed anyone. Sure as hell never needed me.

Luke's thoughts pierced her skull. She gritted her teeth and forced them out. Luke Ransom's head was the very last place on earth she belonged.

"Play nice, Keira," Angus directed in low tone before re-focusing on the map and circling an area of the main building with his dark finger. "We have reports of your target in this area. If you position yourself here"—he tapped the paper—"you have opportunities for shots here and here. This is your point of entrance. This your exit. Got it?"

Keira nodded once, her gaze scouring the floor plan she'd already memorized.

Angus dropped a hand on her shoulder. "Alive is preferred. Dead is perfectly acceptable."

Ice spread through her belly, but she met his intense eyes. "Yes, sir."

"Your call sign is Sniper Six." He gave her a gentle push off. "Be careful out there."

"Yes, sir." She started toward the building without waiting for Luke. Her legs pumped hard in an effort to put space between them, but he caught up to her in seconds.

"Keira." He pulled her around by the arm. "What the hell is going on?"

Her lungs decompressed on a whoosh of air. Three long years she'd imagined all the possible ways they might connect again. What they might say. How it might go. None ever slumped to this level. So many daydreams wasted. So many fantasies shattered.

She dug in her pocket for the two photos. The first landed against his chest with a satisfying thump. "This is the man I'm going to either capture or kill." When he took the photo, she hit him with the second. "This is the kid I'm going to find and rescue. Keep your eyes open. If you spot either one, signal me. And stay out of trouble, Ransom, 'cause you're not on my favorites list. I have enough to think about besides saving your sorry ass."

She started toward the ladder leading to the roof again. Luke easily kept pace with her. "When did you become a fucking *sniper*?"

The dig pinged off her psychic shield, leaving a dent. Everything he did, said, thought, left a dent. "Probably about the same time you became a fucking *ATF agent*."

A local deputy stood at the base of the metal ladder, securing it against the building. "Be careful up there."

"Will do." Keira slanted the strap of her Remington over her chest and whipped the weapon around to lie against her back.

"Watch where you're throwing that thing," Luke groused behind her.

"If I did," she shot over her shoulder, "it would break your perfect nose."

She scaled the ladder with ease. With cool metal beneath her hands, her quads pumping as she ascended, bittersweet memories of her years as a firefighter flooded her mind. The fact that Luke now tailed her only shoved her into a time warp. And as soon as they landed on the rooftop together, crouched and ready to attack, their three years apart evaporated. No two people worked together better—professionally, if not personally.

Only now they weren't focused on drowning a fire. They were hunting a psychotic Russian cult leader holding hostages. Kevlar replaced turnouts, subguns replaced Pulaskis, helmets replaced breathing apparatus. Easy reminders of the bizarre event that changed their lives. All seven members of their hazmat unit had gone into that firefight as ordinary people. Six had emerged permanently altered. One hadn't survived. Keira often wondered if he had been the lucky one.

Focus. Get in, hit the target, find the boy, get out.

She scuttled across the roof toward the single window along the second-story wall, planted her back against the peeling paint, and searched for Luke. He was right there, mirroring her position on the opposite side of the glass.

Despite the intel Angus insisted was accurate, something felt wrong. Wrong location. Wrong target. Wrong . . . something. And Keira couldn't tell if the sensation was expert intuition or some enhanced psychic ability, which was really annoying.

She eased forward, glanced through the window. No one inside the bedroom-turned-office, but the laboratory set up in the corner explained all the sensations Keira had received through Rostov's image. Sink, microscope, slides, test tubes, beakers, floor-to-ceiling glass-fronted cabinets filled with chemicals.

What the hell?

The thought wasn't Keira's, although it echoed her own. Luke also squinted through the glass, studying the mini-lab.

She tilted her chin toward the radio speaker on her shoulder to check in with Angus and pushed the TRANSMIT button.

An explosion rumbled through the opposite end of the

main building, as if Keira's action had detonated a bomb. Her heart punched toward her throat. In mirror reflex actions, she and Luke braced themselves against the wall. When the roar of the explosion dimmed, she tried again.

"Sniper Six to base. Update. Over."

"Base to SS." Angus's cool tone crackled over the radio. "Target has relocated. Hold for intel. Over."

"Dammit." She dropped her head back against the siding, just a second to catch her breath.

Is she really the best shot? What the hell is going on here?

Luke hadn't spoken. At least not out loud. He still peered around the corner of the building, watching the fire.

"Yes," she snapped. "I really *am* the best shot, and you are—evidently—still the jackass who thought I'd fall on my face when I joined the Bureau."

His head snapped around with a *what-the-fuck?* expression, then eased. "I will admit to the jackass part, but for the record, I never expected or wanted you to fall on your face." His eyes narrowed. "Are you reading minds now?"

"Don't be an idiot. Even if I were, which I'm not, your mind would be the last place I'd inhabit."

She darted to Luke's side and followed his gaze around the wall toward the opposite end of the compound. A twenty-foot section of the two-story building in the distance spit flames from every window. Black smoke rolled toward the sky, and somewhere deep inside the structure, sparks surged like a fiery volcano. Cobalt blue sparks. The kind she'd only seen one other time in her life. Five long years ago.

She'd been with Luke then, too.

That reality overwhelmed her. The questions, the repercussions, the complications so vast she simply couldn't process them in the moment. She knew this incident was about to change her life, yet she had no idea how. And, worse, she had absolutely no control over that change. She was on a raft thrown in the rapids with no oars. Hold tight for the ride. Pray you don't drown on the trip.

Every priority in her life altered. Instantly.

Screw following orders. Screw killing Rostov. She had to find that boy.

TWO

Keira jabbed at the radio on her shoulder. "SS to base. *Update*. Over."

She needed more intel to locate the children. This ranch house was a sprawling campus of additions and outbuildings, silos and barns. The kid she'd come for could be anywhere.

"Base to SS. Abort mission. Repeat, abort mission and return to base. Over."

"That's more like it." Luke started for the ladder, reaching for Keira's sleeve when she didn't immediately follow. "Come on, Sniper Girl. Party's over. We'll figure this out on the ground."

"No." She pulled back. "I have to find that kid."

"Keira." Luke's voice fell to a warning tone. "Think about this. You and me on top of this inferno, that lab, those sparks. You think this is all coincidence? Are you sure there even *is* a kid?"

Damn him. She hated the way he dug into her insecurities. Worse, she despised the fact that he could be right. "Not everything in life is a conspiracy, Luke."

But because she fully realized this could be one of those times, Keira crouched, took a deep breath, and let it out slowly as she closed her eyes. As the chaos around her faded, she laid her palm against the black-asphalt roof shingles. The tiles burned from hours searing in the sun and singed her skin. She blocked the pain. Focused. Listened.

Screams rattled inside her head. The screams of a child. Or . . . children. She winced, searching for their origin—present or past? To be sure these were voices and not her own memories, she searched deeper.

I'm scared. I wanna go home.

Where's my mommy? I want my mommy.

Definitely statements from the present. Aside from *I'm scared*, those words would never have come out of Keira's mouth as a kid.

Which meant the children were still inside these burning buildings.

A rolling wave of fear rocked through her, leaving nausea in its wake. Not *her* fear. The collective fear of the children inside. It tilted her equilibrium and she fell forward, hit the asphalt with her knees. Fresh sweat broke on her face in one burst of dampness. She sucked at the hot desert air to keep from retching.

"Are you okay?" Luke's voice came from over her shoulder.

Anger helped distract her from the queasiness. Why so many new powers all at once? Why here? Why now? Even back when she and Luke had been far more connected, her powers had never ramped this aggressively.

She ignored the nagging questions and listened harder, searching through the cries and screams and voices for something more.

Take the children to the south tower.

A man's voice. With an accent. Russian accent. Rostov. Things were finally falling into place.

Protect Mateo with your life.

Keira siphoned a breath. Mateo. He was here. Alive.

When she opened her eyes, Luke was still there, hovering. "And the verdict is?"

"The kids are here," she said. "They're moving to the south tower."

She evaluated the next roofline, connected by slanted, steaming asphalt, then turned back to Luke. "Look, this isn't your fight. Follow orders. Get back to camp. Until I know nothing more can be done, I'm going to stay. I can't just leave them."

Anguished indecision creased the corners of his eyes as he squinted toward the south tower. Those intoxicating blue eyes she'd seen in laughter, love, ecstasy, agony, anguish, fury, and finally betrayal.

She wondered, in that fleeting moment it took him to make the decision between duty and conscience, if he still believed she'd betrayed him in the end. Not that it mattered. Nothing would erase the years of regret that dogged her whenever he crossed her mind.

But the past was the past. She had enough demons to deal with. And there would be more if she didn't get moving.

She pushed to a crouch, resting hands on knees until her head was solid and her stomach was steady.

"If it's your fight, it's my fight." Luke used his weapon to gesture toward the other roofline. "We stick together, right? I've got your back."

A fist of warmth clenched at the center of her body. She knew he wasn't taking on her personal fight. Nor was he following through because he cared. This was loyalty. This was honor. This was sticking with your partner to the end, the way Royal's partner had gone back under fire and dragged him to safety.

She jogged across the roof's heated shingles, her focus homed in on the south tower, but another of Luke's thoughts slipped beneath her skull.

This decision better not haunt me for the next three fucking years like my last one.

Her feet stumbled. She stopped and twisted around. "What?"

"Keep moving." He shoved her forward. "And stay out of my head."

The radios on their shoulders squawked simultaneously. "Base to SS," Angus's voice crackled over the line, his Cajun accent emerging with his increased frustration. "Repeat, abort mission and return to base. Over."

Keira snapped her scattered brain cells into place and responded as she ran south. "SS to base. Headed toward south tower in search of hostages. Over."

"Base to SS. Negative. I repeat, *negative*. Get your ass back here, Keira. Over."

She cringed and picked up speed. The faster she found the boy, the faster she could obey his orders and return.

She reached a dip in the rooflines and leaped from one slanted surface to the other. Luke followed, without pause, without question. He'd always been the best partner, dependable, supportive, loyal. Until everything changed.

By the time she crouched at the window, Luke stood on the opposite side, looking tattered and sexy as hell sporting his rifle and that goddamned semiautomatic strapped to his thick, muscular thigh. Why, why, *why* did she find that so . . . hot?

Because she was freaking depraved, that's why.

"Base to SS," Angus rasped in her ear. "Come in. Over."

"Damn." Irritation rolled beneath her skin. "He's relentless."

Luke smirked. "No wonder you two get along so well."

"Ha-ha." She hit the speaker with one hand and wiped at the sweat drenching her face with her other forearm. "SS to base. Over."

"Keira." Anger shook her boss's typically controlled tone. "Get. Your. Ass. Back. Here. Now. Over."

All she could do was placate and stall. "Yes, sir. Over."

Keira peeked through the glass. Children filed into the room like good little soldiers, ranging in age from toddlers to teenagers. Two women flanked them at the front and end of the line.

"Oh, my God." Excitement surged. "They're here, Luke."

"Do you see the kid you came for?"

"I can't tell from here."

Another woman entered the room with a tray of Dixie-size white cups and passed them out to the children.

"Oh, no. No, no, no." She pushed the speaker on her radio. "SS to base. Two dozen children identified in south tower. Request rescue operation. Over."

Several moments passed with no response while gunfire continued to echo through the compound.

Luke peered back into the window. "What are they giving them?"

"I don't think I want to know."

Looks like a fucking Jonestown rerun to me.

Luke's thought resonated with Keira, both intellectually and emotionally. "Like a Jonestown-slash–Waco rerun."

His gaze shot to Keira's face. "What the hell? You *are* reading minds. That is just . . . wrong. Besides, it's creepy. Knock it off."

"Base to SS," Angus cut in. "*Report back* to base for rescue briefing. Over."

"Like hell." She wouldn't let these kids drink poison just so those testosterone-laden ego-mongers could sit around and make a pretty little plan. "SS to base. No time. Children in immediate jeopardy. Going in. Request air support. Over."

She sidestepped closer to the entry point, flipped the butt of her rifle toward the window, and sent Luke a quick look. "Watch yourself. Glass coming."

With little more than a rough plan in mind—break in, separate women and children, evacuate—she lifted the gun overhead.

Before she had a chance to swing, the window exploded from the inside. The house rocked beneath her feet. Glass sliced the air. A rush of searing heat body-slammed her backward. She went airborne. Thoughts flipped through her mind, fast, disjointed. *Hold on to the gun. Was Luke hit? Don't drop the gun. If I live, I'm so getting fired. Don't let go of the gun. Please let Luke be o—*

She hit hard on her back, knocking all thoughts from her mind. Her rib cage compressed like a sponge. Air squeezed from her lungs. Pain paralyzed her spine and limbs. She skidded across the roof. Hit another vertical surface. Bounced off. Rolled. A brick chimney blurred in her vision on the downward slide. The rifle butt stabbed her stomach. *Don't ever release your weapon.* She tightened her fingers around the Remington. Her knuckles scraped. Burning asphalt tore at her knees. And she kept sliding.

The edge of the steep roof appeared in her head, followed by a thirty-foot drop. Panic sliced in her chest. She struggled for traction, digging with her boots, clawing at the roof with the rifle. Smoke muddled her sense of direction. Pain stabbed through the right side of her head. Gravity dragged her toward the roof's edge.

Her legs plunged over the side. Swung free. Her hips dropped off. Her belly. Her chest.

This is it. Free fall.

She squeezed her eyes shut. Held her breath. Braced for the hit.

The clank of metal vibrated in her head like a gong. Quaked through her hands, down her arms. But no free fall. No hit.

Swinging. She was still swinging. She opened her eyes

and made one last desperate grab for something, anything, to hold on to. Her hand hit metal. She curled her fingers. Held fast. Looked up.

The sky above lunged with furious charcoal billows of smoke. Flames spiked along the roof's edge. Her fingers gripped a rain gutter lining the eaves, her Remington wedged between metal and wood. A perilous savior.

Never release your weapon.

In this case that advice had saved her in an entirely different way than her academy instructor had intended. But she wasn't out of trouble yet.

She glanced down, assessing the risk of letting go and falling as she'd been taught to minimize injury. Only, the ground below her was littered with old lawn mowers, buckets, engines, appliances, tools. If she dropped here, she'd probably break her neck.

The muscles in her arms burned. Fingers slipped on sweat. Vision faded at the edges.

She closed her eyes and opened her mouth. "Luuuke!"

Nothing came back but the crackle of fire, the whoosh of smoke.

A whimper bubbled up her throat. Fear for Luke pressed in, adding to her panic. If he was hurt because of her damned need to push forward when they'd been ordered to retreat . . .

No. She couldn't face that now. Ever.

She'd have to take her chances in the junkyard and drop. Regroup. Search for Luke—

A hand closed around her wrist. She sucked a breath. Looked up as another hand clamped over her opposite forearm. Big, strong, warm hands. Luke's hands.

Relief pushed a mewl from her chest.

He shimmied to the edge of the roof on his stomach, squelching the flames directly beneath him. Fire burned around his arms and shoulders but didn't catch the cotton

tee or scorch his exposed forearms. He remained untouched. Sooty, sweaty, but otherwise untouched. She
knew his powers, had seen them in action before. But now
found herself wondering if he'd also experienced an increase in his abilities during their short time together.

"Climb!" he ordered.

Shit. She didn't think she had the energy to climb. But
neither did she have a choice. She tightened her stomach
muscles to get her feet swinging, building momentum.
With her fingers knotted in Luke's forearms, she threw her
leg up and over the edge of the roof. Luke released one of
her hands, grabbed her thigh, and jerked her the rest of the
way onto the angled surface.

"Oh, my God." She didn't let herself experience the
shock hovering at the boundaries of her mind, for fear it
would take over. "Are you hurt?"

"Me? You're the one who almost fell to your death." He
breathed through the words. "Are *you* hurt?"

"I . . ." She mentally scanned her body, wincing at all the
pains bursting to life in the wake of the adrenaline rush.
"Don't know. Give me . . . a second."

"We don't have a second. Rescue's here."

The familiar roar of fire filtered in, as did the continued
gunshots and mini-explosions throughout the compound.
But the *whap-whap-whap* of helicopter blades drew her
gaze up.

"Let me have a quick look." Luke bent over her, inter-
cepting her view of the circling Black Hawk.

His experienced hands unlatched her helmet and swept
over her skull, down her neck, across her shoulders. The
touch infused her with confidence, easing the stress. Her
gaze held on the pulse at his throat, strong, fast. Familiar.
And she imagined she could still feel it beneath her lips as
they'd made love.

"Hey. What're you doing?" He snapped his fingers in her

face, startling her out of the drift. "Don't go out now. If you make me throw you over my shoulder and hoof you back to staging, I'll drop you at the feet of your team. You'll never live it down."

He patted her arms, picked up her hands, and sucked air between his teeth. "That's going to hurt like an SOB in a few hours."

The warm, tingly, feel-good sensation flowing through her skin everywhere he touched was replaced with irritation.

"Everything's going to hurt like an SOB in a few hours." Worst of all, her heart. She'd made a point of avoiding contact with him for a reason. Recovering from this run-in would not be fun.

"I'm okay." She pulled away from his touch and tucked her feet underneath her, pushing up with significant effort. "Or I will be."

Which brought her mind back around to the reason she was on this roof in the first place.

"Let's get into position," Luke said. "They're picking us up."

She was going to argue as soon as she gained her feet, but then she straightened and looked over the roof peak. Her gaze locked on the second story of the building where she and Luke had been standing just minutes ago. The explosion hadn't just broken the window. It had blown out the entire wall. In the gaping hole, fire chewed at the drywall and two-by-four remnants.

The kids. Oh, God, *the kids.*

"No. Oh, God, no."

"You can't help them now." Luke directed her to the peak of the roof where the helicopter hovered for retrieval.

Screams vibrated in Keira's head. Real or imagined? Past or the present? She needed answers before she left this roof or she'd never sleep again.

"I have to check." She broke from his hold, met his eyes, pleading without restraint. "I have to. Please."

"Keira—"

A high-pitched scream raked across her skin. A girl, no more than eight or nine, stumbled out of the room and onto the roof. She held her arms out to the sides, and fire crawled from her shoulders to her fingertips, like wings of flame.

Shock succumbed to instinct as Keira patted her chest, searching for something to smother the flames. She fumbled for the straps on her vest. But before she got them un-latched, Luke swept by. He enveloped the girl in his arms, using his body to snuff the fire. When the flames were out, the girl collapsed against him, unconscious.

He carried her toward the rescue location. Overhead, the army Black Hawk maintained its float within the angry smoke, the propeller creating a windstorm of debris and embers. The crew dropped a litter out the open door, an-other helicopter hovering nearby with snipers perched on the ledge of each opening, covering the first.

Luke settled the injured girl into the metal basket as more victims emerged from the fiery pit. A young Hispanic boy carrying an even younger child, both cut and bleeding. A Caucasian teenage girl, blood soaking her blond hair and white shirt. Several African American elementary school-aged kids, stumbling and screaming. All covered in soot. Some with charred clothes and skin.

But no Mateo.

She guided the victims toward Luke and the chopper, all while praying Mateo would miraculously appear. But he didn't.

"Keira!" Luke's call came muffled in the chaos surround-ing them. "Let's go."

She peered into the fire, searching for the sweet little face she'd come for. With her hands cupped around her mouth, she yelled as loudly as she could. "Mateo!"

Luke swung her around by the arm. "Dammit. Get to the chopper."

"But—"

"But nothing. This place is going to—"

His gaze snapped behind her.

Keira felt Mateo with a quick, sharp tug at the center of her chest. She swept around and settled her eyes right on him, where he lingered in the background.

"Mateo!" She gripped Luke's arms. "Luke, he's alive. He's there. Right *there*."

Luke's gaze skipped between Keira's face and Mateo's. *Right behind a ten-foot wall of flames.*

"That doesn't matter for you." She didn't even try to hide the fact that she'd read his thoughts. "Please, Luke. I can't explain it, but I *need* him."

A flash of irritation darkened Luke's eyes before he yanked from her grasp. "When did you get so into kids?"

That was low, but she didn't care. Because he strapped his rifle over his back and headed right toward that ten-foot wall of flame. Only one example of why she hadn't been able to get him out of her mind or her heart.

"Base to SS," the radio on her shoulder chirped. "Target sighted headed your direction. Mega firepower enabled. Repeat, mega firepower. Over."

Luke must have heard the transmission the same moment Keira did because he pushed into a run just as a man came sprinting through an inside hallway, directly toward Mateo.

Rostov. Wild eyes flashed with menace. Soot-blackened hair stood on end. Forehead bled in rivulets. And several machine guns lay strapped over his chest. One clutched in his hands.

Luke reached for the semiautomatic at his thigh.

Rostov aimed his weapon at Luke's chest and screamed, "Noooooooooo!"

Muscle memory flexed Keira's arms before she made a conscious decision. Rostov appeared in her crosshairs before she decided to aim. But when her finger squeezed the trigger, she was one hundred and fifty percent invested, mind, body, soul.

The familiar pump to her shoulder delivered an almost indescribable sensation—a mix of triumph and vengeance. The target jerked, stumbled backward, and dropped.

Perfect.

A second later, Luke also dropped.

Not perfect.

"Luke! No!" Fire exploded in her chest as if she'd been hit. She sprinted, dropped to her knees, and swept her hands over his body, searching for the injury. "Luke. Luke. Talk to me. Luke, Jesus Christ, *Luke!*"

His golden lashes brushed his cheekbones, drifting up, and exposing glazed blue eyes.

A wash of agonizing relief softened her bones. "Okay, good. Stay with me, now. Where are you hit?"

"Ve-vest," he rasped. "Hit me . . . in the vest."

She let her hands rest for a split second. Let her eyes fall shut. Let the relief sink into every cell. *Thank you, God.*

She pulled at the hem of his shirt, slipped her hands beneath, and palpated his chest and belly. She found his skin intact. No sticky, warm wetness seeping from any wounds. And despite the dire situation, the hardness of muscle, the softness of skin, and the warmth of his body registered in an elemental part of her mind. He felt good. Really damn *good.*

He caught one of her hands. "Help . . . me up."

She pulled him to his feet. Then suddenly remembered—Mateo. She whipped toward the still-burning building so fast, she nearly fell over. "Ma—"

Something gripped her leg. Heat trailed up her thigh,

trekked through her torso, and tied around her heart. The scar low on her back pulsed and she looked down into a big, soft pair of eyes she knew. Mateo.

"Tó'ksera óti tha erhósoon gia ména, Thia."

Given the circumstances, Luke wasn't sure he wanted to know how the boy had found his way around—or through—the fire and to Keira's side in bare freaking feet and without a scratch on him. He appeared out of the smoke like an apparition, wearing nothing but a pair of shorts.

He was small, maybe three or four years old. Yet he remained silent—no tears, no screams. Hardly a flicker of emotion—except for the clear light of terror lingering in his big, dark eyes.

As soon as he grabbed Keira's pant leg, she swooped him up, and he latched on to her neck with both arms as if they belonged together. As if they'd been waiting for each other.

"Oh, God, I was so worried," Keira mumbled into his hair.

The instant affection set off a firestorm of questions in Luke's head. For a frightening instant, he wondered if the boy was hers, but he quickly calculated the numbers and they didn't work. He and Keira had still been together a little over three years ago, and considering her aversion to children had been the wedge between them, Luke was certain this boy was not her son. But if not hers biologically, then what the hell was he to her? And what did he have to do with this situation?

Resentment tangled with suspicion, but his questions would have to wait.

This time, when he pulled her toward the chopper, she didn't resist. She held the boy tight, one arm wrapped around his bare back, the other holding his head securely against her shoulder.

As they approached the rescue site, a crew member dropped a ladder out the open doorway, the metal rungs rolling toward them like red carpet. The thought of scaling that thing while it whipped in the maelstrom of chopper blades made the pain in Luke's torso throb, but he knew the last child he'd lifted into the chopper wouldn't have been stable enough to move from the litter.

He tightened his muscles against the ache, grabbed the bottom of the ladder, and held it firm. At the top, one of the crew started down, tethered by a harness.

Luke grabbed Mateo around the waist with his free arm. "You're going to have to let go of him."

"I'm not the one holding on." She pushed at the boy's chest, but he clung tight.

"Honey, you have to let go," she yelled over the noise. "There's a man at the top. He's going to help you."

The sweet talk didn't work. The kid didn't budge. And Luke hit his patience limit. He wanted to get the hell off this roof and out of this compound.

With the weight of the other man holding the ladder steady, Luke released the rung and pried the boy's arms off Keira's neck. When he lifted the kid away from her body, Mateo squirmed like a wildcat separated from its mother. Battling a forty-pound child into the arms of army rescue strained every screaming muscle in Luke's body.

Out of breath, pain rocketing through him, Luke lunged for the bottom rung again as the rescuer ascended with Mateo strapped into the harness.

"Get up there," he said.

Keira searched Luke's eyes, then laid a hand on his chest. "You go first. I can't sit up there knowing you're down here."

Heat penetrated his Kevlar, slid under his skin, and eased the ache floating beneath his rib cage. The one that never went away, no matter how hard he worked or whom he slept with. But he didn't need to get kicked in the gut again. He could only survive her abandonment once in his life-time.

"You've got blood oozing everywhere," he said. "You're injured . . ." *I need air. I need to get my head on straight.* "Just go, dammit."

After a second of indecision, she took hold of the ladder and climbed. She scaled the rungs like a chimpanzee—effortless, skilled, almost acrobatic. The Bureau SWAT team had definitely honed the skills she'd already cultivated as a firefighter: climbing, rescue, marksmanship.

She tumbled into the chopper, turned, and hung out the side waiting for him to ascend. And in that moment, look-ing up at her, so warrior-princess-like covered in blood and soot, Luke experienced a deep pang of pride for all she'd ac-complished and a wicked stab of guilt that he had tried to stop her from reaching her full potential.

He took a couple deep breaths, readying himself for the climb, and started up. Knowing Keira waited at the top spurred him on, and when he came into reach, she gripped his forearms and dragged him into the chopper the same way he'd drawn her back from the roof's edge.

Luke rolled to his back on the chopper's steel floor and breathed through the pain.

Keira retreated to one side of the cargo space and pulled off her helmet as the boy scrambled into her lap. She tugged the band out of her hair and shook it free. The long, dark strands fell around her face, giving her that soft, tousled, sexy look she'd always had after they'd made love. That memory combined with those that had invaded his brain on the roof—ones that almost seemed to have come from Keira herself—kicked up that familiar ache in his chest.

The kid fisted his hands in her jumpsuit, curled his arms and legs into his body like a turtle, and buried his face against Keira's shoulder as if he wanted to disappear into her.

Keira's troubled gaze focused on the opposite side of the space, where a crew of medics provided emergency care for the other children. The stench of charred skin wafted through the cabin, replaced by fresh smoke as the blades whipped and lifted them into the air.

Luke pushed himself up to sit. The crew member who'd helped pull him in, a young Hispanic man, his head shaved to the skin, poked at Luke's vest. Luke looked down to find the man's finger engulfed in one of the bullet holes.

"Armor-piercing bullets." He lifted dark brown eyes to Luke's face. "You cheated death, man."

That reminder burned into Luke like a hot poker. An intense panic that often invaded after-the-fact and warped the mind waited at the edges of his mind for the perfect ambush. "My lucky day, I guess."

But he doubted it.

As he rolled to his knees and crawled to Keira's side, he slid one hand beneath his vest to feel the backside where the bullet should have—correction, *had*—penetrated. It lay flush with the Kevlar, the smooth metal cool in contrast to the canvas. The Kevlar hadn't stopped the bullet, Luke's skin had. The vest hadn't saved his life; being with Keira, which had amped his powers and created an impenetrable skin, had kept him alive.

He'd lost those enhanced abilities when Keira left three years before. The sensation had been agonizing, as if his life essence was draining. His powers had grown weaker each day until he'd been left with nothing but his basic resistance to fire.

Now, within a few hours of proximity to her, he was once again bulletproof.

Unnerved more than he wanted to admit, he eased to a

spot beside Keira, leaned against the wall, and braced his boots on the floor.

Her sparkling blue eyes narrowed with concern. "I thought you weren't injured."

"Just sore." He avoided focusing on her by watching the boy. "Who is the kid?"

Keira's eyes flicked away. "The son of a coworker."

"Whoa." Heat flared, which was good. Anger was so much easier than longing. "You're going to lie to me? Now? Seriously? Did you forget who you were talking to? What's wrong with him?"

She tried to pull away from the boy, but he stayed plastered to her body. "What do you mean? Is he hurt?"

"No, I mean what's wrong with his mind? He hasn't made a sound."

Her shoulders relaxed, but she slanted him a glare from beneath her lashes. "You've been off a fire engine too long if you can't recognize signs of shock."

An explosion from below rocked the helicopter. Luke dropped an arm around Keira, bracing her against his body. Kids screamed. Medical supplies spilled from their bins and slid across the cargo area.

"What was that?" Keira looked up at him. She was an inch away, her blue eyes strikingly bright against her soot-stained face. Instinct urged him to drop his head. Feel those perfect lips against his. He couldn't count the number of fantasies he had of doing just that over the years, but intellect told him that would be the most asinine thing he'd done in his entire life. Her breath fanned his cheek, tingled down his neck, and tilted his mind off-line. "Luke? What's wrong?"

He refocused and found her inspecting his face. The chopper banked hard right. Luke's gaze drifted past her shoulder and caught on the destruction below. The entire compound blazed. But what held his attention was a silo at

the west end of the property where purple flames shot sky-
ward. Neon purple flames. Peppered with cobalt blue
sparks arcing out in every direction.

What the hell?

"What? What's—?" Keira's gaze followed his. "Oh, my
God."

Luke's mind flashed back five years to the incident that
had changed their lives, and he saw it all again as if it were
happening in the moment—the fiery interior of that military warehouse, the barrels igniting, the explosion. All
seven members of their team jetted through the air like
missiles. Keira lying next to him on the concrete—twisted,
bones broken, turnouts torn, skin charred, unconscious.
And those bright purple flames and cobalt sparks spitting in
the background just before the darkness closed in on him,
too.

Fresh sweat collected along his forehead, his upper lip.
What wasn't she telling him?

"I don't know anything!" Keira answered his unspoken
question with such conviction, he almost believed her. "I
swear. *I don't know.*"

Kakee andras.

They both looked down at the boy. He peeked up at
them from his hiding spot against Keira's chest.

Kakee andras.

"What is he saying?" Luke asked.

Keira's head jerked toward Luke. "You can hear him?"

Realization hit him with a jab to the sternum. The boy
hadn't spoken aloud. Now, not only was she reading minds,
she was putting shit into Luke's head.

She tightened her arms around the boy, her hand drifting
over his long, gold-dusted curls. "I'm not putting anything
into your head. Do you see me drilling holes into your
already-Swiss-cheese-like brain and pouring words in?"

She turned to yell at the pilot over her shoulder, dislodging Luke's arm from where it was still wrapped around her. "Where are we going?"

"Mercy Medical Center," he called back. "Closest trauma center with a burn unit. ETA five minutes."

She settled back against the metal wall and glared at Luke. "And—just for the record—I'm not reading your mind. You're *projecting*. I can't help it if you're thinking loud enough to be heard over a goddamned atomic bomb."

"Sure, let's make it my fault. That's easy." He sat up and angled to get a better view of the destruction receding in the distance as the chopper cut through the sky. "But speaking of atomic bombs, you can start explaining now."

He pinned her with his don't-fuck-with-me glare, but followed her lead on volume. "I want to know what this kid has to do with all that chaos. What the hell is really going on down there. And how the hell I got wrangled into this mess."

THREE

Luke only half-expected a valid response to his demand, so it didn't surprise him when Keira pushed back instead.

She narrowed her eyes and leaned away, as if the distance gave her a better perspective. "Who the hell are you? You sure as shit never talked to me like that before, and you have even less right to talk to me like that now. So curb your attitude, *Agent,* unless you want a big fat harassment write-up in your personnel file."

"Save it for someone you scare, *Agent,* 'cause it sure ain't me. We both know something ugly is going on here. Considering this involves me on a personal level, I'm owed an explanation."

She snorted a disgusted laugh. "Good luck with that."

"You've still got a talent for top-shelf sarcasm."

"Reserved for the privileged few who earn it."

He'd had enough banter. "Listen—"

"No, *you* listen. I am not one of your ATF groupies. I do not respond to your orders. You have obviously forgotten that you are no longer my supervisor—not that I ever listened to you when you were, but that's beside the point. You have also forgotten that I don't like being bossed around." Her voice dipped in warning. "Let me assure you, *that hasn't changed.*"

A wave of respect washed his anger down a notch. He couldn't remember the last time someone talked back to him on or off the job. All his relationships after Keira—if they could be called that—had been more about distraction than challenge. And watching her eyes sparkle at him with attitude and force now, he realized how much he'd missed it. Damn, he'd loved that spunk. That independence. The way she never let him get away with any bullshit. It still pissed him off, but with an edge of excitement that flipped a switch on his sorry-assed life.

He took a slow breath to tame his temper. "You have also, evidently, learned the politically correct way to tell someone to fuck off."

One edge of her mouth kicked up. "And you have evidently learned to read between the lines." But as quick as it came, the humor died away, leaving a suspicious frown. "How did you get in on this incident?"

"I was deployed with our ATF Special Response Team. We were notified early this morning."

Her eyes went distant. He'd already tried to figure out how they'd ended up here together. Tried to make the pieces fit the moment he'd recognized her face, a second after the shock of her boss's introduction had worn off. But he needed a lot more information to make the connections. Connections he would try to pry from her again at the hospital.

Out the open doorway, the medical center's helipad came into view. Before the chopper even hit the ground, personnel swept in and a rush of triage ensued as transporters whisked the injured children through the open emergency room doors.

Once all the critical patients had been taken to the trauma bay, Luke, Keira, and the boy were hustled into a curtained cubicle in a deserted section of the ER and temporarily abandoned.

Grateful for the break, Luke stood at the curtain and watched the action down the hall. He needed a minute to get his head on straight. Only the more time he had to think, the more questions and suspicions cropped up.

Keira sat on the gurney, still holding Mateo. The developing glaze in her eyes made Luke uncomfortable, as if she were turning inside herself. He'd seen it before. And he'd experienced firsthand her panic attacks that usually resulted.

Distraction had always worked best to divert her attention from whatever had dragged her in. What that had been, he didn't know. She'd never wanted to talk once she'd emerged from the terror. In the past, his distraction of choice had been sex. But as nice . . . amazing . . . as that would be now, it was no longer an option.

"How old is he?" Luke asked.

"Um . . ." She looked up, dazed. "Five. I think."

"You know there's something wrong with him, right? No normal kid is this quiet."

"He's been through hell and back—literally." Her eyes cleared, but her fire was still missing. "I don't expect him to act like a normal happy-go-lucky kid."

"Not happy, just normal. He hasn't so much as squeaked and he doesn't have a scratch on him." Luke crossed his arms. "So let's start at the beginning. Who is he? Where is he from? And how did you get caught up in . . . whatever this *really* is?"

"I told you."

He ticked off arguments on his fingers. "One, nobody risks their life for the kid of a *coworker.* Two, this kid was in some type of commune where the same chemicals that fucked us up were burning. Three, he's not normal. Four, us-here-together, after three years?" He lifted his hands and let them drop against his thighs. "Come on. You think I'm—"

"An idiot?" she finished, that familiar energy renewed.

Finally. "You don't really want me to answer that, right?" Her chin dipped in a sign of dwindling patience. He'd seen that before, too. "My *coworker,* an FBI analyst, was in a custody battle for his son when his ex-wife abducted the boy and ran from commune to commune, seeking protection behind religious walls. We tracked him here, and when social services served a warrant for Mateo's return, Rostov went ballistic. And here we are."

Bullshit.

"If you aren't going to believe anything I say, why ask in the first place?" She stood, dug in the pocket of her cargo pants, and pulled out a cell phone. "I've got better things to do than argue with you."

He swiped her phone away. "You can't just read my goddamned mind and act like it's nothing. When did that start?"

She rolled her eyes toward the ceiling in mock thought. "Hmmm, let's see. Oh, yeah . . ." She looked him right in the eye. "Today. With you. Not exactly what I needed, Ransom."

"Now it's *my* fault that *you* can read minds?"

"How about you? You heard Mateo's thoughts. When did *that* start?"

She didn't wait for an answer. Her hand snaked out and snatched the phone back.

"Who are you calling?"

"My boss. That okay with you, *Agent*?" She punched numbers and put the phone to her ear.

"Hey, Angus, it's me. No, I'm okay. Few bumps, bruises, you know. "

She listened as her boss spoke. Luke watched her shift to a more professional persona as she straightened her shoulders, tightened her jaw.

"Yes, sir," she said. "The target has been eliminated. Yes. Thank you, sir. Yes, I have the boy. I'll call Tony now and— He is? But I told him not to come until I knew for sure—Yeah, I know he's excited." Another shift. A little smile on her mouth. "He's a really cute kid. I know. Tony's going to flip when he sees him. Yes. Thanks. Okay. Will do."

She hung up, still smiling. Jealousy slammed Luke like a fist. He had no right to badger. No right to question. No right to anything. But he couldn't keep it in.

"Tony?" he scoffed. "Coworker, my ass. Tony's your— what would you call him? Boyfriend? Lover? Fiancé, maybe? You can't be married. I would have heard about that. And Mateo is his kid. Yeah. This all makes more sense now. Why don't you just call it like it is?"

She stared at him with brows drawn tight. "Maybe because you think you've got it all figured out already, and once you've got that stubborn mind of yours wrapped around an idea, no explanation will pry it loose. Ever think of that?"

"There is one thing I'd really like to know." And it gnawed a hole in his gut. "Why risk everything for *this* kid, but abandon Kat? What does he have that Kat didn't?"

What does Tony have that I didn't?

Her thick-lashed eyes narrowed. "*Abandon* Kat? Abandon . . . ?" She clenched her jaw. "How *dare* you? I *love* Katrina. I *tried* to be what she needed, what *you* needed. You're the one—"

She sucked in air and held it a long second. Then shook her head. "I'm not doing this with you. Not here, not now. Not ever."

"Excuse me." The soft voice sounded distinctly out of place. In the curtained opening, a young woman stood holding two duffel bags. She was in her mid-twenties, dressed in scrubs. "Sorry to, um, interrupt, but, someone dropped these off for you. Agents Ransom and O'Shay, right?"

"Right," Keira said. "Thanks." She cleared her throat and

moved forward with forceful, angry strides, taking her own bag.

The woman flinched as if she thought Keira might bite her. "Okay. No problem. There's a shower in the doctor's lounge that you can use, right down the hall and around the corner. Dietary is sending up some meals, and um, and the volunteers are looking for some clothes for the little boy."

Keira gave one swift nod. "Sure. Appreciate it."

Luke waited until the girl disappeared, then said, "Jesus, Keira. The poor thing nearly peed her pants."

Keira whipped his way. Even tattered, bloody, and carrying a little boy, she still looked as formidable as any one of Luke's fellow ATF agents at their fiercest. "I'm going to get this boy cleaned up for his father. Then I'm going to take a very long, very hot shower, which will hopefully relax me so I don't rip your damn head off when I get back. I suggest you also think about taking a powder, because if that attitude is still in place when I'm done, I won't be responsible for my actions."

With her duffel slung over one aching shoulder and Mateo cradled in the other throbbing arm, Keira strode toward the doctor's lounge.

"Goddamned sonofabitch," she muttered under her breath. "Pissant piece of shit. Stupid, smartass, arrogant fucking *asshole*."

She pushed the lounge door open and, thankfully, found it empty. Then she turned toward the bathroom door on her left, tucked between two vertical rows of metal lockers, fighting the tears glazing her eyes.

One hard shove and she closed and locked the door at her back, then turned and collapsed against it. Slow deep breaths. That's all she needed to hold it together. Slow deep breaths.

Mateo's hand settled against her cheek. *"Min kles, Thia."*

Maybe it was his sweet voice or the understanding tone, but those unknown words from this unknown boy broke her last barrier. The tears she'd been holding back rushed forward, filled her eyes, and spilled over her lashes.

I won't do this. I won't.

But the emotions washed through in a tidal wave. She'd killed a man—without second thought, without hesitation. She'd almost fallen to her own death off a fiery roof. She'd nearly watched the boy she'd spent a year searching for burn to death. Luke had been shot right in front of her eyes. And to top it all off, after not seeing him for the three longest years of her life, they couldn't stop sniping at each other for ten damn seconds.

Nothing made sense. Everything was out of control. Her tight, cohesive world was falling apart.

"Dammit," she whispered, burying her face in Mateo's soft curls.

As if sensing she needed him, the boy clung tight. He remained silent, but she swore compassion and sympathy and a certain calming essence radiated through his little body and melded with hers. Or maybe it was just the flood of tears that left her feeling wrung out.

Either way, after a five-minute crying jag, her thoughts cleared. She was left with the migraine type hangover of blurred vision, a head like a sandbag, and a dull, steady throb in her brain.

Keira squeezed the wetness from her eyes and took in the room. Sparse, utilitarian, clean, and stocked with hospital-grade white towels and washcloths. Even a rolling cart of first-aid supplies.

She sat Mateo on the counter, wincing at the pain in her arms and torso.

Keira glanced over the boy's head toward her reflection in the mirror and paused at the zombie-like image. Her skin was covered in soot, streaked with sweat and blood. A few nasty lacerations made her wince: one on her forehead over her eyebrow, another angled down the opposite side of her chin, and a nice, deep one across her cheekbone.

"Crap." She pushed her hair out of her eyes and turned her head to get a better look. The cut was jagged and filled with grime. "That is so going to scar."

She immediately thought of Teague and relaxed. Her former teammate's healing abilities had come so far in the last year. If anyone could speed her recovery and limit the scarring, Teague could.

The thought of healing brought all her other aches and pains into focus, and she had the urge to strip and shower to uncover all the damage. She should have a couple things x-rayed, too—like her entire spine, rib cage, skull . . . hell, might as well just radiate her entire body. Those chemicals she'd been exposed to years ago had surely already ruined her.

But first things first, she needed to examine the boy beyond a simple once-over.

"Okay, buddy. Let's get a look at—"

He smiled directly into her eyes, and Keira lost every thought. This was the first time she'd gotten a really good look at him.

Achingly adorable, he reminded Keira of a cherub, complete with round cheeks and bow-shaped lips. Long, thick eyelashes trimmed wide eyes. A dimple indented his chin. And his hair, a golden brown beneath the soot, created a fierce halo of curls, the strands as soft as fleece.

She didn't see the boy's father, Tony, anywhere in his features. But something about the little guy . . . *felt* . . . familiar. An intangible warmth created a dull glow beneath her breastbone, a feeling she'd only had in the best of times with the friends she'd adopted as family—the members of her former firefighting team and their families.

"Stand up, buddy." She lifted him until his bare feet

landed on the countertop, leaving black smudges. "This place is going to look like a fire scene when we get out of here. They'll be sorry they let us use it."

She focused on his body, scanning his bony shoulders, his thin chest where his skin outlined his ribs, the indentation of his flat belly that should have been round and healthy. "Little scrawny, aren't you? Didn't they feed you in that sick place?"

She knew about going hungry as a kid. About being left alone, in the dark, in the cold. About being hit, kicked, cut, burned. And she didn't even want to consider how poorly he'd been treated.

After inspecting him, she found no hint of previous abuse, no scars or misshapen limbs. And even after today's trauma, she couldn't find a bump, a cut, not even a bruise.

Protect Mateo with your life. Chemicals. Purple flames. Blue sparks.

An eerie ice developed at her core and spread outward.

"Iremise, Thia mou." Mateo touched her face. Heat spread from his fingers, penetrated her skin, drifted to the cold spot, and warmed it immediately, leaving her with a pleasant buzz, as if she'd had one glass of wine too many.

Luke's gift and Teague's gift rolled into one?

The thought held for less than a second before she laughed at herself. Mateo laughed, too, even though he had no idea what he was laughing at. Unless he also had *her* gift.

"No." She drew out the word, smiling into his eyes. "I've fried too many brain cells today."

She grabbed a handful of washcloths, ran the water in the sink until it warmed, and tossed them in. At her feet, she rummaged in her duffel and pulled out her travel toiletry bag.

"Sorry about this, but I'd rather you smell like a flower than an operating room."

She went through a dozen washcloths, scrubbing every

bare piece of skin before she had to do the inevitable: get the kid naked. Damn, what did she know about five-year-olds—period—let alone a *boy*? Why couldn't Tony's kid be a girl? At least Keira could have stumbled through this with a girl. She'd done it for a year with Kat, the last day as awkward as the first.

The thought brought back all her guilt from the past, all the turmoil she'd fought within herself those last months, all the arguments with Luke trying to make him understand. And damn him for questioning her love for Kat. *Damn him.*

The only way she was going to get through this, the only way she'd gotten through every day of the last three years, was to focus. Mourning the past did nothing but cause pain. Crippling, debilitating pain.

She scooped Mateo from the counter and set him on the floor. "Let's put you down here. It may not change the reality of the situation, but it will change my geographic location to your little boy parts, and the less I see the better. No offense, buddy."

She peeled off his plain tan shorts and the tiniest pair of tighty whities she'd ever seen and wiped him down.

Something on his skin caught her eye. Before she had even focused on the pale purplish scar spreading over his right hip, down his thigh, and around his buttock, a concentrated fiery throb threaded through the matching scar at the base of her spine.

"Oh, my God." The words came out in a whisper as shaky as her breathing. "Oh, my *God.*"

All awkwardness over his nakedness forgotten, she pushed him back a step and scrutinized the mark. No wonder he *felt* familiar. No wonder those flames had blown purple and the sparks shot blue. She pressed a hand to her forehead.

"Poolaki."

The boy's sweet voice drew Keira out of her dark fog. She looked up at his perfectly innocent face.

Those bastards. How could they?

"Poolaki," Mateo said again, his single word thick with a Greek accent. His fingers touched the scar. "Birdie."

"Birdie?" she repeated. The scar did indeed look like a bird. But not just any bird. "Do you speak English?"

His eyes showed no recognition of her question. He simply gave her one of those half-smiles and repeated, "Birdie."

"Yes, it's a birdie." Disappointment deflated her excitement. She lifted her hand and brushed the soft curls off his forehead. "Who are you? Where did you come from?"

Her own questions echoed Luke's demands in the chopper and brought reality back into sharp focus.

He was Mateo Esposito. Tony Esposito's son. And Tony would be coming for him soon. Which brought a whole new complication into her life. How would she tell Tony about what Mateo had been through at that compound? How would she tell him that his son had not been a religious refugee, but a scientific guinea pig for the same government Tony had chosen to spend his life serving as an FBI agent? And how would she do it without exposing herself and her entire team and their abilities?

Keira squeezed her eyes shut and covered her face. "Can this day get any worse?"

FOUR

Why couldn't he keep his big mouth shut? Luke stared out the small exam room window, waiting for his X-ray results. Outside, several law enforcement vehicles dotted the parking lot, along with a couple of news vans. He let his gaze blur over the scene, now fading in the early evening light.

Keira kept creeping into his mind. The woman pushed his damned buttons. Always had. After today, it looked like she always would. The hurt in her eyes when he'd accused her of abandoning Kat . . . Pain pulsed deep in his gut, but this discomfort didn't stem from his injuries. At least not those inflicted by Rostov. These injuries were self-inflicted.

He dug his phone from his jeans and dialed Teague's number.

"Hello?" Teague's daughter, Kat, answered, her voice drifting over Luke's exposed nerves and soothing him. A smile turned his mouth.

"Hey, princess. What are you up to?"

"Playing with my Barbies."

"Mmm." Luke rubbed his eyes, wincing at the memory of those tiny high heels spiking into his bare instep in the middle of the night more times than he could count during the years he'd parented Kat while his brother-in-law had been in prison. He'd also done his share of dressing, undressing, bathing, hiding, finding, and role-playing with the figurines.

"You're color-coordinating their shoes and purses, right?" he asked.

"Yes." She drew out the word with a dramatic smile in her voice.

"Because we can't have anyone talking smack about our girls."

"Oh," she said. "Alyssa just bought them some new outfits. Cheetah and rhinestones and—you can put them on with me when you come over."

He half-smiled, half-grimaced. Look what he'd started.

"And they come with matching hair ties, for, you know, me, not the Barbies. Can you put my hair up when you come over? Like in that bun you used to do? And use the ties?"

An image of a long-ago typical morning flashed in his head. Kat sitting cross-legged in front of him on his bed, playing with something in her lap. Him clutching bobby pins between his teeth and mentally swearing as he struggled to wrangle every strand of that dark, thick, curly hair into his palm so he could twist it into a roll, then attack it with pins like a voodoo doll until the bun stayed put on the back of her head.

He'd never been very good at the whole hair thing, but the hours of frustration had been worth it whenever she beamed that little gap-toothed grin back from the mirror and said, "It's perfect, Uncle Luke."

"Who's that, Kat?" Teague, Luke's boyhood best friend, former fellow firefighter, and prior brother-in-law, called in the background.

"Uncle Luke," she said. "He's going to come over and dress my Barbies in their new clothes."

There was a scraping sound over the line, then Teague's voice. "I thought you got counseling for that fetish."

"Old habits die hard."

"Are you in Nevada?"

"I am."

"What the fuck?"

Reality pushed back in, smothering all those pleasant memories. "I don't know yet." He looked over his shoulder to make sure he was alone. "When's the last time you saw Keira?"

An extended silence made Luke think he'd lost his connection. Then Teague said, "That's a strange question. I thought that topic was off limits."

In an attempt to let go and move on, he'd asked their friends not to discuss Keira in his presence. But after seeing her today, he realized that not talking about her didn't keep him from remembering or wanting or wishing or regretting.

"It was," Luke said. "Until she showed up here."

"What?" Surprise lifted Teague's voice, then he chuckled. "Her SWAT unit was deployed, wasn't it?"

"You knew she was on SWAT? Why didn't you ever mention that?"

"Does 'subject off limits' sound familiar?"

"Fuck you."

"Oh, man, I'd have paid to witness that reunion. Is that how the fire started?"

"Very funny. Where's that good-for-nothing brother-in-law of yours?"

"Mitch is on his way here. He's tapping sources at Nevada Bureau of Land Management. Doesn't know anything yet. Kai has already called. He's ready to kick asses and take names, as usual. He has Seth on standby and access to his boss's jet."

"Jesus." Luke rubbed his forehead, picturing the two other members of their firefighting hazmat team who'd suffered through the warehouse fire with them. "Those guys are always two steps ahead of me. What about Jessica?"

"Kai said she's in Italy for some conference. He decided not to leave a message on her phone."

"Probably a good idea." He remembered how fragile Jessica, the final member of their team, had been after losing her husband in the fire. How deeply she'd struggled. How far she'd come in the five years since. She'd found her niche, lobbying for firefighters in the political realm. He supposed it was her own personal brand of therapy for dealing with Quaid's tragic death.

And man, loss seemed to be a common thread for all of them, didn't it? Though Luke hadn't suffered through Keira's death in that fire, he'd lost her just the same.

"When can you get here?" Teague asked.

Luke's brain was starting to numb around the edges. "Uh . . . Not sure."

"Are you bringing Keira with you, or are you two going to have to take separate vehicles so you both make it alive?"

Luke scrubbed a hand through his hair. That was something he hadn't contemplated—spending time with Keira. The thought brought mixed emotions—most of them painful. "I'll call you later."

He hung up before Teague could twist the screws any tighter. Keira was doing a fine job of that on her own.

"Agent?"

The male voice drew Luke around to the doorway. The doctor who'd examined him approached and snapped an X-ray film to the light box attached to one wall.

Luke shoved the phone into the front pocket of the fresh jeans he'd put on and squinted at the film. "Ribs and shoulders. That's about all I can make out."

"You've got three breaks, in three different ribs. All beneath the bullet's impact." The older man pointed toward gray lines on the film, but his suspicious hazel eyes stayed on Luke. "Unusual bruising pattern on your chest, though. Never seen that in my thirty years of medicine."

Luke didn't want to get into that conversation. "It was an unusual situation."

The doctor nodded. "You're going to be sore for a while, but there's nothing we can do for broken ribs. Just get lots of rest. Considering what could have happened, and the condition of the others who came in here tonight, I'd say this is inconsequential."

Yeah, he could be lying on a refrigerated metal slab in the morgue. He trailed his fingers over the bruises on his chest, now black and purple and throbbing like a sonofabitch. "That's very true."

Simply by being present, Keira had amped his physical strengths and saved his life. And all he'd done was harass her. Accuse her. Bitch at her. He was such a piece of shit.

"How are they?" he asked. "The kids."

"Lucky." The doctor's brows lifted. "None suffered fatal injuries. Even the girl who was badly burned has stabilized. I guess this is a day for miracles, Agent Ransom. I'd like to think you'll use the opportunity to its fullest. Second chances don't happen as often as people think." The man offered a thoughtful smile, as if a little in awe of the opportunity himself. "I'll get you some pain medication. The nurse will bring your discharge papers."

Luke thanked the doctor and turned toward the window again. He'd had broken ribs before, so he knew they'd just hurt until they healed. And he doubted there would be any rest for him—physical or mental—for a long time.

"Lucas." Keira's voice washed over him from behind. Warm. Familiar. Sweet. It wrapped around him and held tight.

"You know," he said, his tone melancholy from the doctor's talk of miracles and second chances, "you and my mother were the only two people who ever called me Lucas."

"No," she said softly, "I didn't know that."

She couldn't know, because he'd never told her. Along with so many other things he'd kept to himself during their relationship. Including the fact that he'd needed her more than he'd needed his next breath when she'd walked away.

"I needed you, too," she said. "But that didn't keep you from giving me an impossible ultimatum."

He huffed a dry laugh and dropped his head. "Maybe if you'd been able to read minds a few years ago, we'd still be together."

"I shouldn't have had to read your mind to know what you needed or wanted. You should have been able to tell me, like I tried telling you. Besides"—she sighed—"we both needed very different things."

Regret was an ugly, relentless emotion, and it ate away at his gut as he turned to face her. He looked right past the boy she was holding to the cuts on her face covered in Steri-strips and her red, puffy eyes. She'd been crying. Hard. A protective instinct twisted inside him. Maybe she wasn't the warrior princess he'd thought.

Those bright blue eyes traveled over his bare chest with a level of heat he hadn't expected. He could have convinced himself the attraction was his imagination, except for the flare of jet-black pupils against her light irises. That was a signal he would never forget, a signal his body would always respond to, like it was responding now, with heat sparking in his groin.

Her eyes skimmed down and away before focusing on the light board with the X-ray still illuminated. "What did the doctor say?"

"Few broken ribs." His voice came out rough. He cleared his throat and grabbed a clean shirt from his bag. He couldn't remember the last time he'd cared what he looked like, but with Keira standing feet away scouring him like a contestant from the *Bachelorette* show, he wished he'd had a recent haircut, a clean shave, fifteen more minutes added to his daily workout.

He tugged the shirt over his head. When he looked in her direction again, she was gone. Luke swiveled and found her studying the X-ray images up close. Her face was illuminated in the diffused light, outlining her furrowed brow and down-turned lips.

"What?" he asked.

She didn't answer, but she was thinking. He could practically see the wheels turning in her brain.

She stepped toward him, grabbed the hem of his T-shirt, and pulled it up.

Excitement spiked his heart rate. Shock started his mouth. "Hey, hey—" He tried to push her arm down, but she didn't budge. "If you want a better view, we can work something—"

"Shut up," she muttered. "If that shit works on other women, you need to raise your minimum expectations."

She dropped his shirt, turned on her heel, and scanned the room.

"Keira, what—"

Still holding Mateo in one arm, she grabbed his body armor in the other and flipped it over where it lay on the gurney.

Luke clenched his teeth against an overwhelming desire to yank the vest from her view, which was completely illogical. He wasn't hiding anything. What she thought shouldn't matter. Yet when she sucked in a breath and ran her fingers over the exposed, flattened bullet on the inside of the canvas where the metal had hit Luke's skin, he tensed.

Would she insist on taking credit for saving his life? Would she use this as an example of how wrong Luke had been to push her away? Laugh at him for being such a fool?

Her breath leaked from her lips in a slow stream. She folded the front of the vest again and ran the flat of her hand down the tattered front where sections had been ripped and melted. Her touch was reverent, almost loving, as her palm paused over the hole, beneath which Luke's heart would have lain.

"Have you . . . maintained . . . that ability since I've been gone?"

"No," he said cautiously, unsure of her mood.

She nodded.

"How'd you know?" he asked.

"Rostov hit you with a powerful rifle at close range. You should have more breaks than that. And the bruise on your chest, it's"—she shrugged—"strange. An intense, perfect circle in the center, surrounded by stippling in a complete, unbroken radius. It looks the way an actual bullet wound would if the metal had pierced your skin."

That was a sickening thought.

Keira turned to face him, but he couldn't read her eyes. "No more taunting me about new abilities. Deal?"

He nodded agreement.

She wandered to the gurney, where she gently laid the sleeping boy, and Luke experienced an ease in the atmosphere. And an unmistakable and powerful connection. They each knew and accepted that they affected the other— mind, body, and spirit. Like it or not. Accept it or not. Deal with it or not. The facts didn't change.

Luke finally focused on the kid. He was dressed in a T-shirt and jeans, his brown hair a mass of damp, dark curls. "They found him some clothes, huh?"

"Yeah, but he doesn't like wearing them." A smile softened the edges of her pretty mouth, making Luke want to do things that shouldn't even enter his mind. "Absolutely wouldn't put on shoes."

"Sounds familiar." Luke chuckled, his heart warming

over the parenting experience he and Keira had shared while raising Kat for that year before Keira left for the academy. These were the moments that made him long for a wife and children of his own. Only, the more time that passed, the further away that dream slipped.

Keira rested one slim hip against the gurney and crossed her arms over her chest. "How is Kat?"

She wasn't combative. Just sad. Which intensified his lingering guilt. "She's great. Has everything she always wanted—her dad, great new mom, baby brother—"

"On the way," Keira finished. "I know."

Luke bit the inside of his bottom lip to keep from asking about her visits to the area or nagging her about never looking him up when she came. Not even tossing him one damn phone call.

"You had a phone, too," she said. "My cell number hasn't changed."

"I thought we talked about this mind-reading thing."

"We did. It sounded something like *projecting*. Remember?"

"I remember how exasperating you are."

"Ditto."

He scrubbed a hand through his hair. "Just talked to Teague."

"Yeah?" She straightened, her eyes sparking. "What did he say?"

"Doesn't have any info on this yet. Mitch is on his way to Truckee. I guess I'll head home, too, once this quiets down." He hesitated. "He asked if you would be coming . . ." *with me.*

He cut off the last two words, but he guessed she'd probably heard them anyway.

"I don't know." She shifted her feet and dragged the corner of her lower lip between her teeth as she looked at the sleeping boy. "My team may be here until it's over."

Luke met her at the gurney, absorbing the sight of her now in civilian clothes. Dark blue jeans hung low at the curve of her hips. A plain white short-sleeved T-shirt clung to breasts that looked fuller than he remembered in comparison to the narrowness of her waist peeking from beneath a trim-fitting lightweight jean jacket. She'd always been healthy and fit. Perfect, in his opinion. But this little body was a compact machine of muscle.

The metal badge hooked at her waist created pressure beneath his sore ribs, a mixture of pride and regret.

Second chances don't happen as often as people think.

He skimmed the fall of her shiny hair, nearly black. The way her eyes glimmered a brighter blue in contrast. That creamy, smooth skin. And the crème de la crème, her freckles. The caramel-colored dots across the bridge of her little nose, fading as they arced out over her cheekbones. Eighty-three of them. He'd counted every one. Kissed every one.

Was this a day for miracles? Had they been brought together again for that rare second chance?

Keira's brows pulled together. Those silky lips parted, and Luke's chest tightened in anticipation of a *yes* coming out of her mouth.

"Luke, we really need to talk about Mat—"

"Keira?" A male voice called from somewhere down the hall. "Keira? Where are you?"

She startled. Her gaze broke from Luke's, and she spun toward the door.

On the gurney, Mateo's eyes popped wide open, but his body remained stone still.

Kakos andras.

A chill prickled over Luke's shoulders like a cold breeze. The kid's mouth hadn't moved, but Luke knew the words—the same ones he'd heard from the boy in the chopper—had come from Mateo, and he really didn't like this new ability to hear the kid's thoughts.

Keira must have also heard him, because her attention darted back to Mateo and held.

A man stopped at the exam room doorway, both hands on the jamb to halt his forward momentum. A little on the swarthy side with a day's worth of whiskers covering the lower half of his face, dressed in typical office casual, slacks, dress shirt, tie loose at his neck.

"There you are. This place is a zoo." His dark eyes traveled over the room, took in every detail, then latched on to Keira with the heat of ownership. "Beautiful, I owe you. Big-time."

"Tony." Keira's shoulders tightened, her hands dug into the front pockets of her jeans. "Wow, you got here fast."

Tony. The father. The coworker-slash-boyfriend-slash-whatever. Only this wasn't the greeting Luke expected for lovers. Definitely not the way Keira used to greet him, by wrapping her arms around his neck, sliding that perfect body up against his, and latching on to his mouth with her own until he couldn't think straight.

Jealousy burned white-hot. It would have erupted into an inferno if Mateo hadn't distracted him. The boy sat up, his round eyes stuck on the other man with even more fear than Luke had seen on the kid's face when he'd been standing on the opposite side of a wall of fire.

Mateo's fingers curled around the gurney's metal side, his stare intent on Keira. *Thia! Kakos andras.*

Luke reached out and touched Mateo's hand. The boy flinched, and Luke expected him to pull away. Instead, Mateo flipped his hand over and gripped Luke's fingers so hard they stung. He scooted to the edge of the gurney, wrapped his other arm around Luke's waist, fisted his fingers in his T-shirt, and pressed his face into Luke's belly.

An instant, completely irrational urge to shield the boy had Luke drawing Mateo closer, bringing with it a new appreciation for Keira's protectiveness. Luke ran a hand over the boy's head. His curls were as soft as feathers. No wonder Keira couldn't keep her hands out of them.

"*Kakos andras.*" Mateo's murmur vibrated against Luke's stomach.

Keira's eyes rounded in surprise. "Did he just talk?"

He's fucking terrified. Luke found himself thinking at her instead of talking to her. This was all so damned weird.

He picked Mateo up and rubbed his back. "It's okay, buddy."

Tony dropped an arm around Keira, pulling her close. Luke gritted his teeth. Wanted to twist that arm behind Tony's back and break it. The guy stared at Mateo, an uncertain smile turning his mouth. Luke's senses simmered. Where was the awe of seeing his child for the first time in three years? The relief? The excitement?

"Wow," Tony said. "He's gotten big."

"That happens with kids when you don't see them for a while," Luke said. "And judging by your height, he's probably pretty small for his age."

Tony's eyes strayed to Luke's face. "Are you a doctor?"

"Luke is ATF." Keira's demeanor had shifted, as if she'd climbed back inside an uncomfortable shell. "He helped me get Mateo out."

"Thank you, Agent." The gratitude was stiff, but Tony offered his hand.

Luke should have taken it, but he couldn't make himself do it. Something was very wrong with this scenario, with this man, but he had no idea what because his emotions had his mind and body cross-wired.

When Luke didn't respond, Tony's hand dropped. The tension in the room spiked.

Keira stepped into the space between them and looked at Tony. "Mateo's still a little rough around the edges. He's been through a lot in the last few hours."

Mouth tight, eyes fiery, Tony turned his attention to

Keira and relaxed. He reached out, ran a hand over her hair, and squeezed her shoulder, an intimate gesture that spoke of familiarity. One that made Luke want to deck the bastard. "Sure. I understand."

"What is he saying?" Luke interrogated. "What language is he speaking?"

"Probably Greek." Tony's expression had closed. Turned businesslike. "His mother was Greek. Very proprietary about her heritage. She spoke Greek to him from the day he was born."

"Tony," Keira said. "The situation was pretty bad at the ranch when we left and I don't have any news on your wife."

"Ex-wife, and it's fine. My feelings for her died a long time ago."

An awkward silence invaded the room. Luke looked at Keira to check her reaction the same moment she looked back at him. Shared opinion passed between them. One that had nothing to with any mind-reading.

Keira broke the connection and reached out to rub a hand over Mateo's back. "Hey, buddy, your daddy's here. Want to say hi?"

Eyes squeezed closed, Mateo pushed off Luke's chest and climbed into Keira's arms, his movements jerky, almost violent in his need to stay connected to her. Pain wrenched through Luke's ribs, but as soon as the boy was gone, a chill crept into his body. The same loss he'd felt the day he'd watched Keira drive away, headed for the academy. The same loss he'd felt the day he'd given Kat back to Teague when his former brother-in-law had been released from prison.

None of this made sense. And he couldn't take that kind of loss again.

"Keira," Tony said. "Can I have a word with you? Privately?"

"Sure." Keira flashed Luke an apologetic glance. "I'll be right back."

In the hallway they stood close, talking in undertones. With Keira's face turned up to his and Tony leaning toward her, they were only inches apart, Mateo between them.

The image was like looking at a picture of what Luke's life could have been—only with another man standing where Luke should be. Of what Keira's life would be like without Luke in it.

Some part of his damaged psyche still saw Keira as his. His best friend, his partner, his other half. She had been his True North during the darkest times of his life—his sister's suicide, recovering from the warehouse fire, his brother-in-law's imprisonment, the first year parenting Kat. Nothing had dimmed that deep sense of belonging he'd shared with her from their first moment together. Not time, not distance, not even the end of their relationship.

We needed very different things.

Logically, he'd known that. Still knew that. Logically, he knew he couldn't change what he'd needed then or what he still needed. Nor could he change the fact that Keira's needs were entirely different. At least they had been then.

Emotionally, though, looking at her with another man, holding that man's child as if he were her own, the possibility that maybe they hadn't needed such different things after all, that maybe she'd just needed those things with someone else, hit him so hard, his knees went weak.

He turned away, pulled his cell from his jeans, and dialed his boss in Lake Tahoe. His real boss, not the asshole commander at the siege. But Luke's mind was somewhere else. Greek. Greek. Who did he know that spoke Greek? He was dying to find out what the kid was saying.

"Special Agent Carroway."

"Kirk," Luke said when his boss answered. "It's Luke."

"Heard I almost lost you, dickhead."

Luke was too frazzled to smile. "Yeah. Kinda wishing you had."

"What?"

"Never mind. What's happening at the ranch? Did they get any more hostages out? Any more kids?"

"That place is a chemical inferno. Nothin's coming out of there but ashes."

Luke's stomach pitched. "I'm leaving the ER now, headed back to the scene. I'll check in with that jerk incident commander and—"

"Don't bother. The army has taken over. Pushed all other law enforcement out. We're officially released."

"The *army*?" It was happening again. Just like it had five years ago. An explosion. A fire. Deaths. Trauma. The army sweeping in, taking control, classifying the information so they could bury it. "Can they do that?"

"They're the United States Army, Luke. They can do anything they want."

Dread filtered in. A sense of complete loss of control. "What about the FBI?"

"Even the Feds are out on this one."

"You know they're covering." He had to force his voice down. "Where did the chemicals come from? Why didn't we know what we were walking into? We're ATF, for God's sake. If anyone should have known, we should have."

"Good question. The way this all panned out, I'm starting to believe no one knew."

No way. Someone knew.

He spun with a glare ready for Keira. But it was wasted. She was absorbed in Tony. Before Luke turned away again, Tony lowered his head and kissed her. A solid, serious, purposeful, full-on-the-mouth kiss. Luke froze. Pain stabbed the center of his chest.

"Did you hear me?"

His boss's voice pulled him back. Luke squeezed his eyes shut and turned away. He could have gone his entire life without seeing her kiss another man. Sure as hell hadn't planned on being around as a witness.

"Uh, no, boss." Luke rubbed the back of his neck as anger transitioned into hollow loss. "I didn't."

"I said that Delgado is in the parking lot handling releases. He'll get you a vehicle and a hotel room for the night. You can head back to town tomorrow."

"Sure, whatever."

Luke disconnected and waited a few seconds before facing the threesome again. He took a breath, cleared his mind, smoothed a hand over the pain in his chest. Whatever she'd dragged herself into here with Rostov and Mateo and Tony wasn't his problem. She'd relieved him of the need to worry about her when she'd made her choice three years ago. She'd chosen the Bureau. So the fucking Bureau could take care of her now.

He shoved his phone back into his pocket and picked up his duffel. As he approached, Keira took a step back from Tony. She didn't meet Luke's eyes. Guilty. She never looked him in the eye when she felt guilty.

"Looks like you've got everything here under control." Luke tried to keep his tone flat, but even he could tell it came out rusty, pained, and venomous. "In case you're interested, the *army* has taken over control of the incident."

That got her attention. Her light eyes jumped to his and held.

"You might want to double-check with West," he said, "but I was told that even the Feds have been released. So . . ." He cast a glance at Tony, then Mateo, the boy's face buried in Keira's shoulder, hands fisted in her shirt, and back at Keira before he started down the hall. "I guess you can all get on with your lives now."

★   ★   ★

"Luke, wait." Keira peered around Tony's shoulder with an unreasonable sense of panic tightening her throat. *It isn't what you think.* "I need to talk to you."

Luke didn't slow, didn't stop, didn't even turn around. He either didn't care or didn't hear her. Maybe her relationship status just didn't matter. Because *she* just didn't matter. He'd turned his back on her exactly as he had before. Keira felt the rejection all the way to her bones.

And she felt something else, too. An all-encompassing sense of anxiety. Impending disaster. A clusterfuck waiting to happen. Something . . . odd, but dark. Something she couldn't pinpoint or place or attach to anyone or anything.

Tony sidestepped and cut off her view. "Keira, what do you think?"

She didn't know what he was talking about, because once she'd shifted her mind off Luke, her thoughts automatically returned to the irresistible urge to wipe the feel of Tony's mouth off hers with the back of her hand. *That* was probably the root of these disgusting sensations.

"I think you'd better never kiss me again without my permission. I was very clear about our relationship months ago. Nothing has changed."

"Okay, okay." He held up his hands. "I'm sorry. I got carried away. But, it's perfect. Now that you don't have to go back to the scene, we can take a little vacation. Go somewhere quiet, just the three of us. It can be completely platonic. If something happens between us, great. If not, I'll accept it. But that will give Mateo time to get to know me while you're still in the picture. I mean, look at him. What do you think he's going to do when I try to walk out of here with him?"

True. Mateo wouldn't even look at Tony. Wouldn't even allow Keira to put him down. Luke was gone. She'd been released from the scene. There was no excuse not to go with Tony, but the thought of being alone with him for even an hour, let alone days, made her squirm.

"Look, Tony, we both knew this transition was going to be tough. You may have to suffer through a few nights of tears, but he'll get over it. He'll probably forget about me after a day or so."

"That's what you said about me." He smiled, all charm, and ran his fingers over her uninjured cheek. "You're not the kind of girl a boy forgets after a few days."

Oh, no? Ask the man who just left.

"This is already way harder than I expected." The thought of leaving Mateo created an unshakable sense of loss. She had an undeniable connection with the boy, but it wasn't legal or even mental. It was chemical. And Keira still didn't know how to lead into that conversation, only knew that now was not the time or place. "Dragging it out won't help."

The smile disappeared from Tony's eyes, and something uncomfortable niggled along the back of Keira's neck.

"How about this," she offered. "I'll stay close to you two and come see you every day. That will give you both time to acclimate."

"I had a feeling you'd say that." Tony slid his hand around the nape of her neck. "I wish you didn't make me do these things."

His fingers shot into her hair with unexpected force. He yanked her head back. Pain seared her scalp.

"T-Tony, stop." She started to set Mateo down, needing her hands free to knock the living shit out of this bastard. But Tony tightened his fingers, and Keira choked on the new surge of pain.

"Keep your voice down," he murmured in her ear. "Or you won't be the only one hurt."

Something cool and smooth touched the base of her neck. His weapon. He was her tactical equal. Her self-defense skills, her negotiation techniques, they were all rote to him. Panic edged in.

"This . . . this . . ." She didn't know what *this* was. It made no sense. It was so out of character, yet some part of her psyche wasn't completely surprised. "This is really stupid, Tony. Think about your career. Your future. Put the gun away and I won't mention this to West. We'll chalk it all up to stress and forget it ever happened."

"West doesn't mean shit to me. This *is* my career. My future. And I'm damn sick and tired of the delays."

He released her hair and pushed the gun against Mateo's ribs. The boy flinched, buried his head deeper into the hollow of Keira's shoulder, and whined, *"Kakos andras, Thia."*

"We're leaving through that door." Tony lifted his chin toward an exit down the hall and pushed her forward.

"I'll scream." She scanned the room, the hallway, the area, for some type of weapon, for someone to help, but all personnel had been pulled to the trauma bay. "You'll never make it out of the parking lot."

"You won't make a sound, because I don't want you or this kid as much as the others do."

The others. Her chest plunged into a deep freeze.

No. He couldn't be. She'd known him for over a year. Worked with him almost every day at the Bureau. She couldn't have missed . . . The *FBI* couldn't have missed . . .

He pushed the weapon against Mateo's ribs, and the boy let out a sharp squeal of pain. The sound ripped at her heart. "And remember, alive is preferred, dead is perfectly acceptable."

Those were West's words. Keira's mind pinged back to the moment her boss had said them. There hadn't been anyone within earshot. It wasn't a typical FBI euphemism.

She'd always considered Angus a mentor, a muse, someone she'd hoped to emulate someday. Now she didn't know what to think. Or who to trust.

Luke.

Luke, come back! She didn't know why she tried to contact him telepathically. He might have heard Mateo's thoughts, but he hadn't indicated he'd been able to hear hers. The truth was she had no idea how this mind thing worked, because the strange web of communication they seemed to have developed was different from anything she'd experienced before. Still, she screamed in her head. *I need you. Help me. Luuuuuke!*

Keira let Tony shove her forward. No one wandered the short hallway, and when Tony opened the door, no alarm sounded. The rear parking lot was deserted.

She stumbled into the warm, dry evening air. Dusk mixed with the smoke drifting from the fires at the ranch, and a gray tinge settled over the landscape, dulling all edges and colors like a muddy painting.

He opened the driver's door of a familiar Crown Victoria and shoved her across the bench seat toward the passenger's side. She glanced at the lock. At the door handle. She could run, shield herself and Mateo behind the other cars until someone came into the parking lot.

"Don't bother." Tony pounded the lock on his door with a fist. "Your locks are disabled. You're not going anywhere."

He fired up the engine, screeched out of the parking lot, and turned onto the main road, heading east. A sleepy desert town spread out to the west. Flat, barren land stretched in all other directions.

Luuuke!

FIVE

Luke slammed a fist against the shower controls in the dinky hotel bathroom and swore when a pansy-ass stream of water emerged.

"What do you expect in the middle of bumfuck nowhere?" He shucked his clothes, trying like hell to keep his mind off the day's events.

Fire, explosions, mayhem: fine. Keira kissing another man: torture.

After testing the water temperature, he stepped under the wimpy spray and let go of the tension in his neck, his shoulders, his arms.

Luuuke!

He winced as Keira's terror-filled cry ricocheted around his brain, more distant than in that moment on the roof when he'd been frantically searching for her after the blast. But it still brought back the sight of her hanging off the edge, the fear tearing at him like that of a dream in which he'd been falling, only to wake just before he hit the ground, sweating, panting, heart jumping from his chest.

He closed his eyes and let his head drop back and under the water. And there she was, imprinted on the back of his eyelids—kissing Tony.

Anguish closed his throat around a groan. "Fuck me."

His cell rang. He pushed the shower curtain aside and leaned out to grab it off the counter.

"What?" he barked, ready to take off the head of any unsuspecting victim.

"What the hell is wrong with you?" A female voice met his ear. A perturbed female voice. One he couldn't place. "Tell me you're stuck in traffic or make up some other elaborate excuse, 'cause I'm about as pissed as you sound right now."

His mind tangled, searching for her identity. Since his mother had passed over a decade ago, his sister, Teague's first wife, had committed depression-induced suicide, and Keira had gone off in search of something better with the FBI, there were no constant women in his life. But there had been attempts, women he'd hoped to connect with in an effort to forget Keira. So many attempts. So many failures. And after seeing her today, he finally knew why.

"Um . . ." Instinct told him to tread lightly. "By the sound of your voice, I'd say I should be somewhere I'm not."

A second of dark silence brought the tension back to his shoulders.

"Where are you?" she asked.

"I'm . . ." He had a feeling this was going to start World War III. "In Nevada."

"Nevada?" she nearly screeched. "That's not even funny, Luke."

"It's not meant to be funny," he said, resigned to the fallout. This had happened many times over the last two years, since he'd begun dating again after returning Kat to Teague. After realizing Keira wasn't coming back. The arguments over the demands of his job, the lack of connection, of even the *desire* to connect with anyone. "I was dispatched to an incident here this morning. Have you been watching the news?"

"No. I've been getting ready for our date. Do Bon Jovi tickets mean anything to you? Front row center?" Her voice rose with anger. "I spent a week's pay on these tickets, Luke."

Oh, shit. That did mean something to him.

"Jesus, Carly, I'm sorry." He closed his eyes and hung his head. Such a loser. "There's no way I can make it back in time."

Nor did he have any inspiration to try. A really big fucking loser.

Silence.

The beginning of the end. He'd been here so many times.

"We're in the middle of nowhere." He attempted to sound apologetic, but somehow the absurd disparity between his reality and hers—burning children versus Bon Jovi tickets—limited his depth of sympathy. "I've had lousy cell service and this is a damned war zone."

Another extended silence followed by a long, drawn-out, frustrated sigh.

Luke leaned his forehead against the tile. He would have thrown in his near-death experience if he'd thought it would have mattered. He didn't. "Why don't you take your sister? Or your friend, what's her name, Sunny?"

"Summer."

"Right, Summer."

"Or maybe," she said, her voice now cool, "I should take Damon. He's been after me for months."

A tired, defeated laugh slipped out. Carly was an incredibly beautiful, intelligent woman who shared Luke's desire for children and a family. Yet, he couldn't summon even an ounce of jealousy.

"You know what? That's a great idea." *A fucking fantastic idea.* "This obviously isn't working out for either of us. You and Damon have my blessing. Good-bye, Carly."

Luke disconnected with a combination of remorse and

relief, and tossed his phone on the counter. It clattered hard as he put his head back under the spray and ran the hotel soap over his hair and body.

The phone rang again and Luke growled. He didn't have the patience to go through the easy letdown. Couldn't summon the compassion he needed to justify the situation to an irate, hurt, emotional female. But guilt made him pick up his phone anyway.

"Ransom." He sighed, watching the water drip off his body and onto the chipped linoleum floor.

Nothing.

He frowned, looked at the display. Still connected. He put the phone back to his ear and listened. A scrape. A whisper. The rustle of cloth.

Luke. Thank God.

The water layering his skin turned cold. Goosebumps rose on his arms.

"Hello?" he queried again, then, for a reason he couldn't explain, said, "Keira?"

"Yes." The word came in barely a whisper, but the frightened tone drifted through loud and clear. "It's me."

He hit the shower control and cut the water. "What's wrong?"

"I need you." The words reverberated through his body like a mini-quake, and the desperation in her voice pumped his heart rate higher. "I couldn't call anyone else. It's Tony. He's not Tony. I mean, he's not who he says he is. He's not Mateo's father. I don't know—"

"Don't know what?"

"What's happening. You were right. Nothing about this is what it was made out to be. I need you to . . . Come get me, Luke. Mateo and me."

"I'm coming. I'm there. Where are you?" He barely swiped a towel over his body before grabbing his jeans and pulling them on with one hand.

"I . . . Hell, I don't know. He took us from the hospital after you left. We've been heading east on back roads for about an hour. But it's dark and deserted and I can't see anything. Damn, Luke, I left all my weapons in the chopper. He has a gun and he's twice my size and he's trained and . . . I have Mateo . . ." She paused to drag in a shaky breath. "Luke, if I don't see you again . . ."

"Don't." He forced the possibility from his head. "I'll find you."

"I'm sorry I didn't stay. I'm sorry I didn't come back. I should have tried harder."

His heart split open. "Jesus, Keira—"

"He's coming," she whispered. "Luke, whatever you do, don't trust *anyone.*"

The other end of the line went quiet in Luke's ear.

"Keira?" He gripped the phone harder. "Keira!"

Those same sounds that had initiated the call now ended it, a murmur, a shuffle of fabric, then nothing. But the line didn't go dead. She'd left her phone on. Which meant it probably had GPS tracking.

"Damn," he murmured. "You are one smart girl."

He grabbed the hotel phone and connected to an outside line, then dialed the operator. As he waited, he set down his cell and threw belongings into his duffel with his free hand.

The operator came on the line.

"Yeah," Luke said. His mind fragmented into a dozen pieces, his heart pounding too hard and too fast. "I need the number of the nearest—"

The words *FBI field office* never made it out of his mouth. *Don't trust anyone.*

"Hello?" the operator queried.

"Uh . . . Never mind."

He hung up. Stared at the phone. Who exactly did *anyone* encompass? Her boss? Her agency? He didn't know. But if Tony was supposed to be FBI and wasn't, if the incident had been taken over by the army, if it had included several different law enforcement agencies, there was no telling how deep the conspiracy went.

He needed help. Needed someone with connections. Someone who could get information. Who could elicit answers.

His mind calculated routes and miles and speeds. Tony had a good seventy-, eighty-minute jump on him. It would take him hours to catch up, even if he knew where he was going, which he didn't.

Without disconnecting his cell, he punched into the directory, searched until he found the number of the only person who had everything he needed, and dialed the hotel phone again.

"Mitch Foster," the other man answered in a brisk business tone.

"Mitch, it's Luke."

"Oh, it's only you. What number are you calling from?" Mitch didn't wait for an answer. "This better be important, Ransom, 'cause my Padres are spanking your Giants, and if I miss even one good pitch, I'm going to be pissed."

"What the fuck? You're supposed to be on a plane."

"I am. Haven't you ever heard of in-flight television? You really need to get out more, cop. There's even in-flight Internet nowadays, and—"

"There is no in-flight cell service. Where the hell are you?"

"On the tarmac, taxiing in. They're entertaining us through a delay at the gate with a rerun of the San Diego–San Francisco game, which I happened to miss last night because I was, shall we say, *entertaining* one very beautiful, enthusiastic young Harvard law student on break for an internship at—"

"I couldn't care less about your sex life, Foster."

"You should pay more attention. Maybe you'd learn

something. *Get* something once in a while. It would improve that constantly fucked mood—"

"You are such a prick. Under any other circumstances, I'd tell you to go screw yourself." Luke cut off the casual banter he and Mitch typically exchanged. "But I need you to track a cell transmission. And I need you to do it fast."

"Wait. Did you just tell me to go screw myself and then ask me for something?" Mitch let out a superior chuckle. The no-harm, no-foul ribbing usually entertained Luke. Not today. "And I'm supposed to care? Why aren't you turning to your fellow boys in blue to handle this?"

"Because I can't . . ." *Trust anyone.*

Mitch hesitated. "Are you still in Nevada?"

"Yes."

"Whose phone?"

"Keira's."

"Oh, my God." Mitch drew out the words in disbelief. "You are stupid, Ransom. You get the chance to pull your head out of your ass and you screw it up. What idiotic stunt did you pull to send her running this time?"

The fact that Mitch knew every detail of Luke and Keira's history without ever having known them as a couple was a testament to how their pseudo-family operated. Everyone got into everyone else's business. And they all told each other how they felt about said business, whether any of them wanted to hear it or not. The only thing that kept the whole group from a bloody brawl was that each one of them knew the opinion was imparted in his or her own best interest.

"She's not running from me, asshole." Luke's teeth ground as he searched for patience. "Someone abducted her."

"Fucking A." Mitch's voice lost all joviality. "This better not be a joke, Luke, or I'll pull your teeth out with a pair of rusty pliers."

"Colorful. You've been practicing criminal law too long."

The sound of paper crackled over the line. "Give me the number."

Luke recited it. "She said she's been heading east of the incident on back roads for about an hour. Her cell is still on and connected to mine."

"Why'd she call you? It sure as hell wasn't for a dose of your lousy charm. Why didn't she call the cops?"

"Do you really have to ask?"

"Goddammit," he muttered. "I'll have a location for you in twenty minutes."

"Make it ten, and, Mitch, I need one more thing."

"You're a demanding SOB, Ransom. What?"

"A plane and a pilot."

"That's two things, you stupid cop."

Jocelyn Dargan paced the wall of windows in her office at the Department of Defense, arms crossed as she stared through the glass toward the lights of Arlington glittering against the night. Behind her, the wall-mounted flat screen continued to spit out the latest CNN news on the firestorm still raging out of control at Rostov's compound.

"What a mess," she grumbled, her mind formulating damage control strategies. "Stupid, stupid people."

The cell clutched in her hand rang. She looked at the caller ID, held her breath, and hit the RECEIVE button. "Tony, do you have him?"

"Yes, ma'am, I have him."

The confidence in his words reassured her that not only did he have the kid, but that Tony was in charge of the situation. Jocelyn let her eyes close and her shoulders sag.

The army already had control of the scene. The other agencies had been debriefed with perfectly orchestrated lies.

The press had been fed a load of horseshit. Senator Schaeffer would never know how close they'd come to discovery. To disaster.

She shook her hair back. "Very good. Nice work, Tony. Where are you?"

"About thirty minutes from the exchange point." Jocelyn opened her mouth to praise him again; then Tony said, "I have someone else, too. I have O'Shay."

Jocelyn's shoulders tightened. The only O'Shay that came to mind—Cash O'Shay—was imprisoned at the Castle, on the verge of a developmental breakthrough, promising to catapult the United States military into the next century as the leader in warfare. One that would have Jocelyn's name all over the credits.

"*Which* O'Shay?"

"Keira O'Shay."

Confusion crisscrossed her brain. "Exactly what do you mean you *have* her?"

"I mean . . ." Tony hesitated. "I took her . . . when I took the boy."

"How in the hell . . . ?" She stopped herself from exposing any more ignorance. Besides, the how didn't matter at this point. "Why would you do that?"

"Ma'am, didn't you read my briefing on the heredity aspect of Rostov's work?" He sounded like a ten-year-old asking to stay up ten minutes past his bedtime. "I sent it to your office by special delivery four months ago."

Oh. My. God. He was one of those. She would never have suspected.

Anger built, heating her base temperature ten degrees. "This mission does not in any way, shape, or form include Keira O'Shay. You have seriously jeopardized our role in this investigation, and you have dangerously overstepped your authority."

"I had to take her." His voice turned cold and professional. "I couldn't take the boy without taking her. He would have drawn attention. It was a command decision."

Jocelyn's office door opened and Owen Young stepped in, looking as tall and fit as he had back in their military years together, two decades before in Iraq. A few white papers dangled from his hand, and as he read her expression, a questioning furrow creased his brow. She didn't need any more aggravation at the moment, but she did need information, so she waved him in.

"You had strict orders, Tony," she said into the phone. "Do you realize the ramifications of your actions? Do you realize the shit storm that will explode when the rest of her team realizes she's MIA?"

"I can get rid of her if you want," Tony said, bitterness creeping in now, "but you should at least see them together first. Read my report. Rostov was onto something. This could be a once-in-a-lifetime opportunity."

Okay, he wasn't just one of those. He was a raving lunatic. Worse than Rostov. And he had custody of Mateo and Keira O'Shay. Beautiful. Just beautiful. She was going to strangle Tony's handler. Personally.

"That is exactly why we want to get him back to the Castle with his father." The lie gave Jocelyn an idea. She drew in a slow, furious breath, searching for patience—not her strongest trait. "Take a picture of them together and e-mail it to me. Go ahead with the drop already planned for the boy, but just hold on to O'Shay for now. I'll call you back with orders. And, Tony. If you screw this up any worse than you have, don't expect to make your next annual review."

"Yes, ma—"

She hung up, jammed both hands to her hips, and turned toward Owen. He'd settled his large frame on the loveseat across the room. One ankle rested on the opposite knee, one arm stretched easily on the back of the sofa, tapping the papers against the leather cushion.

His dark hair, just now threading with gray at fifty-five, needed a cut, but she liked it that way. She'd spent too many years looking at him nearly bald when they'd served together. And the sight of any shaved head now brought back memories of that village in Iraq and all those soldiers with similar crew cuts, strewn out across the dirt, dead. All because the Iraqi army had been one step ahead of the U.S. Better weapons. Better intel.

Owen had been with her that day, and the experience had created a unique bond. Nothing less would have been strong enough to hold their professional relationship together after the painful end to their personal one. Owen had been handsome back then as well. Maybe even more so, but in an entirely different way. More savage. More primal.

And he'd been good in bed. An amazing, tireless, demanding, sex maniac. Not a lover. He'd never been a lover. If he had been, she wouldn't have kicked him out of her bed. Out of her heart. Would never have turned to Jason, another unit member and friend. She'd stayed with Jason off and on for nearly twenty years, but never loved him the way she'd loved Owen in their few short months together.

"I came in here to tell you that O'Shay was at the incident." He shrugged, his wide shoulders challenging the fabric of his sage dress shirt, still pressed and tucked into gray slacks, even at the end of a long day. The only testament to his frustration was the tie pulled loose at his neck and the deeper-than-usual crinkles at the corners of his eyes. "But it looks like you're one step ahead of me. Like always."

"At the . . ." She squeezed the bridge of her nose and shifted through facts in her mind. "My God, the incompetence boggles my mind." She threw her arm to the side and let it drop, then leaned against the desk. To avoid watching Owen's gaze roam down her narrow skirt and over her legs, Jocelyn scrolled through the contacts on her phone until she reached the number for Tony's handler. "No. I didn't know she was at the incident."

"Good to know I can still keep up with you." Owen's grin loosened, turned flirtatious. His eyes sharpened as he sat forward and pressed elbows to knees. "You are right about her team, though. They'll go ape-shit when they find out she's gone. Mitch Foster's going to be crawling up your ass before sunrise."

Just the mention of that cunning, manipulative piece-of-shit lawyer made Jocelyn's skin ripple.

A man's voice sounded in Jocelyn's ear. "Deputy Dargan, ma'am?"

She held up a hand to Owen and spoke into her phone. "Redland, I don't want your excuses. Do you hear me?"

"Yes, ma'am. Absolutely, ma'am. I—"

"Esposito," she cut him off with a curt snap of her voice, "was your responsibility, soldier. The results of his actions today remain to be seen. They are deep and far reaching and will affect our department, our careers, and ultimately the security of our nation. You will take care of the problem you created with your oversight."

A heavy moment of silence wafted over the line. Redland was a former decorated Marine. Where he'd gone wrong with Tony, Jocelyn didn't know. What she did know was that addressing him as "soldier" would bring out all his loyalty and the dig about national security would cut deep.

"Are we clear, *soldier*?" Jocelyn asked.

"Crystal clear, ma'am."

Jocelyn disconnected after his promise to contact her with status updates.

When she looked up, Owen's expression held a mixture of decades-old emotions that stirred her heart and her libido. Those eyes in crazy-beautiful shades of caramel and moss stared back with pride, awe, and plenty of heat.

"You always did have a way with words, Jocelyn."

Owen's deep, slow speech reverberated around the office, rolling through her like a heat wave. Sexual, predatory, challenging. Since Jason had died—correction, been killed by Teague Creek and the hell that miserable team stirred, Owen had picked up his prowl around Jocelyn as if twenty years hadn't passed since their wild fling while stationed together during Desert Storm. As if Owen hadn't ever gotten married, had children. As if Jocelyn would be interested simply because Jason wasn't around anymore.

Idiot.

Whether Jason was around or not, she wanted Owen. He had a maddening way of making her want him and hate him at the same time. She could have entertained the idea of an occasional sexual interlude with Owen now that she was mature enough to remain emotionally distant, but there was a large and, Jocelyn often thought, convenient roadblock between them: Owen was still married. Jocelyn had never been, and would never be, a mistress.

She pushed off the desk and wandered to the windows again, her gaze blurring over the city lights. "If we let O'Shay go, she leaves with information about the boy, about Rostov. If we eliminate her, the others will crawl out from their quiet holes."

She thought of Foster, and all his evidence. The photos and documents and taped phone conversations linking a dozen top officials—most important, Senator Schaeffer—to a slew of unethical, unauthorized, unsavory scientific projects funded by taxpayers. Information that would be strewn to various major media sources should anything happen to Foster or his team.

Jocelyn's mind churned with options. "If we can make it look like she was killed in the incident—"

"No chance." Owen's voice cut into her plans.

She glared at him over her shoulder. "Why the hell not?"

He slapped the papers on the walnut coffee table at his knees. Pointed at something highlighted on the page. "Because Ransom was there, too. Reportedly aided her in the boy's rescue. He knows she didn't die in that incident, and he'd never rest until he found and killed everyone involved in her death. Besides, the news is already across the wires."

Jocelyn's stomach dropped. She rushed to the table and picked up Owen's papers. Interdepartmental news updates. Next worst thing to media. This would be spread throughout every department in every government agency within hours.

"How did Ransom show up there? And you're off base on their relationship. They broke up three years ago. Not a word since."

Owen sat back and reached up to pull his tie a little looser and unfasten the second button on his shirt.

"Time doesn't erase emotion," he said. "At least, not for some of us."

"Only those of us who *have* emotion would know that, Owen."

"Low, Joce. Low. As far as I can tell, Ransom ended up there by statistical chance."

"That's the same as coincidence, and I don't believe in coincidence."

Owen tipped his head, narrowed his eyes, his thick dark lashes nearly obscuring the light irises. "What about fate, Joce?" His voice softened to what Jocelyn would have misconstrued as a vulnerable tone if she didn't know him better. But she did. "Do you believe fate brought Ransom and O'Shay back together?"

A stream of heat poured through the center of her chest. She crossed her arms and clenched her fingers around her biceps. "Why are you screwing with me, Owen? Frustrated? Is Libby going through the change? Not in the mood?" She raised her brows. "Having an affair?"

He didn't react. Unusual. A new tactic in his arsenal? If so, it was unnerving. But Jocelyn didn't show it. She held her ground and his stare.

"Ransom is part of a Special Response Team with ATF." When he finally spoke, his voice was even, but subdued. The fact that he hadn't picked up her challenge hinted at something painful and personal brewing for Owen. Maybe he had developed emotion sometime over the past twenty years after all.

"His team covers the northwestern United States. Normally, the Los Angeles SRT would have gone to the incident with Rostov, but they were, and still are, dispatched to a hostage situation along the border of Mexico and Texas in a little hellhole by the name of Langtry. Some Mexican drug lord smuggling through a tunnel across the border.

"Esposito wrangled O'Shay into finding and retrieving this kid. Ballsy and innovative if you ask me, only it backfired on him when it became a siege and Ransom's unit was deployed. Once Ransom and O'Shay were within fifty miles of each other, they were bound to end up together. We can monitor, we can manipulate, but we can't control every move every member of their team makes."

"Not every member," she said. "But we should be controlling Ransom and O'Shay. Considering how their powers intensify, definitely *them*. And Creek. And Foster. And . . ." *Shit*. "Okay, yes, every member. Keeping them all apart is the best possible situation short of killing them."

She lifted her fingers to her temples and rubbed small circles at the fresh surge of tension. "Schaeffer should have gotten rid of them all at that damned fire. It would have been so easy. This should have been handled five goddamned years ago. It's not my issue."

Owen's superior chuckle scraped Jocelyn's raw nerves. "Wishing you'd stayed in the private sector, Jocie?"

A fiery spear of pain slashed her heart. "Don't call me that." Halfway through the bark, she wished she could pull it back. Only Jason called her Jocie. And Owen knew it. Owen could call her Joce. But not Jocie. Never Jocie.

"Hey, hey . . ." He held up his hands in surrender and enlisted that purring voice he used when he wanted something. "I'm sorry, honey. You're still a little sensitive." He shrugged, all innocence. "It's been over six months now. I guess I figured . . . I didn't realize. I'm sorry."

She ground her teeth to keep from responding. If she admitted to still hurting over Jason's death, aching over his absence, mourning over how much time she'd wasted at work instead of spending it with him when he'd asked, she'd expose her weakness. If she got angry over Owen's sentiment, he would take it as admittance. There was no win. Manipulative bastard.

"No, I don't belong in the private sector," she said instead. "But neither do I belong working with such incompetence, and I won't stand for any manipulation. I'll take care of this situation just like I would in any sector—public or private. Professionally and permanently."

Owen pushed to his feet, left the papers on the table, and pulled an envelope from his back pocket. He tapped the paper against one palm, a pensive expression pulling at his mouth. "This came for you while you were on that conference call with Schaeffer a couple of hours ago."

Crap. What now? "What is it?"

"I wasn't sure . . . I mean, I was trying to find a good time to give it to you, but . . ." He looked up, an uncharacteristic sympathy in his eyes. "I guess there really is no good time."

Unease curled through her stomach. "*What* is it?"

"I don't know. It came by messenger from, um, Carl Sutton's office."

Jason's attorney.

Jocelyn managed to tighten her throat around the sound trying to escape. Managed to keep her face frozen against the pain.

Owen lifted cautious eyes to her face. "I thought Jason's estate was all settled."

She swallowed, cleared her throat, and managed a weak, "So did I."

. . . *You should see them together . . . once-in-a-lifetime opportunity . . . Rostov's heredity research . . .*

Keira was still trying to piece together that bizarre stream of information when Tony smacked his BlackBerry against the steering wheel with a curse. She flinched and came fully out of the half-hypnotic state she'd been using to tap into Tony's thoughts. Not that she'd been getting anything anyway. Whispers of possible messages continued to linger just out of reach, and his new flash of anger not only tossed a black sheet over his mind, but it added to Keira's anxiety, interfering with her abilities.

Mateo stirred where he lay against her chest. He'd finally fallen asleep half an hour ago, allowing her to focus.

Tony dropped the phone into his left pocket, close to where he held his gun, resting against his thigh. Well out of Keira's reach.

She'd had nearly two hours to consider escape plans—none of which was appealing in the middle of a quickly cooling, pitch-black desert night with no cover, no weapons, no food, no water, and no freaking idea where they were or which direction she should take. But tidbits of Tony's conversation—specifically the part about getting rid of her and being thirty minutes from an exchange point—told her she'd better do something. And given the risks and her limitations, fucking with his head seemed to be her best bet.

"You've gone and done it now." She projected a bored, knowing tone as she stared out the passenger's window at the black expanse she hoped to be sprinting over soon. "You've gone and made a decision on your own. Don't you know you're not supposed to think, Tony?"

"You really don't get it," he said, his attention steady on the road. "You never did. You look at the trees and miss the forest. You just don't have the vision."

After working with Tony for a year, she knew he wasn't the clearest thinker when he was pissed off.

"You mean the one that involves sacrificing individuals for the sake of experimentation?" she said. "Using human guinea pigs to test your latest inventions or scientific discoveries so you can turn around and give that information to soldiers who can then apply it in warfare to destroy other human beings? *That* vision? No, Tony. I don't have that vision."

"This is the problem." He slammed his palm against the steering wheel. "You completely twist the idea. If you'd been more sensible in the first place, none of this would have been necessary. I could have gone at this mission from an entirely different direction."

Yeah, he could have used her more completely than she'd already allowed. "Are you working for the same men Jason Vasser was working for? Are you working for Jocelyn Dargan? For Senator Schaeffer?"

Tony's mouth compressed in frustration. He had a narrow face, broad forehead. His dark hair was too long at the bottom, too thin at the top. His dark eyes set too far apart. He was an attractive guy when you looked at his face as a unit, but no one feature alone was the least bit handsome.

"Don't start," he warned. "Vasser has nothing to do—"

"It's called manipulation, Tony, not the greater good.

The common thread here is manipulation and control, not American freedom and safety. Framing Teague Creek for murder, rigging the trial so he'd go to prison and stop asking questions about that warehouse fire—tell me, where was the greater good in that? A little girl lost her only living parent. Teague's escape from prison—for something he didn't do in the first place—caused the deaths of innocent bystanders. Forgive me, but I'm not seeing a benefit to the American people anywhere in that scenario."

"Creek's got nothing to bitch about," Tony said. "He and Alyssa Foster made bank on that situation. After her brother raked in double settlements, they're living in fucking Fort Knox in Truckee. Neither will ever have to work another day of their lives if they don't want to." He rested one elbow on the window ledge, his fingers rubbing hard strokes over his forehead. "Besides, that situation was different."

"No, Tony, that's the point. It *wasn't* different. Let's compare that to what happened today. For whatever reason, Rostov went off the reservation. He'd made progress with Mateo, and your . . . psycho scientists . . . wanted the new and improved toy, but Rostov said no. Finders, keepers. Your job was to find out what was really going on, to find a way to steal Mateo back. You knew about me, about the way I acquired my powers through similar chemicals. Hell, you work for the people who caused them in that fire. So you used me."

Though how he knew she'd feel this deep connection to the boy, Keira had no idea. Maybe the people who'd exposed her to the chemicals in that explosion five years ago understood more about how she and her teammates would develop their powers than they did.

"But what happens, Tony, when things don't go exactly as planned? What happens when someone finds out about these chemicals and Rostov and Dargan and Schaeffer and all the games they've been playing? *Manipulation* and *control*. They turn the scene over to the army so they can classify information and destroy evidence." Before she went on, Keira coated her stomach with an imaginary steel lining, because the facts she was going to hit him with would otherwise make her puke.

"Did you do your homework on the ranch, Tony? Do you realize there were thirty-four children living there? *Thirty-four*. Sixteen adults. Your people slaughtered them, Tony. Slaughtered them. Because of *you*. Because of *your* plan."

"Stop."

"Have you ever seen that many bodies? In pieces? Burned? *Women*, Tony. *Babies*."

"Enough!"

She paused. Gave him a minute to wipe the sweat from his upper lip, slow his breathing, then pushed on. Going for the break.

"I've studied Dargan for a long time. Schaeffer, too. You know all that overtime I spend at the office, Tony? That's what I'm doing. Investigating *your* people. That's how I know they're all about *manipulation* and *control*. Life means nothing to them. Loyalty means less than nothing. It's all about power, and all they want are yes men. You went beyond yes. You put your mind to work. What do you think they're going to do to you after you drop us off? When they realize they can't trust you to stay in line?"

"What happened at the ranch . . . wasn't us. It was Rostov." Tony cast an uncertain look her way, as if he were searching for affirmation in her eyes. "Our organization cares more about life than most Americans. We're fighting to sustain and better all Americans' way of life by doing the work the public wants done but doesn't have the guts to approve."

"Straight out of the DoD black ops manual. Nice."

"If one kid could save thousands, are you saying you'd let thousands die to save that one?"

Her arms tightened around Mateo. "That's a theoretical question that can't be answered."

"It's not as theoretical as you think. Any threat to America threatens our children."

Our children. Mateo's weight seemed to double. Something unnerving shifted in Keira's belly. "And whose child is this, Tony? Who has he been snatched from to be used as a pawn in your war games?"

Tony's teeth clenched hard. His fingers choked the steering wheel.

"Who is he, Tony?" An indescribable need to know stoked her anger. "Where did he come from?"

"Some ghetto in Greece." Tony spat the words, his hand flying with the confession. "He's a fucking street urchin who begged for food like a dog. Even a restricted life in America is better than how he existed."

An uneasy tingle slithered under her skin and sank into her stomach. He was lying. She didn't know how she knew, but she knew. "You're saying you pulled him off the streets?"

"*We* didn't do anything. *Rostov* did."

That part felt true. But which streets remained in question.

"If you're not involved, how do you know that?"

"The same way you know things, Keira—information, research, observation."

"Stalking. The way the rest of your department watches our team. We all know we have shadows."

Surprise registered in his dark eyes.

She snorted a laugh. "I'm an FBI agent. You don't think I'm going to notice someone following me? Don't think Teague Creek is watching every damn move around him?"

He looked away, shrugged. "Each of you has value. Each of you poses a risk. It would be stupid not to monitor you."

Mateo lifted his head from Keira's shoulder and rubbed his eyes.

Lucas.

Mateo's single word filled Keira's head.

"Stamata t'aftokinito, Thia. Stamata to," he murmured.

Frustration sizzled over her skin. He could have been speaking an alien language for all she understood. The only thing she got out of that was Lucas. Maybe Luke was close. And even if he wasn't, Keira had to make a move soon. Who knew what would happen in thirty minutes?

"He probably has to pee," she said.

"He can wait."

"You obviously don't know kids. This car is going to reek of urine in about two minutes. You got to take a piss over an hour ago." Which had been a very good thing. If he hadn't, she wouldn't have been able to call Luke. "But you expect a kid to hold it?"

Tony looked at his watch, rubbed his hand over his mouth.

"Stamata t'aftokinito, Thia." Mateo's voice rose in a whine.

Keira looked down into his earnest eyes. He was trying to tell her something, and she didn't think it was that he had to pee.

"Fuck." Tony took his foot off the gas pedal and slowed to a stop in the middle of the deserted two-lane road. "If you try to run, I will shoot you. Do you understand me? Even in the dark, I'm almost as good a shot as you are, Keira. Don't make me prove it."

SIX

Keira kept her mouth shut so she didn't ruin this opportunity to escape. Maybe her only opportunity.

Tony scanned the surroundings and dragged Keira across the driver's seat and out the door. She struggled with Mateo's weight. The boy tried to hang on instead of standing, causing all her injured muscles to pull.

The cold night closed around her, adding gravity to her circumstances. The air was frostier than she'd guessed from inside the car, but as long as she kept moving, she'd be okay.

Tony pushed her off the cracked asphalt to a dirt strip. "Get busy."

Keira set Mateo on the ground, guided him a few feet away, and crouched in front of him. She searched the terrain from beneath her lashes, or at least what she could see of it in the sliver of moonlight and the diffusion of headlights.

A whisper of calm blanketed her shoulders. Unjustified, but real. Familiar, yet unknown.

The sandy dirt pitched and rolled in hills so slight she hadn't noticed them from the car. Ones that could provide temporary seclusion as she ran. But she'd have to do something to disable Tony first. She was fast, but carrying Mateo, she'd never outrun the man.

"And while we're out here, you go, too, Keira," he

snapped, nervous eyes darting right and left in the car's faded side beams. "I'm not stopping again. For anyth—"

A wave of energy splashed her with heat just before a fleshy smack split the air. Tony grunted and stumbled sideways, then whipped around, his weapon pointed into the darkness, wavering from one area to another, searching for the threat.

"She doesn't like being bossed around."

Luke. A mixture of excitement and relief pushed the breath from Keira's lungs in one long whoosh, and she smiled. A big, face-splitting, cheek-pinching smile.

His voice snaked through the quiet night from what seemed like every direction, but she could feel him kicking off surge after surge of emotion on Tony's right. Volatile, complex emotions she couldn't label.

Tony twisted one way, turned another, unable to pin Luke's location. Another crack of flesh on flesh, and Tony flailed backward. The flash of his gun burst red against the black surroundings. The sound exploded in Keira's ears. Her heart jerked at the same time Mateo grabbed her shirt with both hands and squealed in terror. She scooped him into her arms and darted to the opposite side of the car.

Once she'd set him on his feet, Keira pushed him back by the arms and looked him in the eye. "Stay here." With a shake of his shoulders and a determined gaze, she repeated, "Don't move."

When she turned and scuffled toward the trunk, she anticipated the grab of his hand, the sound of his voice calling her back, but neither happened. Peering around the bumper, Keira watched the men's silhouettes struggle. Both were tall. Both lean and muscular. Both trained fighters. But Luke's blond hair shimmered golden in the moonlight.

In a crouch, she started toward them. The vibrations flowing off each were so different, she would have known who was who even if she hadn't been able to see the shine of Luke's blond head. She followed her senses and angled behind Tony. Grunts, kicks, smacks, scuffles. Another gunshot. Keira's heartbeat spiked.

Her gaze hooked on to the neon flash, and she lunged. She caught Tony's wrist from behind and yanked his arm backward. When he turned a shocked look her way, Luke plowed his fist into the side of Tony's face. He jerked, spun, and dropped. Keira stomped on his forearm, wrenched the gun from his hand, and pointed it at his chest. But Tony didn't notice. He was already unconscious.

"Goddamned sonofabitch!" Luke clutched one fist inside the other, both held tight to his body. "I think I broke my fucking fingers to go along with my fucking ribs."

A laugh bubbled up from her throat. A traumatized, Tinker Bell–like laugh. When she lowered the gun, her hand was shaking. Her gun hand never shook. Never. The laugh twisted into a pained moan of relief as her shoulders sagged and her mind shorted out.

Luke advanced on her, shaking out his fist, a grimace on his scruffy face. His energy or aura or whatever the hell it was she felt spilling from him traveled in tandem, and his approach pressed in on her like an impending tsunami. She fell back a step before he closed his arms around her, yanked her against his body, and lifted her off the ground.

Sizzle. Pop. Buzz. The current mellowed to a soothing hum. Warmth coated every inch of her body. She melted into him. Dropped her arms around his neck, her face against his shoulder. He was warm and hard and strong. He smelled so good, fit her so perfectly.

Oh, yes. This is where I belong.

"Jesus Christ, Keira," he muttered against her neck, where he'd buried his face. Where she wanted it to stay. Where she wanted him to kiss her. "You just took ten goddamned years off my life."

She skimmed the fingers of her free hand through his hair. Still as rich and soft as she remembered. "Only ten?"

"The *second* ten. The first ten came off when I saw you hanging from that roof. At this rate, you're going to dig my grave in a week."

She grinned. "You always said I'd be the death of you."

He loosened his hold and let her slide down his body. And, oh, wow, how had she forgotten the steely, searing beauty of it? By the time her feet touched the ground, her hips were wedged against his erection, her belly pressed to his, her breasts flattened against his chest, and fire ripped over every inch of her.

Luke started to pull back, but Keira held on. She shouldn't. She knew. But her arms wouldn't release his shoulders. His hands gripped her waist, fingers digging into her flesh and holding her against him, as if he, too, was having a hard time letting go.

He looked into her eyes, and she could have fallen back in time—to when she could read his mind with one look into the beautiful blue irises. Now, she saw traces of that man. Relief, lingering adrenaline . . . desire. Yes, definitely desire. Need pulsed deep in her abdomen. She lowered her gaze to his mouth, so very hungry for the taste of him again. His lips looked fuller outlined with several days' worth of whisker growth, and they were so close.

"Back then I was talking about how you wore me out in bed."

She watched his mouth move with the words, basked in the way his voice showered over her, and smiled at the same time fire exploded at the center of her body. Her fingers slid into his hair, head tilted up until her mouth was on a trajectory with his—

"*Thia.*" Mateo gripped her jeans.

Her eyes snapped up from Luke's mouth and met his;

found them mirroring her flash of surprise. Then they crinkled at the corners with his slow smile, and Keira's heart
flipped, twisted, and floated to her throat.

"Thia." Mateo bounced restlessly at their feet, his arms
stretched up to her. *"Aggalia."*

Reality check.

She released Luke, and as if the three years separating
them whirled in to take over, contentment and love washed
out on one wave, disappointment and heartache swept in
on another.

Definitely a reality check. What in God's name was she
thinking? Kissing Luke was like inviting catastrophe into
her carefully secured world. She needed to get back to
Sacramento—way the hell far away from him.

Mateo clawed at her clothes, panic shining in his eyes.
Exhaustion crept into Keira's muscles. As much as she wanted
to wrap that little bundle of heat into her arms, she just
didn't have the energy.

She set the safety on Tony's weapon, stuffed it into the
waistband of her jeans, and dropped into a crouch. Mateo
immediately crawled into her lap. And while one type of
heat ebbed, another grew. She closed her eyes and let her
face drop against his pillow of curls. This was all so damned
confusing.

"I can't carry you anymore, kid." She glanced up at Luke.
"He may not look big, but he gets heavy after a few hours."

Reality seemed to have crept in for him as well. His smile
was gone. The light, crystal-clear eyes she'd looked into just
moments ago had turned dark and veiled. Scowl in place,
one arm crossed protectively across his abdomen, he used
his foot to roll Tony onto his back.

"This from a woman who maneuvers her body like a
freaking acrobat." He leaned down and grabbed the collar
of Tony's shirt. "You're going to have to handle the kid.
I've got this mess to deal with."

With a firm hold on Mateo, Keira pushed to her feet. Luke hauled Tony across the dirt and onto the asphalt, dropping him alongside the still idling vehicle. Tony's head smacked the road, and Keira winced. Luke pulled handcuffs from the back of his jeans, clamped one around Tony's limp wrist, the other around the passenger door's handle. He paused for a moment, bent over, hands on knees, breathing hard, face scrunched in pain. Then started going through Tony's pockets.

"What are you doing?"

He plucked the wallet and phone from Tony's trousers and shoved them into his own jeans. Then he tugged off the unconscious man's dress shoes and chucked them into the darkness.

"What does it look like I'm doing? I'm making sure he doesn't go anywhere anytime soon."

"But . . . Shouldn't we take him in . . . or with us . . . or something?"

Luke's eyes cut to hers, looking more silver than blue in the moonlight. "You were the one who told me not to trust anyone. Do you want to explain all this to local deputies?"

"Well, no." It sounded absurd now that he'd spelled it out. Still . . . "It just doesn't seem right to let go of someone who knows so much. He has information—"

"That I doubt he'd give us short of torture."

"How did you find us?"

Luke opened the back door. With one long leg extended behind him, the other knee braced on the backseat, he rummaged through the car's contents. She didn't notice he hadn't answered. She was too busy staring at his butt. She couldn't say it was her favorite part of the male anatomy, she preferred the tan, sinewy strength of a man's forearms. Or hands. Broad palms, long, strong fingers, short, clean, well-shaped nails. Good hands were hard to find. But Luke's hands . . . Oh, Luke's hands were . . .

No, no, no. Keira snapped a mental stop sign into place. Really, *don't go there.*

She had to admit, Luke's butt had always been exceptional, too. Perfectly shaped, muscular . . .

"Why don't you make yourself useful instead of staring at my ass?"

She was startled out of her daydream, her face heating all over again. For a long second she wasn't sure if he'd said it or thought it, but the words still rang in the cold night air, and her embarrassment ramped up faster than she could shift Mateo to her other hip. "Get over yourself. I've seen better."

He straightened from the car and shot her a smirk. *No, you haven't. You've said so yourself.*

The memory of telling him what a great ass he had and how much she loved it every chance she got so many years ago sent a rush of heat up her neck. And the way Luke was projecting his thoughts as easily as if he'd spoken was really starting to bug her. "You sonofa—"

"You really should stop swearing in front of the kid." He rounded the car to the driver's side.

She narrowed her eyes and beamed her next thought at his head like a softball. *Fuck you.*

"Baby." He pulled open the car door and crossed his arms on the roof, his eyes intent and direct on hers. "Don't let that smart mouth write checks *your* sweet little ass can't cash."

She wasn't going to take the bait. It would just start a senseless fight. "You're reading my thoughts now, too?"

"I guess so. Lucky me, huh?"

Luke ducked into the car and rifled through the glove box and center console while Keira tightened the reins on her temper. He knew exactly how to push her buttons. This must have been where she'd learned how to mess with people's minds.

He shut down the engine and pulled the keys. The silent night rushed in and filled the void, shaking her back to her barren surroundings and the near freezing temperatures. She shivered.

Before she could broach a discussion on plans, Luke turned, drew back his arm, and chucked the keys into the night.

Keira's mouth dropped open. "What . . . ? Why did you . . . ? How are we . . . ?" Her mind clicked in and she peered around the darkness again. "You didn't answer me. How'd you find us? How'd you get here?"

"I found you the way you expected me to." He came back around the car, took one last satisfied look at Tony, and put a hand on her arm, urging her forward. "The GPS on your phone. Brilliant, by the way. I'm impressed."

She shouldn't be bolstered by the offhanded compliment, but she was. "Where are we—"

Her gaze fell on a black sedan parked in a shallow valley.

She held the rest of her questions until he was behind the wheel, pulling out onto the road. "You're going the wrong way."

"No, I'm not."

She turned and looked at his profile. So different from Tony. All balance and symmetry. Square jaw, high cheekbones, full lips. Too handsome. Too damned sexy. Frustration burned. "Your hair's too long. You look like a girl."

He lifted a brow, cast a *where-did-that-come-from?* look out of the corner of his eye, and raised his chin toward Mateo. "That's funny considering you can't keep your hands out of those curls."

"He's a little boy, not a grown man. When's the last time you shaved?"

"I was about to when *someone* called begging for my help. I got a little . . . distracted."

Distracted. Keira's mind shifted to another place, another time, another distraction. To Luke standing in front of the mirror in his bathroom at his home in Truckee, with nothing but a white towel wrapped low at his hips. She could still see the tan shade of his skin and the muscles of his chest and belly rippling beneath. The strip of fine gold hair starting at his navel and disappearing beneath the edge of the towel shimmered in the fluorescent light as he bent over the sink with a razor in one hand, shaving cream in the other.

She had uncoiled from their warm bed and walked in on him. The animalistic look he'd tossed her way then made her blood simmer even now.

"Baby," he'd said, with a hot, sweeping glance down her naked body, "don't distract me when I've got a razor blade in my hand."

Luke hit the brakes. The car jerked and slid on the sandy highway. Keira held Mateo tight with one arm, slapped the other hand to the dash.

When they came to a stop, Keira's gaze scoured the landscape, searching for a threat. "What? What's wrong?"

Luke's low growl filled the car. "What the fuck was that?"

"What was . . . ?"

Keira swung her attention to Luke, and the expression on his face stopped her midsentence. Then the sensation penetrated. Lust. Vivid, fiery, nearly painful desire danced around the car's interior, pierced her chest, and prodded a similar awareness deep inside her to come out and play.

Lucky for her, Luke didn't give it a chance. He lowered his chin, raised his hand, and pointed at her. "Don't you dare start putting shit like that—"

"Shit?" She raised her brows. "I see. Our memories are now *shit* in your book?"

"That's not what I meant—"

"Let's make this clear—I'm not putting anything into your head." She swung her hair over her shoulder and lowered her voice to a velvety tone he used to thrive on. If she had to suffer, she might as well have company. "Because if I were, I would have added the incredible smell of that shaving cream. Mmm, yeah." She closed her eyes, dropped her head back, and took a long, slow, deep breath through her nose, filling her chest. "I would have added the memory of how I pulled that towel off you and started drawing—"

"Keira! Stop." He shifted in his seat and tugged on the leg of his jeans as if they were too small. "For Christ's sake, I remember just fucking fine, thank you very much."

"How does that saying go?" A zing of accomplishment made her grin. "Don't let that smart mouth write checks your sweet ass can't cash?"

"Christ," he muttered, releasing the brake and starting forward again, wiping his forehead as if he were sweating. "I don't even want to hear what others say aloud half the time. I sure as hell don't want to hear what they're thinking. Why the hell am I here again?"

A flutter of guilt dulled the enjoyment of seeing him suffer. He *had* saved her. She didn't know if she would have gotten away from Tony on her own or not, although she would have tried. She could have very well died out here tonight. Mateo could have died out here with her.

Keira released her seat belt and shifted Mateo in her lap so she could lean across the console. She pressed her forehead to Luke's cheek. Absorbed the gentle scratch of his whiskers on her skin. So real. So alive. Closed her eyes and breathed in that familiar sexy scent of pure Luke. The blend of sweat and soap and skin went straight to her bloodstream. Who needed booze? Who needed drugs? He was the only controlled substance she'd ever wanted. Only, coming off the high? Not so fun.

She pressed her lips against the hollow of his cheek. Just for a second. Only a second. Forced herself to pull away. "Thank you for coming."

"Suck-up." His voice came out rough as he reached

around and gave her head an affectionate squeeze against his before pushing her away. "Get back on your side of the car and fasten your seat belt."

Yeah. Good idea. *Note to self: Don't do that again. Your control isn't as strong as you think.*

Keira redirected her thoughts to the desert view in the headlights as she resettled into her seat when all she wanted to do was climb across the console and straddle Luke's lap. "How did you beat us here?"

"I flew."

She raised a brow. "I assume you mean that figuratively."

"No, literally. I flew. You know, in a plane. One with wings and a propeller—"

"Smart ass. There's no . . ."

Her words died. In the distance, lights twinkled against the night, illuminating a rudimentary airstrip and a couple of industrial buildings surrounded by chain link. Within the confines of the fence, one small engine plane sat waiting.

"Oookaaay," she said. "Did you get your pilot's license in the last three years in addition to changing careers?"

She couldn't help throwing in a dig about his job change, considering the hell he'd given her when she'd decided to leave firefighting.

"I didn't change careers," he said. "I'm still in the fire service."

"Last time I looked, firefighters didn't carry subguns."

"So, I'm a fire cop." Luke slowed the car and squinted through the windshield. "And, no, I didn't get a pilot's license."

Keira followed his gaze to a man descending from the plane. "Is that your pilot?"

The car came to a complete stop a half mile away from the plane. Luke leaned forward, both arms folded over the steering wheel.

"No," he said. "That's not my pilot."

★   ★   ★

"Goddammit." Luke sat back and pounded the steering wheel. "Could one freaking thing go right today?"

"We're alive."

"Thanks, Pollyanna."

Keira kissed Mateo's head. "Don't grow up to be an ass like some people, okay?"

Luke ground his teeth as the creep inspected the plane. The pilot he'd met at the Las Vegas airport had been wearing black pants and a white shirt before donning an olive-colored air force flight suit. The prowler wore tan cargo pants and a jean jacket. And he was Caucasian. Luke's pilot, Joe Marquez, had been Hispanic.

Before Luke could figure out the next step, another man emerged from one of the hangars. Still not Joe.

A touch grazed his arm. He turned to look at Keira, but the heat traveling up his shoulder and across his chest came from Mateo. The kid was sitting up, his big brown eyes glazed as if his mind was somewhere else. *"Einai entaksei, Lucas."*

He had no idea what the boy had said, but was reassuring nonetheless. He reached over and ruffled the curls Keira loved so much. "Guess we need to go to plan B, huh, buddy?"

"What's plan B?" Keira asked.

"Don't have one."

A hard knock clattered on Keira's window. All three of them startled. Luke and Keira drew their weapons at the same time and pointed at the glass.

A man stood outside in a partial crouch, hands up, palms out. "It's me. Marquez."

Luke released the air caught in his lungs. "I'm going to die of a heart attack before this night is over. It's my pilot."

Keira didn't move. "How do you know you can trust him?"

"Because he's Mitch's friend."

Her gun lowered, and she twisted to look at Luke over her shoulder, eyes bright with renewed interest. "Mitch? Mitch got the plane?" A smile drifted over her mouth as she hit the button to roll down the window. "I'm going to be giving that man an appropriate thank-you next time I see him."

"Over my dead body," Luke muttered.

"That can be arranged."

"Hel-looo." He pointed at himself. "I'm the one who's here. I'm the one who's risked his ass half a dozen times today, not that pansy wannabe."

"You're so exaggerating. Twice, and one of those is washed out by the fact that I saved your ass once. Don't worry, by the time this is over, I have a feeling we'll be even."

"That doesn't exactly make me feel better."

"Hey, there, ma'am." Marquez offered his hand through the window. "Colonel Joseph Marquez, United States Air Force, retired."

They shook. "Keira O'Shay, Special Agent, FBI, seriously *wishing* I were retired."

Marquez chuckled.

"You forgot your SWAT title," Luke muttered.

"Oh, yeah. That, too." She looked down at Mateo, who was peering at the man from his customary spot leaning against Keira's chest. "This is . . . well, we think his name is Mateo."

Marquez reached in to take the boy's hand. Keira expected Mateo to shrink, but he didn't. He let Marquez engulf his hand and shake.

"Hey, little man. You sure are cute."

Keira lifted her chin toward the airstrip. "What's going on over there?"

"No idea." He glanced over his shoulder. "Sure would love to know how they got out here so fast, though."

"Probably followed the flight plan," Keira said.

"Nope." Marquez leaned one forearm on the window ledge. "Flying under the radar tonight."

"Get in." Luke hooked a finger toward the backseat. "We'll figure it out on the move."

"Nah." A glint of excitement sparked in Marquez's dark eyes. "I've got a few buddies and the cops coming. Those guys will never mess with one of my planes again."

He reached into the front pocket of his jumpsuit, fishing around for something. "Take this road back the way you came. In a quarter of a mile, turn right. The road dips into a shallow valley, so no one coming this way will see your headlights. It'll dump you back onto the highway past the road the cops will take to get here. Hawthorne is a hundred miles northwest. Carson City is another sixty."

He pulled out two business cards from his jumpsuit and handed them to Keira. "If you run into any trouble, if you need anything, these guys are pros. One in Hawthorne and one in Carson. They're also indebted to Mitch, so you can trust them. I've called ahead. They're ready if you need anything. And if I get any info out of these yahoos"—he nodded toward his plane—"I'll pass it on to Mitch."

Luke relaxed into the first sense of control he'd had since he'd set foot on this baked Nevada dirt. He reached across Keira and shook Marquez's hand. "We owe you, man."

"I could do favors for Mitch the rest of my life and not adequately repay him. We're good." He popped a hand against the window ledge. "Now get out of here before the cops show."

Marquez jogged into the darkness. Luke swung a U-turn and started back.

After an extended silence Keira said, "Do you know . . . exactly . . . what Mitch does?"

"I know he defends criminals. Does a lot of work for military guys."

"I know creeps come in every shape, size, and color, but Marquez sure doesn't strike me as a criminal. And if they're dirty, why are all his clients found innocent?"

"Because he's a damned shark," Luke muttered. "A good one."

Keira turned those sharp blue eyes on him. "Why do you hate him?"

"I don't *hate* him. I just don't particularly *like* him."

"Jealous?"

He scoffed. "Of what?"

"His money, his power, his lifestyle, his intelligence, his success. His looks."

"No." Luke slanted her a glance. "You hot for him?"

She grinned. "I could be."

He narrowed his eyes in a glare before refocusing on the road. "What irks me about the guy is his arrogance."

"Confidence."

"Whatever."

"That's interesting coming from the most confident man I've ever known."

Luke slid her a look, sure he'd just heard her wrong, only his chest was warming with an uncomfortable sensation.

"When you turn off," she said, "pull over and switch seats with me. I need a break from this living appendage."

He didn't like the idea of stopping. Not here.

"It'll be fast," she said. "I'll just slide across the seat."

Irritation rolled through his shoulders. "Only if you'll tell me how to get you out of my head."

"You banished me from your head a long time ago, Ransom. This is just a temporary setback."

He stopped, put the car in park, and held his thoughts until he was outside. Whether or not that would keep her from hearing them, he didn't know.

Temporary. She would walk out of his life again when this was over. And where would he be? Back to women he couldn't connect with? Who didn't understand him or his life?

The cool night air washed over him but didn't ease his distress. When Keira was situated in the driver's seat, Luke dropped into the passenger's side and took the sleeping boy into his lap.

He pulled Tony's wallet from his pocket, unfolded it, and peered at the driver's license. "Oh, well. What can you expect from the DMV?"

Keira ignored him.

He opened the billfold and whistled, pulling out a dozen twenties. "Looks like drinks are on Esposito."

"Luke," Keira chastised, as weak as water.

"Keira," he mimicked, then brought reality into play. "Do you happen to have any cash on you?"

She quirked her lips and looked away.

"I didn't think so." He stuffed the money in his pocket and started pulling cards from the wallet slots. "Visa. This sure as hell isn't where I want to be."

"That's not their tagline anymore."

"What is it?"

"Life takes Visa."

"I like the other one better." He pulled out another. "MasterCard. Whatever money can't buy—doesn't interest me."

Keira rolled her eyes. "Why doesn't that surprise me?"

"Men's Wearhouse. I didn't particularly like the way he looked. But *you* may have had a different opinion."

"Don't start."

He yanked several more cards. "*Seven* department stores— Nordstrom, Macy's, Saks Fifth Avenue . . ."

She shot him an incredulous look. "How can he afford to shop there?"

"I'm guessing the shadow agent business pays well. Is this guy a fucking clothes whore, or what?"

"You should really stop swearing in front of the kid," she said in a voice that mimicked his earlier condemnation of her language.

"Funny." Another compartment contained more plastic. Luke sifted through them. "Furniture. Tools. I don't even know what these other places—oooooh." A black card with red cursive writing across the face sparked his interest. Then shot a stab of anger through his chest. "This is interesting."

Keira's head turned toward him. "What?"

Luke watched her expression as he turned the card to face her. "Frederick's of Hollywood."

One side of her face crunched. "That's not interesting. It's . . . *Ew.*"

He went back to the wallet. "He never brought you home a teddy?"

"Don't *even* go there."

"Or the stockings you like with those things . . ." He waved his hand to nudge his memory—for the name, not the image. He'd never forget how she looked in those sheer black stockings that stopped at the top of her toned thighs, held up by straps attached to some thread of silk tugged low on her flat belly. The way he'd been able to slip off the matching panties—if you could call the scrap of fabric she'd been wearing panties—and slide into her with that sexy lingerie still on.

Keira hit the brakes. In a reverse déjà vu, Luke held tight to Mateo and hit the dash with the opposite hand.

"They're called garters, and the answer is no," she growled before he had a chance to figure out why she'd stopped. She stared straight ahead, jaw pulsing, voice low. "You really don't want to get into this game with me, Lucas. It would be wise of you to remember that it's my gift, not yours. I've had it for five years. You've had it for five minutes. If you insist on playing, not only will I win, I won't show you any mercy."

He shouldn't find that threat sexy. There was something really wrong with the way his mouth went dry and visions of dominatrix role-playing—which he'd never engaged in, nor even been interested in—flashed in his mind. Considering who and what she'd become, personally and professionally, his heart should have been terrified to a dead stop by now. This was not the tentative young woman who'd walked away from him three years ago—smart, independent, but still growing and reserved in so many ways.

This was a woman who had found herself. Had tapped into her strengths and polished them to a blinding gleam. Mature, intelligent, savvy. Definitely a handful, as her boss had so accurately described her. And she was blazing hot.

But there was still some of that softer side underneath. The side she tried to hide. He'd heard her back there in the desert whisper against his shoulder. *This is where I belong.*

"Like I said before, O'Shay"—he leaned back in the seat, confused over the complex new feelings of both loss and excitement—"save it for someone you scare."

Once she'd reached cruising speed again, he added, "And just for the record, this is not a competition. And you're right, I don't have control over my brain the way you do, so I'm sorry if my thoughts offend you. I'll try my best to . . . *un*project. Or whatever."

Keira remained silent—both verbally and mentally.

He finished studying the credit cards, checked a few other empty slots, then found a stack of business cards. "Well, he carries more credit than cash. Definitely lives the American way."

"He's no American." The edge in her voice drew his gaze. Her fingers squeezed the steering wheel until they were white. "He's a psychotic mini-Hitler wannabe."

Luke waited a beat. "Do you want to expand on that?"

"Not at the moment."

"Oooookay." He sifted through the cards. "CPA, Attorney, Hair Stylist, Masseuse, Manicurist . . ." Luke raised his brows, tilted his head in her direction. "Metrosexual, huh?"

"I wouldn't know."

"Right." He returned his attention to the cards. "Chiropractor, General Physician . . ."

The next card shocked him into silence. If he thought the Frederick's credit card lit him up, this one jacked him one hundred eighty degrees. He couldn't be seeing it right, because it looked like . . . He held it closer to the ambient light drifting off the dash's clock. Yep, it was a . . . well, porno might be a little strong. Then again . . . maybe not.

"What did you find?" Keira asked.

"Uh . . . Well . . ."

He wasn't sure how this would hit her. Wasn't thrilled with the possibilities, either. Best to just get it over with. He held the business card between his fingers and faced it toward her.

She squinted; then her eyes popped open along with her mouth. "What is that?"

"I believe *that* is fondly referred to as the reverse cowboy." He turned the card back around and looked at it, one edge of his mouth turning up. Goddamn, he had a hard-on. Didn't take much nowadays. "Surprised you don't recognize it. Isn't it one of your favorites?"

"It shouldn't surprise you that I don't recognize it if you can't even remember what sexual position I like."

Oh, he remembered. But it was damn fun to bait her.

"Rapture." He read the card, caught between turned-on, disgusted, and so jealous his hair was about to catch fire. "A full-swap or soft-swap swingers club for the exclusive couple."

She rested her forehead in her hand and slid her fingers

down to rub her eyes, then returned her gaze toward the road with a shoulder-rocking sigh.

"So." Luke snapped the wallet closed, tossed it into the glove compartment, and tapped into the Internet on his own cell. He wanted to be distracted when they went through this part of the conversation. "Give me the real deal on Tony. And when did you pick up this . . . swingers fetish? But, wait." He looked up from his phone. "First, I have to clarify. That's like . . . everything goes, right? Even women on women? 'Cause the thought of you . . . and . . . oh, babe." He laughed, held up a hand to her. "Stay out of my head right now."

A fist slammed his chest. His broken ribs shook. Breath stalled. Pain radiated. Lungs seized. He coughed, holding his chest against the shooting stabs.

"We weren't seeing each other," she growled through gritted teeth. "We *worked* together."

"Right." He sucked in air as the pain ebbed to an ache. "I always *kiss* my coworkers."

"Yeah, I heard that about you, Ransom. Heard you get around. Wife shopping, they say."

His head swung toward her. "Who says?"

"Everyone."

"Who's everyone?"

"It's a small town. Word gets around."

"You don't even live there anymore."

"You think I don't have any friends? You think I don't talk to anyone anymore just because I live a couple hours away? Have you ever heard of e-mail? Skype? Social media? I keep up."

A sinking sensation burned down the length of his belly. He didn't like the possibility that she knew everything he'd been doing the last three years. He'd made his share of mistakes. Every damn one of them out of a search to fill the void she'd left. And seeing her again, experiencing her quick mind and sharp wit, made him feel even lonelier than when she'd left. How humiliating was that?

"Nobody says a word to me about you," he said, trying not to pout.

"That's your own doing." She snorted an irreverent laugh. "You think I don't know about your directive?"

Fuuuuck. Luke looked out the passenger window at the darkness. The cold slid in through the window and over his shoulders. "I hate that town," he muttered.

"Have you found your fairy tale yet, Luke? A woman who will bring your slippers and fill your house with babies?"

Who-oa. That jab hurt worse than the fist. And it landed way lower. His anger built again. But it gave him hope, too. Maybe she didn't know *all* the inept details of his life without her.

"I thought you kept up," he snapped. "Still as judgmental as you used to be, I see. Why are you deflecting the conversation? You think starting a fight will make me forget I watched you kiss that ass?"

"I didn't kiss him. *He* kissed *me.* And if you'd waited at the hospital, instead of turning your back on me—something you're evidently good at—I could have explained. I told you the truth. We dated *one* time, nearly a year ago. He never let it go. At least, that's what I thought. Should have known no one would pine for me that long. You sure as hell didn't."

Luke heaved a breath and forced his mind away from the automatic thought that came in response. Instead, he visualized a barrier coating the inside of his skull. Then he let the internal words go.

No, I pined for you much longer.

And waited.

"Dammit, it's none of your business, anyway. I'm not discussing this with you again." She lowered her chin, took a breath, and repositioned her hands on the steering wheel. "I also wanted to tell you something about Mateo."

She hadn't heard him. If she had, she'd have picked up and run with it. Could he have found protection against his stupid self?

"What about him?" Grateful for the change of subject, Luke tapped into his Internet browser and Googled "Greek translation."

"He's . . . special. I mean, he's . . . like us."

For some reason, that resonated with him. "Why would you think that?"

"He has the mark. I found it when I was washing him."

Luke looked down at the boy sleeping against his chest. "Where?"

"Same place as yours."

He set his phone on the dash, repositioned Mateo's limp body, and pulled at the waist of the boy's jeans. Sure enough, on the front of his right hip, where his leg met his pelvis, faint purplish marks stained his skin.

Luke's own scar heated as if in response to the connection. He hit the overhead light to get a better view.

"See?" Keira said. "It's the same. The wings, the body. Looks just like a—"

"Phoenix." He looked up at Keira, shocked, suddenly breathless. "What's his power? What can he do?"

She shook her head. "I have no idea."

Silence filled the car. The road noise joined the tension, creating an ominous air.

Luke's cell rang. He answered, distracted. "Ransom."

"Do you have her?" Mitch asked, voice filled with concern.

"Yes, I have her. She's . . ." *A pain in the ass.* "Fine."

"Same to you, Ransom," she muttered.

Luke rubbed his eyes, reminded himself to pull up that shield before he thought something, dammit. Then he refocused on wrapping his mind around everything that had happened. Everything that could still happen. "There was a problem at the airstrip—"

"I know. Marquez called me. Listen, just keep driving straight to Teague's. I'm waiting for information, but should have something by the time you get here."

Luke ran a hand over Mateo's head. "No, we can't go there. Too risky."

"This place is a fortress. There's nowhere safer."

"These people want this kid bad, Mitch. They've already killed dozens to get to him. I won't risk Teague and Alyssa's family." *My family.*

A long silence fell over the line before Mitch asked, "What kid?"

SEVEN

Keira drove in silence, stealing glances at Luke every few minutes. Okay, maybe it was every few seconds. He hadn't spoken again since he'd hung up with Mitch. She wanted to talk to him about her confrontation with Tony in the car. Then again, she didn't. Seemed the more they talked, the more they argued. And since he was definitely in a mood, their already high probability of fighting doubled.

His frowning face glowed in the light reflected from his phone as he continued searching translation websites. Without looking up from the phone he said, "Bad man."

"Huh?"

"That's what he's been saying. *Kakos andras*. Bad man. And *kakee andras* is bad men."

She thought back to the moments she'd heard Mateo think or say the words—on the chopper, when Tony walked into the ER. "But . . ."

"How would he have known?" Luke turned off the Internet and rubbed his eyes. "I don't know, but I can't think anymore. Hawthorne is coming up. We need gas, need to get this kid something to eat, and figure out where the hell we're going. I'm fresh out of ideas for the next step."

The edges of town passed by the windows in a dark blur. Keira spotted a Chevron and pulled up to a pump. Aside from a cashier lingering in the snack shop, the station was deserted.

She turned off the car and looked at Luke. "I'll get the gas if you take him to the bathroom. He hasn't peed in hours, and I don't think I'd be a very good mentor in that department."

Luke grinned, the first real grin she'd seen since they'd set eyes on each other earlier that day, and her heart tightened uncomfortably. "I suppose. Come on, champ. Let's take a leak."

Keira rolled her eyes and pushed her door open. "Spoken like a true male of the species."

Mateo woke up, his dazed dark eyes darting around like little arrows. He held out his arms to Keira and pushed off with his feet, forcing a grunt from Luke. *"Thia."*

She took hold of his hands and squeezed. "Shh, you're okay. Look." She pointed at Luke, and Mateo settled right down. "When you get back, look up that word, *Thia*. And will you drop money with the cashier before you go to the bathroom, please?"

"Here's a lesson, kid: they never stop making demands or asking for money. Get a good job when you grow up. And remember, civil service pays crap." Luke tsked and pulled the wad of twenties he'd taken from Tony's wallet out of his pocket, tipping his head in consideration. "Except for maybe shadow DARPA agents. That might be the way to go."

"Don't put more crap in his head." Keira climbed out of the car. "You're going to ruin him."

She waited at the pump and watched the boys disappear into the mini-mart. Luke carried Mateo even though his broken ribs had to be hurting like hell. Sacrifice. That's what parenting was all about. And, damn, Luke would make a good dad someday. He'd been a fantastic surrogate for Katrina while Teague was in prison. In retrospect, Keira

realized that Luke had found the meaning he'd been looking for in life with Katrina: a family of his own.

The death of his parents years before had hit Luke hard,
but it had been his sister's suicide that had left him barren
and searching. When Kat had been thrown at him, he'd
stumbled and fumbled. But within days, Luke had fallen
into the role of loving, doting, fun-loving, purposeful father
to the then toddler. It had been a beautiful sight to
behold—again, in retrospect.

In the moment, the ease of Luke's transformation and
Keira's utter failure to follow had been terrifying. Her own
lousy childhood had come back to haunt her in vivid Tech-
nicolor with the man she loved watching and a child's life
affected.

When the Bureau's employment offer came through, the
sixteen-week academy seemed like the perfect opportunity
for Keira to take a break, make a fresh start with her career,
get her head on straight. Luke had seen it as abandonment.
She'd wanted to go back to them after the academy, but
Luke had issued an ultimatum—the Bureau or them. He
never understood the decision had been far more complicated for her.

Luke stepped out of the mini-mart, set Mateo down,
took his hand, and swung it in an exaggerated, playful arc.
Mateo's curls bounced, the fluorescent lights above gleam-
ing off the little teeth showing in his big smile. She'd never
had a real family. Couldn't truly say she'd ever had even the
semblance of a family. But that didn't keep a familiar yearning from pulling at her heart as she watched the two of
them together.

Before disappearing into the restroom, Luke stopped,
turned, and looked at her. Mateo's happiness was reflected
in Luke's handsome face, and the joy shot across the distance like a light beam, warming Keira's heart. And for the
millionth time in the last three years, Keira wished she'd

make half as good a mom as he would a dad. But she wouldn't. Couldn't. There were just too many odds against her—historically, environmentally, genetically. And a child's life was not something she would ever use as a testing ground. She'd been there, done that, now she'd witnessed it as well. No child should live that way.

Disquiet created a subtle storm in her belly as Luke and Mateo disappeared into the bathroom. Keira took a deep breath, propped the pump nozzle in the tank, and started fueling.

A quick glance around the area and she realized they had limited food resources. No fast food. No restaurants. A blue sedan pulled into the station and parked two pumps back. Behind it, a light caught Keira's eye. Looked like a small grocery might still be open.

A middle-aged man emerged from the sedan, slipped a credit card into the neighboring pump, and pressed buttons. She swept his work boots, jeans, and flannel shirt with a cautious look and opened her mind. No unusual bulge in his clothing indicating a concealed weapon. No obnoxious penetrating thoughts.

Her own pump kicked off. She pulled the nozzle from the tank just as Luke and Mateo emerged from the rest-room, holding hands. She couldn't help smiling even as the distant storm in her belly grew stronger. Luke was definitely dad material.

She turned to replace the nozzle. A zap of lightning shot down her spine. A clap of thunder rolled through her stomach. With a hand on the pump to steady herself, she searched for Luke, as if seeking reassurance. His eyes focused behind her, his smile gone. A concerned frown switched off all that light filling his face just moments ago. He pulled Mateo into his arms with too much force. Pushed into a run.

Behind you!

Everything collided in her consciousness at once: Luke's warning, the sensations, the man at the other pump.

She started to turn—too late. The man's arm cut across her throat. Metal jabbed the side of her skull. She didn't need to look to know the barrel of a gun was pointed at her head.

"Run!" she yelled before the man jerked her head back and clamped her airway.

"All I want is the kid," the man called out so Luke could hear. "You two can go. Tony never should have involved you."

The crack of a single gunshot sounded distantly inside her head, making her flinch. A draining sensation left her icy cold. "You . . . killed him?" She tested the words against the sensations, but this ability was still so new, she couldn't tell if they fit. "You *killed* Tony?"

"All I said was that he shouldn't have involved you."

Keira closed her eyes, calming the panic and allowing other sensations to penetrate. The gas nozzle hung heavy in her hands. The weapon in her waistband lay cold against her spine. The man's breath blew warm on her cheek.

Find cover. She directed her thought toward Luke, hoping he was clearheaded enough to receive it.

When she opened her eyes and tilted her head to scan the area, Luke had taken Mateo behind a gas pump on the opposite island. Better. But it would only take one stray bullet in this fuel dump to rip open the sky with a fireball.

"Come on." The man's breath made smoke signals in the frigid air. "Let's get this over with. When the cops show up, not only do I get the kid, but you two go to jail. That's unnecessary, don't you think? I'm trying to give you an out here. Bring me the kid."

On three, sprint to the car. Keira counted in her head. *One. Two. Three.*

She sucked air, held it, and ripped the pump nozzle up

and over her shoulder. It met the man's head with a *thunk*. He grunted. Wavered. The gun drifted away from her head. But he didn't let go. She swung again. Something on his face crunched near her ear. Blood spurted. Splattered her face and neck.

The attacker's grip broke. He stumbled backward. Tripped. Fell.

The nozzle dropped from Keira's hand. She had the gun in her palm before the pump hit the ground.

"Drop your weapon." Her demand scraped her throat. "Drop your weapon, now!"

The man writhed on the ground, the gun still in his grip. He wiped blood from his face, lifted his weapon toward her chest.

She squeezed her trigger. Again. And again. And again.

Too good. Too comforting. Too easy.

Keira didn't know how many times she fired before Luke's voice penetrated the ringing in her ears.

"Keira, stop! He's dead. Keira!"

Somewhere in her mind, she registered a hand on hers, the tug of her sleeve, warmth around her shoulders. Then she was in the car. She couldn't hear anything but that obnoxious buzz. Couldn't see anything but a fuzzy black background. Couldn't feel anything but cold. Bone-deep cold.

"Breathe, baby." The voice came from inside a tunnel very far away. "Just breathe. You'll be okay."

The car whipped her back, right, left. She pressed her head against the seat, closed her eyes, and used the inside of her jacket to wipe the sticky blood from her face. "I'm going to be sick."

"Not yet," Luke said. "Give me a couple minutes. Come on, sweetheart, breathe. Deep, slow breaths."

Warmth crept into her lap in the form of a little body. Mateo's palms rested against her cheeks. His forehead pressed against hers.

"Irémise, Thía moo."

Whatever he'd said calmed her instantly. She shut her brain down and reveled in the sensations pouring from his touch, filling her with light and chasing the dark away. She circled his wrists with her fingers, pulled his arms around her neck, and enveloped him in her arms. And as if he were purging the trauma and anguish from her body, the sense of doom lifted.

By the time Keira opened her eyes, the car had slowed. They passed through an automatic gate and crawled up a dark hill. The metal clattered closed behind them, and an unwarranted sense of safety eased her shoulders.

"Where are we?"

"One of the contacts Marquez gave us."

How Luke had known to come here, she couldn't guess. She hadn't heard him talking on his cell. But then, she hadn't heard or seen much between the gas station and now. Couldn't remember much, either. Her brain seemed frozen in a twilight zone.

As she struggled to focus on the shadowed surroundings, her mind cleared, but it wouldn't completely engage. The dirt road ended at the door of a small building. At the edge of the headlights' beam, a man emerged from the darkness and waited as Luke cut the engine and got out of the car. Their host was built like a compact truck, dressed all in black with a shaved head and stern face. Not someone she would have trusted on sight.

The two men spoke quickly, and Keira didn't have the least interest in what they were discussing. Didn't care to know their next move, let alone take it. She needed to get into a hot shower to scrub this blood off, wanted to sink into a soft bed and forget this violent world existed.

Luke came to the passenger's door, his gaze intense and searching her face through the window. Before he'd even opened the door and dropped into a crouch, Keira felt his genuine concern embrace her. He pressed his fingers against her throat, peered into her eyes.

"I'm not a science experiment." She pushed his hand away and sat up, turning Mateo to face Luke. "And take this guy, will you?"

"Well, there's an improvement." He lifted Mateo, then took her arm and eased her to her feet.

Her head seemed to lift off her shoulders. She swayed. Luke secured her against his body with an arm around her shoulders. "Not quite seaworthy yet, but we've got that shower and that bed you want. You'll feel better in a few hours."

"Stay out of my head, Ransom."

"Okay, maybe a few minutes. You always did bounce back on a dime."

Once she was out of the car, Keira forced herself to stand on her own. She wouldn't face this stranger like a wimp.

His sharp eyes studied her and Mateo as they approached.

"Ma'am," he greeted, his face a solid brick of concrete, but his voice surprisingly soft and reassuring. "Hear you've been tracking through hell."

"Singed and lived to tell about it."

The man returned her minimal grin and gestured to the door. "A safe haven from the devil himself for as long as you need it."

He unlocked the metal door and flipped on an interior light, illuminating a spacious single room with two queen-size beds against one wall, a flat panel television against another. A desk in the corner housed a computer, with a mini-fridge beneath. Everything from the brown, tweed-like blankets to the gray metal nightstands was military grade and pristine.

But it didn't feel safe. It felt cold and barren and . . . hopeless.

"Drinks and snacks in the fridge. Bathroom through that door," he said, pointing to the far side of the room. "Linens in the cabinets. But this is the important stuff."

He walked toward the computer, leaned down, and pulled up an area rug, exposing another metal door. "Escape hatch."

Keira's throat shrank. Reflexively, she stepped back.

The man pushed a metal slide embedded in the floor, gripped the indented handle, and drew it open. Keira turned her head away as unexpected memories banged on the gate of her psyche, their reaching, distorted fingers digging around the edges for leverage. She chewed the inside of her cheek to control the growing anxiety.

"The light is here."

A click sounded, and light flashed in Keira's peripheral vision. Light. There was a light. Her throat released and Keira dragged in air. Not so similar to her childhood hell after all. Damn, that little phobia had blindsided her. She hadn't even thought of that fear of dark, damp, earthen spaces in years. It had cropped up initially during her training at the academy, until she learned that they wouldn't be rapelling down mine shafts or playing hostage beneath buildings. Tight spaces were no problem. Tight spaces beneath structures or earth, however . . .

Luke's hand pressed between her shoulder blades, bringing warmth and support. Then slid beneath her hair, rested against the base of her neck, and gave a strong squeeze.

Everything's fine. You're safe. I'm here.

A bittersweet sensation pressed beneath her ribs. Having someone who knew you so well could be a beautiful thing. Unless that someone ignored what you needed even when they knew it was essential. Then it could be damn painful. But Luke's reassurance settled her crawling skin. She inched toward the hole, craning her neck to look inside. Steps led into a tunnel with rock walls and a cement floor. Her dungeon had been dirt and rotted wood. A damp, bug- and rodent-infested hole under the house. More tension eased. The fewer the similarities, the better.

Their host looked up from his crouched position. "This tunnels beneath the property about a quarter mile, exits in a safe room just below a back road." He pulled keys off a hook by the light switch. "Keys to a Jeep parked ten feet from the exit, equipped with two Glock nines and two Colt subguns."

Luke nodded his understanding, but Keira's mind had turned from her troubled past to new questions. The reality of a place like this in the middle of nowhere held disturbing connotations. As did the fact that the man owed Mitch favors of this magnitude.

He turned off the light, closed and locked the floor hatch, kicked the rug back into place, then pointed to a speaker on the wall. "Intercom directly to my house. If we need to communicate, we use this. Your cells won't work in here. There's no phone that could be tapped."

The four of them stood there in a moment of silence. Keira cleared her throat. "I'm . . . speechless."

Luke smirked at the man. "Lucky you."

Their host laughed, and the smile that cut across his face took fifteen years off his appearance. "If you need to use the car and the weapons, just give me a call to let me know where I can pick them up when you're finished."

Luke stretched Keira's jean jacket across the desk and scrubbed at the blood. Fresh clothes were not an option, and he didn't want her having to put on bloody ones in the morning. After the way she'd reacted to that tunnel, he wished he could wrap her up and take her far, far away. Anywhere those stomach-churning fears would disappear.

Her fragmented thoughts as the owner of the safe house had shown them the escape hatch had shredded Luke. He couldn't piece together what had terrorized her about the tunnel, and was furious with himself that he didn't already know. How could he have spent so much time with her, been so intimate with her, loved her so much, and still not known something that had shaped her so deeply?

Whatever it had been stemmed from her childhood. That part of her life she'd never wanted to talk about when they'd been together. Tonight, the thoughts that leaked from her mind had been in the eerie voice of a little girl.

I'm sorry. I didn't mean it.

Please, don't make me go in there!

Can we come out now? The babies are hungry.

The shower turned off, and Luke's brain veered back to the present. He chucked the washcloth at the jacket. "Fuck!"

Mateo, already asleep in the bed closest to the bathroom, stirred. Luke moved close and rubbed his back, murmuring apologies. The exhausted kid went right back to sleep.

Luke picked up the washcloth and tossed it on top of the towel he'd used after his shower. Keira had been putting Mateo to sleep.

Now she emerged, hair in tousled wet black waves, long legs extending beneath the hem of his gray T-shirt. He ignored the squeeze of his chest and brought her a bottle of water and several ibuprofen tablets. "Take these."

"Thanks for the shirt." She scanned his bare torso before tossing the medicine back and taking a long drink of water. "You look really good, Luke. Aside from the bruises, I mean."

You look . . . beyond amazing. He kept that thought to himself and turned toward the bed. "I got most of the blood out of your clothes." With a flick of the covers, he opened a spot beside the boy. "Get some sleep. We'll talk in the morning."

"Can we, um, leave the bathroom light on? I'll close the door. I just want . . . to be able to . . . see."

His heart tugged. He'd never known her to need a light before. "Sure."

"It's just that this place is kind of freaky and after everything that happened today—"

"You don't have to explain. It's fine."

She closed the bathroom door so only a slice of light flowed underneath and returned to the bed. Still holding the water bottle, she hesitated, her gaze on the bed as if considering and hope skyrocketed in his chest.

Tell me you want to sleep with me. Keeping thoughts from crossing his mind was far more difficult than keeping something from coming out of his mouth. He wanted to hold her so badly. Wanted to feel that tight body up against his. Wanted to feel her hands on him again. Hear her whisper his name. Slide his hands up her sleek thighs, over her ass. Pull her against him. Slide into her. Deep into her . . .

She flicked a look his way. Then set the water on the nightstand and settled under the covers alongside Mateo.

His air exited in a long, slow stream of relief, disappointment, and loss.

Smart girl.

With her dark hair fanned on the pillow, her face freshly cleaned, new strips secured on her cuts, those freckles smiling up at him, it took all his willpower not to climb in right next to her. He braced his arms on either side of her chest and looked down into those sparkling blue eyes.

"It's really good to see you, O'Shay," he whispered. "And for the record . . ." He hesitated, scanned that sweet, sweet face again, his chest so filled with regret he could barely breathe. "I'm sorry, too. And I should have tried a hell of a lot harder."

When a little smile turned her lips, he leaned down and pressed his mouth to her forehead. She sighed. Her warm breath caressed his chest. And he wanted more. So much more.

Push away now. Before you can't.

He reached up and clicked off the nightstand light, then forced himself to shove off the bed. The bathroom glow cast a barely there shimmer over the room. In the dark, he peeled off his jeans and eased his broken, aching body onto the other bed. When he closed his eyes, the day's events flashed before him. Endless questions, teeming uncertainty, excessive fear, senseless loss.

He floated in and out of an uncomfortable doze, sometimes waking from pain in his body, sometimes from a violent memory. This time, he came around for no apparent reason. He lay still, staring at the ceiling, trying to fade off into the edges of another dream. A pleasant dream that included Keira and him, naked . . .

A shadow moved in his peripheral vision. He tensed.

As slowly as he could make his muscles move, he slid his arm up, scooted his hand beneath the pillow, and wrapped his fingers around the grip of his Glock.

Sniffle.

Luke turned his head, just enough to get a better view of the intruder. The shadow slid along the wall. Stopped. Drifted the opposite direction.

Sniffle.

His breath slipped through his lips in relief. Not an intruder. Keira. Up and pacing the room. Fighting tears.

He released the gun. Another ten years down the drain.

Turning to his side, Luke readjusted the pillow and watched her wander as his heart rate slowed. His mind reached out, tried to connect with hers.

Who the fuck am I? What have I turned into?

An amazingly gorgeous, sexy force to be reckoned with, that's who she was, what she'd turned into.

She shook her head, moaned, and dropped her face into her hands to cover the sound.

You're torturing yourself. How long is it going to take before you ask for what you need?

She lifted her head and whispered, "Are you awake?"

"Yes."

Silence.

Her breath leaked out of her lungs. "I'm sorry. I was trying not to wake you."

"I know."

Another silence.

"Keira?"

"Yeah?"

"Come here."

She didn't move. "W-why?"

"You know why."

"I . . . don't think—"

"Keira?" He closed his eyes, visualized his body cooling. He couldn't be wound this tight when she finally caved. And she would.

"Y-yeah?"

"Come to me."

She hesitated. Took her first step. Crossed the room and stood beside his bed. He scooted back, making room for her. Still, she waited. When he lifted one arm in invitation, she finally dropped onto the bed and curled into him, much the way Mateo curled into her.

She pulled her knees up against his thighs, pressed her face to his shoulder, her hands to his chest, and broke. Her sobs raked through the knots in his chest, pulling and ripping. He held her tight, smoothed his hand over her hair.

"Shh, baby," he whispered. "It's okay now. We're all okay. Shh."

God, she felt heavenly in his arms. Warm and soft and curvy. She smelled mouthwatering. But it was the vulnerability that cut through every argument for pushing her away. The weakness she never showed anyone else that had made him fall in love with her the first time around. And this was no different. Only, when his heart surrendered and opened, he realized he'd never stopped loving her in the first place.

If he'd thought his life was rough since their breakup, it was now headed for severe turbulence if he had to continue living without her.

Ten minutes of crying was all it took for her to detox. As she calmed, her breaths slowed from chaotic spurts to shaky wisps of warm air with an occasional hiccup.

"I . . . I . . . I killed them."

"Because they would have killed you. Or me. Or Mateo."

She sniffled and nodded. "Have you ever . . . killed anyone?"

"Does wanting to count? 'Cause I was about to take Tony's head off at the hospital."

She laughed softly. Her legs uncurled, and that warm skin brushed his as they stretched the length of the bed. Excitement spiked through his body. Want rushed his system. All he could do was shift his hips away from hers. But not before his erection brushed her thigh. He sucked air against the flash of white-hot lust. Knew by the way her bright eyes darted to his face that she'd noticed. Goddamn, it had been a long time. His body felt as if it were twisting inside out with need, and everything he wanted was lying in his arms, yet he couldn't risk the reach.

He purposely averted his mind from searching hers. Any negative thought would hurt like hell. Any positive thought would push him over the edge. He wasn't stable enough in the moment to control either emotion.

Her lashes swept down to cover the sharp glint of her eyes as she looked at his bare chest. "He's a lousy kisser. Does that help?"

"Uh . . . No." *Hell no.*

"Hmm. Sorry." She bent her knee and slid it along the outside of his thigh. His throat thickened. "He's not near as hot as you. Does that help?"

"Hardly."

Her hands slid over his shoulders, his back, rounded forward to stroke his belly. Luke's body jerked in response. The warmth of her touch pushed a moan out of his throat. At her back, he closed his hands into fists to keep them from roaming, but had to open them again to grab her hands and still them as her fingers toyed with the waistband of his boxer briefs.

His breathing had picked up by the time she slid her fingers into his and flattened their palms. "His body doesn't even begin to compare to yours."

"You know . . ." He was caught between searing jealousy and a sexual need so primal he was ready to chew his own arm off to fill it. "The fact that you've kissed him and seen his body doesn't make me feel all warm and fuzzy inside."

A short, disgusted laugh scraped her throat. She pushed his hands back, rolled toward him, and whipped one leg over his hips until she was straddling him on her knees, his hands secured on either side of his head. God help him, she was gorgeous. She looked down at him with those eyes, those freckles, tossed her hair to one side, and licked her lips. "If you really want to ruin the moment, I could drag out all your . . . affairs . . . since we broke up."

Impatient for the weight of her hips on his—even while knowing it would be better for them both if she changed her mind and climbed off him—he moved beneath her. "You make it sound like I had a different girl every night. I don't know what you heard, but—"

"But it doesn't matter now. Unless you're seeing someone." Her eyes grew intense, her body still. "Are you?"

"Uh . . . no." A flicker of panic—that she might actually

go through with this seduction and he'd be so pathetically helpless to stop her once it started—had him struggling to get up. Actually struggling. She was a hell of a lot stronger than she looked. Which only turned up the heat in his flaming body. "Keira, let's back up a second—"

"Let me clear this up for you, because I know how you can beat one subject to death." She made one hard push of his hands against the bed, stilling them. Her eyes shone with residual wetness, but the mind behind them had shed any weakness. The warrior was back. And she had her sights set on him.

She bent her knees and lowered her hips until that sweet, hot center pressed against his straining erection, separated by only two thin layers of fabric. Lust kicked through his system. His eyes closed, hips rose automatically. Keira responded by rocking against him, the silk of her panties sliding along his length.

"Ah, God. Baby, what . . . ?" He'd started to ask what they were doing, but he knew damn well what they were doing. He also knew asking that question might very well stop what they were doing, and he didn't think he could. Not now. After so long without her. So many dark nights. So many unfulfilled fantasies. "Christ, Keira."

She stilled against him and waited until Luke cracked his lids to continue speaking. "Not including tonight, because *he kissed me* without my consent, Tony and I kissed once. I've seen his body during workouts at the gym. I was not involved with him, nor did I sleep with him. Nor did I ever want to." She lifted her brows, lowered her face closer to his, which pressed her hips harder against him. "Better?"

"Aaaah . . . God, yes."

"We were amazing together, Luke." She leaned closer and whispered. Her breath caressed his jaw, his neck. He squeezed her hands hard and curled his toes to keep from pushing against her. "Do you remember? How hot, how sexy, how fun? Do you remember how you taught me everything? How to touch you, how to ride you—"

"Keira." With an irritated, wanton bark, Luke opened his eyes and stared past her beautiful face toward the ceiling.

He hadn't been her first lover, but neither had she been experienced when she and Luke had finally slept together. He'd never dreamed she would end up being as much a teacher as a student.

She released one of his hands and caressed his jaw. His mouth opened against her palm. *Don't kiss her. Don't do it. If you start, you'll never stop.* He growled and closed his teeth on her skin instead.

She gasped, the sound more surprise than pain. He hadn't put enough pressure behind the bite to hurt her, just enough to snap them both back to reality. "You're playing with fire here, baby." He looked directly into her eyes with all the fierceness built up in his body, wanting her to understand exactly what she was unleashing. "It's been one hell of a long time and I'm locked and loaded."

Something hot jumped in her eyes, and a slow, wicked smile slid over her face just before her hips tilted in a slow erotic lunge. "Bring it on."

Excitement shot through his hips, up his chest. He arched and groaned. She combed her fingers through his hair, pressed her mouth to his chest. An electric wave of sensation flowed from her body to his. An overwhelming passion surged in one wild undulation, shoulders to thighs. His cock swelled until it ached.

Whoa. Whoa. Whoa. The fire mellowed and his brain came back online. "What the hell was that?"

"That was *us,*" she whispered, her mouth at his ear. "You're so right; it's been one hell of a long time, Lucas. Too damn long."

Longer than he cared to think about. Far longer than she knew.

"What?" She lifted her head, a frown of suspicion on her face.

He slid his other hand out from under hers and cupped her face in both hands. Ran his thumbs over her freckles. This reading minds thing was getting dicey, especially under these conditions. "What, what?"

"Don't what, what me. What did you just think?"

If he wanted to ruin the mood, all he had to do was answer that question honestly. Fess up to the fact that it had taken him a year to even come to terms with the realization that she wasn't coming back. That he would actually have to attempt to move on. After which he'd spent another year haphazardly dating and sleeping with every type of woman from corporate executives to free-spirit artists just to find out where he belonged. Only to discover each morning after that the hole inside him had grown a little wider, a little deeper, a little darker. Until he couldn't face one more excavation.

His solution had been to stop having sex altogether. About a year ago.

And at this moment, he would give almost anything to be able to take every one of those nights back just to be able to tell her he'd never been with anyone after her. Wished he'd been smart enough to know *this* was where he'd always belonged. That he hadn't shoved that barrier between them and broken the bond they'd shared.

Second chances don't happen as often as people think.

"You're thinking pretty hard there, Ransom. And working pretty hard to keep me out." Her fingers drifted across his forehead, down his nose to his lips. "How long is it going to take before you ask for what you need?"

He caved. It didn't even take a second.

He lifted his head, drove his fingers into her hair, and kissed her mouth before he could change his mind. She sucked in a breath of surprise, siphoning the air from his throat, then returning it on a groan as she sank in and kissed him back.

Her mouth was just like he remembered, supple, warm, wet, and so willing. Unable to wait, he swept his tongue inside. And groaned again. She still tasted wild and sultry, and now with the tang of salt from her tears, a little forbidden, a little frightening. Her tongue met his in a slow, circular sweep that made his muscles quiver.

"Oh, God," he said against her mouth. "So good, baby. So good."

Her hands wrapped around his shoulders, nails clawed at his skin as if she couldn't get close enough fast enough. He tilted his head, took her mouth harder, faster, deeper. Ignoring the pull of his ribs, he rolled them to the side, then onto her back.

She wiggled, positioning him just right between her opened legs and fully drew his hips in. And Luke felt like he'd come home. The level of joy flooding his chest frightened the hell out of him. He couldn't just have sex with her and walk away. He couldn't lose her again.

He rested high on his elbows to look down at her, that shiny black hair dark against the pillow, her face scraped, bruises developing in various places along her jaw, forehead, and cheek. "You're so beautiful."

With sultry, heavy-lidded eyes, she slid her hands down his back, gripped his ass, and pulled her hips into her as she lifted and rocked. Luke nearly climaxed. And, Jesus, wouldn't that have been a beautiful screwup?

"Slow down, baby." He clenched his teeth, moved his hips back to break the connection. Yeah, he wanted her fast, but not that fast. "You're gonna make me lose it here."

She groaned in complaint and tried to pull him back. "I love that. When you can't control yourself. When your mind blanks out and your body takes over. I want it. I want *you*."

"You are so sexy." He pushed the T-shirt up, exposing her tight abdomen, complete with a couple ridges of muscle. Pressed his hands to her waist and slid them up her ribs. So soft, so hard, so perfect. "Goddamn, you feel good. When did you go all Rambo?"

She laughed. The sound filtered through his head, squeezed every last thought from his mind, and then wrapped around his heart. Tied it off with a big fat bow. He was history. What ever made him think he could go through life without her?

He slid down her body, pressed his mouth against her belly. Her fingers raked through his hair.

"Lucas." His name was part groan, part sigh. "God, I've missed you."

Ah, shit. He squeezed his eyes against the burn. He couldn't count the number of times he'd dreamed of hearing her say those words. Only now, holding her, kissing her, loving her again, did he realize he'd also been waiting for them. Had put his entire life on hold secretly hoping, praying, this moment would come.

"Make love to me, Lucas." She pulled at his hair, squirmed beneath him, searching for contact. "I need you. I really need you."

Life didn't get any sweeter than this. He wanted to savor it. But after so long without sex, without her, his body was in the driver's seat.

He skimmed teeth, lips, and tongue up her stomach, pushed the cotton over one luscious breast, and sucked the nipple into his mouth. She fisted his hair, arched, and let out a little cry of pleasure that sparked him deep inside.

"I . . . God, I can't wait." She gripped his face and pulled his mouth from her breast. "Condoms. Do you have any?"

A light flicked on in his head. A blindingly bright light that made his brain wince. Condoms. Common sense.

"Luke?"

With his chin on her belly, he looked up at her. His stomach squeezed with dread and hope. "What . . . if I said no?"

"No, what?" She was breathing hard, eyes hazed with lust, brow pulled in confusion.

"No, I don't have any."

She stared a blank second, then released his face, pushed herself back, sitting up. The T-shirt fell over her perfect breasts. Thoughts passed through her eyes, but not her mind, at least none that he could hear. And judging by the flashes of disappointment, that was probably a good thing.

"I guess I'd say . . ." She blew out a breath, squeezed her eyes shut, and combed both hands through her hair. "Shit." Wiped both hands over her face. "Dammit, Luke. Why'd you let that . . ." She gestured helplessly. "Why'd you let me do that if you didn't have any?"

He lifted an eyebrow, barely restrained an absurd laugh. "Keira."

Anger and embarrassment tightened her expression. She pushed out a heavy breath and tried to escape from beneath him.

"Wait." He grabbed her hips before she got away and pulled her back, pressed his forehead to her shoulder. "I really want to be inside you. Really want to feel you, Keira." It was true. So damn true. He ached to feel her again. And he really *didn't* have any condoms. "We can still . . ." He kissed his way up her neck to her ear and whispered, "Let me make you come, then I'll pull out. I promise."

Her head fell back on a groan, half pain, half pleasure. He took the opportunity to bite a gentle path back down to her collarbone. "You can't be serious. Luke, you *know* that doesn't work."

He dropped his head against her shoulder again. *Would it really be such a bad thing if it didn't work?*

"Whoa." Her head came up, eyes dazed. "Did that mean what I think it meant?"

"What?" He searched his head. Had it? Well, yeah, but not exactly.

She scrambled out from under him and tossed those long, bare, gorgeous legs over the side of the bed, but didn't get to her feet. "Did you really just wonder if it would be such a bad thing if I got *pregnant*?"

"No. I mean . . . You're . . . misunderstanding."

"Am I?"

"Yes." He hesitated, then added, "Sort of."

She looked at him as if he'd grown horns.

A sense of urgency clicked on—straighten out this mess or lose the progress they'd made. He sat up, leaned close, and cupped her cheek, tightening his hold when she tried to lift her head. "I want you. I want us."

"And you want kids." Her eyes slanted with a familiar stubbornness. "Which aren't on my agenda. My mind hasn't changed."

Luke's heart pounded hard. How had this happened? He felt like they'd fallen back in time, into the same old argument they'd had more and more often after Kat came into their lives. His niece had opened up a world to him that he hadn't even contemplated before he'd been assigned as her guardian, one that he'd discovered he loved, one that completed him: fatherhood.

And the thought that Keira truly didn't want children was ludicrous. Maybe three years ago, when the trauma of the warehouse fire and the team's newly acquired paranormal skills were fresh. But now, as she neared thirty?

If there was such a thing as a natural parent, it was Keira. From the moment he'd met her, she'd gravitated toward children—signed up to give talks at schools, jumped to be the one to give tours at the firehouse. She'd taken on the role of not only mothering Kat without hesitation, but of teaching Luke how to be a parent to his own niece. And for Mateo, a kid she'd never met before this afternoon, she'd risked her life several times over.

And while he really didn't want to talk about this here or now, nor could he risk sinking his heart into her only to suffer that loss again.

"But why?" he asked, searching for patience as he remembered the strange thoughts wafting from her when they'd opened the tunnel. "You're so good with them. You were such a good influence on Kat. Mateo can't stand to be away from you for two seconds."

"I didn't say I hate kids. I love them." She gestured as she spoke, betraying intense emotion. But he couldn't tell if it was frustration or fear. "I said I don't want any of my own."

"That just doesn't make sense." Her irrational arguments pumped the heat of his anger. "Is this about the genetics thing again?"

She pushed to her feet and turned on him. "Don't mock me. You know my fears are founded. You may be willing to stick your head in the sand and procreate with this toxin contaminating our bodies, but I'm not. Especially not with someone else who also has it, doubling the chances—"

"Of what?" He stood, purposely pressing to his full height and leaning over her. "Of having a doubly gifted child?"

Not only did she mirror his posture, fully facing off with him, she lifted her chin and looked him directly in the eye. "No, of having a doubly fucked-up child."

"*Mi malonete, Thia. Mi malonete,*" a little voice broke in.

Luke darted a look behind Keira. Mateo was sitting up in bed, his hand held up in a 'stop' gesture, fear bright in his eyes as he looked at the door.

"*Kakee andres. Irthan kakee anthropee.*" He yelled, angelic face tense with fear. "*Mas vrikan kakee anthropee.*"

EIGHT

After so much time, that ugly, complex argument still hung between them—the triple sword against Keira having children: history, environment, and genetics.

And Luke still didn't get it.

She turned to Mateo with ready arms to take him in, but he shook his head, just as the lights in their room flicked on. She glanced at Luke, who stood there in nothing but boxer briefs. Muscled shoulders tapered to ripped abdomen, straight hips, awesome bulge in his shorts, thick thighs, and calves. Amazing. Edible. But, evidently, they still weren't compatible.

"Did you—?"

He held his hands up. "I didn't touch the lights."

The speaker on the wall crackled. "Rise and shine, folks. You've been tracked. Time to move out."

"Get dressed." Luke jumped into action, dragging his jeans on, tossing a fresh shirt over his head. "Come on, we gotta go."

"How'd they find us?" Keira shoved her legs into her own jeans.

Luke wrestled Mateo into his clothes, pushed the boy into Keira's arms, and headed for the trap door. "I don't know, and it doesn't matter right now."

He paused at the speaker, hit the intercom, and said, "Thanks. We'll return your vehicle ASAP."

"Godspeed, friend."

Luke pried open the metal door. The rich scent of earth filled the room. Mateo's hands fisted in Keira's jacket, and his frightened whines clouded her head. Keira's mind slid sideways. Everything faded at the edges. Sound garbled and slowed. Children's cries grew louder. Pressure built around her shoulders, pushing, pushing, pushing, until she felt powerless. She covered one ear with her palm, the other holding Mateo tight.

Please don't make me go down there, again. Please.

"Keira. Honey, look at me."

"It's cold. Dark . . ."

"I'm right here." Luke's warm hands cradled her face. "Open your eyes. You're safe. There you go, breathe. Look at me now. Into my eyes. Right here, good."

She blinked. Focused on dragging air through a constricted throat. Her eyes darted around the room. Into Mateo's worried face.

"Thia."

Embarrassment swamped her. She hadn't had one of these panic attacks for years. Luke had witnessed a couple— when things had gotten rough with Kat and those moments had mixed with a trip to the park or a hike in the woods, but he never knew why. She'd always lied.

"Keira." His voice came calm but urgent. "Where's your gun?"

"M-my jeans."

"You *have* to clear your head, baby. We have to go."

Cold. She was so damned cold. Still felt bugs crawling up her legs, over her shoulders, in her hair. She let her training take over and move her muscles while her brain recovered in standby.

Luke pulled Mateo from her arms and waved her down the ladder. "You first. I'll hand him down."

Keira hesitated at the top of the stairs. Terror ripped at her gut. The pressure of fearful tears tingled behind her nose and rose to her eyes. There was light. This was not her hole under the house.

She sucked a shallow breath and started down. At the bottom, with concrete beneath her feet, her throat relaxed. Air came easier. With air, her brain worked better.

She looked up and extended her arms, catching Mateo by the waist.

"Go," Luke said. "And don't look back. I'll catch up."

"No. I can't . . ." *Go without you.* "Luke—"

"Yes, you can," he snapped. "Go!"

She tightened her arms around Mateo and pushed into a jog down the tunnel. Bare bulbs hung on a wire every three feet, illuminating rough-hewn rock walls. The damp, musky scent of earth kept her stomach clenched tight. Kept the endless cry of children echoing in the back of her head. Kept a constant chill deep in her bones.

She felt as if she'd fallen into an Indiana Jones movie or an Elisabeth Naughton novel, in possession of a treasure everyone wanted, on a quest she didn't understand, running a race for which she had no timetable, no map.

She couldn't remember where she was going or why. Her feet slowed. She looked ahead, looked back. Both directions appeared identical. What if the guy who'd let them stay here wasn't as trustworthy as they thought? What if she was running into the arms of their enemies instead of escaping them?

Luke sprinted up behind her and skidded to a halt. "What are you doing?"

"I don't know anymore. How do we know this is right?"

He grabbed her shoulder, spun her around, and pushed her forward. "Sometimes you've got to have faith in the unknown. Move."

She let him plow her toward an all-metal room. Only when Luke shut the door behind them and dropped a thick metal bar into place could she take a full breath.

He immediately climbed the metal rungs cemented into the wall. Keira lunged for him, grabbed his shirt. He turned a confused look on her.

"Luke . . . are you sure?"

He pried her fingers open and squeezed her hand. "No. But there are very few assurances in this life, Keira. You know that as well as I do."

Yes, she knew that all too well. But she'd always had a plan. And a backup plan. And a backup, backup plan. She didn't dive into anything blindly. She'd learned that growing up in foster care. Then again in the warehouse fire.

He reached the top, held his gun in one hand as he unlatched and cracked the door with the other. Keira held her breath as he peered out.

He ducked back down, gestured her up with his gun, and climbed out of the hatch. Keira passed Mateo off to him and climbed the rungs. By the time she reached ground level, Luke had the Jeep fired up and Mateo belted in the backseat.

She dropped into the passenger's seat. Luke had the car moving before she'd even closed the door. "How'd you do that?"

"Do what?"

"Get him to sit back there?"

"I didn't give him a choice. You okay?"

"Yeah. Better."

"Good. I need you." He peeled onto the main road and tossed a map into Keira's lap. "Tell me where I'm going. He's got a route lined out on there."

Keira hit the interior light, hand still shaking. "Turn right in about two miles on Reservation Road. You can follow that to the highway or take a bunch of other back roads he's got marked. But if they could find us there, they can find us anywhere. Shit, how are they doing it?"

"Don't know." His gaze flicked between the windshield and the rearview mirror. "But it looks like they've done it again."

Keira spotted headlights out the windshield. Another set of lights coming from behind. And they were moving fast.

"I told you," she nearly screeched. "*I told you.* This is why I don't have faith in the unknown."

"I also recall you telling me that not everything in life is a conspiracy."

"Shut up." She whipped her Glock from her jeans, then remembered she only had a few shots left. "Where did he say he put the other weapons?"

"He didn't."

"Just fucking beautiful." She clicked her seat belt free and climbed into the back.

"*Thia.*" Mateo instantly reached for her.

"Okay, buddy, okay." She unfastened his seat belt and he climbed into her lap. "Shh, shh. You're all right. I'm staying right here."

She settled him on the floor, eased him onto his back, making him as small a target as possible.

"If we get out of this," she growled at Luke, "I'm going to beat you into a coma with I-told-you-so's."

"When we get out of this, you can beat me with anything you like."

"Men, I swear. You could twist anything into a sexual connotation."

"Just one of our gifts. Look under the seats."

She scoured the cargo area, found nothing. Turned back to dive under the seats and found Mateo holding up a submachine gun with both hands.

"Crap." She snatched the gun from his hands. "Baby, don't touch that."

He reached under the seat again. Keira caught his arm and dipped her head to look into the compact space. She found another subgun and two Glocks.

When she sat up, all four weapons in her lap, Luke shot a grin over his shoulder. "Oh, looky there."

"Shut up and drive. I'll shoot."

"Then get ready, 'cause they're boxing us in." The car coming toward them turned across the road to cut them off. "Hold on."

Luke braked, swerved. Keira leaned down and covered Mateo, bracing for a crash. But somehow Luke missed the other car and skidded off the road, onto the desert terrain.

Shots ripped through the night. Punched the car's grille. Mateo let out a screech.

Luke gunned the engine. The back wheels spun in the sandy dirt, grabbed, and shot them forward. Keira looked out the back window. One vehicle trailed directly behind them; the other turned to follow the first.

She rolled down both rear windows, set the subs on either side of the seat pointing out so she could raise and shoot fast. "Slow down. Let them come closer."

She sank low for cover just as the car behind them gunned its engine. Keira set one of the weapons on the edge of the open window. Aimed. Fired.

The tire of the other car popped in what sounded like another gunshot. The vehicle tipped and rolled. A thick dust cloud erupted in the night air.

"Un-be-lievable," Luke muttered from the front seat. "You took them out with one damned shot."

"Two. Always a double-tap," she corrected, but the combination of shock and reverence in Luke's voice made Keira smile. Payback for those thousands of hours on the range. "Told you I really am the best."

"Good thing," Luke said, " 'cause the others are coming on fast."

They were also already shooting. Keira resettled into position, tuned out the pings of bullets hitting their car.

"They're going for the tires," Luke said. "I'm going to make this a little tougher for you."

He swerved to the right and back. A shot hit the rear window. It shattered. Mateo screamed, clutching her leg. Another bullet hit the driver's window at an angle. More glass shattered. Luke's head whipped sideways. The Jeep jerked, then straightened out.

"Fuck," Luke bit out.

Keira's attention turned forward, where Luke pressed a hand to his temple. "Are you hit?"

"I'm fine. Would you get rid of those motherfuckers already?"

She aimed out the freshly opened space. "Thank you, *kakee andras*."

More shots rang out, snapped against the body of the car as Luke's haphazard driving made it hard for Keira to sync up.

"Give me a rhythm, Luke."

He did, steering and whipping the Jeep into a perfectly wild, chaotic rhythm that reminded her of the way their passion used to dominate them as they made love.

She pushed that thought from her mind and focused. Gave herself over to the swerves and curves. Watched the other driver's reactions. And, once she recognized the pattern, squeezed the trigger.

Four shots pounded through the windshield of the other car. It veered, hit the embankment hard, and went airborne. An extended moment of eerie silence floated as the vehicle flipped, midair. Then came down on its roof with an ear-piercing crunch of metal and rolled off into the darkness.

Keira laid her forehead against the seat. She was sweating and shaking when Luke's voice pierced her adrenaline crash.

"You are—officially—fucking amazing."

She laughed through shaky breaths. "Remember that . . . when I'm . . . making you crazy."

"Fováme, Thia." Mateo clawed at her jeans, his voice a high whine. *"Kráta me."* Keira pulled him into her arms. "It's okay now, baby. You're safe." She realized those were the same words Luke used to bring her back from the edge of the anxiety attack. "I'm right here."

"He's talking more. That's a good sign."

"Wish I could understand what the hell he's saying." She smoothed a hand over his hair. "Luke, he's shaking."

"Baby, after that fiasco, *I'm* shaking."

"This is *so* royally messed up."

Luke sputtered a laugh. "You're just figuring that out?"

She rubbed Mateo's round cheek with her thumb. "What is it about you, little guy? I mean, heck yeah, you're cute as can be, but even I wouldn't go to these lengths for a cute guy."

"Well," Luke drawled, "that's reassuring."

Keira pulled at the tight little curls at the base of Mateo's neck, as if she could straighten them if she tugged enough.

That's when she felt it, a ridge beneath his skin, just above the hairline. She probed to get a better idea of its size and shape, worried she might have overlooked an injury.

But the more she assessed, the more confused she became. She repositioned the boy in her lap and tilted his head forward. "Put your head down, baby. Let me see this."

Keira hit the overhead light and brushed the curls away. The linear bump she'd felt was a scar. Above the scar, something else lurked beneath his skin. In the shape of a square.

Her stomach went cold, then hot, then nauseous. "Oh, my God."

"What?" Luke looked back, frowning.

"At the first safe opportunity, pull over," she said. "I think I've found an answer to at least one of my questions."

"Which one?"

"How they keep finding us. I think he's got a tracker."

Cash O'Shay barely noticed the chill radiating off the tall rock walls of the hallway leading to his cell. He rubbed at his eyes. "Where did I go wrong?"

Gomez, the guard of the day, stopped at the door to Cash's cell and turned the lock. The clank echoed off the surrounding stone. "Get some sleep, Cash. It'll come to you. You're close, man. Real close."

Cash's mind cleared for a second as he looked at Gomez. The older man's dark face held a familiar expression: pity. Cash had come to recognize and read all the people here over the last three years—lab technicians, scientists, administrative personnel, guards, even the cleaning staff.

He'd attempted to befriend and even manipulate and bribe just about every one of them in an effort to escape, but he'd come to realize there was no greater motivator than fear. And all the people here were clearly still here because if they tried to leave, they feared for their lives and the lives of their families. Everyone was a prisoner of some sort.

Cash could have easily overpowered Gomez, despite the weapon strapped at his hip, but he knew from experience the guards weren't his true gatekeepers. The motion detectors, the alarms, the cameras, the Comanche helicopter surveillance, and the U.S. Army soldiers posted twenty-four-seven outside the massive facility in the middle of nowhere—those were the insurmountable obstacles for one man with no resources.

"Not close enough, Gomez."

Cash turned into his room, scanned the space he'd seen

every day for the last three years. A space they—whoever the hell *they* really were—tried to pretend was some fancy city loft with polished granite floors, frosted glass enclosures, stainless-steel fixtures, and furniture with fine linens. What Cash saw was industrial, indestructible flooring, tempered, unbreakable glass, bolts holding in fixtures and furnishings, and linens that didn't degrade, stain, or tear.

A familiar fear tapped his thoughts: the fear he'd never see the sky again. Never feel the grass. Never smell fresh air. Or never hold his son again. That hope was all that kept him going, day to day, month to month.

"Go home and enjoy your family, Gomez," Cash said. "It's all any of us really have."

With a sage nod, Gomez backed out of the room.

Cash steeled himself for the harsh sounds that inevitably came next, but it didn't help. The slide of metal on metal twisted his stomach. The clank of the lock made him flinch.

And as he stood surrounded by his cold, hard furnishings, a film of hopelessness inked his insides. After today's failure, he just couldn't take one more day of this life.

Repressed rage boiled up from his very core. His vision blurred. He leaned in and swept the contents of his bookcase to the floor with a guttural yell. Shelf after shelf of science texts and fiction hardbacks smacked the floor. He ripped his bedcovers off, overturned his mattress and box spring.

At the dining table, he hoisted the single chair over the tabletop, brought it down with all his strength. Metal clanked on glass and bounced back, smacking him in the head. Blood seeped from his skull, but he barely felt the pain.

"Mother*fuckers!*" He pounded until the metal band bordering the glass broke and a piece of the table chipped off. Then he swung the chair one final time and let go. It sailed across the room and slammed against the cement block wall without leaving so much as a nick.

Cash's mind broke. He didn't have any solid thoughts as he continued to demolish his room, only thrived on releasing the years of pent-up violence.

He was bleeding from his face, head, arms, and hands when pure exhaustion finally brought him to a stop. When his mind cleared, he was right back where he'd started. Imprisoned. Hopeless.

The single glass shard glittered in the light filtering in from the corridor. He picked up the substantial triangle and stumbled backward until his spine hit a wall, then let his muscles go and slid to the floor. He wrapped his arms around his legs and pressed his eyes to his knees.

He would go for his carotid. Forget the wrists. If he was going to kill himself, he was going to go fast. He didn't want them finding him too soon and patching him up. No, when he left this hell, it would be for good. And tonight seemed like as good a night as any.

Nothing in his army training, not even courses in surviving enemy torture, had prepared him to make it through this. He was in the fucking United States, not Iraq. He was a damned American citizen. Joined the military at eighteen and dedicated his life to protecting his country. Yet the government he'd served in good faith was the very one that had imprisoned him here.

"Fucking *sonsofbitches!*"

He tilted his chin back and set the point of glass against the pulse at his neck. If he pushed hard enough, he could cut both the carotid and the jugular with the first slice. The faster the better.

Cash took a solid hold on the glass wedge, squeezed his eyes closed, took his last breath—

"Hold it down, man. Some of us are trying to sleep."

The distant, familiar voice lanced Cash's chest with a silver light.

"Q?" Hope created a painful pressure beneath his ribs. He searched for the vent at the base of the concrete wall supporting him. It wasn't as if he could see the man through the vent, only that the metal grate provided their lifeline of communication. Was this his imagination? Cash had been going a little crazy without his friend for conversation and support. "Q, is that you?"

"Who else do you think it would be, bonehead?"

Cash dropped the glass, suicide postponed, and scooted closer to the vent. "Where have you been? It's been like a month. I thought they'd finally killed you."

"They killed me one hell of a long time ago, Sci-Fi. Now they just fuck with what's left of my brain until they get bored."

The nickname Q had given Cash when they'd first talked through the walls and Q had discovered Cash was a military scientist brought tears to the backs of Cash's eyes. Over their sketchy years in this dungeon, through the slats of this vent, they had built a bond stronger than Cash had once had with any of his military buddies, stronger than any childhood friend. The only relationships that meant more to him had been those with his wife, Zoya, his sister, Keira, and his son, Mateo.

"I . . . I don't think I can do this anymore, Q."

"You have to," Q said. "You've got a kid to think about."

"Do I? I don't even know if he's still alive. They're probably using that lie as a fucking carrot."

The possibility had always been out there, lingering in the back of his mind, but he'd never said it aloud. Now he knew why. Even the remote chance his son was dead gutted him.

"What if it's not? What if he *is* out there?" Q paused, then said, "I take it your shit didn't gel tonight."

Cash thought back to the moment his experiment had failed. He'd hoped to create the substance for a bulletproof, fireproof, flexible, breathable material for the American troops, but it hadn't hardened from a sticky liquid into the projected neoprene-like "skin." There would be no success. Which meant no freedom. No Mateo. No new life. "No. It didn't gel."

"Did you let the mixtures breathe before you joined them, like I said?"

Cash couldn't bring himself to think about the circumstances of the experiment failure. Q had learned everything he knew about science and experiment from Cash over their years of talking through the walls. They either talked about Cash's previous life, science, or fiction, because Q didn't have any memories or self-knowledge to discuss prior to his time in the Castle. He didn't even know how old he was.

Cash often wondered if the man stayed sane precisely because he had nothing else to live for—at least that he knew of—outside these walls.

"I told you that won't make any difference," Cash said.

"You also told me that the polymers have to split before they join." Q's tone remained patient. "And you told me that these polymers have the ability to split at a certain temperature, which could only happen if you let them rest in a controlled environment for a certain amount of time before you joined them."

Cash's mind stopped spinning. Q's words took on amazing clarity.

"Oh, man." Cash squeezed his head between his hands. "Why didn't I see that?"

"Because you've been embroiled in this for three damn years. Sometimes it takes an outside perspective to see all the options."

Cash clicked through the changes he'd have to make in the experiment to fit Q's scenario.

"What the hell are you waiting for, Sci-Fi? The sooner you get that shit created, the sooner you get out of here."

Cash pushed off the floor, dragged himself to the cell door, and pounded with his fist. "Gomez! I need to go back to the lab!"

NINE

"**Y**ou are such a good sport." Luke fitted the final pieces of Mateo's foil helmet into place. "Kat would have kicked and screamed and ripped this thing to pieces by now."

On the other side of the car, Keira scrunched up the remaining scraps of foil from the box they'd purchased at a mini-mart on the way to the Fallon airport. "If this weren't so screwed up, it would be funny."

"Are you kidding? It would be hilarious." He patted the boy's metal head. "I'm sure we'll look back on this and laugh our asses off."

"I hope so." Keira continued to scan the small Nevada air strip. At this hour of the morning it was deserted. Another reason Luke was able to relax a little. Between them, Mateo fought to keep his eyes open. "I wish we could have gone there. I hate making her come all the way here so late in her pregnancy."

"Good Lord, don't say that to her. She's only seven months along and she'll never let us hear the end of how she's fully capable of doing everything she usually does. Besides, it's a quick flight and we have more anonymity here."

Keria tugged at the edges of the foil at Mateo's neck to maintain coverage. "You think this will work?"

"It's better than the metal strip I had wrapped around his

neck earlier." Desperate people did desperate things, like ripping up the floorboard to access a piece of metal that would do that job. "And nobody has jumped down our throats in hours. Yeah, I'd say it's interrupting the signal."

"What if they're just waiting? What if we're putting Alyssa and Teague in danger by dragging them into the middle of an ambush?"

"Why do you always have to think in worst-case scenarios?"

"Because that's my reality." Her eyes sparked in the dim overhead lights peppering the industrial site. "Because that's what I was born and raised with. What I've lived with my whole damn life. Forgive me if I'd rather be prepared than blindsided."

Luke's jaw tensed in a combination of anger, frustration, and pity.

"Let me check your head," she said.

He rubbed his temple. "There's nothing wrong with my head."

"I beg to differ. Turn toward me."

He relented, resting the right side of his face against the driver's seat so she could inspect his left temple.

That bullet had made a direct hit. If it hadn't been for the abilities that Keira had strengthened, his brains would be splattered all over the passenger's seat, freezing in the desert.

Her fingers parted his hair away from the injury site. "I knew you were lying. Damn, you are so lucky."

"Just what every man wants, a woman who knows when he's lying." He pulled away from her touch, stared out the window, frustration growing. "And my luck is only temporary. It will be running out soon enough, won't it?"

A mixture of pain and guilt darkened her eyes before she glanced out the windshield. "I think that's Teague and Alyssa."

On the runway a Cessna floated in for landing, and Luke's hopes sank in tandem. He reached for the door handle, but Keira grabbed his arm.

"No, wait. Let's make sure before we open ourselves as targets."

"Would you be more comfortable if they were shooting at us?"

The venom in his tone must have penetrated. Her eyes shot to his as she released his arm. "Yes. Yes, I would. That's the big difference between us, Luke. That's where I'm comfortable—behind a scope, not a picket fence."

"You are in such denial it's pitiful." He looked pointedly at the way Mateo rested against her, completely at peace. With a shake of his head, he pushed the car door open. "And who said they had to be mutually exclusive?"

He'd stymied her right into an open mouth with no response.

"How many agents do you know with kids?" he asked.

"A lot, but—"

"SWAT members with kids?"

"Well, yeah, but—"

"But what?"

"I'm . . . different."

He suppressed a bark of absurd laughter. "You mean you're fucked in the head?"

"Shut up." She pushed open her own door and climbed out. "Like you're perfect? Don't even get me started."

"I never claimed to be perfect."

"Neither did I." Mateo awoke and reached for her. Without even looking, she drew him into her arms and rubbed his back. She was a natural and didn't even realize it. "You created that unrealistic fantasy all on your own."

Luke rounded the hood, his temper heating. "No, I based that opinion off what I saw when we were together."

Her mouth clamped shut, eyes darted away.

"You were the sexiest, most fun-loving, generous, compassionate, gorgeous woman I'd ever known," he said. "You may not have been raised with any sense of a normal family, but you created a family of your own with the firefighters you worked with, and you loved that family. You would have done anything for any one of them."

He closed the distance between them, took a handful of her hair, and fisted it gently, with just enough bite to get through that thick skull of hers. She lifted defiant eyes.

"That's the woman I fell in love with," he said. "And after seeing you again, I'm not ready to give up hope that she is still inside the shell you've built around yourself. I've already seen pieces of her."

She pulled away. "That's because pieces are all that's left."

The airplane tires hit the asphalt, and a squeal sliced into their argument. Luke stuffed his hands into his pockets and clamped down on his anger. He couldn't change her, couldn't make her see herself as he did. And he sure as hell didn't need her rejection again.

The plane came to a stop and the doors opened. Luke started forward as Alyssa climbed from the passenger's seat. Her legs came first, followed by that big pregnant belly as she maneuvered her way to the ground.

The sight pushed his hurt and frustration to the background. He didn't know how, but she managed to look more beautiful every time he saw her. Pregnancy had lent her long black hair a deeper shine, her Asian-Irish skin a brighter glow, and those pretty hazel eyes a sharper spark.

With her feet on the ground, body finally balanced, she hit him with a warning glare. "Don't you dare laugh."

"Never." He put an arm around her shoulders and kissed the top of her head. "You look great. How's the boy?"

She laid a hand on the baby. "Kicking up a storm. Wanna feel?"

"Ah . . ." The reality that he might never feel his own child move inside the only woman he wanted seemed a little too stark at the moment. "Not right now."

Alyssa's curiosity melted into understanding. She kissed his cheek. "Where's Keira? Teague was worried you might have chopped her up and left her body in an oil drum by now."

"There's a thought," he muttered. "She's right here. Where is that lousy husband of yo—?"

Two men came around the nose of the plane, one dressed in a black jumpsuit similar to Keira's SWAT uniform and carrying a submachine gun. The other swaggered over wearing worn jeans, white shirt, and a camel-colored leather jacket, his arm draped around Keira's shoulders.

Mitch Foster. Alyssa's twin brother.

A long, slow sigh pushed from between Luke's teeth. "Foster."

"Ransom." He put out his hand and shook Luke's. "You look like hell."

"You, too. Where's Teague?"

"Home," Alyssa said. "He didn't want to leave Kat alone with Mitch. Said he'd have her mastering bongs and roach clips by the time we got back."

"That's so sixties," Mitch said. "I would have taken her straight to heroin."

Alyssa cast Mitch one of her signature stares. "And he's not happy about me coming here with anyone less skilled than a Special Forces soldier."

"Ow." Mitch slapped a hand to his chest and winced, then gestured to the other man. "I complied with his asinine demands. Sergeant Nelson is our pilot and protector."

Luke greeted Nelson, an average-size, plain-faced, all-American guy Luke wouldn't have taken special notice of on the street.

Keira, still holding Mateo, unwound herself from Mitch's arm and hugged Alyssa. "I'm sorry you had to come all this way."

"Never a problem." She smiled at Mateo. "That's quite a costume. I bet Uncle Luke made that for you. He's good at dress-up."

"I'll just bet he is." Mitch laughed. "Bet he prefers the feel of lace on his delicate skin."

"Don't start firing off that mouth of yours, Foster."

Mitch shot Luke a shit-eating grin. "I'm going to help Nelson tie down the plane."

"I'd offer to help," Luke said as Mitch planted his hands on the back of one wing and Nelson took the other, pushing it into a parking space. "But it looks like you could use a little manual labor. Sitting behind that desk is making you soft."

"Prick," Mitch muttered.

"Mitch," Alyssa scolded, reminding Luke he'd have to watch his language. Lys was a stickler on swearing. At some point, she'd attached a charge to each curse, and if he didn't watch his mouth, Luke would be handing over his retirement.

She smiled at Mateo. "What a little heartbreaker."

Keira grinned down at the boy, whose eyes kept skipping between faces. "Cute, huh?"

"Beyond cute. Look at those curls."

"To die for, aren't they?"

"Yet you bitch about me needing a haircut," Luke muttered, then held up a hand. "Sorry, Lys. I'll work on it."

"Sounds like somebody's jealous," Alyssa said. "Will he freak when I try to examine him?"

Keira shrugged. "He let Luke put that thing on his head without a squeak."

"And no English at all?"

"Not that we can tell."

Alyssa smiled at Mateo. "I won't hurt you, sweetheart. I just want to see what you've got back here."

Mateo let Alyssa probe and inspect the scar.

"Interesting placement," she murmured. "There are easier locations to put a simple tracker. But the implant is superficial. Should only take fifteen minutes to get it out. The hospital is only a mile from here. A friend I interned with is letting me use an exam room in a wing of offices. We'll have everything we need."

"That our ride?" Mitch came up beside them, brushing his hands together. He squinted at the Jeep. "Damn, Ransom, looks like you've been through hell and back in that thing."

Luke rubbed his face. "Feels that way, too."

Keira climbed into the backseat with Alyssa. Mateo cozied up between them while Luke drove and Mitch took shotgun. Nelson rolled into the rear cargo space as if he were on a training maneuver.

Keira hadn't even closed the door before Alyssa started in. "Why does it take a crisis for us to get to see you?"

Mitch shot a look over his shoulder from the front seat. "Yeah."

"You have no room to talk." Alyssa cut her attention back to Keira. "So? Why are you avoiding us?"

There was a myriad of reasons Keira kept her distance from Teague and Alyssa. She loved them. Dearly. Would fight to the death for them or either of their children. But their seemingly perfect life increasingly reminded Keira of all her own life lacked. And the less she saw Teague and Alyssa, the less she had to be reminded of what she'd lost, what she still didn't have, and what she'd seriously begun to doubt she'd ever find.

"Don't even think about using Sacramento as an excuse," Alyssa said. "It's only two hours away."

"I'm working a lot."

"She's too busy doing that surgeon in Davis," Mitch said.

A disgusted sound gurgled from Keira's throat. "Mitchell Foster—"

"What the fuck?" Luke cut in.

"Luke," Alyssa chastised, then turned to Keira. "Is that what's keeping you so busy?"

"No." Keira sent Mitch an *I'll-kill-you-later* glare. "I told you he is the husband of another agent."

"Being married never stopped anyone from screwing around." The darkness in Mitch's tone stemmed from something deep and painful. Keira recognized the signs. But it didn't erase her anger over his bringing this up in front of Luke, which she knew he'd done on purpose. "I saw how he was looking at you that night at dinner. He'd have been feeling you up under the table if I hadn't sat between you."

"Dinner?" Luke said. "When did you two have dinner together? And who the hell is this surgeon?"

"We get together every month, Ransom," Mitch said. "Just 'cause you're too stupid to realize how hot she is doesn't mean all men are."

"There is no surgeon." Keira rubbed at the pain in her forehead. There was nobody. There hadn't been anybody since her pathetic attempts at dating shortly after breaking up with Luke. Even the thought of trying again made her queasy. Until she'd set eyes on Luke, of course. Why was the universe so damn cruel?

"Stop stirring the shit, Mitch," Alyssa said.

"Holy crap." Mitch's gorgeous hazel eyes whipped around to land on his sister. "Did you just swear?" He turned to Luke. "Did you hear that?"

"I heard it."

"I think that might wipe out our debt. What do you think?"

"I agree."

"I hate to be a wet blanket," Keira said, "but can you two stop screwing around before I choke you both?"

"Oh, baby." Mitch slanted her a grin. "Promises, promises."

Luke's fist hit Mitch dead center in the chest. Mitch sputtered a pained laugh.

"Mi malónete." Mateo's voice brought everyone's gaze around to the boy's worried face. *"Lucas, mi malónete."*

"That's what you need, Ransom." Still grinning, Mitch rubbed his chest. "A five-year-old to keep you in line."

They pulled into a parking lot alongside the rural community hospital and stopped at a wing of office buildings.

"Pull up to that second building on the right." Alyssa pointed over Luke's shoulder. "There's a side door . . . yeah, right there. My friend owns the building and he turned the alarm off remotely from his home. Said there's a spare key attached to the corner of the building between the foundation and the framing."

Nelson exited the vehicle first, his gaze sweeping the area, weapon held ready. The parking lot was deserted, dimly illuminated by sparse overhead lighting. He retrieved the key, unlocked the door, and disappeared inside.

"Are you sure no one will see us?" Keira asked.

"It's a nine-to-five-type place," Alyssa said. "No one will be here until tomorrow morning."

Nelson emerged and waved them in. Outside the car, Keira handed Mateo over to Luke and drew one of the Glocks from the Jeep. Mitch held a weapon he'd dragged from somewhere beneath his leather jacket and followed Alyssa and Nelson inside. Luke waited for Keira, then scanned the area before closing and locking the door behind him.

Inside an exam room, Alyssa unpackaged medical supplies and set up a procedure tray.

Keira crossed her arms, scanning all the white and blue–wrapped bundles. "How bad is this going to hurt?"

Mitch wandered to the counter across the room and opened cabinets. "She's not cutting on you, Pixie."

Luke's brow went up. "Pixie?"

"Yeah, she looks like a pixie." He picked up an object from a shelf and fiddled with it. "You know, like one of those things with wings in Kat's books."

"You mean a fairy," Luke said. "Hence the term *fairy* tale."

"Should have known you'd be a fairy expert." Mitch lifted his chin at Keira. "Look at her. That little nose, the angle of her eyes, those freckles. She looks like a pixie."

Luke shot her a scowl. "Too bad she doesn't have their sugarplum personality."

"You two are *so* not funny." Keira was ready to pop out of her skin. Something about being cooped up in that room with all those supplies and instruments, knowing there were people outside who wanted them all dead, just didn't bring out the jokester in her.

Unlike Mitch. Who approached the exam table with a mischievous grin and an anatomical model in his hands. A detailed, three-dimensional, life-size model of a penis and testicles.

"What in the hell?" Keira sputtered.

"You don't recognize Big Jim and the Twins?" Mitch pulled pieces out, put them back, pulled others out, looked inside. "I can fix that, sweetheart."

"Mitch, put that down," Alyssa scolded. "I swear, if you break something—"

"Why does this guy have a puzzle like this in his office? Is he gay? Not that I care. I mean I'm a San Franciscan transplant. Besides, gay guys have *the hottest* girlfriends."

"I swear he was switched at birth." Alyssa glared at her twin brother. "Doctor Henle is a urologist. I'm sure if you ask nicely he'll give you a free prostate exam, Mitch. Now put that *very expensive anatomical model* down."

Mitch set the model back on the counter. "Killjoy."

Luke laid Mateo on the table as Alyssa directed. Keira combed her fingers through the hair at his temple, whispering reassurances the boy didn't understand and Keira didn't feel.

"You're going to numb him or something, right?"

"Yes, with a tiny needle. He may feel a little stick and burn, but that's it."

The boy made it through the numbing better than Keira. Just the sight of the needle tightened her throat. She had to look away when Alyssa injected. Mateo, on the other hand, barely made a murmur of complaint.

His eyes grew heavy and closed before Alyssa had even picked up a scalpel. But as soon as she pressed the tip of that knife into the skin of Mateo's neck, the second that drop of bright red blood bloomed on the boy's olive skin, Keira's head went light. A distant buzzing grew louder until it encompassed her brain.

"We're gonna lose her," Alyssa murmured somewhere close.

Luke's arms circled Keira before she even realized she was melting toward the floor.

"She's pale." Mitch's worried voice came at her from the left. "Is she okay?"

"She'll be fine." Alyssa's gaze remained locked on Mateo's neck. "It happens to parents a lot. Should have seen Teague when Kat hit her head on the coffee table and needed a couple stitches."

He's not my kid. But Keira didn't say it. Couldn't say it. Nausea boiled too close to the surface. Alyssa could have been digging to Mateo's spine the way she prodded and tugged.

"What's going on, Lys?" Mitch asked. "You said it was superficial."

"The chip is," she murmured, still working, "but it's attached to something."

Keira's mind engaged. "What do you mean?"

"Could be scar tissue. Could be a tendon or a muscle. I'm not sure." Alyssa drew back with a frown and wiped her forehead with the back of her arm. Keira's gaze caught on the forceps in her hand, the tips covered in blood.

"Oh, God." She pressed a hand to her stomach.

"A little blood makes you woozy," Luke muttered, "after you've killed at least four—"

"Luke," she snapped.

"What?" Mitch straightened away from the counter.

Alyssa's gaze came around.

The hollow in Keira's stomach squeezed tight. She wrestled herself out of Luke's grip, pressed her back to the wall, and slid away from him, arms crossed over her chest again. "Thanks. I needed the reminder."

"Damn, you are so extreme it's freakin' hot," Mitch said with too much excitement. "What the hell happened?"

"Foster," Luke bit out. "Don't be a—"

"Don't you two start again." Now cold and clammy, Keira wiped at the sweat breaking across her face. "Let's just say it's been a rough day."

Keira didn't look at Mitch, who she knew wanted to press for details. She couldn't watch Alyssa dig into Mateo's perfect, precious flesh. Wouldn't even glance at Luke for fear she might knock out a few teeth. Instead, she paced the opposite side of the room and let her gaze roam the detailed cutaway poster of a kidney.

"Got it," Alyssa announced.

Keira spun around. "Is he okay? Is it all out?"

"He's fine." Alyssa lowered the chip to a silver tray. "But unfortunately, no, it's not all out." She pointed to one end of the thumbnail-size chip. "See those holes? About a dozen of them? Each was attached to a wire."

"A wire? I don't understand. Can't you get the wire out, too?"

"Wires. And no." She set the forceps down and picked up a needle already threaded with black filament. "Those wires seem to be attached to something else . . . higher up."

Keira waited for Alyssa to expand. When she didn't, Keira prodded, "Higher up? Like in his scalp?"

"No. They're too deep to be in his scalp. I think they'd have to be . . . in his brain."

Denial hit Keira first. Then panic. Then searing anger, burning away the chill.

"Those—" *Motherfucking bloodsuckers.* "I'm going to—" *Kill them.*

The realization that she'd already killed some of them gave her grim satisfaction. But not near enough for what they'd done to this baby.

"How do we know they can't track him with whatever's still in there?" Keira asked.

"I guess we don't." Alyssa stitched the tiny incision. "I know a little about how these types of implants are used in medicine, and they're still experimental. But we already know these probably weren't implanted for medical reasons."

Keira closed a hand over her eyes. "This is too much," she murmured, more to herself than the others. "Just too much."

"Help us out here, hotshot." Luke's strained voice brought Keira's head up. He was glaring at Mitch. "You've got contacts everywhere else, what about in the IT field?"

"Be careful whose throat you're jumping down, Ransom. Next time you need a fucking plane, you may not get one."

"Mitch—" Alyssa didn't take her eyes off her work.

"Quit swearing or I'll reinstate the payment rule, and you have quite a tab running already. Answer him."

"I'm thinking." Mitch's gaze dropped to the floor. "Techies aren't the types who usually need my help. More like the Ransoms of the world, who screw up at every turn and ask for shit like planes and pilots, and, oh, yeah, one more thing . . ."

"Fuck you, Foster."

"That's it. You both start off owing me a hundred bucks." Alyssa fixed them each with a solid glare before she set down her needle and stretched her back. "Twenty more per curse from here on out."

A new dark swirl of emotion distracted Keira from the group's banter. She checked Mateo, but found him asleep. She looked at Luke, but this sensation didn't have the same quality as the other feelings he'd emitted.

"It doesn't count when the kids aren't around," Mitch grumbled.

Alyssa gestured toward Mateo. "And who is this?"

"He doesn't even speak English."

What office?

Keira held up her hand to the others. "Shhhh."

The room went silent.

An Adam Henle. Opposite side of the building. We can go through this corridor.

Fear exploded in her belly. "They found us."

She swept Mateo off the table.

"I didn't hear anyth—" Mitch started.

A knock sounded on the door just before Nelson poked his head in, gaze homed on Mitch. "The primary security alarm just sounded. Worst case, they're here. Best case, the cops will arrive in a couple minutes."

"I didn't hear the alarm, either." Alyssa chucked supplies into the trash.

"It's a low buzz at the receptionist's desk," Nelson said.

"The loud one will kick in after about three minutes if the primary isn't deactivated."

Luke intercepted Keira and took Mateo. "I'll carry, you shoot. Mitch, grab the foil. Wrap that chip."

Keira pulled the gun from her jeans and followed Nelson out the door.

Alyssa was still trashing supplies when Mitch grabbed her arm. "Earth to Doctor Foster. Come in, Doctor Foster."

"I'm just observing a little professional courtesy. Will you ever grow out of being such a bully?"

"If I was going to, it would have happened by now."

Alyssa snapped off her gloves and tossed them into the garbage as she passed through the door.

The others climbed into the Jeep. Nelson lifted the hatch and rolled into the back. Mitch handed the foil to Alyssa, who fashioned a rudimentary cap over the back of Mateo's head and neck. "Sorry, little buddy. Not near as cool as Uncle Luke's."

Luke crept through the parking lot with the Jeep's lights extinguished, pausing in between buildings to cover the area with a quick, sweeping search.

"That's them." A dark sedan sat in a shadow between overhead lights at the rear of the building.

"Drop me off," Nelson said. "I'll make sure they think twice about following you again."

The sentiment resonated with Keira. "Let me out with him." She'd already started to shift Mateo across the seat toward Alyssa. "I haven't met my quota of kills for the day."

Mitch scraped out a dark laugh. "It's official. I'm in love."

Luke cut a look at Mitch that could have severed a limb, then shot a glare over his shoulder at Keira. "Chill."

"There's another exit at the opposite end of the parking lot," Alyssa said. "Turn around."

Nelson scowled. "Where's the fun in that? At least let me slice their tires or something."

"Too risky," Luke said. "I've had enough fun for one day. Where's the chip?"

Mitch held it up, wrapped in foil. "Here. They must have tracked us while Lys was taking it out. They're damned close, man."

"Or they're everywhere." Which Keira thought more likely.

"We'll just keep it triple-wrapped in foil until I can get it to someone who knows what to do with it." Mitch turned in his seat, looked at the sleeping boy, and dialed his phone. "Can you wake him up?"

"Why?"

"Because I have someone who can talk to him."

"Who?" Keira asked.

"Relative of someone I represented a couple years ago. Lives in Greece, but they don't call it Greece. They call it Hellas. And Greek is Hellene. I've been told using the other terms is considered derogatory, so don't use it and piss him off. He said he'd be happy to help . . . Hey, Panos," Mitch said into the phone. "It's Mitch. Yeah, he's right here. I'm putting you on speaker."

Keira gave Mateo a gentle shake. "Honey, wake up. Mateo?"

The boy's eyes dragged open. He rubbed them with little fists and turned back into Keira's chest.

"Yá soo," Panos said, *"pos se léne, pedí moo?"*

Mateo twisted in Keira's arms and stared at the phone.

"Pió íne t'ónomá soo, kalé moo? Me akoós?" Panos tried again.

"Ne." Mateo drew out the word, uncertain.

"Ah, ya soo! Ti kánees? Me léne . . ." Panos started off in a streak.

Not until the tension eased from Mateo's shoulders did Keira relax as well. Then the boy started talking. He and Panos delved into an animated conversation and that old saying, it's all Greek—or Hellene—to me, took on a whole new meaning.

Keira soaked in Mateo's voice as she waited for translation, the sweet tone twining around her heart and doing strange things to her stomach. She didn't have to hear the words to pick up Mateo's intelligence. His words were well enunciated, his voice filled with inflection.

"His name *is* Mateo," Panos said. "He doesn't know his last name. When I ask him where he lives, he says it's a big white house with barns but no animals."

"Can you ask him if he knows where his family is?" Keira said.

She waited as Panos and Mateo spoke again. When she heard the word *Thia*, Keira's stomach knotted.

"He says his mother is in heaven, his father is somewhere at a place called the Castle, and he's sitting in his aunt's lap."

The scar on Keira's back lit up like a firecracker. Heat skimmed her flanks, her ribs, and wrapped around her heart. She'd never felt this type of intense connection with a child. Yes, she loved Kat. Already loved Alyssa and Teague's unborn son. But nothing like the overwhelming unconditional feeling she'd developed for Mateo literally overnight. Still, she was not his family. She had no family.

"He was probably taught to call the women who cared for him at the ranch aunts," she said.

"According to him," Panos went on, "he knew you would come for him someday. He's been waiting. He says he's watched you search for him for a long time, and that his father is working hard to get free and return to him."

Keira's chest tightened. "To get free?"

"Do you have siblings, Keira?" Alyssa asked.

"No." Thoughts of her brother caused a fresh stab of pain. "I mean, I did. An older brother. He died in a house fire when I was five."

Luke's attention veered from the road. "You have a brother? You never told me that."

"I *had* a brother. He's been dead for twenty-five years."

"Ask him how long he's been at the ranch," Mitch said. "Ask him what they did there."

Panos had a short discussion with Mateo, then said, "He doesn't know how long. He doesn't remember living anywhere else. They did schoolwork. But what he's calling schoolwork sounds more like testing. Looking into other spaces, talking without words, guessing games with cards, matching games . . ."

Anger burned through Keira's body. Mateo leaned into her, pressed his face into her chest as if to hide.

"Mitch," she whispered, not wanting to offend Panos. "Enough for now."

Mitch disconnected after a hearty thank-you to Panos and a promise they would contact him again when things calmed down.

A phenomenon that Keira could barely imagine.

Luke frowned at Mitch. "Fill us in on the rest of the information you've got."

Mitch opened a folder in his lap. "What do you want first? Rostov? The Ranch? The research?"

Dark desert zoomed by the Jeep windows. Keira let her eyes glaze and focused on the feel of Mateo's warm body in her lap. "Start with Rostov."

"Born in Russia when it was still the USSR," Mitch said. "Noted scientist. Spent seven years as the director of Russian research on cultivating paranormal abilities in soldiers for use in military warfare—specifically telepathy and remote viewing."

"Remote viewing," Keira murmured.

Between different members of their team, they encompassed many paranormal abilities. Luke was fireproof, Keira clairaudient, Jessica specialized in scrying, Teague was a thermokinetic healer, Kai had powerful and various empathic abilities, Seth was psychokinetic, and Quaid . . . Quaid was just dead.

When she couldn't define the term, her frustration resurfaced. "What is remote viewing?"

"When someone psychically travels to another location and can see and hear everything going on in real time, in the moment," Luke said. "Whether it be in another room, another city, or even another country."

"That's it. That's his ability." She focused on the bundle in her lap. "That's how he knew Tony was bad before he showed up. And how he knew the attack was going to happen at the safe house."

"Then that has to also be how he knew you'd been searching for him," Luke said.

"If that's true, then he's got a screwed-up sense of relationships, because I can't possibly be his aunt. My brother is *dead.*"

Her bark bit a chunk from the conversation, leaving silence.

"*That's* not a touchy subject," Luke finally muttered.

Mitch darted glances around the car from beneath his brows, then cleared his throat. "About eight months after Soviet research efforts were canned, Rostov immigrated to the United States and—surprise, surprise—was employed by the Department of Defense from the day he set foot on U.S. soil to the day he bought that property in the Nevada desert."

"What about the ranch?" Luke asked. "The chemicals?"

"The ranch was classified as a religious organization," Mitch said, "at least according to IRS records. But shipping companies have been delivering all sorts of chemicals to that address since its inception."

The facts confirmed Keira's leap to a conclusion she'd made in the car with Tony—that Rostov had gone off the reservation, was using the chemicals in unauthorized ways, made progress with Mateo, and DARPA wanted the kid now.

Fingers curled into a fist, she slammed the Jeep's armrest, wishing she'd gotten a chance at some hand-to-hand with Tony. "They used me . . . as an *assassin*."

Mitch released a long, heavy breath. Still sitting sideways in the seat directly in front of her, he wiped a hand over his face and rested his fingers against closed eyes. "This has turned into an epic nightmare."

Keira laid her head against the window. "It's going to get a lot worse before it gets any better."

TEN

Luke shifted in the front passenger's seat of Alyssa's Audi Q5, but even the padded leather, luxury SUV bucket seat couldn't provide him with any relief. Previously ignored or unknown injuries had come alive. Including that bullet to the temple, leaving him with an almost ear-bleedingly painful headache. He was wishing he hadn't bolted from that ER before getting drugs.

Twenty-four hours hadn't yet passed from the time he'd set foot at the siege, yet more had happened in his life in those hours than in the last three years. With the short flight and minimal drive, they'd reached the hospital in those barely morning dead zone hours. The familiar exterior of Tahoe Basin Community Hospital came into view. Lights washed the river rock and cedar entrance, illuminating the dark night.

"You think you can hook me up with some pain meds while we're here, Lys?"

His question penetrated the car's heavy silence. With just Alyssa, Keira, Mateo, and himself in the car, it was quiet. Everyone was tired, stressed, freaked out, and silent.

Mitch had gone to Alyssa and Teague's house to brief Teague, while Alyssa drove the rest of them to the hospital so she could utilize the equipment there to get more information on the . . . things . . . in Mateo's head.

Alyssa turned a suspicious look his way as she parked in the hospital's side lot. "Why do you need pain meds?"

"He got shot," Keira offered in a dark tone from the backseat.

"What?" Alyssa asked. "Nobody said anything about getting shot."

"Twice," Keira added, like a freaking six-year-old tattling to Mom.

"Keira." Luke twisted in his seat, which slashed another dose of pain across his ribs and stole his breath. *Shut up.*

Keira had closed him out of her thoughts in the plane and hadn't opened up again since, but that didn't mean *she* couldn't hear *him.*

"Why didn't you tell me so I could examine you?" Alyssa's gaze swept over his torso. "Must not have been bad."

"No, I'm just banged up. Have a few cracked ribs. And after all the climbing and lifting I've done today, they're killing me. Something other than Vicodin. It makes me—"

"Puke." Alyssa shut down the engine. Her distracted hazel eyes searched the darkened lot as if she expected a stalker to pop out of the bushes. "I remember. I've got some Oxycodone at home."

Luke followed her gaze, his unease returning. "You said this was kosher."

Alyssa pulled on the door handle. The crisp, fall mountain air swept in and grabbed them in a brisk hug. "It is."

"Then why are you uncomfortable?"

Alyssa grabbed her ID badge from the center console with a look that translated to *you-are-so-damn-stupid-sometimes.* "We're being chased by powerful people who want this boy bad enough to kill. Forgive me if I'm a little nervous. Let's get in, get out, and get home."

With Keira carrying a limp, barefooted, foil-capped kid, Luke followed the women toward the side entrance with his weapon held close to his thigh. But nothing about *get in and get out* felt or sounded right.

At the glass door Alyssa peered down the empty hallway before swiping her badge, then held the door open.

But crossing that threshold brought to Luke's mind all Alyssa had to lose by breaching hospital protocol. "You shouldn't be risking this. We could have brought him in through the emergency room and gotten a doctor's order."

"I'd like to have heard that story," Alyssa said. "Why doesn't he speak English? How did he get that cut? He's got *what* in his head? The cops would have shown up twenty minutes after the ER doc reported an abducted or abused child with psychotic parents."

When they reached the office door, Alyssa slid her badge again. "No security guard, no night technologist, no housekeeping. We're on a roll."

She pushed the door open.

"It's about damn time." The deep voice vibrated from inside the room.

Luke's fingers tightened around the grip of his gun. Then the voice registered. Teague. Air whooshed out of Luke's lungs.

"Jesus, Teague." Alyssa put a hand over her heart and stood aside so Keira and Luke could enter. "You scared me. How'd you beat us here? How'd you get in? Who's with Kat?"

"Mitch called on the way from the airport. I didn't stay to talk." Teague stepped into the light cast by six different computer screens, holding up an identification badge just like the one Alyssa had, his expression stern. "You know those badges you can never keep track of? And it's better I scared you, considering the options, don't you think? Mitch is at the house with Kat, and she's asleep. This isn't smart, Alyssa."

"It's got to be done."

Teague wrapped his wife in his arms. "I know what you're trying to do, Lys, but think about what you're risking."

Teague was right. In Luke's need to get answers for Keira, he'd overlooked the toll this could take on Alyssa's career—one she'd worked so hard and sacrificed so much for.

"Let's just bail," Luke said.

Keira didn't say anything. She stood immobile just inside the door, her light eyes jumping from face to face with pained indecision as she stroked Mateo's curls.

"We can't," Alyssa said. "There's no better time. This place is deserted; Mateo's asleep."

Teague let her go with a sigh and stepped forward with an extended hand for Luke. When he took it, Teague pulled him into a quick hug. "I see you're still too damn stubborn to die."

"You know it. But I almost shot you, dumb shit."

Teague smirked and put both hands on Keira's arms, his eyes scouring her face. "Those cuts are going to scar. Better let me work on them."

"Tomorrow." Keira offered a weak smile. "I promise."

"No, later. I can't do anything with tissue that's already healed . . . or died." He kissed her forehead, then dropped his gaze to Mateo. "This is the little waif causing all the trouble? Hard to believe. He's barely bigger than a string bean."

"Luke," Alyssa directed, "lock that door behind you. Keira, bring him in here."

Alyssa entered a separate room housing a state-of-the-art CAT scanner. Keira followed, her bright eyes running over the machine with a mixture of awe and fear. Still, her thoughts remained blocked.

"It's good he's asleep." Alyssa pulled a lead apron off

hooks on the wall. "I won't have to sedate him for the test if he stays still on his own. Put this on and you can stay in here with him. It'll only take a few minutes."

Alyssa took the sleeping boy from Keira's arms. He shifted, coming awake slowly. His eyes weren't even open when he reached in Keira's direction as if he could sense her. *"Thia."*

"Right here, baby." Keira fastened the Velcro and took Mateo again.

"Okay." Alyssa patted the bed of the scanner. "Lay him on his back."

Keira took one step toward the scanner before Mateo's eyes opened. *"Mee!"* He struggled in Keira's arms as she tried to keep the boy from twisting right out of her grasp. *"Stamata, Thia . . ."*

He screamed in a language no one understood and clawed at Keira's clothes, climbing her body like a kitten cornered by a Doberman.

Luke darted into the room and caught the boy just before he pitched himself to the floor. "Shhhhh, buddy," he murmured, rubbing his back as he rocked. Mateo's heart knocked so hard on Luke's ribs he could feel it in his own chest. "Shhhhh, it's okay."

"Bring him in here." Alyssa returned to the first room with the CT controls and approached the medication dispenser. "Looks like I'll have to sedate him after all."

"I say we call the whole thing off," Luke said.

Keira stood nearby, arms crossed, fingers squeezing her biceps so hard she drained the blood of the indented flesh. She was torn. He didn't have to read her mind to know. He could still read her expressions.

"Lys, he's right." Teague put a hand on Alyssa's arm. "It's one thing to sneak into the hospital, use resources without authorization, and expose a child to radiation. It's another to medicate a patient you know nothing about. You're risking everything here. Your position, your reputation, even your license. Not to mention his health."

"Screw that," Luke said as Mateo continued to whimper against his shoulder. "We're all in enough trouble. We're not dragging you down, Lys."

"Wait, wait, *wait*." She turned fully toward them. Met each of their gazes deliberately. "You want to talk about his health? Let's talk about the fact that there is something experimental implanted in his brain tissue. The risk of this sedative is negligible compared to the potential damage these implants could cause. This study could save his life."

The room remained quiet. Luke was caught in an impossible dilemma between the people he loved most.

"Aren't you all *getting* it? This isn't about me or Mateo or any one of us individually anymore. We need to know what they put in his head and why. The answers are critical to our survival. The implications of what those people did to this boy affect every child, every person, in the nation. And we are the only people in a position to gather evidence and information to *stop* them. Am I the only one who sees the *enormity* of this situation?"

Gazes dropped to the floor. Luke's chest grew painfully tight.

"I didn't think so." Alyssa faced the Pixus machine again and punched more numbers, pulled a drawer open, and took a small bottle from a compartment.

"So it's, um . . . pretty safe then?" Keira's worried voice broke the tense silence.

Alyssa held up a tiny bottle. "This is the safest sedative made. I'll use as little as possible to calm him so I can get images. Unfortunately, no other study will give us the information we need, and they all require him to remain still just like this one."

She put her hands over Keira's. "I'm sorry I don't have a

better solution, but whatever is in his head has life-threatening potential. The benefits far outweigh the risk. Keira, you are the closest thing he has to a mother at the moment. If you say no, we'll leave."

Keira didn't balk at the surrogate mother reference as Luke expected, only pressed her lips together and nodded. "What do I need to do?"

"Just try to keep him quiet while I give him the medication."

Keira stepped close to Luke. She steadied herself with a hand on his back, then rested her head against his shoulder so she was face-to-face with Mateo. She kissed the boy's nose. Laid her cheek to his. Whispered soothing reassurances.

Luke couldn't ignore the rightness of the situation. Her, him, a child. Not necessarily Mateo, although the kid was an absolute doll. But that connection. That uniting force. The completion of a family.

Alyssa drew up the medication. Mateo took the shot with as little fuss as the numbing medication at the doctor's office.

"Okay." Alyssa rubbed at the spot on his arm to ease the sting of the needle. "That should kick in pretty quick. Let's not take him back in there until his eyes close."

Keira brushed the wetness from the boy's cheek with her thumb, her own eyes brewing with tears. "What the hell did they do to you in that place, baby?"

Luke's muscles kinked with tension as he considered the possibilities. Mateo's body softened against Luke's. The hand fisted in Luke's shirt fell to his side.

"He's ready," Alyssa said. "Let's go."

Keira remained in the room, sentinel at Mateo's side. Luke, grateful for the distance, stood beside Alyssa as she punched buttons on the CT console and started the scan.

Images flashed across the screen as fast as subliminal messages. Before Luke could begin to assimilate the first image, Alyssa was pushing buttons again.

"Done," she said. "I'm transferring the images to a DVD so I can take them home and look at them there. Get everyone to the car." She lifted her eyes to Luke. "And, Luke. You owe me another twenty bucks."

Keira was still struggling to numb herself as they reached Alyssa and Teague's house. She wanted to completely shut down, a self-preservation technique she'd learned a long time ago, one that had seen her through the toughest moments of her life. But it wasn't working.

Everyone she'd tried so hard to distance herself from over the last three years was back, all at once, and all together. Then there was the beauty of what she considered home— Truckee and a family unit she loved. One that gave her the understanding and support she needed, but that also mucked in her business, which she hated. And just to top it all off, she was saddled with this kid who stirred yearnings and fears she'd thought she'd settled long ago.

This, all of it, was exactly why she didn't come back to visit anymore.

Two men dressed in fatigues, carrying M14s and looking like they'd just walked off the Rostov compound, opened the gate leading to Teague and Alyssa's mountain property.

Keira straightened in the backseat of the SUV. "What's wrong?"

Teague waved in greeting as they passed through columns of towering pines and broke into an open space beneath the trees where their lodge-style home stood in a clearing overlooking a mountain meadow. "Just extra security. We call in a little muscle when junk like this happens. Otherwise our own system does the job."

Their own system would do the job for Bill Gates. It included the most advanced shit Mitch and his military buddies could think up—infrared movement detection, video surveillance, silent alarms, automatic locking mechanisms, even state-of-the-art booby traps along the border of the ten-acre property.

And while they'd never fessed up, Keira would bet each member of Teague and Alyssa's family had a tracker implanted somewhere on his or her body. One that verified each person's whereabouts with an independent third-party service. Teague would never go through what he'd been through with these DARPA animals again. He'd never let anything happen to Alyssa or Kat or their unborn baby.

She thought of her conversation with Tony and his cavalier attitude about the money Teague and Alyssa had received in settlements—Teague from the federal government for wrongful conviction and Alyssa from the state for negligence on the part of the guards who'd left Teague, their prisoner at the time, alone with her, resulting in her abduction. Luke had been right when he'd said Mitch was good. When it came to slaying dragons, Mitch was the best.

But no amount of money could restore a person's identity. Or their sense of security. Keira had lost both, and she didn't need a ton of money to know it wouldn't be any type of fix for either problem.

As they neared the house, Keira spotted Kat standing in the glow of the open front door. Guilt coated her belly. As did fear. She felt the same way every damned time she had to face Kat, which was just freaking stupid, because Kat had never once rejected Keira—before or after she'd left for the academy.

Keira hadn't even climbed from the car before the seven-year-old burst from the house. For a split second she considered asking Luke to run interference so she could avoid the whole reunion, but she decided just to face it. It had to happen sooner or later.

Kat headed straight for Luke, who dropped to one knee and pulled her into a hug.

"What are you doing up?" Teague asked Kat, but looked behind her at Mitch for the answer.

Mitch shrugged in that carefree way. "You woke her when you left. I let her stay up. That's what uncles are for. Breaking rules."

Teague tossed a look at Alyssa as she met him at the passenger's side. "*That's* why I didn't go to Fallon with you."

"Sorry, Kitty-Cat," Luke said into Kat's hair, eyes squeezed in an expression of pleasure and pain. "I can't pick you up. I've got sore ribs."

Kat didn't seem to mind. Her angelic face, one that Keira swore had its own light source, turned toward her and Mateo.

"Auntie Keira!" She bounced on her toes and tore from Luke to reach for her. Only when it was obvious the boy in Keira's arms would prevent Kat from giving a proper hug did the girl seem to notice Mateo. She cocked her head in that oh-so-innocent way. "Who are you?"

Keira crouched. Mateo was already alert, inspecting Kat with those matter-of-fact chocolate eyes. "This is Mateo."

"I'm Kat." The little extrovert didn't waste a second. "I'm seven and I'm in first grade. How old are you?"

Mateo just stared.

"He doesn't speak English, Kat."

Her brow furrowed, as if trying to understand that phenomenon. "Where did he come from?"

"We're trying to figure that out. He's five and he's had a really rough night. Do you think you could be extra nice to him? Share some of your toys?"

"Sure." The frown vanished. She reached out and wound her fingers around his hand and tugged. "Come on. I'll show you my new Barbie clothes."

"Hey, now," Luke teased. "Wait a minute."

Teague snorted a laugh. "You've been swept by the competition."

Mateo's dark eyes darted around the circle of faces. Keira nodded and nudged him off her lap. "It's okay."

Kat's chatter seemed to hypnotize the boy, and he followed obediently. Their feet crunched on the pine needles scattered along the stone walkway.

Teague swung an arm around Alyssa's shoulders and led her toward the expansive, authentic log home's front steps and double-glass-door entry beyond, all flanked by a covered wraparound porch. He grinned as he watched the kids wander ahead of them. "Another one bites the dust."

Keira didn't realize she was still standing in place until Alyssa's voice broke her trance. "Are you coming?"

Keira startled, then headed toward the door, but felt more like she was floating than walking, she was so exhausted.

Alyssa waited in the foyer and closed the door behind her. "Why don't you take a shower? I'll bring you some of my pajamas to change into and have Teague start a fire in the living room."

Another shower? She'd turn into a prune. "But the CAT scan—"

"I need some time to study the images. Go take a few minutes to decompress."

Normally, Keira would have bristled at the suggestion, but she nodded in agreement. The thought of decompression sounded good, but . . . She darted a nervous look toward the living room.

"You saw those guys out front?" Alyssa asked. "There are

four more around the property. I'll make sure either Mitch, Teague, or Luke checks on Mateo every five minutes. Okay?"

Keira's shoulders sagged as she nodded and retreated to the bathroom. Her mind felt like a piece of cooked rice: soggy, swollen, and stupid. The rote tasks of adjusting the water, gathering fresh towels, and stripping became nothing but reflex as thoughts in the foreground shut down. But on some level her brain still worked. Still chewed on things she would never allow when she had more strength for control.

Because she knew this semiconscious state could be dangerous, she fought the brain fog and quickly rinsed off. The hot spray stung cuts all over her body, but also eased sore muscles, and she let it pound on her shoulders, tilting her chin to her chest to stretch her tight neck.

A magenta splotch expanded across her left flank, the border shadowed a deeper plum that reached out to brush her belly button.

Her fingers feathered over the edges of the bruise. Her mushy brain slid sideways into the past, into one of her many foster homes.

Instead of the butt of her rifle jabbing her in the stomach in the aftermath of the explosion, in her mind she saw the bottom of a man's boot come at her. The source—maybe a foster father, maybe a boyfriend of a foster mother, maybe another kid in the house—wasn't as clear as the boot's size: nearly the width of her ten-year-old shoulders. Or the tread pattern—arrows. Arrows creating an X in the sole of the boot. So vivid, she could still remember pushing one hand in front of her chest to ward off the blow, wrapping the other arm around her torso. She curled into a ball, as tight as she could. Still the heel caught her side. Pain crackled through her ribs. Another kick. A scream—her own—as her insides ripped.

"Keira?"

The female voice forced Keira's eyes open. She found her arms wrapped tight across her belly, breaths coming fast and labored. She was naked. Hot water pounding on her back. Pain throbbing through her belly and chest. Where—?

"Keira?" The voice again. "I brought you some pajamas. I'll leave them on the sink. Bring your clothes out so I can wash them." A hesitation. "Okay?"

Alyssa.

Keira's brain clicked back to the present.

"Ye—" Her voice cracked. "Yeah."

"Are you . . . okay?"

"Uh, no," she murmured. "Not okay. Lys. Wait."

She flipped off the water and wrapped the towel around her, chest to thighs, without bothering to dry off. She didn't want to miss this opportunity to be alone with Alyssa; there were so many questions running through her head.

But she needn't have worried, because when she pushed the curtain open, Alyssa was sitting on the sink, hands flanking her hips, ankles crossed, feet swinging, and that pregnant belly creating an overinflated basketball beneath her V-neck black sweater.

Alyssa's eyes went straight to Keira's shoulder. She pushed off the sink and landed on her feet in a move far too lithe for a woman seven-months pregnant. "Oh, man. Can you move that arm?"

"Yeah, sure."

"Show me."

Wincing, Keira lifted and rotated her injured shoulder the best she could. Alyssa probed the joint. "How'd you do this?"

"Hit a chimney. I think."

"What were you doing on a roof?"

"Breaking into a house."

"Your job is so much more exciting than mine."

"And yours is so much safer, and pays so much better."

Alyssa moved in front of her, lifted both hands, grimaced. "Bend your fingers."

Keira obeyed, gritting her teeth.

"How did you do this?"

"Sliding down that roof."

Alyssa shook her head, dropped into a crouch. "I suppose you had to have matching knees."

"Absolutely."

She rose, propped a hand on her hip, looked Keira in the eye. "What else?"

Keira opened one side of her towel to expose her ribs.

"Oh, how cute." Alyssa bent and inspected. "His and hers matching broken ribs. Who got theirs first?"

"Me." Keira closed her towel. "He always has to try and show me up."

Alyssa straightened. "You two are . . ." She lifted her eyes to the ceiling as she seemed to search for the right words. "A lot more connected than I expected. After three years, all the stories I heard . . ." She shrugged. "I guess I thought there would be more animosity or indifference or . . . I don't know."

Keira still had a hard time reconciling the fact that she hadn't known either Alyssa or Mitch when she and Luke had been together. She felt like she'd known them both forever. "Yeah. I don't know, either. Can I ask you some questions?"

"Of course."

Keira dropped to the edge of the tub with her towel tight around her chest again. Alyssa leaned against the sink.

"So, you know I'm almost thirty. And, uh, women have kids late now, like even into their forties, right?"

"Yeeees." Alyssa drew out the word cautiously. "But it's better to have children earlier because after a certain age, typically thirty-five, risks for certain types of birth defects and complications increase with every year."

"Right, but I'm not talking about a normal woman. I'm talking about me, and what kind of, you know, birth defects our baby could have." She met Alyssa's surprised eyes, cleared her throat. "Mine and . . . you know, Luke's," she clarified, unable to believe she'd actually said the words.

"Well, duh. I figured the Luke part, which I have to admit is . . . both shocking and exciting." Alyssa grinned, then got serious again. "I've done some research on your particular situation. I'm half in your situation, remember. I've checked with colleagues, and while there are, of course, no prior studies to go on, based on what we know of medicine and science in general, I'd say you and Luke are at only a slightly higher risk than the general population."

Keira scraped out a dry laugh. "Gee, that's helpful. Some real specifics there, Lys. What does a slightly higher risk mean?"

"What it means is that birth defects are a fact of life. It happens, across the board. Risk is inherent in pregnancy— to the mother and the unborn child. Certain people carry more risks for certain defects than others. Given you and Luke have perfect health," Alyssa said, "and no known history of familial defects—"

"I didn't know my father. Who knows what could be on his side of the family?"

"That's true, but let's look at what we do know. You're healthy, you're strong, you're young. Plus, none of the team directly affected by the chemicals at the warehouse has contracted any diseases or cancer. That's another very healthy sign in favor of your strong genetics.

"In fact, if you think about it, none of you has had so much as a common cold since the incident. I've been keeping records, and everyone is healthier than they've ever been, except psychologically, of course. Which may indicate that your genes are even stronger than the average person's, not weaker.

"And if you did get pregnant, you could have an amniocentesis to make sure the baby's chromosomes were normal. It doesn't rule out all the potential problems, but unfortunately . . ." Alyssa shrugged. "There are very few assurances in this life, for either the normal or the paranormal."

"Yeah, I keep hearing that."

"For what it's worth, Keira, I like you and Luke together, and you know I wouldn't say that unless I meant it. Having known you both as individuals, now seeing you together . . ." She nodded. "Good fit."

Keira laughed again. "Um . . . did you happen to miss the fact that we haven't spent one moment together *not* fighting?"

"You've been apart for three years. Teague and I bicker if we've been apart three hours. It takes time to get used to each other again. Besides, arguing is healthy. It's keeping everything inside that'll kill you."

"Yeah, about that." Keira's fingers tightened in her towel as her chest squeezed with embarrassment. "Could you, uh, recommend a good, you know, shrink, psychologist . . . whatever you call them?"

Alyssa's brows rose. "Looking into counseling?"

Keira sighed. "I think it's about time."

"Smart move." Alyssa reached out and squeezed her arm. "It's really helped Teague and Seth. I'll get you names and numbers. Anything else you want me to check?"

She hadn't known Teague and Seth had been to counseling. That knowledge somehow eased her mind. "Not unless you can crawl inside my crazy head."

"You're going to be just fine." Alyssa gave her one of those reassuring smiles that made Keira feel she could do anything. "If your shoulder swells, we'll need to take you in for an X-ray, maybe an MRI. Gentle stretches if you don't want it to freeze up on you." She put her hand on the doorknob and turned back to Keira with a wink. "I like the belly button ring. After the baby, you'll have to take me to get one. Surprise Teague for his birthday."

Keira grinned. "Deal."

"Come in my office when you're dressed. I'll get you some painkillers and we'll look at the CT."

The door closed and Keira finally felt as if she'd found some sort of balance again. She dressed in the spaghetti-strap, formfitting cami and tissue-thin silky pajama pants Alyssa had left for her. The soft fabrics felt nice on her bruised, torn skin.

Keira wandered down the hall toward the living room, open to an airy kitchen on one side and a family room on the other. The house was warm, and the men's low voices floated from the kitchen, where they stood talking.

Beyond, a light shone from a partially open office door, and Keira could just make out the fall of Alyssa's long, black hair where she sat at the desk. As promised, a fire burned in the hearth across the open space in the family room.

Keira crossed the foyer, passed through the kitchen on the way to the office. The men's conversation stopped dead. All three stood at the counter, a drink in one hand, the other pressed against the tile, stance negligent as if they had nothing more important on their minds than the latest play-off game. And all three stared at her as she walked toward the office.

"What happened to your shoulder?" Teague asked. "Why didn't you tell me about that earlier?"

Mitch, who had just taken a swallow from his glass, choked on the liquid and shot Luke a grin. "Going to be a long night for you, Ransom."

Her skin tightened with sudden self-consciousness. "I know. I look like hell. I don't want to hear it. Would one of you pour me a drink?"

Like hell and sin and Satan all in one package. My God, what was Alyssa thinking?

That thought had come from Luke and heated her from the inside out.

"Mitch." She picked up an empty glass from the counter and tapped it to get his attention. "Alcohol, please."

Mitch was still grinning that poor sonofabitch grin when he reached for the vodka bottle in front of him and tilted it toward Keira's glass.

Alyssa stepped up to the counter and put her hand over the rim, then offered her two pills instead. "You can't have both."

"Lys?" Luke muttered with a quick glare before starting for the office. "Can I have a word with you?"

Jocelyn leaned forward in the plush chair in the sitting room of her office. Her assistant had started the gas fireplace and ordered Jocelyn's favorite Thai takeout before she'd left for the night, now nearly ten hours ago. But Jocelyn hadn't touched the food, nor had she taken notice of the fire. She'd been engrossed in the files pulled from one of the confidential vaults and couriered to her office the prior afternoon upon first word of the siege. Files on every member of that godforsaken firefighting team.

She'd had access to them last year, when all that shit had broken with Creek escaping prison. But since only Creek and Ransom had been heavily involved at the time, she'd glossed over the rest of the team's information. Currently, she was halfway through Keira O'Shay's dossier, and her stomach was knotted so tight that if she'd eaten that Thai, she'd have puked it up by now.

Movement blurred to her left. She started, twisted toward the shadow, hand at her hip, a natural response after so many years carrying a weapon. But no metal lay along her waist anymore.

Owen stood at the door separating her office and sitting

room, one hand in the front pocket of his navy slacks. His pretty eyes darted to the file, then back to her face. "That must be interesting. You were lost. I knocked, called your name."

His voice, smooth, warm, immediately calmed her.

"Owen." She spread her hand over her heart. "You scared me."

"You? Scared?" He smiled. "Not possible."

"You're in early." She glanced at her watch, ignoring the charming grin, and shored the defenses already weakening at their foundation. "What pried you out of Libby's warm bed at this hour of the morning?"

The twinkle in his eyes died. "Just got some news. Thought you should know."

"What now?"

He strolled toward the fire. She purposely kept her eyes locked on his head. That head full of dark hair she'd never gotten to feel. Not once.

"Kai Ryder just went wheels up in Wyoming."

Her mind sharpened. "With what? He doesn't have a—"

"Yes, he does. His shadow just called. He's borrowed his boss's private jet. A Hawker Six Hundred with a capacity of eight. Filed a flight plan for an overnight stop in Redmond, Oregon, with a final destination of Truckee, California, which means he's picking up Seth Masters on his way to Teague Creek's place."

Jocelyn spread out the files in front of her. That meant the whole team would be together. All their powers clustered in one place. "Damn. I was afraid of this." She looked back up at Owen. "Who the hell does Ryder work for that he can borrow a Hawker Six Hundred? And where did he learn to fly one?"

Owen leaned in and opened Ryder's file to a headshot. Tousled brown hair, serious rugged features, eyes squinting against the sun, Ryder stared straight back at Jocelyn, and even through the photo his sky-high sexuality quotient stung her gut.

"Works for a retired air force general now doing security contract work for some big corporations," Owen said. "Ryder served under him for six years before leaving service for civilian firefighting."

Jocelyn rubbed at the tension in her forehead. "Get someone on that general. See what he's working on, what Ryder's working on, what clearances he's got."

"Your wish . . ." Owen said, letting the *is my command* go unsaid, but Jocelyn didn't miss the innuendo in the undertone and hated the way her body tingled.

"And Seth Masters?"

"Still licking his wounds from his wife's incarceration at the mental facility. He's never given his shadow much to report. I guess when the woman a man thought he loved cracks, kills someone, and sends a lifetime friend to prison just to get a kid . . . it makes a man question himself."

Tara Masters's instability had come in handy when they'd needed to shut Creek up, but it had become a huge liability once he'd escaped.

"Is Masters working?" she asked.

"Yes. He's a battalion chief for Placer County Fire. That's all he does. It's his life since Tara went into the loony bin."

"Fine. Masters has never been a big problem. Now, Jessica Fury I worry about. Definitely a sleeper. She has some tight ties to very powerful people in Washington. If she were to pick up interest in the team's mission . . ."

"She hasn't," Owen assured her. "She's got three shadows, two of which are in Italy with her at the moment where she's in the middle of some international hazardous materials conference with the partner in her lobbying firm."

"It's not that long a flight," Jocelyn said.

Owen shook his head. "Only one call was placed to her

hotel in Rome. By Ryder, and he didn't reach her. He left a message that we killed. She won't be jumping on any flight back to the States to join this powwow. Besides, with the distance she's created between her and the team over the last five years, I doubt she'd dive into the deep end now."

Oh, yes, she would, if she knew what Jocelyn knew. But that could never happen, which was only one reason Jocelyn needed to get that kid back.

She slapped the file she'd been reading down on the table. "Have you read this? O'Shay's file?"

"No, but I pretty much know . . ." Owen glanced at the file. His eyes skipped to the corner of the table. Jocelyn followed his attention—to the envelope from Jason's attorney. Dammit. "You haven't opened it yet?"

"Focus, Owen."

"Why not?"

"Because I don't want to be distracted. Because *this*"— she tapped the file—"is my mission. And it's a damn good thing, because if I was even a millimeter off my game, O'Shay would take her shot and nail me right between the eyes. Did you know she won Top Shot at the National Inter-agency competition this year? She beat the man who's held the title for seven years."

"I know she's the region's best sharpshooter."

"Not just the region, Owen. The *nation*."

"You've never been impressed by titles or ribbons, Joce."

He wasn't getting it. She returned her attention to the file and summarized. "She had an absent father and an abusive, alcoholic mother. Went into foster care at age five. Had a dozen different sets of foster parents by the time she was released from the system at eighteen." Jocelyn turned to another section of the file. "There are various signs of mental and physical abuse, yet she made honor roll every year in school. Top of her class at the fire academy—"

"I'm getting nauseous, Joce. Were you going to nomi-
nate her for citizen of the year or make a point?"

"I'm making it." *Idiot.* "Don't you see a pattern? She ex-
cels against all odds. When she sees an obstacle, she doesn't
back down, she fights harder to overcome it. When someone attacks her, she doesn't succumb, she fights back. Unlike her brother, who has an amazing IQ of one hundred
seventy-two, she's an above-average one hundred twenty-
nine. She's not a genius. She's a fighter. Which would be
great if she was on our side—"

"You sure you're not identifying with her just a little,
Joce? The alcoholic mother. The absent father—"

"Are you missing my point on purpose or just trying to
piss me off?"

"I'm trying to give you another perspective. But as always, you've got your blinders on." He leaned his shoulder
against the fireplace. "She's not on our side, which makes
her dangerous. And the longer she has the kid, the more
chance they have of discovering what he can do, who
he is."

"I don't see how." Though this was her biggest fear. "He's
only five years old, he only speaks Greek, and even he
doesn't know who he is."

"You have no idea what abilities Rostov developed in
him."

"That's ridiculous. The informant inside the ranch—"

"Was relatively worthless," Owen finished. "She was
only with him a few hours a day and is now dead. My
point, Joce, is that nothing where this kid or this team is
concerned is ridiculous. We have limited information on
their abilities, and they've proven their fierce loyalty when
one has been threatened in the past. And by the way they're
staging in Truckee, it's obvious that hasn't changed."

She bit the inside of her cheek, staring at O'Shay's file.
Jocelyn knew the secrets surrounding that kid would be

devastating in O'Shay's hands. Not to mention Foster's. At a loss, Jocelyn folded her hands in her lap, straightened her shoulders, and lifted her face to Owen.

"What would you suggest I do?"

Owen shrugged, pushed off the fireplace, and sauntered toward her. He'd gained grace over the years, his body smooth and strong, the kind that a knowing woman could spot regardless of the clothes he wore. And Jocelyn definitely knew his body. Couldn't forget it no matter how hard she'd tried.

He stopped next to her chair, reached down, and lifted the soft fringe of bangs off her forehead, smoothing them to the side. Jocelyn couldn't keep her eyes from falling closed.

"Might have to take a chance, Joce." His voice was low and soft, his finger caressing her temple. "Might have to just jump and take the risk of exposing yourself for the chance of gaining something even better."

She leaned into his hand, then nudged it away. When she looked up at him, he was smiling, his mouth and eyes soft.

"Cash," she said.

He shrugged one shoulder, slipped his hands back into his pockets. "It's an option."

"It's a huge risk. We'd be completely exposed."

He turned toward the door and slowly made his way across the office, giving her plenty of time to look at his ass. Jocelyn didn't mind. She rarely let herself indulge, and it was such a fine piece of male flesh.

"The bigger the risk, the bigger the payoff."

"Or the bigger the fall," she said.

"True. But if you never try, you'll never know."

He put his hand on the door handle, and Jocelyn's chest tightened. Dammit, she didn't want him to go. Didn't want him to stay. So she stalled with, "Headed back home?"

"Uh, no." He lifted his hand from the door, wrapped it

around the back of his neck, and turned halfway toward her. "I'm . . . not living at my house anymore, Joce. I moved out."

Her mouth fell open. "But . . . You . . . *What* . . . ?" Her heart pushed air out of her lungs on each hard, heavy beat. "Why?"

"Libby and I . . ." He pushed his hand back into his pocket. "We haven't been happy for a long time. I don't know if I've ever really been happy in the marriage. But that doesn't matter anymore. We just decided to stop pretending. We're getting a divorce."

"I . . . I . . ." Her mouth went dry. Her loss of Jason seemed to boomerang out of nowhere and smack her at an angle she hadn't experienced before. "I'm so sorry, Owen. Really. Truly sorry."

"Like I said, it's been over. Maybe it never started for me, because, honestly, Joce, I never really got over you."

Oh, God help her. "Owen—"

"I know it hasn't been long since Jason died. But I'm not in any hurry. I've waited twenty years for you, Joce. I can wait until you're ready." He pulled a card from his pocket and dropped it on a bookcase near the door. "My new contact info. Just in case you decide . . . you want me."

Jocelyn stared at her office door long after Owen exited. Finally, she wiped her fingers across a damp brow. "I don't need this."

But now that she was distracted, she might as well open the letter from Jason's attorney. Get all distraction of the male persuasion out of the way at once.

Jocelyn reached across the table and picked up the envelope. Heavy. Something was inside other than paper.

She wedged her thumb under one unsealed corner and ripped along the seam. Poured the contents into her other hand. A key hit her palm. Light, thin, gold. Familiar, because she had one of her own. A safe-deposit box key.

Her eyes closed for a brief second. "Great."

She unfolded the letter. The sight of Jason's handwriting did something to her guts. They clenched, quivered, went cold, then warm, and kept changing with each emotion like a kaleidoscope.

Jocie,
I hope this makes your future choices easier.
I wish you every happiness.
All my love,
Jason

ELEVEN

Keira wanted a drink. Needed a drink. Would give her next paycheck for a drink.

If she got another paycheck.

Crap, she needed to call her boss. First thing tomorrow. Wait, it was tomorrow. Okay, as soon as she got some sleep.

She watched Luke walk toward the office and lifted her chin to his retreating back. "But he's drinking."

"Water." Luke lifted his glass as he disappeared around the corner, still talking. "The drugs are way better than the booze. Guaranteed."

"But they take longer," she muttered as she took the heavy-duty pain relievers from Alyssa, then the glass of water she offered. "Where are the kids?"

"Watching a movie." Alyssa walked to the office with Keira. "Mateo's already asleep on Kat's bed. Kat will be out any second. A soldier is stationed outside their window."

"This is crazy." Keira rubbed her forehead.

Mitch was the last to file into the office, a pair of scissors and a comb in one hand, a spray bottle in the other. He grinned and held them up to Keira. "I have something to keep your hands busy. I'm past due on my cut, pixie."

"I'll say," Alyssa muttered, and plopped into the big black leather chair in front of two huge flat-screen computer monitors where X-ray images already filled the space.

Keira cut Mitch's hair every time they got together. Had even accused him of calling her every six or eight weeks for dinner as an excuse. To date, he'd never denied the allegation. And she loved his company. He was fun, intelligent, sharp, insightful. And he never made moves on her. This bark was all for Luke's benefit. Or, rather, torture. She and Mitch loved each other differently. The same as she and Teague loved each other. Or she and Kai. Or she and Seth. They were friends. They were family.

"You sure?" she asked. "I haven't slept in . . . I don't even know how many hours it's been."

She took the supplies from Mitch. With a triumphant grin, he pulled a desk chair from across the room, dropped it in the middle of the office, and straddled it. "I trust you, babe."

"Are we all settled now?" Alyssa asked.

"Sure, sis. Go ahead." Mitch picked up a remote from the nearby coffee table and pointed it toward the flat screen in the corner. "ESPN2 is replaying the—"

"No." Alyssa swiped the remote and took it with her to the desk.

"You can mute it. I just want to—"

"No."

"I can do more than one thing at a time, Lys—"

"No."

"Mom always said you were kicking me in the balls from the womb."

Keira threaded her hands through Mitch's familiar jet-black hair. A coil of dark emotion spiraled at her from Luke's direction where he sat on the arm of the loveseat across the small room. Jealousy. Clear and sharp.

She'd done a good job blocking him for hours. But she was tired and hurting, and honestly, she wanted him. Wanted him to fold her into his arms, let her rest there.

"How short?" she asked Mitch.

"I'll leave that up to you, beautiful. Just make me hot enough to turn you on."

Keira resisted the urge to roll her eyes. This man was the biggest shit stirrer she'd ever known—and she'd lived in a firehouse.

"Are we ready to get serious?" Alyssa turned her attention to the computer screens. "These image slices start at the top of Mateo's head and go through the base of his brain. These are sagittal. For you nonmedical people"—she shot Mitch a look—"that means vertical, and run right to left. And these are transverse, or horizontal, running top to bottom. Here, you can see all the gyri, the folds of brain matter. As you come down toward the spine, there are other structures."

She pointed them out and named them. Some sounded familiar, some sounded like something out of a science fiction movie.

Keira sprayed Mitch's hair with the water and combed through.

"What is all that stuff in there?" Luke had his arms crossed over his chest, angst wafting off him in tight waves. "The bright white things? The lines?"

"Those lines are the wires I told you about at the clinic." She pointed to one of the rectangular specks seated within the gyri and followed the wire to the brainstem. "The ones connected to the chip I took out of his neck."

Keira sifted pieces of Mitch's hair between her fingers and snipped, trying to focus so she didn't yank and chop in accordance with her emotions. "Do you know what they are? Can you tell what they do?"

"Typically, they're used to repair problems such as hearing deficiencies. Only these aren't in the right location in his brain to aid with hearing loss. Nor are they in the right location to aid in depression or seizures or limb movement, which are some more recent advances in the use of implants."

Keira's hands stopped moving through Mitch's hair. "Then what the hell are they doing in there?"

"I don't know yet." Alyssa waved toward the myriad of open volumes spread over one end of the desk space, another computer screen above displaying a web page with what looked like a research project on the subject. "I may find something in here."

"But you have an idea," Mitch said. "I know that look in your eye."

She set her gaze on Keira and cleared her throat. She always cleared her throat right before she had to deliver ominous news. Keira leaned closer to Mitch.

"Implants are simply microchips. They're called brain-computer interfaces. They collect and redirect the electrical currents already running through the brain.

"Recently, researchers have added amplifiers, which increase and transfer the voltage to a master or control chip, like the one we removed from Mateo's neck, which then becomes, in effect, an all-in-one power source and micro-computer, harnessing the power of the mind. Those chips have the impetus to perform whatever task they are programmed for. In the last decade, that's typically been to move a prosthetic limb."

"Well, he obviously doesn't have a prosthetic limb." Luke sat forward and rested his elbows on his knees. "So what else might they be doing in his brain with all this . . . current?"

Alyssa shrugged. "The possibilities are as endless as the imagination. I don't know enough about these implants to guess."

Everyone went silent for a moment, each lost in his own thoughts. Keira blew out a frustrated breath, rounded in front of Mitch, and started on his cut again. She needed the distraction.

The stress in the room whipped like a hurricane. She'd lost track of where it was coming from. Her walls were now paper-thin. She'd spent years learning to control her abilities, only to find herself at their mercy again after less than twenty four hours of havoc.

"From what I can see"—Alyssa pointed at an image where several little bright spots clustered in the center of Mateo's brain—"the majority of implants are centered around the nerves. Specifically the ocular core where nerves like the optic, occulomotor, trochlear, and abducens nerves are located."

Teague rubbed a hand over his face. "Baby, English. Please."

"Those are nerves that affect the muscles and functions related to vision, like eye movement and pupil constriction."

A hot rock dropped in Keira's stomach. She stopped cutting. "Vision." It made complete sense. "They were trying to manipulate his powers as a remote viewer."

Alyssa lifted her brows in consideration. "That's the most logical conclusion."

"Do you realize what this could mean?" Keira fisted the scissors and stepped away from Mitch, panic sizzling through her bloodstream. "If they discovered or even believed Rostov could manipulate or control Mateo's power of remote viewing by implanting electrodes in his brain and hooking him up to a computer, what would they do to manipulate or control *our* abilities?"

She waved a hand at Luke. "If boiling water doesn't scald Luke's skin, what would happen if they implanted electrodes to amp that power? Could they make his body resistant to three hundred degrees? Five hundred? A thousand?

And if flame doesn't scorch him, what about acid? And if he's bulletproof, what about knife-proof?"

"Keira." Luke grimaced. "You're making me sick."

"What about Teague's ability?" she continued. "If he can heal cuts at a certain temperature, stop bleeding at another, what would they have to do to enable him to cure cancer? Eradicate disease? And who would they test his abilities on?

"And then there's me. My abilities aren't that different from Mateo's, only I hear, he sees. Do I need to go on?"

Here we go. Worst-case scenarios again.

She turned to Luke. "Maybe you should open your brain a little wider."

The room went silent. Keira bit the inside of her lip.

"You two . . ." Mitch's light eyes darted between them. "Having your own private conversation?"

Keira closed her eyes on a sigh.

"Holy shit," Mitch muttered. "I sure as hell hope you can't hear what I think."

"Mitch," Alyssa said. "You are so careless with your money. That's another twenty into Kat's college fund."

Teague held up a hand. "Keira, don't get ahead of yourself. We don't even know that's what these implants are for. Come over here and let me work on your cuts."

Mitch wrapped his arm around her waist in the most offensive move he'd ever made toward her. "But not before you get a proper thank-you for my new style."

The move didn't feel threatening, just . . . awkward. Mitch leaned in, clearly with the intention of kissing her, but slowly. Too slowly. A direct contrast to the way he'd grabbed her. And no, she couldn't read what was on his mind. But Luke's thoughts pierced her skull like a knife.

Over my dead body.

Luke fisted the back of Mitch's T-shirt and yanked him

backward. "You don't want to know what I did to the last guy who kissed her in front of me."

Mitch shot Keira a wink before pulling from Luke's grasp, shaking him off and hitting him with a scowl.

"Get off me, cop. She's a free entity."

"Guys." Alyssa's irritable tone made it clear her patience was low. "Knock it off. Keira, let Teague work on your cuts."

Keira was too exhausted to take much interest in Luke and Mitch's power struggle, one that was more about Mitch's ability to needle Luke and Luke's ability to stab back than it was about either one's feelings for her.

Boys. They never changed.

She dropped into the loveseat facing Teague, curled one foot underneath her, and let her friend inspect her cuts. She'd peeled the loose Steri-strips off after the shower, leaving her injuries clean and exposed.

Teague's warm fingers started on the cut at her temple. His sure touch sent pulses of heat into the first centimeter of flesh before it dissipated, and along with it, the throbbing ache. With every inch of healing, her stress decreased another notch.

"Mitch," she said. "Were you able to find out about the other kids who survived?"

"As soon as they were stable, the army flew them out to military hospitals. We'll never find them now."

"In the car," she said, "Tony talked about Rostov's hereditary research; said the kids that came out of the ranch were of different nationalities."

"He probably chose different nationalities and genders and ages to test for variations in response to the chemical exposure." Alyssa rubbed a hand across her eyes. "My God, he's a modern-day Joseph Mengele."

"Mangled what?" Mitch asked.

"Mengele," Alyssa repeated. "World War Two." When

that didn't stimulate a response, she started gesturing with her hands. "Scientist. Experimented on kids, took a keen interest in twins, injected dye into their eyes to see if they changed colors, performed amputations without anesthetic . . ." She put up both hands in a "stop" gesture. "Oh, wait. I remember now. Nicole Jamison sat next to you in that class. You almost flunked out. Mom grounded you for a month."

Mitch's expression went wistful. "Nicole Jamison. Mmm-mmm. Now there's a blast from the past. Haven't thought of ol' Nickie in a long time." A grin edged his mouth up. "She was so worth that D, and Dad softened Mom down to a week."

"The double standard in action." Alyssa looked at Keira as if gaining support from the only other female in the room. "She had an overbite, her mouth was too big for her face, and she was as dumb as a brick wall."

"Now, now. Be nice if you want me to tell you where these came from." He leaned over Alyssa's shoulder, picked up the magnifying glass on the desk, and inspected the implants in Mateo's brain. "Someone's got to manufacture these little beauties, which means someone had to invent them first, which means someone knows what they're used for. Write down these numbers, Lys."

Alyssa scribbled numbers on a piece of paper as Mitch read them from each microchip. Her gaze flicked between the images and the numbers. "They're arranged in a numerical pattern. The shape of a star where the points are multiples of three."

Mitch's head tilted. "Your brain is so twisted, Lys. How you can see shit like that is beyond me."

She looked at him and fingered her earlobe. "Maybe I'll bypass that college fund for now. She's only seven and I could use a pair of diamond earrings."

"Just write down anything else you know about the implants—what they're used for, what they're being re-searched for, what type of companies manufacture them and possibilities of what they might be called, like implants, brain-computer interfaces, whatever." Mitch plopped the magnifying glass back on the desk with a clunk. "If you're getting diamond earrings, you're going to earn them."

Luke still sat on the arm of the loveseat, not quite sure of his next move. Mitch had bailed after he'd taken the information on the implants with mutterings of research. Alyssa and Teague had gone to make sure both Kat and Mateo were safely tucked into Kat's bed before they turned in themselves. And Luke was alone with Keira, who was still strung so tight he could have plucked an E note off her.

He'd been contemplating asking for a haircut. Not only did he need one, but she wanted him to have one, and, as an added benefit, he'd get to feel her hands on him. But in her current state of mind, the thought of her having sharp instruments near his head—not appealing. Besides, it was nearing five a.m. and they both needed at least a few hours of sleep.

"We're still in America, right?" Keira planted her fists on the desk ledge in front of the computer screens,. "Liberty and justice for all? One land under God and all that?"

Luke didn't respond, giving her time to vent. In the meantime he soaked in the sight of her—the toned muscle shaping her tan arms. The way her shoulders sloped to a sleekly tapered back and waist. His gaze dropped to her ass, the curves outlined seductively by the ultrathin silk pajama bottoms . . .

His eyes jumped back to the waistband. To something peeking over the edge, something black and lacy. Not underwear, 'cause she sure as hell wasn't wearing any. Was that a . . . *tattoo?*

Her head came up and she straightened from the desk, quick, defensive.

Before she could turn, Luke planted his hands on her hips. "What is this?"

Her fingers closed over his and pushed, but she wasn't trying to get away. Not really. If she wanted to kick his ass, she certainly had the ability.

He pushed against her grip and shoved her tank higher, her pants lower, to reveal what was indeed a tattoo. An intricate, artistic, truly stunning tattoo. One that followed the lines of her scar, the one she'd developed after the warehouse fire. One every member of the team shared in different sizes and in different locations on their bodies. Hers encompassed the width of her hips, extended downward in the shape of a V toward her ass.

"Damn, Keira." He couldn't keep the shock from his voice. He continued to nudge her clothes until he'd exposed the majority of the artwork along with a very sexy portion of her body, complete with twin dimples at the base of her spine. "When did you do this?"

"Luke . . ." Her voice came out a little breathless as she pried at his fingers.

"When?" He held tighter, his fingers indenting the firm flesh of her hips. "Why?"

"About a year ago." She finally put effort behind her attempts at release and broke his grip. "Because I decided it was time to accept my abilities instead of fight them."

His blood pulsed as she turned to face him. But her statement lit a fuse of hope somewhere inside. If she could recognize, fight, and win a battle of that magnitude within herself, maybe . . . maybe she could do it again.

"It's . . . amazing." His gaze skimmed up the front of her body, over the swell of her breasts cradled tight in the cross of her arms, and stopped at the spark of those blue eyes. "That's not . . . something I ever thought you'd do."

"What? The tattoo or accepting my abilities?"

"Either, I guess."

"Yeah, well . . ." She dropped her arms and stood tall, chin proud. "I'm not the same person you knew three years ago."

No. Not the person he'd known three years ago when she'd left, or five years ago when they'd first dated, or seven years ago when he'd first set eyes on her in passing at a firefighter class.

He was uncovering slivers he hadn't even known existed. Fascinating new shiny slivers. And he wanted to explore every last one. But he found himself in this never-ending spiral where she blocked him because she didn't trust, and she didn't trust because she blocked him.

She flicked her wrist and the scissors flashed in the light. "Do you want a haircut or not? I won't give you a Mohawk, for God's sake."

"I'm more concerned about losing an ear."

"Eh." Keira shrugged. "You've got another one."

Luke studied the chair and debated. Maybe, if she was touching him, he could hear her. Or project. Maybe, he could soften her a little, get her to talk, get her to listen.

Worth a shot. Not talking, or rather—fighting—sure wasn't working for them. He threw one leg over the chair and dropped in. Crossing his arms over the back, he rested his chin on his forearms and emptied his mind.

She squirted him down, and he flinched against the cold spray. While she swept the comb through his dripping hair, he tuned into her, reached out with his mind, searching, but all he got back was a low, vibrating hum.

"When are you going to call your boss?" he asked, his voice muffled against his arms. "And what are you going to say?"

She sidled up alongside him until her leg brushed his thigh and hip, reaching in to comb strands into her fingers with one hand and snip with the other. When she'd finished cutting and started combing again, Luke lifted his head and rested his chin on his arms so he could see her, watch her move.

"In a few hours, when he's back in the office. But I'm not sure what I'll say. If he's involved in this, I'm screwed. He could bury me if he wanted to. Now would be the time to cut me off at the knees, now that I know about Mateo, about Rostov, about the ranch, and the chemicals. We're one very big step closer to the truth. They aren't going to let that slide."

"What are you going to do if that happens?"

"I guess I'll hire a good shark to cajole, manipulate, and blackmail. Then think about another damn career move. ATF hiring?"

Luke chuckled.

As Keira moved behind him, Luke closed his eyes and simply focused on the feel of her hands. The way her strong fingers massaged his scalp and tugged at his hair. The same as when they used to make love.

"Luke," she warned. "If you want a lousy cut, keep it up."

His mouth turned in triumph. "I'm a guest in your mind again? You've been blocking me for hours."

"I still would be, but I just don't have the strength right now. Besides, it's not that easy. Unfortunately."

She continued to move around him, swaying to one side, leaning to the other, comb, snip, comb, snip. She swept her hand over his shoulder, across his forehead. He could sit here forever like this, with her body heat circling him, her fresh scent toying with his senses. His world felt so right, so complete when she was within reach.

He opened his eyes as she stood in front of the chair, lifting her arms to reach for the top of his head. Her tank rode up her flat belly, and a flash caught his eye. One he'd never seen there before.

"Whoa." His hands landed on her hips, thumbs pushed her cami up to reveal a diamond stud in her belly button that teased him with a wink. "Well, look at this. You are just full of sexy surprises, aren't you? How long have you had that?"

" 'Bout two years."

"How did I miss that last night?" he murmured, his thumb skimming across the little gem and her warm, supple belly. "I was right there."

Her muscles tightened, and she shifted out of reach. "Preoccupied, I guess."

"No shit." Just the thought of how close they'd been to making love was sending him back to that preoccupied state. And his body responded just as quick. "I like it."

The steady comb-and-snip motion of her hands faltered. "Thanks."

"Sexy. Really freaking sexy."

"Luke," she warned again.

"Does Mitch know about it? About the tattoo?"

"You know he's just messing with you, right? You know there's nothing between us. He's like my . . ."

The word *brother* hung heavy in the air.

Backfire. He'd take the perfect opening to talk about the things she'd kept from him in the past.

"Tell me about him." He wasn't about to live with that elephant in the room. They already weren't talking about the gorilla swinging on the lamp or the giraffe chewing ficus leaves by the fireplace. "Your brother."

She groaned. "I don't—"

"What was his name?"

She hesitated. Sighed. "Cash. His name was Cash."

"Cash and Keira. That's cute."

"I guess." She picked up the water bottle and resprayed his hair. "Though our life wasn't the least bit cute."

It seemed so odd now how little he knew of Keira's childhood. Yes, they'd been coworkers, friends. Lovers. But that had been during a beautiful time in their lives when the past didn't matter and their futures were light-years away.

A time when they lived in the excitement of the moment. When their companions were the fellow firefighters they loved and admired, their jobs exciting and rewarding and downright freaking fun, their off-duty hours spent at pubs, family barbecues, and inter-agency softball tournaments.

Once Keira and Luke got together, they'd spent their days putting out flames in the field and their nights lighting them up in the bedroom. It had been a perfect life. One Luke had started to believe would last until death did they part.

The warehouse fire changed everything.

Now, he wanted to know the woman he should have known back then, who she'd become in the years they'd been apart, and who she'd been before he'd met her.

The tunnel, her thoughts, and fears filled his mind again. But he'd be lucky to get her to stick to the subject of her brother tonight. He had a feeling they'd be taking baby steps fleshing out her past.

"Turn around," she said. "Look up at me."

He turned on the chair and tilted his head back. Her fingers skimmed through his hair, testing the length. Not yet satisfied, she started combing and snipping again.

"How did the fire start?" Luke asked, watching those perfect, unbound breasts jiggle beneath the thin cotton top, nipples tight.

She moved to his right, leaned in, her belly pressing his upper arm. All his attention slid in that direction. "Stupid. Little kitchen fire."

A little kitchen fire didn't kill people. Luke looked up.

When she didn't meet his gaze, he stilled her hands with his. "What happened?"

She waved the comb in frustration and broke from his grasp. "It caught. Blew up. I got out; my brother didn't. End of story."

Luke knew Keira hadn't known her father. Remembered she had once said she doubted her mother had even known her father. But then changed the subject and veered away from it every time it came up again. "What about your mother?"

"She got out, too," she muttered with a clear *piece-of-shit* tone. "Unfortunately."

"But I thought you told me she was dead."

"She is. Points for God on that score. She died in prison."

"Prison?" The word came out with candid shock.

Keira laughed, the sound dry and harsh. "Not so sorry you got rid of me now, are you?"

He ignored her jibe. "Why was she in prison?"

"Because her drunken temper turned that tiny fire into an inferno, burned down the house, and killed my brother. I have no doubt she's rotting in hell, right where she belongs."

The air rushed out of Luke's lungs. With that kind of baggage, it was no wonder Keira had mother issues.

I cared about Kat. I tried to be what she needed . . . I tried to be what you needed . . .

Keira's words spiked through his heart. Luke could imagine how Keira had internalized Kat's inconsolable grief at losing both her mother and Teague. Blamed it on her lack of maternal skills or genes or whatever, although she never once complained, never once pushed Kat away, never once confessed her fears. And Luke had been oblivious.

He never considered the toll it might have taken on Keira. Not until long after she'd gone. But now, knowing about her childhood, feeling her abilities firsthand, his appreciation for her torment was that much sharper. His guilt that much keener.

Imagine going into a burning building, being able to hear people crying for help upstairs, but only in your head. How would you convince your chief you had to get up there without telling him you were hearing voices? How would you live with yourself if you were allowed to go, but the fire was impassible and you had to listen to them burn to death?

Her words to him in one of their last and most volatile arguments surrounding the subject of her quitting firefighting and taking the FBI job replayed in his head. She'd been trying so hard to explain. He just hadn't heard her.

He was damn well going to listen this time.

"He was only fifteen when the fire started?" Luke asked, now with a million questions running through his head.

She nodded.

"Big age difference between you two."

"We were accidents with different fathers. Good-for-nothing losers. Our mother never missed an opportunity to tell us that. And we both looked like her, which really pissed her off." She set the scissors down on the desk behind her. Standing directly in front of him, Keira made one more pass at his hair, sliding both hands through, then stepped back. "You're done."

Luke caught her waist before she was out of reach and pulled her between his legs. He wrapped his arms around her hips, rested his chin on her belly, and looked up at her. "I guess that's one good thing you got out of the deal. Those dark Irish good looks."

Her fingers flitted through his hair, a little frown on her lips. "You're not so bad yourself, Ransom. But, I'm beginning to think that haircut wasn't such a good idea."

A slow smile drifted over his mouth. She'd always preferred his hair short. Said it showed off his eyes, the angles of his face. Said just looking at him made her hot.

He spread his hands over the curve of her spine and tucked his fingers underneath her tank, sliding them up her back. "Appreciating your work, O'Shay?"

Her frown turned and a soft, almost self-deprecating grin lit her face. The first sight of those pretty white teeth in . . . he didn't know how long, just that it had been *way* too long.

"Appreciating the canvas." But as quickly as it appeared, her smile drifted away. "What happened to us, Luke?"

His own smile died, but the fact that she'd asked after everything that had happened sparked hope. He reached up and ran his thumb over her soft cheek and that fringe of freckles.

"What *didn't* happen, baby? We went from utopia to hell in one night. Somebody we loved died. We all nearly died. We spent months recovering physically, years recovering mentally. Our lives changed forever. *We* changed forever."

Keira squeezed her eyes shut and nodded against his hand. "I miss those early days. I miss you. *Us*. How good it used to be." Tears crept over her bottom lashes. "I miss the life we had, all the possibilities before everything changed. God, how I miss it."

"Oh, baby." Her confession ripped at his heart. He locked his arms around her hips and pulled her onto his lap. Her legs parted easily to straddle him, her arms circled his neck, and she pressed her forehead to his. "We're together now. Things may be different, but they could be better."

She opened her eyes, her blue irises glimmering with wetness, searching his with a mixture of hope and fear, yearning for . . . something.

He slid both hands into her hair and held her gaze. "Trust me."

TWELVE

When it came to her heart, Keira couldn't truly say she trusted anyone. Not even herself.

But then he kissed her. Slid his hands deep into her hair, pulled her face to his, and tasted her lips, again and again until she couldn't keep from responding.

Just like the last time they were together, something happened between them. Something different, even better than three years before, which she hadn't believed possible. But their new abilities connected them on a higher, more intimate level. Just as his ability to fend off fire and bullets had become stronger and her ability to hear thoughts and voices had expanded, their sexual chemistry had intensified.

Now, Luke's entire essence flowed through his body and burned in his kiss. He infused her with his passion, not just adding to her own, but doubling, tripling, quadrupling the desire between them.

She kissed him back, skimming her fingers over his freshly cut hair, pulling his mouth deeper, pushing her tongue past his lips and seeking his. Luke groaned long and deep, and a spike of heat and satisfaction drilled to her core. Then he pulled back, holding her face steadfast, looking into her eyes with something that almost resembled pain.

She ran her hands over his shoulders, down the hard muscle of his sides, his belly, and covered the generous package between his legs. He was as hot as he was hard, and an urgent need pulsed deep inside her.

Luke sucked air. "Keira. *God*. I've missed you."

He lifted his hips, rocking into her. Raw pleasure flooded her body. She wanted him inside her, filling her, completing her like no one else ever had, ever could.

She scraped her nails under his T-shirt and up the soft skin and hard muscle of his torso, pushing the fabric out of the way.

Luke growled, skimming his hands down her back, gripping her hips. "Keira, you're killing me."

"I'd love to make sure you die happy." She kissed him deeply with an erotic play of her tongue, scooted back, and searched for the button of his jeans. She would take him right there. Straddling him in the chair. Shedding only enough clothing to get him inside her. That's all she needed right now. The long, hard, hot length of him burning inside. She'd take more later. But now, she couldn't wait.

Anticipation dried her mouth. Her fingers fumbled with his zipper, her mind already on all that silky heat in her hands.

But his fingers closed around hers. Tightened. He pressed his cheek against hers, his breath hot and whispered, "No."

"No?" Dazed, she pulled back to look into his eyes. All she found was a mirror of frustration and need. "No what?"

His pained, humorless chuckle transitioned into a moan. He kept his eyes downcast. His cheeks tinged pink—a rare sight that hit Keira's chest with an unfamiliar apprehension.

"No condoms. Remember?"

Grudgingly, yeah, she remembered, with enough frustration to scream. Which brought up a question she'd been wondering about since the safe house incident. "Why aren't you carrying at least one?" As soon as she voiced the question, a sickening thought popped to mind. "Lucas Ransom. You told me you weren't seeing anyone."

His head jerked up, a look of shock on his face. "I'm not."

"Then what is this? If you tell me you took some bizarre, New-Age oath of celibacy I'm going to kill you here and now."

"That's not what I intended, but . . ." He grinned, but it disappeared quickly. "I'm sorry, baby. I can't even tell you how sorry, but I don't carry condoms because I never need any." The quirk of his mouth showed a heavy dose of nerves. He cleared his throat, dropped his gaze to her chest. "I never need any, because . . . well, like I told you last night . . . it's been a long time."

A zing of shock burned along her sternum. "I . . . I thought you meant . . . us."

"I know. Didn't see the point in . . ." He shrugged. Beneath her, his knee started to bounce. His fingers dug into the flesh at her waist and released. He darted a nervous glance from beneath his brows, then looked away again. And when Keira opened herself to deeper sensations, a dark lightning cloud settled over Luke, filled with angst.

She tried to wrap her mind around his admittance, battling her own emotions. *"Why?"*

He heaved a breath, seemed to shore himself up, and looked directly into her eyes. "The short story is: you. Because I got tired of trying to fill your place only to be disappointed. Because nobody else was you. Because I always just wanted *you*."

"Oh, my God," she whispered, heart tearing. She cupped his face, touched by the flush along his cheekbones, by the way his gaze lost its strength to hold hers once the admission had been made. "Why didn't you ever . . . God, you never even . . . A phone call? An e-mail? I was only two hours away; you could have come to see me. Christ, Luke, did you expect me to read your mind?"

"I don't know what I expected." His eyes closed for a second as he shook his head. "I didn't know what was wrong with me. Thought I had gone a little . . . I don't know . . . crazy." His hands slid up her sides, over her shoulders, and clasped the back of her head, pulling her in and pressing his forehead to hers. "But it all makes sense now. I couldn't be with anyone else anymore because my head and my body had figured out what my heart had always known. It's always been *you* for me. *Only you.*"

Her heart pounded, afraid to believe. There were still unresolved issues between them. Big ones. But when he tilted his head and touched his lips to hers, she found strength and security in the warmth of his mouth. His tongue drifted in and sought hers, and her passion exploded. She tightened her arms, arched her back, tilted her head, and devoured him with his words floating through her head.

Only you. Only you, baby.

Luke responded with the same hunger, his tongue hot, lips relentless, fingers digging into her back as he smashed her chest against his.

She broke the kiss, fisting her hands in his T-shirt. "God, I want you."

Luke's mouth dropped to her neck, his teeth adding an exciting pinch to the passion. One hand came around, slid between their bodies, and palmed her breast. Pleasure filled her, made her restless. She rocked her hips against his, and he groaned against her skin. Found her nipple. Rolled it between his fingers. Keira whimpered, scraped her fingers along his scalp. He pinched, and need tugged deep inside her.

"Goddammit, Luke," she growled. "I want you inside me." She dropped her hands to the generous swell beneath his jeans and rubbed.

Luke's head came back, lids dropped halfway, his lips parted on a low moan. "Ah, Christ." He grabbed her hands and pulled them away from what Keira wanted most. "Baby,

I want that, too. Wish I could give it to you right now, but there's plenty of time. I'll go to the store in a few hours."

"Not soon enough. You know by then everyone's going to be awake. Alyssa and Mitch sniping at each other. Kids running all over the place."

"Thia."

Keira startled at Mateo's voice. She pushed off Luke's chest and turned. The boy stood behind her, rubbing his eyes with his fists.

"Crap, that scared me." So much for finding any relief for this nagging three-year-old ache. "Right on cue. Guess we have to wait anyway."

She reluctantly slid off Luke's lap and lifted the boy, who now had both arms held out to her. Luke remained in the chair, shoulders slumped, huge hard-on filling his jeans, unfulfilled desire darkening his expression.

Still, his mouth turned in a lopsided smile as he ran a hand over Mateo's head where the boy nestled against Keira's shoulder and closed his eyes. "Kinda reminds me of when we first got Kat."

Oh, yes. The end of spontaneous, hot, crazy sex as they knew it, which was the least of their painful moments. Far worse were all the blind parenting attempts, all the sleepless nights, the tears, the angst and pain, and ultimately, the failure— of everything.

There was a mood killer.

Keira pushed the memories back. She wanted to hold on to the faint shine of hope Luke had polished in her heart.

"Let's lie down." Luke pushed to his feet and nudged her toward the couch with a warm hand at the base of her spine and a sexy smile. "Get a little sleep before I venture out to the store. You're gonna need it."

"I like the sound of that."

He lay on his side and scooted back, lifting his arms in invitation. Keira faced him, transferring Mateo's weight to the cushions between them. Peering at Luke over a child's curls did feel familiar, but in a bittersweet, anxious sort of way.

The past is the past. Let it go.

His brows dipped between heavy lidded eyes. "You okay?"

Better watch those thoughts. "Unsettled."

He gave her a sleepy smile, reached over Mateo, and ran a hand over her head. A sweet, familiar gesture that swept her back in time. The mixed memories had her brain sloshing from one emotion to another, a ship on rough seas.

"What are you going to do about him?"

"Hmm?" Luke's question helped her refocus on the present. "What? About who?"

"What do you mean who?" His mouth tipped as his eyes darted toward Mateo and back. "Him."

"Oh." Keira looked down at Mateo's face, so completely angelic in sleep, reminding her so much of Kat at his age. No two ways about it, that was a sweet thought. "I don't know what you mean. He seems fine."

"I mean, if he's truly an orphan. If he's truly from Greece. If his life there was truly as dismal as Tony described."

Uh-oh. The drift of this conversation was not good. That sliver of light she'd experienced just moments ago faded.

"I think it's a little early to be deciding his fate, Luke. I'm sure Tony was lying about where he came from."

"Why? Mateo does speak fluent Greek."

She shook her head. "I don't know, but it doesn't matter. It's not my decision to make."

Luke's fingers stilled in Mateo's hair, then moved to Keira's cheek. Trying to get her attention. "Keira." His tone said everything she didn't want to hear, a combination of you-can't-avoid-this and you-need-to-do-the-right-thing.

"There is clearly something between you two. Beyond a child's need for comfort."

Yes, she knew. She'd known the first moment she'd seen his photograph. Only, she still didn't know what that something encompassed. And the longer she had Mateo, the murkier the source of their connection became. "We're connected by the powers. I'm protecting him. Caring for him. It's just natural."

"It's natural for a child to cling to someone who cares for him, but you clearly love him, too."

She pushed up on her elbow. Mateo's head was cradled on Luke's shoulder, and Luke's fingers ran over the boy's hair, cheek, arm, then back to his hair. Lord, he was a sweet man. But he was also stubborn. And right now that stubbornness was making the walls close in on her.

"Yes, I love him, like I love Kat."

"You have to recognize that you love him differently. Even I can see that."

Her answers were never good enough. "What is this about?"

"It doesn't really matter where he's from. Those implants in his head, that mark on his skin, his powers, change everything. If he is from Greece, you can't just dump him back there with cutting-edge technology in his head and military-grade psychological powers. If anyone ever caught wind of that, what happened to him here would be a spa date compared to what they'd do to him in Greece.

"If he is from here and we can't reconnect him with his parents, which doesn't seem likely given the results of Mitch's research on reported missing children, he'll end up in foster care. That alone is absurd—*you* letting *him* end up in foster care. Plus, you know DARPA won't let him stay there. They'll snatch him and send him who knows where to do who knows what."

Her chest grew tighter with every word. "I can't believe you're dumping all this on me. Now. After the day we've had."

He slipped warm fingers beneath her hair to squeeze her neck. "I want you to think ahead. You like to have plans, right? Plan A, plan B, et cetera."

She could see where this was going. "You're boxing me in, Luke."

"I'm giving you options."

"Do any of those options include just being me? Who I am right now? Or do they all require me to change into a person more suitable to who you want me to be? Specifically, a mother."

"It's not about a label. I love who you are right now. I love who you are but won't allow yourself to be. I see a boy you love, who also loves you and needs a home. And I'd love to be part of making that family."

Her heart rattled in its cage. She wanted to let it free, but the fear of what would happen to it if she did was overwhelming. What lurked outside those bars?

If she let her heart out . . . If she let it live . . . People could hurt her.

And there were a lot of people out there who wanted to do just that.

When she didn't respond, Luke shook his head with an expression of disbelief. "You can't use the genetic excuse here, Keira. Who would be better suited to raise him than people who understand his powers?"

The word *excuse* hit her wrong. His impatient, demanding attitude hit her wrong.

She sat up, angled toward him. "Have you ever considered that you're seeing what you want to see? That I'm not fighting against the inevitable, but that you're fighting for the impossible?"

"Your fear is talking, Keira, not your heart."

She pushed off the sofa and stood, so filled with competing emotions she was shaking. "Don't judge me."

"Keira." His voice turned stern. "Open your damn eyes. You are the strongest, warmest, most capable woman I've ever known. There is no one more suited to be this boy's mother than you. More than that, you want to. You just won't let yourself. And you don't have to do it alone. I care about him, too. But you won't let me in, either. Not really. You always hold something back. You always have a safety net. An out."

Keira's fight died. Pain and confusion melded into a rock wedged beneath her ribs. Those were terrible, cold, mean things to say. Yet, they were true. Which added more shadows to her cloaked psyche.

In direct contrast, Luke's light eyes were filled with confidence, his expression drenched with hope. He struggled toward his goal of family like a moth seeking light. And no matter how much he and Keira wanted each other, maybe even still loved each other, it wouldn't be enough to overcome that primal instinct that drove him, the same one Keira longed for yet pushed away at the same time.

She couldn't do this anymore. Not tonight. Not with him. She needed some time and space to clear her head and calm the fears heating her temper.

"It's good you care about him, Luke." The relative safety of the guest room beckoned. She took in the sight of the two of them together and yearned for a different past, a different future, and an end to all this pain inside. "That will make it easier for you to decide whether or not *you* want to adopt him."

This time when Cash returned to his room, he didn't have the energy to throw furniture. He didn't have the energy to do anything but sink his head into the pure down pillow they provided as if it would somehow make up for holding him prisoner.

"Hey, O'Shay. How'd it go?" Q's raspy voice drifted through the vent at the foot of Cash's bed and clawed its way into his brain, drawing him from the edge of sleep.

They often talked like this until they drifted off—at least on the nights Q was there and not MIA on one of their testing frenzies where they took him off-site for days or even weeks at a time.

"I tried it your way," Cash slurred without opening his eyes. "But I won't know if it worked for twenty-four to forty-eight hours."

"What are you going to do if it works?"

Cash's eyes opened. He stared blankly at the dark ceiling turning gray with the morning light filtering through the glass block that was his only window. The first thought that came to mind was, *that's a stupid question.* Only after a millisecond, it wasn't so stupid.

After he'd found out what these animals had done to Q, Cash had realized the chances they would release him as promised were nearly nonexistent. But there was always hope. There had to be, or he'd have killed himself years ago. He'd never been this close to a solution, and the possibility these fucks might not release him now was beyond his pain threshold.

The cell door clanked. Fear flashed through Cash's chest. If they heard him talking to Q they could move his friend to another cell, and Cash had come to rely on Q's presence for his sanity.

He sat up in bed, still dressed after he'd simply fallen there when he'd walked in. His face still cut, stained with dried blood, and his room still trashed from his earlier tirade.

The steel door swung open, the lights flipped on, and a

woman walked in. Cash's eyes took a moment to adjust. When he recognized her, everything inside him shut down.

Dargan strolled in, her icy blue eyes taking in the havoc Cash had wreaked. In her tailored taupe suit, with bleached-blond hair straight to her shoulders, every speck of makeup perfect, she was ludicrously out of place.

"I like what you've done with the place, Cash." Her voice was as smooth and cool and hard as glass. "But you don't look so good." She cast a glance at the guard they called Domino because of his mixed African American–Caucasian ancestry. "Send a medic when we're done here."

Domino gave a quick nod.

"Something big must have brought you, Jocelyn." Cash stood, put his hands on his hips, gaze searching the room for a weapon should he need one. He edged toward the metal chair lying on its side near the wall it had bounced off earlier. "You're either here to release me or kill me."

"You're so melodramatic, Cash. I really would love to release you. Had your experiment tonight panned out, I would be asking Domino to escort you to a car waiting to take you to a brand-new life."

"Then why are you here? Annual visit? At . . ." He glanced at his watch. "Five-fucking-o'clock in the morning?"

She smiled, but there was no warmth in it. He doubted there was an ounce of warmth in her entire body. "Duty never sleeps, right, soldier?"

"The patriotic crap stopped working when you killed my wife and stole my son."

Her brows lifted, head tilted with a minuscule shrug. "We *did* warn you, Cash. A number of times."

Fury gushed in his veins. He lunged for her, his head filled with a vision of squeezing her neck until that pale skin turned alabaster, those blue eyes stared wide with vacancy.

He made it as far as her blazer. Fisted his hands at her collar. Two guards came from behind her, jerked on his arms, and hauled him backward, slamming him against the cement wall.

The satisfaction in her gaze stirred his rage, but whatever he'd pulled off her neck, the metal now tangled in his fingers, distracted him. With his hands tight by his sides, he wound the chain into his palm and closed his fingers, then jerked out of the guard's grips.

"Mateo is already dead, isn't he?" Cash breathed hard, searching, maybe hoping, for a reason to quit. "He died with his mother, didn't he?"

"No," she said, completely unflustered. "No, he didn't. In fact, that's why I came tonight. When I heard how close you were, that your earlier attempt failed, I wanted to give you that extra incentive to keep going. The sooner you finish, the sooner you get to be with them."

"Them? Who's *them*?"

She pulled something from her pocket and approached. A photograph. Cash's chest tightened, but he kept himself from reaching for it. He couldn't let her see his desperation.

"In fact, not only do I have a current photo of your now five-year-old son for you, but of him with your sister."

Cash's jaw went slack before he found control. No one had ever mentioned his sister. He had assumed they didn't know about her. Assumed she'd been adopted early on in foster care and changed her name.

She'd been such a cute kid, with those big blue eyes, those freckles, the deep sweetness and endless loyalty to those she loved despite their mother's attempts to quash her. He was sure there had been childless couples fighting over her. He was also sure he used that rationalization to ease the guilt he often suffered over running after the fire, over not letting her know he was alive.

So much guilt where Keira was concerned. And now, that much more if these fucks had drawn her into this.

He considered denying Keira's existence, but remembered who he was dealing with. The darkest agency of the government with the deepest power. So he said nothing.

"Amazing, isn't it?" Jocelyn held up the photo. "How paths diverge, then cross at another place, another time?"

The restraint he had to employ to keep from ripping that photo from her hand made him shake. "What do you want?"

"I want what I've always wanted—safety for our troops, security for America. And I'm here to remind you that your work not only contributes to the greater good of our country, but to show you the rewards waiting for you personally."

She held the photo out to him. Cash didn't drop his gaze from hers, but he couldn't keep from reaching for the photo. Because if they did know about Keira, if she and Mateo were both still alive and Dargan had a photo of them together, they were probably held captive somewhere. Which meant Cash could no longer think about dealing with the next step when his experiment succeeded. He would need a plan. Now.

He snapped the photo away from her, held it in his free hand, keeping his other clenched tight around the chain and what felt like a substantial charm, and brought the image close for scrutiny. One part of his heart hoped it was a fake. The other prayed it was real.

He inspected the faces—the boy first. His son. Mateo Ryan O'Shay. Yes. He would know those big brown eyes anywhere, no matter how many years later. They were his mother's eyes. Zoya's eyes. Oh, God, how he missed that woman. Missed the child they'd created.

He closed his throat around a sob. Blinked back tears

burning his eyes and turned his gaze to the woman. Keira. Yes. He might not have seen her since she was five years old, but the woman in this photo was definitely Keira. He recognized the defiance in her bright blue eyes, the same look she'd often given their mother, which had always earned her a good smack across the face. Sometimes worse if their mother had been drinking.

His eyes flicked between them. Did Keira know Mateo was her nephew? Did she know her brother was alive? Or did she still think he was dead?

"Where are they?" Cash's voice came out as a venomous rasp. "Where are you holding them? How do I even know they're still alive?"

Jocelyn smiled that thin, frigid smile and shook her head in that dainty way that made Cash want to strangle her. "Of course they're alive. We know how intelligent you are. We aren't going to try and trick you. And whether we have them in custody or not doesn't matter. We can reach anyone, anywhere, anytime we want. You know that.

"The only way to get your life back, Cash, get *their* lives back, is to finish what you came here to do so we can part on good terms. You're so close. It would be a shame to give up now." She gestured to the photo. "He's only five. And Keira, almost thirty. Lots of life left to live. With you or without you."

Jocelyn sauntered toward the door. "Good luck with your work tomorrow."

Her guards followed, both casting a guilty look his way before closing and locking the steel door.

Cash turned his back on the entrance and uncurled his fingers. A bead chain lay in his palm, the kind he'd worn for years with his military dog tag hanging on the end. But attached to this chain lay a key. Little smaller than average, thin, multiple notches all along the length, narrow top. Not a house key. Not a car key. Maybe a safe. Whatever it was,

Dargan would notice it was gone soon. And she'd know where it had been lost.

His attention turned back to the photo. Cash was entrenched in memories of Zoya and Mateo by the time Q spoke again. "Is it him?"

"Yes. It's him."

"Hey, man, you never told me you had a sister."

"That's a really long story."

"Can I see your picture? Can I see your family?"

Cash continued to study their faces. He'd never get enough.

"I'll give it back," Q said. "I just want to see that little guy, put a face to the name and the stories."

Cash's fingers tightened on the photo. He didn't want to give it up, but he trusted Q. He leaned down and slid it through the vents, holding tight until Q's fingers secured the other side. "Be careful. It's all I've got."

As he let go and the picture dropped out of sight, Cash's chest knotted in a moment of panic. Then double knotted as Q didn't immediately say anything.

"Q? You have it?"

"Yeah, yeah," he murmured. "They're . . . They're beautiful. Does your son look like you?"

Cash's mouth turned up in an ironic half smile, realizing he and Q had never actually seen each other. "No, he looks like his mother. But my sister and I look a lot alike."

"Can't look that much alike," he quipped. "She's pretty. So you've got black hair and blue eyes?"

"Yeah."

"She's younger than you?"

"By ten years."

"Married? Kids? Where does she live?"

Cash closed his eyes, guilt coating his guts. He often missed Keira, but had spent years justifying his lack of effort to reconnect with her. Early on he'd told himself any connection to him could hurt her chances of getting a good family. Then, he'd justified not seeking her out because surely she wouldn't want an ex-con for a brother. And finally, the army had given him the perfect excuse, instructing everyone involved in highly classified projects that the less contact with family the better.

"Cash?" Q said. "How come you never talk about your sister?"

"I don't . . . know her. I mean, now—I don't know her now. We were separated when she was five and I was fifteen."

"Separated?"

"I'm tired, Q. Give me the picture back so I can get some sleep."

"You've piqued my interest, buddy. And I can sense you need to talk about it."

"You sense shit." Cash slammed a hand against the wall. "Give me the picture."

"Tell me what happened with your sister, and I'll give it back."

"You son of a—"

"Time's wasting. Thought you were tired."

Cash clamped his mouth shut and heaved a long breath. "Our house burned down when we were young. My mother went to prison for murder, my sister went to foster care. I ducked out because I didn't want to end up in foster care, too. Got in some trouble with drugs, went to prison for a few years. Got out, joined the army, went into classified work. There was never a good time to reconnect."

Q remained quiet a moment. "You said your mom was dead."

"She is. Died in prison."

"Who did she murder?"

Cash leaned his head left and right until his cervical vertebra popped. "Me."

Another long silence.

"Can I get the picture back, now?"

"Hold on. You skipped out? You faked your death in the house fire and let your mom go to prison for murder?"

Cash didn't have one iota of guilt. "If she hadn't gone to prison, she'd have gotten custody of Keira again. If that had happened, I guarantee my sister wouldn't be alive today."

"And Keira? She thinks you're dead?"

"As far as I know. It wasn't until I met and married Zoya and we had Mateo that I realized I needed to find Keira. Then Zoya was killed, Mateo taken, and I ended up in this hellhole. Hence, my lack of success in contacting her again." He slammed the wall. "Picture, please. Now."

Q passed the picture through the vent. Once Cash had it in his hands again, one fear dimmed, but another flared.

"Now what am I going to do? If my experiment works, like you said? How am I going to make sure I get Mateo and Keira back alive? And even if I get them back, how can I make sure we all stay alive? I've never gotten this far with my experiments before. I guess I never thought this far ahead."

"You know what they say about geniuses," Q quipped. "No common sense."

"Asshole." But Cash couldn't help wondering if that's what Jocelyn and her team were counting on.

"I won't hold that against you, Sci-Fi. You're under a lot of pressure. It's simple. What they want is inside your brain, and only you can give it to them. So just don't."

Cash pinched the bridge of his nose. "I've been up for about thirty hours straight. Would you mind spelling it out for me? I'm a genius and all."

"What do you do in your experiments that gives them all the answers? Fill out a form? Video the process?"

"I write a lab report. Have to turn it in at the end of every day and every experiment."

"So, from here on out, doctor your reports. Between the two of us, we can get you the fuck out of here. By the time they figure out you've been writing bogus shit, you'll be gone. Once you're out, you contact them with the key information and make a deal—a trade for your freedom and your family."

"Won't work."

"Why not?"

"Because Mario is a genius, too." Cash thought of the lab manager. "As lazy as they come, but brilliant. He would skim the report and know immediately." He remained silent a moment, forming an alternative. "I'll just finish the report, let him look it over, take it back at the last minute to make one minor correction, and slip out the Method pages. Then I'll eat them or something. They can't re-create anything without those notes. Those are the key."

Q chuckled. "Eat them? Very *Mission Impossible*–like."

A sudden burn slid down Cash's spine. He frowned hard at the wall wondering if he'd just spilled his entire plan to a mole. "How the hell would you know about *Mission Impossible*?"

"They do let me read, Sci-Fi, remember?"

Cash wiped a hand down his face. God, he was losing it.

"However you do it is your call," Q said. "But I've been in and out of this place so many times, I know the compound inside and out. I know the guards, their schedules, their quirks, their habits. If your sci-fi brain can rig something to get you out of a cell, I can get you off this unholy ground. Your Special Forces training will have to take you the rest of the way."

"I want you to come with me, Q."

Even as he said the words, he knew the plan wasn't feasible. The right side of Q's brain had been damaged in one of those crazy experiments several months ago, and the left side of his friend's body had suffered so severely, there had been weeks after the incident when Q said the doctors told him he'd never regain use of his arm or leg.

Since then, Q had made great strides on his own with a training regime he and Cash had created together. One Q could perform in his cell, just like the one Cash had designed for himself to stay in top physical condition.

"Would love to," Q said. "But my dance card is full, buddy."

Cash didn't push the issue. They still had a little time. If he could come up with a plan where he could take Q, or come back for him . . .

"One thing I don't get," Q said. "If Keira still thinks you're dead, if you haven't seen her in twenty-five years, how in the hell did she end up with your kid in that photograph?"

"That, my friend, is the sixty-four-zillion-dollar question."

THIRTEEN

Sleep had completely eluded her. Keira's exhausted eyes gazed beyond the guest bedroom window where the caramel sunrise nudged the indigo night into another hemisphere. Mountains blanketed with pines and aspens waited silently for the change from shadow to light.

Even going on fifty hours without any rest, Keira's mind continued to fight. Her heart continued to struggle. But worse and most painful, her soul continued to reach. For Luke.

At times over the night, she swore it was a two-year-old throwing a tantrum. At times she'd come so close to letting it have its way. Going to Luke and promising him anything if he'd just vow to love her forever in return. Love her like he used to. Before everything went wrong.

And that was the very memory that kept her pacing the room instead of lying by his side—all that had gone wrong.

The soft carpet beneath her feet had flattened from hours of travel. She threaded both hands through her hair and yanked at the strands. Her scalp pulled, the sting a welcome relief to the tension that made her think her head would explode.

"Why am I so screwed up?"

Stupid question. Stupid, stupid question. She knew exactly why. The real question she'd stopped asking a long time ago, but which was creeping up now in her moment of helpless crisis, was *why me?* She'd never had the luxury of self-pity. Besides, she wasn't the type.

"So knock it off." She pulled her hands from her head and shook her hair back. "Just go out there and deal with it. Stop being such a coward."

She realized how messed up she was. She got it. The problem was, Luke didn't.

Luke, the sick, crazy bastard, looked at her as the mother to whatever brood he had dreamed up in that gorgeous head of his. And he pushed and pushed and *pushed*. Every time he brought up the subject, as he'd done last night, she felt like he was smothering her. As if he'd crushed a pillow over her face and she had to kick him in the balls to get him to let up so she could breathe.

She was trapped. Because now that she'd seen him again, kissed him again, touched him again, she realized she'd never stopped loving him and knew why her attempts at life—a real life—for the last three years had failed. Miserably.

She needed him. She wanted him. He had been the part of her life that made it rich and spontaneous and joyous and . . . meaningful. Through the fights, the fun, the loss, the love. It was Luke. Luke made her feel like . . . herself. Luke made her feel real. Unique. Authentic. Luke made her feel alive.

Without Luke, she worked. She ate. She trained.

Without Luke, she *existed*.

You won't let me in. Not really. You always hold something back. You always have a safety net. An out.

As far back as her memory would take her, Keira had lived with a bag packed and hidden away. A change of clothes, snacks, her favorite blanket, a stuffed animal. Yes, she always had an out.

But if she was going to make it work with Luke this time, she'd have to go all in. She knew that. Which was why she was still in her room pacing, not out in the family room with everyone else eating breakfast like a normal person.

Because she was so not normal.

"This is ridiculous. I can't keep living like this."

She didn't know what the answer was. Didn't know how they'd find it. But she was committed to crawling through those dark spots to figure it out, as long as Luke was crawling with her.

Keira turned toward the door. She took a deep breath and blew it out slowly. "We'll talk." She nodded once. "We'll fight." Her lips compressed. "We'll fight some more." Resignation sank in and her chest grew heavy. "We'll . . . probably fight a lot . . ."

Tears of fear snuck into her eyes. For a flicker of a second she considered rejecting the idea. Then her mind darted toward returning to her life in Sacramento. To her eighteen hours at work. Two hours at the gym. Four hours in bed—alone.

A void opened in her chest. Trying to live without Luke was like trying to breathe in a smoke-filled room. Trying to run under water. Trying to hold back an ocean wave.

She reached for the doorknob and hesitated. As if she was split in two, one half of her urged her to stay put, keep her mouth shut. But the other half, the half that knew she couldn't keep living this way, pushed her feet forward.

In the hallway, a child's giggle met her ears. The sweet sound slid over her shoulders, crowded her chest, and squeezed. Mateo. The kid could turn her inside out without even trying.

As she made her way down the hall, scents of breakfast wafted in the air as well as the playful chatter of both children. Sensory overload sent her back in time, to Luke's house. To her days off duty when he would let her sleep late. To the way he would sneak Kat from her toddler bed next to his California king and set her up with toys at his feet in the kitchen to keep her occupied while Keira slept and he made breakfast. To the way he used to wake Keira with kisses on her neck and a perfectly brewed cup of coffee.

Her feet stopped moving. Her eyes closed. Oh, what a beautiful memory. Could it be that good again?

I see a boy you love, who also loves you and needs a home. And I'd love to be part of making that family.

A wave of contentment eased through her. As if her two halves fused into one whole, heat radiated through her body and filled her heart. She continued to the end of the hallway and peered around the wall toward the living room.

Mateo and Kat sat on the floor in front of the fireplace, a huge plastic bin between them filled with naked Barbie and Ken dolls, miniature clothes strewn around them on the carpet. Mateo held a half-dressed doll, struggling to get a shoe the size of a fingernail on its foot. His brow was creased, his tongue tipped out the side of his mouth in concentration.

Keira broke into a full smile.

Kids playing in the living room. Parents working in the kitchen. It seemed so . . . right.

Could she do it? Could she have *this*? All she had to do was reach out for it. Luke was offering this and so much more.

"Maybe you can barbecue tonight." Alyssa's voice floated from somewhere in the kitchen around the corner. But it was a little off. A little too . . . appeasing. "I can pull tri-tip and ribs from the deep freeze."

"Whatever."

Teague's clipped response brought Keira up short. The thrill still tingling over her skin from her realization faded. What was wrong now?

She cocked her ear toward the kitchen. Food sizzled and pans clanged. No Mitch. No Luke.

"Don't let him ruin your day," Alyssa said. After a moment with no response from Teague, she added, "How long are you going to stay mad?"

"Probably until he pulls his head out of his ass."

"You might be waiting a while," Alyssa grumbled.

Teague was either talking about Mitch or Luke. Keira had a fifty-fifty chance of guessing which one he was ticked at, and if it was Luke, that would derail her plans. Broaching the topic of their relationship would be volatile enough. She didn't need him pissed off before they even started.

Keira stepped into the kitchen. Teague stood in front of an open refrigerator door, dressed in light blue jeans and a tan stonewashed tee, surveying the contents. Alyssa leaned over the granite island, her pregnant belly pressing against the edge, her chin propped in one hand, pencil poised over a pad. Bacon cooked in a pan beside her.

"Green salad or fruit salad?" Teague asked.

"Both." Alyssa scribbled on the paper. "I'll pick up kiwi and mangoes at the store for Seth."

Teague shut the fridge. "And bread. But don't do garlic."

"I remember," Alyssa said. "Kai's allergic."

"They're both coming?" Keira asked, excited and nervous to see her friends and former teammates. "Why?"

Teague turned toward her. His heavy frown lightened, but the tension was still there.

"Look who's up." He removed the bacon from the pan and set it on a paper towel to drain, then picked up a mug from the counter and flipped it right-side up. "Coffee? We've got hotcakes in the oven. This is the last of the bacon."

"You didn't sleep, did you?" Alyssa's sharp eyes checked Keira's face. "You don't look so good."

Teague pointed at her cheek. "All except those cuts. Those look fantastic, if I do say so myself."

"Mmm, true." Alyssa tipped her head in consideration. "You do good work, babe."

"When are Kai and Seth coming?" Keira asked.

Teague's gaze dropped to the coffee cup in his hand. Alyssa didn't respond, but didn't look away. Distress snuck into Keira's belly.

"Kai had a layover at Seth's last night," Teague said. "They'll be here this afternoon. They want to help figure this out, and they want to see everyone. We tried to get hold of Jessica, but she's at some conference in Italy."

Keira winced. When she was having a bad day, all she had to do was think of Jessica to realize her life could be worse. Jess hadn't just lost her sense of security in that warehouse fire, like the rest of them; she'd lost her newlywed husband and the love of her life. She'd never been the same. Not only had she made a huge career leap, but she'd moved to the other side of the nation. Running as hard and as fast as she could to get away from the pain.

"I'm glad you didn't get her," Keira said. "She doesn't need any reminders. But you'd better tell me what's going on, because I know Kai and Seth aren't dropping everything to fly here for your barbecue, Teague—as good as it is."

"You know Kai," he said, filling the mug with steaming coffee even though Keira hadn't agreed to have any. "Always looking for trouble."

"And usually finding it." The man had amazing empathic abilities. And when it came to the team, he seemed to be able to sense danger even across the country. "So what trouble is he feeling here all the way from Wyoming?"

Teague dropped an arm around Alyssa's shoulders. She didn't exactly dart a look at her husband. Her nervous glances were more of a slow, cautious slide, and she sent him one before returning her eyes to Keira's. "He's never specific, you know that. But he's feeling some sort of . . . elimination plan brewing."

"Elimination?" Keira's said. "Expand, please."

"He didn't say more," Teague said. "Just that he felt danger circling the team and an inevitable confrontation. He wanted us to be together when it hit so we could get a jump on . . . whatever the situation turned out to be."

Keira waited a beat for more information. "That's it?"

"That's it," Teague said.

"Beautiful."

Keira glanced around the space again, the anticipation of seeing Luke bubbling through her system. "Where are Luke and Mitch?"

"Mitch is on the phone in my office," Alyssa said. "Researching Mateo's implants."

"And Luke?"

"Went home."

Teague's hard voice cut off Keira's retreating tension. "When will he be back?"

No answer. Teague's jaw tightened. Alyssa made another cautious eye-slide.

"What happened now?" Keira asked.

"The same thing that always happens when the subject of you comes up." Teague's lips pressed together before he blurted, "He's an idiotic, stubborn *ass*. And he just pisses me off."

Teague set the mug down with a hard *clink*. He picked up the bottle of liquid soap from the sink and squeezed it directly into the hot grease. An angry sizzle filled the kitchen in a chaotic burst of bubbles mimicking the roil of emotion in Keira's chest.

When the chemical reaction calmed, Teague ran hot water in the pan and started scrubbing.

"Teague," Keira said, "I have to take a lot of the blame. I mean, you're right, he can be . . . stubborn . . . but we all know I'm pretty screwed up. The two of us are just constantly clashing."

"Fight all you want," he said, scrubbing harder. "Yell,

scream, swear, but you don't leave." He looked up at Keira with anger and pain in his eyes. Alyssa stepped close and laid a hand on his back. "When you love someone, you *stay* and *fight*."

Her chest squeezed as Teague's words sank in. She'd sure done her share of leaving. Learn by example. That's what she'd done to Luke three years before. Instead of staying and fighting for him, for *them,* she'd run. From her past. From her future. From all those fears she couldn't face.

"Which is something he can't actually advise from experience, but from hindsight," Alyssa said, patting his back. "Right, babe?"

Keira knew the complicated story of how Seth's previous wife and Kat's co-guardian had kidnapped Kat and attempted to take her over the Canadian border when Teague escaped prison. Of how he'd abandoned Alyssa, his lover at the time, to save her from involvement in his drama, and had gone in search of Kat on his own.

But Teague didn't answer and something else nagged at the fringes of Keira's brain. Something drifting off him in angry waves.

"What's *I'm done*?" She narrowed her eyes on him. "Is that coming from you?"

Teague's gaze dropped back to the sink. "Jeez, Keira."

"That's something Luke said before he left," Alyssa said.

"Meaning he was done fighting with Teague?"

Alyssa glanced toward Teague, then Keira, with characteristic candidness. "It sounded more like he was just done, you know, with . . ."

This couldn't be happening, not when she'd just come to the point of acceptance. "With *me*?"

Teague's head came up, his light eyes on fire. "Do you see why I'm so pissed?"

A cold slide of panic cut through her belly. The glowing

warmth she'd cultivated this morning leaked out. Had she already missed her chance? Was she too late? God, when that man made up his mind about something . . .

She looked to the window as one of the men guarding the house strolled by the kitchen. Her fear of having lost her opportunity at a second chance with Luke blended with a new unease. "Did one of your guys drive him? Is someone staying with him?"

"No," Teague said. "Why?"

"He's alone?" she asked. "After Kai sensed danger, he left on his own?"

"Kai felt danger for the team, not to any one individual. And he's a big boy, Keira. He's also a cop. He can take care of himself. Besides, they want Mateo, not us."

Keira's terror streak calmed with the injection of common sense. "You're right. I'm just . . . wound up. How did he get home? Did he take one of your cars?"

"No, he ran," Teague said.

Keira's brows lifted. "Ran? What do you mean ran?"

"I mean he *ran*. You know, with feet. Legs. Ran. Borrowed a pair of my running shoes."

"His house is, like, ten miles away."

"Eight," Teague said. "He usually runs five a day anyway and said he needed to think."

He must have needed to think pretty badly to borrow a pair of shoes for an eight-mile run. He was going to have blisters for a week. The sign of a man needing to rid himself of a great deal of frustration or anger or . . . cleansing himself of an erratic, unstable, volatile ex-girlfriend.

No. She had to talk to him. Explain. Tell him all the things she'd held back before.

She swung around and started toward the front hallway. "Where are your keys, Lys?"

"You can't go out like that, it's cold." Alyssa followed. "What's wrong?"

Keira looked down. She was still in the pajamas Alyssa had lent her—the pale blue cami and silk pants. It didn't matter. What mattered was reaching Luke before he'd had a chance to think too much. Make too many decisions.

"Nothing. I mean, I just need to talk to him." She reached for the SUV's keys hanging on a hook. "Where's my gun?"

She'd forgo the purse, the shoes, the phone, but she didn't go anywhere without her weapon.

Teague disappeared into the kitchen, where he kept all the weapons in a locked cabinet.

Alyssa pulled a thin, white sweater from the hall-tree and tossed it at Keira. "Wouldn't hurt to cover up a little. Shoes might be good, too." She kicked a pair of flip-flops sitting by the door toward her.

Teague rounded the corner and held out her weapon. "I'll go with you."

"No, no," she said. "He and I need to talk."

Before Keira could turn for the door, a little body pummeled into her legs, knocking her off balance. Heat sizzled through the scar lines on her back.

"Thia?"

Keira winced at Mateo's worried tone. She'd been so caught up in getting to Luke fast, she'd forgotten about Mateo for a moment. Forgotten she should have said goodbye. Forgotten he might get upset she was leaving.

Great mother material.

She dropped into a crouch and slid her hands down his arms, fighting back the fear. His straight, dark eyebrows angled down as he frowned, his little lips puckered into perfect cupid buds. He looked so familiar to her after just hours of being with him, as if she'd known him her whole life. Her chest squeezed—with a deep affection and . . .

You have to recognize that you love him differently.

God. She really did love him differently. And Luke had seen it.

"I'll be back. I promise," she said, her voice rough. When Mateo only searched her eyes, she added, "I'm going to see Lucas."

His fingers released their grip on her shoulders. "Lucas?"

Keira tried for a reassuring smile. "Yes, Lucas."

Kat slipped into the group and distracted the boy with another Barbie, and Keira took the opportunity to disappear out the door.

She tried not to dwell on the bizarre state of her life as she backed Alyssa's luxury crossover through the gate of their property, but it was hard when two men in camouflage with M14s strapped over their backs guarded the entrance to the small mountain estate.

She didn't admire the snow-tipped mountains on the ten-minute drive to Luke's house. Didn't appreciate the contrast of gold aspens against evergreen pines. Didn't turn melancholy as she sped through the single downtown strip.

All she kept thinking was . . . *five miles a day*?

Five miles wasn't a marathon or anything. She ran that just to stay ready for the heavy demands of SWAT training. But Luke hated to run. He'd play basketball. Baseball. Racquetball. Hell, he'd play volleyball. And he was good at all of them. Athletic and agile. But he hated running. Always said it bored him. Nothing to do but think. Now he was doing it on purpose? Specifically *to* think?

She didn't disagree with the method, only that he'd chosen today to do it. Today, right now, she didn't want him thinking. Not alone and angry and hurt.

As she turned onto Luke's street, Keira tilted the rearview mirror toward her. One glance and she couldn't help grimacing. Teague's touches had helped, but she still had healing cuts and bruises over nearly every surface of her face. There was nothing she could do about that, and Luke had seen her in far worse condition—covered in soot at fires, covered in blood at accident scenes, covered in gasoline at chemical spills, covered in fire at the warehouse.

The remembered tranquility of the area where Luke lived held true—deluxe, custom cabin-style homes nestled among pines and along ridges, looking out over Tahoe National Forest. Luke's, a small, one-bedroom, craftsman-style, brought heavy emotion rushing Keira's throat as she approached and pulled into the driveway. Through the square windows along the top of the garage door, she could see his black Explorer parked inside.

She slammed the car into park and let it idle as uncertainty and anxiety grew to an explosive boil in her chest. Her fingers gripped the steering wheel and twisted as if she were wringing out a wet towel. Would he reject her? Tell her, after thinking about it, he'd changed his mind? That their differences were too major? That it was too late?

Sound drifted through the glass and into her thoughts. Her attention shifted from the garage to the wraparound front porch. Music. The familiar classic rock Luke favored. Only, far louder than she'd ever heard him play it, which for some intangible reason, made her uneasy.

She shut down the engine, picked up her weapon, and exited the SUV. She paused to tune in to her senses. She looked up, searched the quiet neighborhood. Nothing appeared out of place. But then nothing ever did, yet she knew damn well that somewhere out there two pairs of eyes watched. One pair belonged to whoever was assigned to watch her that day; one pair to whoever was assigned to watch Luke. She'd tried on countless occasions over the years to tap into the thoughts of her shadows, but had always failed. And she didn't have time to mess with them now. More important matters waited inside.

Keira held her gun tight and crossed her arms against the cold. As she climbed the steps toward the front door, memories pummeled her from every angle. The fuchsia and grape pansies she'd planted at the base of the porch and along the stairs were long gone. The white wicker rockers she and Luke had bought from a secondhand store, refurbished, and spent so many hours sitting in out here on this very porch had been put away for the winter.

Creedence Clearwater Revival wailed about hearing it through the grapevine and drew her attention toward the front door.

Knock or go in? Neither felt right.

She lifted her hand and pounded on the door to be heard over the music. "Luke!"

She braced herself for his less than enthusiastic response to her visit. But she would face it. And she would face him. If he'd answer the damn door.

She pounded again with the side of her fist. "Luke, it's cold out here. Open the door."

She crossed the porch and peered through the window. Unlike the front of the house, where the reminders of her life with Luke had vanished, everything in the living room was immediately familiar. Same camel sofa, same pine coffee table, same colorful abstract area rug—everything she and Luke had picked out together on a snowy Sunday shopping spree in Reno. That had been so long ago, but being there, seeing it, brought her right back to their life together. Yes, there had been pain, anger, frustration, but the love between them and the happiness they'd once shared in this house far outweighed any lingering negativity.

She scanned the dining area, the kitch—

Her gaze halted on something lying on the floor between the kitchen and the dining room. Something barely in view. Shoes. The soles of athletic shoes.

A burning spike of fear tore through Keira's chest. She pushed to her toes, craned her neck, but couldn't maneuver a better view.

She took hold of her weapon with both hands. Returned to the door, her back against the wood siding.

Don't freak. Yet.

Her gaze scoured the neighborhood again. Nothing new. Eyes fell to the doorknob. Hand reached out. Settled. Twisted.

Don't turn. Don't turn.

The metal turned.

No.

Her stomach burned cold like dry ice.

Don't overreact.

Bizarre possibilities filled her head. What if they'd come to question Luke and he'd resisted, like the bullheaded ass he could be, and they'd hurt him? What if they'd finally just had enough of the team's interference—their questions, their quest to know what or who had started that warehouse fire, what they'd been exposed to and who had been responsible, and planned on killing them all, one by one?

Don't. Overreact.

Focus.

With two quick, deep breaths, she pushed the door open and swept the living room, dining room with her weapon. Empty.

Steeled herself. Swung into the kitchen.

Shoes.

Just shoes. Not attached to an unconscious Luke, but kicked off haphazardly and left strewn in the middle of the floor.

The breath whooshed out of her lungs. *"Fuck!"*

She pressed a hand to her stomach, quelling the rush of adrenaline-induced nausea. When her legs felt steady, she walked to the front door and slammed it.

An instant later, the song ended. A moment of booming silence filled the house before the edges of her amped senses softened and another familiar noise drifted in.

The shower.

Between the water and the music, it was no wonder he hadn't heard her at the door. Some of her fear released from her tense shoulders and stiff arms. But she wouldn't lower her guard until she saw his perfect, healthy, handsome face.

She eased toward the bedroom and checked the space before going in. She could have been stepping back in time. Everything was exactly the same as when she'd left. Same furniture arrangement. Same unmade bed with the same rich, solid blue comforter and same white and blue pin-striped sheets they'd had twisted around sweaty, sated bodies. Same simple cobalt area rug covering the home's old hardwood floor that she and Luke had refinished by hand. Same prints on the walls they'd picked at a local art fair one summer. It all made a melancholy joy seep in and eradicate the momentary fear.

Yet something was different. Something was missing. She couldn't pinpoint what exactly, but it left her with a hollow ache.

Keira focused on the closed bathroom door, where light filled the seam between the bottom edge and the floor. A jumble of clothes sat on the floor to the side—gray gym shorts and an olive green T-shirt he must have borrowed from Teague, and the navy boxer briefs he'd been wearing at the safe house. The ones she'd wanted to rip off him before their conversation had brought them to an impasse.

She was just about to lower her weapon when an uncomfortable sensation skidded down her spine like tipped dominoes.

She stiffened. Cut another glance around the room. Tuned into her clairaudience and listened. But got nothing. Was he still blocking her? But why when it took so much effort and he didn't know she was there?

The unease spread from bone to bone, muscle to muscle,

until the serpent-like invader coiled around her body, chest to hips. A slow squeeze made it hard to breathe.

She thought about calling to him through the door, but something cautioned her. With her weapon at her thigh, Keira leaned in, listening. For what, she wasn't sure, but no sound came from the bathroom except the unbroken stream of water.

Unbroken.

The hair on her arms prickled. She tightened her fingers around the butt of her gun and listened harder. No splashing. No interruption. Which meant no movement. And suggested another possible reason for Keira's inability to tap into his thoughts. He wasn't having any.

Oh, God.

Focus.

Her memory roamed the landscape of the bathroom she and Luke had remodeled just months before she'd left. Toilet to the left, double sinks and huge mirror directly ahead, open, half-wall stone shower to the right, the same direction the door opened.

She solidified her stance, the grip of her gun, the hold on the door handle. Her gaze caught on a reflection of light against the floor. On a pool of water seeping out from beneath the door. Growing. Sliding across the slate beneath her feet.

With the shower on the other side of the room and the lack of movement sounding in the shower, there was only one reason Keira could imagine for that water to be leaking from the bathroom—Luke lying on the floor. Unconscious. Dead.

She turned the knob and prayed she was wrong.

FOURTEEN

Muscles strung taut, back pressed against the cold wall next to the door, Luke stared at the door handle, but his mind kept scattering through the contents of the cabinets on the opposite side of the bathroom.

He was naked, dripping wet. Not one goddamned thing he could use as a weapon within reach. Yeah, he could hold his own in a fight, even against others with weapons, but he'd really rather have the gun he'd left in the bedroom.

And with every moment that passed since he'd heard that front door slam shut with no one calling his name, his muscles coiled tighter in preparation.

Come on.

He forced his mind into combat mode, shaving off all distractions until he had beamlike focus. And waited.

The doorknob turned. So slowly, he almost couldn't decipher the movement. He pressed harder against the wall, fingers stretched toward the handle.

Luke hesitated, gave the person an opportunity to announce themselves. Teague, Mitch, maybe one of the guys they had guarding the other house had come to check on him.

But he heard nothing. Including thoughts.

In the half-inch opening, the bathroom light flashed over a dark weapon. He made the split-second decision to act.

He forced his hand through the door and gripped the wrist of the intruder. Wrapped the fingers of his other hand around the open edge and yanked the door back. His eyes never left the gun as he fought for control.

"Luke! Wait—"

The use of his name registered. Then the female voice. But all too late.

His leverage on one arm whipped the intruder around as he covered the weapon with a controlling fist. He had just enough presence of mind not to slam her up against the shower wall as hard as his adrenaline would have driven.

"It's me. Luke. It's me."

Every muscle quivered with the need for action, but Luke kept his body forced against hers, pinning her to the stone wall. Kept his fingers closed over hers, covering the gun.

Not only was Keira the last person he'd expected to see, she was the last person he wanted to see. "What the fuck? I could have hurt you."

"You *are* hurting me."

He growled and leaned back to release some pressure. The shower spray hit his shoulder and ricocheted into her face. She squeezed her eyes shut and sputtered.

"What do you expect when you walk into my house, my goddamned shower, unannounced?"

He took the gun from her loose fingers, set it on the ledge of a small window above her head as the shower stream soaked her, and concentrated on easing off the adrenaline high.

"I was not unannounced," she said. "I banged on your door. I called your name. Then I get these dark vibes . . . I hear the water . . . you're not in the shower. And I couldn't hear your thoughts. And the water, it's leaking. It . . . under the door. It . . ."

Her eyes connected with his, and the terror there took him off guard. He'd expected her typical anger.

"I thought something had happened to you." She bent her head, laid it against his chest, and wound her arms around his back. "God, you scared me."

The sound of the shower filled the following moment of silence. His mind skipped around but couldn't land on anything to straighten out the growing confusion. "Did I miss something between you basically telling me to go fuck myself last night and now?"

"I know I was harsh last night." She pulled back. Regret filled her eyes, and as soon as he saw the familiar look, something pulled in his chest. The first sucker red flag. "I didn't sleep at all."

"Join the club."

He didn't need this. He was still hurting. Still angry. Still grieving. Their argument the night before had been the tipping point for Luke. The moment when all their discussions and fights on the topic of having kids conglomerated into one solid rock. One he realized couldn't be broken, cracked, or even chipped away.

Never had he loved anyone the way he loved her. Never would he love anyone like this again. Which left him with the impossible decision: live with his true love and give up his dream of a family? Or fulfill his dream of a family with someone other than his true love?

"I stayed up all night thinking about what you said," Keira started, "and—"

"I can't do this." He gripped her arms, still locked around him, pried them off, and stepped back. "I'm not going through the same old bullshit with you again. You weren't the only one up all night thinking, and my head feels like a bowling ball."

"But, I want to tell you—"

"Keira." His bark cut her off. He sucked in a breath and gathered the threads of his patience, worn bare by pain. "Here's the thing. When I see you with Mateo, I ache, the way I used to ache when I saw you with Kat. A beautiful, this-is-what-life-is-about stolen moment ache. An if-only-I-could-stop-time ache.

"And it's not just about having kids. It's about you and me being a family. A real family. It's about finding strength in the sum of our parts instead of fighting life alone. Knowing that no matter how bad it gets we'll be there together, sticking it out.

"Don't you think I'm scared, too? That all of this, what's happened to us, doesn't make me worry about how I would protect a family? But when I look at you with Mateo, I know I want that connection with the woman I love. I need to be a part of something greater than myself. Especially now, after everything I've been through."

He clenched his jaw, knew he was about to cross a line he couldn't ever cross back over. "Keira, I can't go back to the way things were before . . . I can't do it. I want more. I want the whole package—you, kids, and, yes, the white picket fence. I can't sit back and watch Teague and Alyssa together and know we're never going to have that bond. I can't watch you smother Kat with love and know that's never going to be our child. It's too painful. I'd rather spend the rest of my life alone."

As he said the words, words he hadn't fully thought through before this moment, he knew they were true. Even if they absolutely broke his heart. "I'm done fighting with you about this —"

She pushed up on her toes and kissed him. Her lips were warm, soft, wet. They immediately scrambled his thoughts.

He leaned back. "That's not going to—"

She kissed him again. Her arms escaped his grip and wound around his neck. Her mouth opened under his. Her tongue darted in.

Ah, damn.

Heat. So much heat.

One taste and his resistance wavered? Not this time. Not again.

He pushed her away. "Keira—"

"What I want to tell you, if you'd listen a second," she said before he could cut her off again, "is that you were right. About so many things. I do love Mateo differently. I do always hold something back. I do let my fear rule my heart."

She darted a nervous look from beneath those dark lashes sparkling with water droplets. And he found himself hesitating.

"I'm listening," he said cautiously. "But I'm not going to hear the same bullshit, Keira."

And he wasn't giving in. Even if that tank she was wearing was so wet it was now translucent and layered to her like a second skin. Even if the sight of her skin all glowing and slick made him want to rip every shred of clothing from her body. Because that would only be a temporary fix to a permanent problem.

"I have issues with feeling . . . closed in." Her eyes slid to his chest. "So when you push me on the whole kid thing, and you use all your logic and all your examples and I can't fight back, I get scared. Walls start pressing in on me, like they did last night. And I say things that I don't always mean or that don't always come out right."

She lifted her eyes to his. "But I did mean what I said when I called you from Tony's car. I should have tried harder before, and I want to try harder now. That's why I'm here. I know how screwed up I am. And I know we have . . . issues. I don't have all the answers; I can't say I even fully understand the problems. I love kids, I love family, but having my own scares me into panic attacks.

"I obviously have a problem, Luke. One that's not going to be fixed overnight, but one I'm willing to work on. I won't lose you over this. Not again. I'm ready to try . . . I mean, to think about . . ." She took a deep breath. "I want that connection with you, too. Desperately. Maybe . . . I mean, if you're still willing . . . maybe we could talk about having . . . a family."

He felt as though he'd been pulled into a river, the water eddying around rocks, dragging him from one rapid to another, with never enough time to catch his breath. Her words, the look of sincerity and seriousness and self-deprecation in her eyes gave him so much hope. More than he'd ever imagined he'd feel again. This was the first time she'd been the one to mention children. She'd never gone as far as to say she wanted a family with him. And she'd never, not once, brought up the subject on her own.

But he'd been here a few too many times in the past couple of days. Had his heart twisted and torn more than he could handle. If she was willing to back up her words with action, he might be able to take that leap one more time.

He wrapped his arms around her back and pulled her against his body. His wet skin slid against her silk, sparking every cell. His erection jerked against the softness of her belly.

She rested her hands against his chest, watching him with hope in those beautiful eyes.

"Tell me about the tunnel," he said.

Fear flashed a second before the warm blue irises hardened to glass. Luke's heart took a cold hit of disappointment. She wasn't going to do it. She wasn't going to open up. He'd expected too much.

She lowered her eyes to his chest. Clenched and released her fingers. Cleared her throat. "One of my foster families, they lived in Sparks, Nevada. It was before the town grew. Still the middle of nowhere. There were eight of us—kids. I was the oldest. Took care of the others. All of them had some type of physical or mental disorder from previous parental abuse. The youngest was seven months old."

Her heart picked up speed and beat harder against Luke's chest. *Keep going. Get it out. Talk to me.*

"The dad, he was a good man. Worked for the railroad. Traveled. Gone long hours. When he was home, everything was fine. He was good to us. But the woman, she was . . . I don't even think she was human. We were animals to her. When chores were done, she locked us . . ." Keira shuttered a breath. "Under the house. Winter and below zero, summer and a hundred-ten, she didn't care. She couldn't listen to the babies cry. Couldn't be bothered to feed us. Even looking at us made her angry."

Keira rested her forehead against his shoulder. Her warm breath rippled over his skin. "So, sometimes when kids cling to me, like Mateo has been, I get claustrophobic. When I feel responsible for a child's well-being, like I did with Kat, the pressure reminds me of that feeling I had when one of the babies had been crying for hours and I couldn't soothe them no matter how hard I tried. When those mix with certain smells, the smell of earth—dirt, plants, mold—I . . . I kinda lose it. I don't know what happens. My mind tilts, my heart speeds up, I start sweating. I panic, basically." She pressed her eyes closed with a shake of her head. "I never panic. I'm a sniper, for God's sake. Panic is not in our vocabulary.

"It's not logical. I know that. But it doesn't keep those dark moments from coming. I can't control them. I lash out. I retreat. I told you, I'm fucked up. I don't even know why you want me. Or if you still do."

All his walls came tumbling down. She'd taken that first step toward him. She'd finally let him in to a place she kept locked down tight. It wasn't a solution to all their problems, but it was a start. And that was more than they'd ever had before.

He took her face in both hands, pushed the dripping strands away from those beautiful eyes, and covered her mouth with his. Her fingers curled around his palms and held on. She pushed up on her toes, enveloping his mouth, pressing every perfect curve against him.

Her lips opened. Her tongue swept in, glided over his, swirled until he groaned.

She slid her hands up his arms, over his shoulders, around his neck, and tilted her head, digging in with the kind of passion that burned his brain clean through.

He wanted to say her name. Wanted to talk to her, tell her how good she felt, how he'd dreamed about her, how the years had dragged on, interminable, without her. But he couldn't pull his mouth from the feast.

The inner recesses of her mouth were so warm and wet and welcoming. Which turned his mind to other parts of her body, and the urgency to fill those spaces burned white-hot.

He tore his mouth from hers. Dragged in air as he shoved at the fabric on her hips. It dropped to the stone floor with a squishy plop. "Naked. I want you naked."

She swayed, breathing hard, eyes hazy. Sex-crazed brain. He'd seen it before and thanked the universe for it now.

"I want skin." He gripped the edge of her tank and pulled it up, over her breasts, cleared her head, and tossed it aside. Lust and need killed his patience. Appreciation of her beauty would have to come after satiation.

"Hell, yeah," he growled, hands gripping her tight waist, thumbs skimming the ripped abs. "Lots and lots of skin. Fuck, you're gorgeous."

Unable to stand the distance another second, he wrapped his arms around her slender body and drew her into him.

Oh, the feel of her in his arms. Perfection. Completion.

"Keira." He had to hear himself say her name while he was holding her, equivalent to a pinch assuring him he wasn't dreaming. "Keira."

She planted her mouth on his throat, sucked. Grazed her

teeth toward his ear. He rocked in a full body shiver and let out another moan, gritting his teeth. Her hands swept down and around to his belly, lower, squeezing between their bodies. Fingers wrapped around his shaft.

A zing of pleasure-laced pain cut off what little air he'd gathered, and a strangled grunt stumbled out of his throat.

"I remember just what you like," she whispered in his ear as her strong, smooth, talented fingers proved her one hundred and fifty percent right. "You taught me everything."

Fire spit into his blood. He hadn't been able to even kiss another woman without thinking about Keira in either desire or comparison. And now he had her. Authentic Keira O'Shay. Her freckles sparkling in his shower, her perfect breasts molded to his chest, her amazing fingers working his cock in that inquiring, demanding signature way that drove his dreams and woke him panting and sweating in his empty bed. A way he hadn't taught her at all, but one she'd explored and discovered all on her own in her never-ending desire to find the most visceral ways to blow his mind.

"Keir—" His tongue felt as swollen as his dick, now filling her hands. Brain felt as swollen as his balls, throbbing to get in on the action. "I can't—"

"Then don't."

One small hand released him, pushed between his thighs, rose to cup his balls. Squeezed.

Pleasure gushed through his groin, his pelvis. He groaned, long and deep. His eyes fell shut. White light burst against closed lids.

Not yet. Goddammit, not yet, you pathetic SOB.

"It's okay," she encouraged as if she'd heard him, her voice layering with the motion of her hands and enticing him toward climax. "It's been so long."

The muscles of his thighs shook, fought to keep his knees from buckling. His fingers cramped from where they'd clenched in her hair.

He cracked his lids and found Keira's bright eyes intense on his face. Mischievous. Knowing. Powerful.

"Keira . . ." His voice was gravel, his brain dust. He didn't know what he wanted to say. Couldn't form the words. He was gone. Slipping off the ledge without another sliver of strength to hold on to.

"I know, it feels good. So good," she whispered. Seductive. Erotic. One hand massaging between his legs, the other alternating stroking the underside of his penis, wrapping the head. "And when you come, I'm going to watch. You remember how I love to watch?"

Her hand rocked, letting the slick skin slide through her palm. Pumping. Fast and hard.

Not yet. Not fucking yet.

"Yes, now." Those blue eyes glittered at him with excitement and challenge and lust. "Right fucking now."

Her words exploded on impact. The orgasm bolted through his system without warning or permission. Bursting through his groin, up his torso, out his limbs. Searing, fiery, liquid pleasure.

Keira braced herself on the stone wall behind her as Luke's body arched and his sex lunged in her hands. Eyes closed, jaw clenched, face awash in fierce pleasure, he was the sexiest thing Keira had ever seen. She ached to have him inside her, but she'd blown that chance with this impulsive move.

When his body made one last hard jerk, then quaked in mini-shudders, she decided his gratification was completely worth postponing her own.

She closed her eyes and leaned in, kissing his chest, soaking in the feeling of power and love and hope flooding in until she thought she'd burst with a happiness she hadn't felt in years.

Luke's chest rose and fell with panting breaths. He

coughed, slapped a hand against the rock wall behind her, and groaned again, dropping his forehead against her shoulder. And she couldn't help but chuckle.

"Laugh while you can, baby." He bit the hollow between her neck and shoulder. Tingles shot across her skin. " 'Cause you are so going to pay for that."

"Soon, I hope." She kissed his chest, turned her head, and whispered in his ear, "Real soon."

He caught her mouth with his own and she draped her arms around his neck.

"I'm thinking now," he said against her mouth, then swept his tongue between her lips. He pushed off the wall, put both hands at her waist, and lifted her off the floor.

She held tight, wrapped her legs around his waist, smiling against his mouth. "Dreamer. Maybe in half an hour."

"Wanna bet on that?" Grinning, he stepped out of the shower and reached for a towel, dragging it around her back. "A blow job for the winner?"

She snorted, rubbing her fingers over his beautiful lips, imagining them between her legs doing all the amazing things that made her lose brain cells. "That's stupid. Bet for something you're not already going to get."

He tripped, caught the wall with one hand. Keira squeaked and tightened her arms around his neck.

"Christ, Keira." He glared at her with mock anger. "Don't do that."

She waited for him to right himself, open the bathroom door, and step into the bedroom, then leaned in and nibbled on his ear. "Don't do what? Tell you how I'm going to put my mouth on you? Lick you? Suck you until you scr—?"

She was the one to scream. He threw her. Just tossed her in the air like she weighed nothing. She landed in the middle of his bed, covers fluffing, hair flying. Before she could clear the wild strands from her face, he was on top of her, pinning her with his body.

She stopped struggling, sank into the soft mattress, and reveled in all his hot muscle and warm skin. "Oh, yeah, now this is more like it."

She ran her hands down the cords of muscle roping his arms as he levered himself over her. Wiggled beneath him and sucked in a breath of surprise when that hard, hot length rubbed her thigh. "No way."

A slow, sexy grin turned his mouth and crinkled the corner of his eyes. "Not quite a hundred percent." He rocked his hips, rubbed against her. "But soon. In the meantime . . ."

He maneuvered his knees between hers and pressed them open. A jolt of lust hit her.

He slid lower, dropped his hot, wet mouth over one nipple and closed down hard. Pleasure wiggled its way down her torso, filled her sex, and made her rub against his hips. His tongue licked, circled, teased. His mouth sucked. Keira's head dropped back. Her feet dug into the mattress, her hands into his wet hair.

"Luke . . ." Jesus, she could barely speak. "Luke. We still need . . . There's a lot, I mean, to talk about . . ."

He lifted his mouth only to shift to the other breast and plump it with his hand as if preparing his attack. "I picked up condoms."

His mouth came down. Teeth scraped across her skin. She groaned. Lifted her hips. He met her pressure and rocked, their rhythm instinctively perfect.

"What?" She jerked at his hair. "After that speech in the shower?"

"I picked them up before I knew I'd be giving the speech."

His mouth closed over her breast, suckled hard. Sensation rocketed through her body. She arched under him, cried out.

"Where?" If he didn't stop, she'd come right now. "Where are they?"

"What's the rush?" He grinned up at her. "I'd like to see you come this way. That would be new."

"Not funny." She scooted back, levered herself up on her elbows, unable to think straight let alone contemplate the ramifications of him reading her mind during sex. "If you want that blow job, tell me where they are."

His eyes darkened with lust. "Nightstand drawer."

"Nice. I'm looking forward to that." She smiled, twisted, and reached for the drawer at the edge of the bed. "But right now, I need something else."

She fumbled with the drawer, her mind already three steps ahead—package open, condom rolled on, slow and torturous, the length of his cock rubbing over her, getting nice and slick for the first tight ride in.

"Keira," he moaned.

She grinned. Okay, this mind thing could be really fun.

Her fingers searched blindly as his tongue traced the tattoo on her lower back and the upper curve of her ass.

"This is so sexy." His voice came out in a low growl and spiked heat down her chest. "I can't even tell you."

His mouth closed over the skin at the base of her spine as his fingers floated up her back, out over her ribs, and down her sides. His hands slipped underneath her hips. His fingers spread toward her aching center.

Her eyes glazed over. Her hand grasped the drawer for support. She closed her eyes, dropped her forehead to the mattress. "Yes."

Just a little more. A little more.

His fingers dug into her skin, holding her still. His hot mouth covered her center, kissed.

"Luke," she cried. "God, Lu—"

His tongue seared a path along her opening, cutting off her ability to speak. Then he moved on, his teeth closing around the flesh at one hip.

"No," she rasped. "Don't stop."

"More later," he promised. "I have a lot to see. A lot to do. Don't rush me."

Frustration rippled through every muscle. She snatched the box from the drawer, shoved a finger under the edge, and pried open the thin cardboard. That's when the cover caught her eye.

"Multicolored and . . . tropical flavor?" She shot a *what-the-hell* look over her shoulder.

He dragged his mouth toward the curve of her ass, lifted her hips a little higher, separated her legs a little more. Keira's breath caught in anticipation. *Yes.*

"It's all they had," he murmured against her skin, moving away from the spot that needed his mouth most. "Beggars and choosers and all that. Wasn't sure I'd ever get to use them anyway."

"All they had? Where did you go, a gas station? And only three?" They would need so many more. "Are you on a budget or something?"

He laughed and looked up. "I grabbed ten bucks from Teague on the way out the door and, no, not quite a gas station, but it was a mini-mart with limited options."

"You couldn't have bought *two* packages?" She poured the contents into her hand. "Or did they sell out? I can imagine multicolored, tropical flavor condoms are in high dem—"

Luke's strong hands closed around her waist and flipped her on the bed. He cut off her squeal with his mouth, kissing every thought right out of her brain.

When he pulled back, he was breathing hard, his eyes fierce and hot. "There are plenty of things I can do to you that don't require a condom."

One hand pushed between their bodies, slid down her stomach, and stopped at the thin strip of hair. His fingers feathered the edge, making her hips rock toward the motion, searching on a moan.

"I will give you as much as you want. As fast or slow as you want. As hard or soft as you want. In any goddamned position you want. Condoms or no condoms, you will want for nothing. I promise."

"Show me," she whispered. "I'm starting to think you're all talk, Ransom."

With a slow, sexy smile, he slid his hand lower. Keira held her breath as he brushed his fingers past her pounding clit so gently she almost believed she'd imagined the touch. Then one finger made a deep sweep over her opening and pushed inside.

Oh, God. Her eyes squeezed closed. Body clenched around his touch. Hips lifted to drive him forward. A sound emanated from her throat, followed by a long, drawn out, *"Yeeeees."*

With slow, deep movements, Luke thrust and rubbed until she was panting. He purposely stayed away from the very spots that would have led her to release three times by now. If he'd wanted to he could bring her from zero to climax within sixty seconds. He'd done it countless times before—in the hushed back row of a movie theater, a temporarily deserted engine bay at the fire station, the center table in a crowded restaurant.

She broke their kiss, where his mouth mirrored the movement of his hand. "Luke," she growled through gritted teeth. "Come on . . ."

"Baby, you're tight. Spread your legs."

The order spit lust into her bloodstream. Her need to have him inside her climbed toward anger. She spread. And she lifted, too. "The only thing that's going to help is getting your dick in there and working me over."

His head lifted from her shoulder, eyes serious as they settled on hers. When he pulled his hand from her body, she couldn't tell if her dirty talk had excited him into moving forward or disgusted him into pulling back.

He shifted his body, lying half on her, half on the bed. Down the length of his body, his scar drew her attention. Pale purplish lines and curves created the outline of a phoenix across his hip and down his strong thigh. So sexy. She reached down to trace the pattern, but he grabbed her hand.

"How long has it been since you had sex?" he asked.

A twinge of fear burned in her chest. "Where did that come from? What difference does it make?"

"How long?"

She hesitated, considered lying. "You already know."

"I want to hear you say it."

"Why do you want to talk about this now?" She was torn between mortification over the subject, fear of his rejection, and the physical and emotional need to reconnect with him. "I just want you. I want to make love with you. I want to be with you."

"Which is why you should be able to tell me. I told you." His brows lifted. "And in a very similar situation."

Why did it feel so different?

Because she held back, just like he'd argued last night. Because it was safer to be closed off than open and vulnerable.

She drew a deep breath. Best to just do it fast. Like removing a Band-Aid.

"Over two years. Okay, let's mess around." She pushed on his chest and rolled him onto his back.

Before she could get her mouth on his, he got hold of her wrists and pushed back, throwing one heavy thigh over her legs and pinning her in a twist. "Good try. Why so long?"

"Um . . ." She rolled her eyes in thought. "Because men are pigheaded imbeciles?"

He smirked. "True, but not the answer I'm looking for. Try again."

"Haven't I made enough confessions for one day?"

"Sounds like we've got years and years to make up for."

She scowled, licked dry lips, dropped her gaze. "I first tried three months after I left." She released a nervous breath of pent up air. "A friend of a friend of a friend at the academy. I was so beside myself without you I was about to flunk out."

She chanced a glance from beneath her lashes. Luke's smile dropped. His fingers slid from her wrists to thread with hers.

"I was determined to prove to myself that I could get over you. I'd be damned if I'd fail because of a *guy*." She sank her teeth into the flesh of her inner cheek as heat rose in her neck. "I had to get so drunk just to work up the nerve to go back to my apartment with him that I blacked out. Passed out. I don't know. I have no idea what happened. I don't know if we did, if we didn't . . ."

Luke's leg slid down hers; he shifted his body so hers uncoiled from the awkward position and dropped one hand over her waist, pulling her up on her side and against his body.

Good. Now she wouldn't have to look at him when she explained the next one. She could stare at his shoulder.

"Six months after that, I met a really nice guy. Another friend of a friend thing. Treated me like gold. We dated a few weeks but there was nothing for me, no spark. My friends told me I'd never get over you if I didn't try."

She squeezed her eyes shut. Tried like hell to pass over all the painfully awkward memories of his fumbling foreplay, drooling kisses, selfish focus.

"So I tried. And . . . well . . . I finally learned where women came up with that remark about, you know, counting ceiling tiles."

Luke barked out a laugh he obviously hadn't expected,

making Keira smile. Almost washing away all those terrible memories.

"But since I'd always had the best lover, I'd never known what in the hell they were talking about." She lifted her chin, relished the clear, intelligent blue eyes that looked back at her. "You ruined me, Luke. Ruined me for any other man on the planet. Since then I haven't tried to get over you. I haven't tried to have sex with other men. I knew it was a waste of time."

His eyes softened. He rubbed a thumb over her cheek, and under his touch, she felt wetness there for the first time.

"Give me those." He reached for the condoms.

She jerked them out of his reach. "No." She sniffled and ripped a package open. "That's my job."

He rolled to his knees over her, that shaft jutting out, stealing the spotlight. She wet him with her mouth, not anywhere close to the blow job he'd get later, but enough to make him close his eyes, sway, and lose his balance. Then she rolled the piña colada condom over his length, taking her time, stroking him as she went.

As soon as her fingers hit the base of his erection, Luke gripped her by the waist. "Roll over."

"Why? I want to—"

"Because." He leaned down, keeping his hot blue eyes on hers as he licked her bottom lip, then her upper. "That's the best position for . . . as you so nastily put it . . . getting my dick in there and working you over. Besides, it's hot as hell and I happen to remember—one of your favorites. You come so hard you nearly cut my dick off. Flip over and I'll remind you."

He twisted her toward her stomach, and she didn't resist. He was right on all counts. Just the thought of it turned up the heat between her legs until she was burning.

Flat on her stomach, she felt vulnerable, exposed, out of

control. The fact that those were all things Luke loved about the position made her stomach flutter. She pushed pillows out of her face and pressed her nose to the sheets, inhaling deeply of Luke's unique, masculine scent.

His hands swept down her legs, reached between her thighs, and pulled them open. He pressed the inside of his knees to hers, slowly opening her wide. Baring her.

"Beautiful," he whispered.

Cool air stroked all the overheated, oversensitized tissues. Tantalizing and teasing.

"That is much better." His voice was deep and appreciative. "So much better. God, you are so hot."

His warm fingers traveled up the insides of her thighs, pulling her knees up, opening her further. Then he stroked her, slow, one finger, two. Palmed her. Sparks speared her core. She lifted her hips, pressed into his touch, and whimpered. Both hands covered her ass, squeezed.

"Luke—" She fisted the sheets. "Don't make me wait. Play later. Fuck me now."

"I like that talk. But we've got work to do." He leaned over her, skimmed his teeth over her shoulder as his hands caressed her ass to the rocking movement of her hips. "That's it," he murmured against the back of her neck. "Let's get you good and wet."

With one hand on her breast, the other slipped between her legs from behind and caressed a scream from her throat she hadn't known was coming.

"You feel amazing," he whispered against her shoulder, taking small bites where he could, his fingers continuing to pull mewls of excruciating pleasure from her throat. "Tight and wet and hot. How many times do you want to come, baby? You name it, I'll deliver. Three? Five?"

"One. How 'bout just one, Luke?" She gritted her teeth. Their chemistry had always been good; now it was explosive. "Like *now*."

He laughed, low and throaty. "I am loving this . . . whatever the hell this extra boost between us is. Damned amazing, baby."

He took her whole breast in his hand and squeezed hard. Bit the sensitive flesh at the base of her neck and did, God, something with the hand between her legs. What, exactly, she wasn't sure, because she couldn't think. He pressed a thick finger deep inside her while others continued to stroke and roll and slide easily. As she thrust her hips against the pressure, Luke penetrated and withdrew, rubbed and pinched and squeezed Keira right into a toe-curling, mind-melting, full-body climax.

Electricity still arced and buzzed through her cells, fingers still fisted in the sheets when Luke whispered, "Oh, yeah. That's what I'm talking about."

She wasn't following. Couldn't make her mind pull from the beautiful buzzing white cloud to pay attention. Until he lifted her hips from where she'd melted flat to her stomach after that wickedly delicious orgasm. She was about to complain about giving her a minute . . . until his body slipped between her legs and his knees pushed hers apart again.

"Oh, my God," she groaned, unable to believe she was ready for him. Wanting to feel him inside her after that rush. But she was. She did.

With one hand on her ass, he held the head of his cock to her opening and rubbed it over her. "So hot," he murmured. "So wet."

"Not . . . enough." She hadn't caught her breath from the last climax and yet she was already panting again, careless of her hair falling in her face, blowing with her breath. "More."

"Demanding," he crooned in a voice so sexy her heart skipped. "Have I ever told you how much I love that?"

He pushed in, just the head, but his size was enough to make Keira suck in a breath. Delicious stinging pressure slid through the lower half of her body.

"Oh, yes. God, yes." She pushed back, searching. "More. Lots more."

Instead of obliging, Luke pulled out. Keira opened her eyes, was about to turn and say something filthy to rile him enough to slam that cock into her, but he pushed back in on his own before she had a chance. And he continued the maddening pattern until Keira thought she'd go insane.

"Deeper, Luke. Harder." Impatient, needy, she lifted her hips, and hurried the process. A sultry burn erupted along the walls of her vagina, and the bite pushed a long moan from her chest.

Luke leaned over her, pressing his chest to her back, big, strong hands gripping her hips, husky voice in her ear. "Like that?"

Before she could answer, he dug his fingers in to the flesh at her hips and rocked into her, pushing deeper. Deeper.

She gasped. Held her breath until the burn transitioned into pure pleasure, then moved against him, the rock of her hips dragging him out and driving him back in. The pleasure of it swallowed her. So intense. So consuming. She bit down on the corner of a pillow with a throaty growl.

"What about that?" His voice came at her earlobe, clearing her mind and bringing back the reality of their positions, of his dominance, his control. "That's right, baby. You're mine. I'm not letting go. Now answer me." He made another powerful, purposeful thrust, driving a rippling level of pleasure Keira had never experienced through her body until she screamed against the pillow. "Do you like that?" he asked deliberately in her ear.

She turned her head and dragged in air. "Yes."

"Want more?"

"I want more." She arched the small of her back, tilting her pelvis, trying to take him deeper. "I want it all."

"It's all for you." Luke made a low growling sound in his throat and pushed his hips forward, filling her another inch.

They picked up a quick, perfect rhythm. With each of Luke's thrusts, Keira angled her hips up and back. Inch by inch, he drove deeper on each push. By the time he finally filled her, sweat dripped down her temple and stung her eye.

Wedged deep inside her, Luke pushed up on his hands. "My negotiation skills . . ." he panted, wiping his forehead on his bicep, "have been exhausted. Time to rock and roll, baby."

Christ, wasn't that what they'd been doing?

He pulled out slowly, made a few shallow thrusts, then drove deep, burying himself once again. The slide was electric, the pressure luxuriant. Keira arched, clenched her fingers in the sheets, tasted that sweet moment of anticipation just before release. With Luke buried inside her. So long. It had been so damn long.

Then Luke pulsed his hips. The head of his cock rubbed on some hot button she hadn't known existed. His shaft stroked her tender walls with fire. And the resulting strikes of pleasure shot her toward the edge of a canyon, with the sun overhead, beckoning.

"Luke." She barely managed his name. Every muscle contracted, one fiber at a time, preparing her for liftoff. "God, Luke."

"Right here, baby." His chest pressed to her back, his cheek to her cheek. "Rock into me, Keira. Hard. Going to be so good."

With her hands fisted in the sheets, teeth clenched around the corner of a pillow, Keira tilted her pelvis back and up. Luke met it on a strong thrust. Pleasure spiked through her pelvis, straight up her chest. She cried out against the pillow.

"Harder," he rasped against her ear.

Luke pulled out. She rocked again, squeezing her glutes for punch.

"Come on," he taunted. "Use that gorgeous ass. Give me some goddamned power."

She tried again. Harder.

"Ah, yeah. That's it. Again, baby."

Each thrust pushed her another step toward the cliff, the slap of sweaty flesh like quick footsteps until Keira took a running leap off that canyon ledge and flew directly into the blinding light of the sun.

Fifteen

Keira felt someone watching her as she bubbled to the surface of consciousness. But she wasn't scared or anxious. A deep, soothing sense of well-being warmed her right down to the core. She cracked her lids to peer through her lashes.

White wall. Afternoon light coming from a window somewhere else in the room. She flicked her gaze down. Rich navy blue comforter.

"Thought you'd never wake up. Had to count your freckles twice to keep from prodding you."

A slow smile lifted her mouth as she turned toward Luke's voice. Then muscles pulled and joints rolled and skin rubbed.

She winced. "Ow."

He laughed, slid an arm over her middle, and scooted close, pushing one long, warm thigh between hers.

She only turned halfway before she gave up and sank back into the bed. He was propped up on one elbow, looking down with those light eyes, an easy smile on his face. But something hung in the shadows as if he was covering some sort of unease.

Searching her senses, she came up empty on a source and decided to stall the impending, inevitable step back to reality. "How many do I have?"

"Eighty-nine." He leaned in and kissed the tip of her nose. "Picked up a few extras in the last three years."

She glanced around the room with a leisure she hadn't had the first time she'd come in. Everything was exactly the same as she'd first thought, only now the towel they'd dragged from the shower lay on the floor beside the bed, as did all three empty condom wrappers.

"What time is it?" she asked, reluctant to leap back into life, yet already feeling guilty about the amount of time she'd spent away from Mateo.

"Does it matter?"

"I wish it didn't."

Her eyes followed the swath of light beaming from the window and a memory clicked. Her gaze swung toward the blank wall she'd been looking at when she woke up.

"That's it." Her stomach plummeted.

"What's what?"

"That's what's missing." She stared at the spot where the light dissipated into a soft pool, lightening the hardwood two shades. "I knew something was missing as soon as I came in the house, but I couldn't figure out what." She pushed up, twisted in that direction. "Kat's bed."

Keira could still see the little girl napping there, the late sun hitting her dark hair and making it shine like patent leather. Could still see the warm glow of her porcelain skin under the light, reminding Keira of a perfect angel.

"Her toys, her books, the crayons she left everywhere." How many times had Keira stepped on one of the crayons Kat had eternally gripped in her chubby little fist? How many times had she repainted these walls where Kat had gotten creative in a rare moment she wasn't being constantly watched? "That's what's missing."

Luke didn't immediately respond. He didn't need to. Keira felt the loss streaming through him.

"Guess I've gotten used to it." But his tone hinted that he'd never get used to it.

A familiar, haunting guilt twisted in Keira's stomach. The stark reality of what Luke must have suffered when he'd given "his princess," as he'd called her, back to Teague and Alyssa hit her so hard, tears swelled in her eyes.

An inkling of how hard it would be to let go of Mateo edged in.

If he goes back to Greece, he'll die on the streets. If he stays here, DARPA will snatch him from foster care.

"If I can't find Mateo's parents," she said, "I'll have Mitch start on adoption papers." Her throat grew tight with a mixture of love for the boy, fear for his future, and anxiety over her own role in that future. "It's going to be complicated and risky. I'll need a ton of false documents. But I won't ever let those DARPA bastards get him."

Luke nestled his face against the side of her neck, kissed her there, slid his arm across her waist, and squeezed her close. He kissed his way across her shoulder. Under the covers, the hand on her waist slid to the flat of her belly, then lower. "You feel like heaven, baby."

Keira smiled, groaned at the feel of those long, strong fingers pushing between her legs. "Luke—" She drew out his name. "We don't have any more condoms."

"We have to." He pulled her earlobe between his teeth. "I still want you."

She laughed and pulled his hand into hers, dragging it to her mouth for a kiss. "Are you listening to me?"

"Mmm-hmm." His thigh slid between hers, pushed high, rocked.

"Lu-uke." She rolled over, easing him to his back and straddling his hips.

"Hell, yeah." His hands gripped her hips, his eyes traveled the length of her body, a huge, hot grin slid over his face. And a huge, hot erection rode across her entrance. "Now this . . . baby. *This* is what I'm talking about."

Tracing the muscles on his abdomen, she felt a mixture of apprehension and excitement coil inside her as she brought up the subject she wanted to get hashed out and behind them so they could relax together. "Do you still have your heart set on that baseball team?"

His eyes darted up from her belly button stud, which his thumb flicked back and forth so it twinkled in the light. "Baseball what?"

"You know, kids. You used to say you wanted enough kids to make your own baseball team." All she could do was hope she kept the cringe out of her voice when she said, "You were kidding, right?"

His grin turned lopsided, his gaze more playful than devilish. "I'd like to practice for first string, but only draft the first pick, if you know what I mean."

"Uh, not really. Sounds like you've been hanging around Mitch too much."

"I'd eat my gun first. It means practice makes perfect. One perfect kid is fine with me."

Her brows shot up. The tightness in her chest evaporated. "One? You're saying you'd be happy with one child? What happened to the brood you wanted?"

"Kat happened." He laughed. "After raising that girl for a couple years on my own . . . Man, she about killed me. The tears, the moods. My shoes don't match my dress, my hair's not right, Tiffany's mom brings her lunch every day, I'm too old for daycare, why do you work so much?"

He met her eyes again. "I'd be very happy with one. Boy or girl. Now or later. If we add Mateo to the mix, great. If we find his parents and they're good people and we can return him home, even better." He slid his hands to her shoulders and pulled her down on top of him, then pressed a sweet, slow kiss to her lips. "As long as I still have you.

Everything hinges on that. *You* are the key to the family that means everything to me."

Her heart skipped, then started again with a hard, but pleasant, kick. One child? Yes, she could do that. She could handle that. She could give him that family he wanted so desperately. Something she'd always wanted, too, but never believed she could have. She closed her eyes and lowered her mouth to his.

His fingers caught her face, her mouth an inch from his. "I love you. So much."

Surprise popped her eyes open. The words sank in and glowed around her heart, mending all the pains from her past as if Luke had Teague's healing powers.

She lifted her hands overhead, pressed them to the wall, and scooted her body down Luke's, readjusting for the perfect fit.

Who else is in there with them? The curt female voice pierced the easy white cloud in Keira's head. She gasped.

"What?" Luke looked down the length of their entwined bodies. "Did I hurt you?"

"No," she whispered, her mind searching. "Wait."

"Why are you whisper—"

"Shhh." She put gentle fingers on his mouth. Realization dawned in his eyes.

No one that we can tell. A man's voice joined the conversation in her head. *Just her and Ransom.*

"Crap." Keira pushed against Luke's chest and slid off him. "They're here. Outside."

Luke was out of bed and at the window in fluid, catlike moves. Her own body didn't move quite so easily. Muscles ached and pulled as she stole into the bathroom and retrieved her weapon from the shower.

She moved to Luke's closet, jerked a pair of his jeans from the shelf, and leaned around the doorjamb to toss them on the bed. "Who is it?"

He picked up the pants and stepped into them. "I can't tell. Black SUVs. Two of them."

"Dargan." Keira grabbed an ATF sweatshirt and pulled it over her head. Then dragged on sweatpants, tied them at the waist, and rolled the waistband down three times so they didn't swallow her. "I heard her voice."

"How do you know my voice?" These words didn't ring in her head. They were clear and crisp.

Keira dropped the cotton tee she'd grabbed for Luke, gripped her gun in both hands, and swiveled out of the closet toward the voice. But when she faced the female intruder, she found two males accompanying her, both with guns already pointed at her and Luke.

Arms crossed, Jocelyn took in the scene. Luke in nothing but faded jeans, zipped but not buttoned. He could have been the poster boy for Abercrombie and Fitch. Keira, on the other hand, looked like a homeless rag doll, men's clothes hanging off her small frame, her hair tossed, face mottled with bruises and healing cuts.

Far from a homeless rag doll, though, she held that Glock like it was an extension of her arm, and the intensity in her expression stung with a familiarity Jocelyn couldn't quite place. If Keira wanted to, she could put a bullet in the forehead of all three of them before either of her men got off a shot. But she wouldn't. She was a consummate professional. Owen had been right on at least one level. Jocelyn identified with many of the other woman's fierce fighter characteristics.

"So?" Jocelyn asked again, curious. "How do you know my voice?"

"You're not the only ones who tap phones and plant bugs," Keira said.

A chill rattled Jocelyn's chest. The hunted hunting? Why hadn't she considered that a possibility?

She smiled, then laughed as Keira's cunning came into

sharp focus. "Does the FBI know you're misusing resources? Could get you in hot water."

"Who said I'm using FBI resources?"

"Touché. I suppose with Mitch Foster's connections you
wouldn't need the Bureau's toys. You're even sharper than
I expected."

Too bad Keira was on the wrong side of the game. Jocelyn would love to have someone so skilled, so gutsy, on her
team. As it was, she didn't doubt that Keira's reputation as
a killer shot had her men ready to pee their pants.

"Why don't you put the weapon down so we can have a
civilized discussion," Jocelyn said. "The gun only creates
more tension."

"There's nothing civilized about you or your people.
And if you want to see tension, live my life for a few days."

Jocelyn's gaze cut to Luke, scanned him. A very similar
physique to Owen. And judging by Keira's disheveled appearance, equally as primal in bed.

"Luke, you should probably get dressed so we women
can think straight. Keira, when you're ready to talk, I'll be
in the living room."

"Scott—" Jocelyn addressed the older of her two men
as she turned and started for the door. "You're with me.
Davis, holster your weapon and watch Ransom. We're just
here to talk."

In the living room, Jocelyn fingered the photos in her
pocket and took a deep breath to loosen her chest. If her
judgment of Keira's honor and intelligence was accurate,
that calculated risk wouldn't come back to bite her in the
ass. Not like Tony's had. If it weren't for him, none of this
would be happening.

At least that problem had been eliminated.

Jocelyn looked over the single thin bookshelf on the far
living room wall housing photos of Ransom's niece, Katrina, and his deceased family members—father from heart

attack, mother from cancer, sister, and Teague's first wife, from suicide. A suicide DARPA scientists had surmised stemmed from postpartum depression exacerbated by secondhand exposure to the raw chemicals in that warehouse. The ones her unsuspecting, loving husband, Teague, and her brother, Luke, had dragged home with them.

Oh, the irony. Life was full of irony.

Her own irony came clearly to mind—the way her thoughts flipped between Owen and Jason relentlessly. She reached up to finger the chain around her neck holding the key nestled between her breasts. The key to Jason's safe-deposit box. Then she remembered it was missing, and unease nagged at the edges of her mind. Her memory fought to track her movements from the time she'd opened the envelope to the moment she'd first noticed it missing. Where hadn't she already looked twice?

"This is a bold move," Keira said from behind her. "Even for you."

Jocelyn turned to face the other woman. The perfect shot had tucked her weapon into the waistband of her baggy sweatpants. A rather comical sight, although Jocelyn passed up the opportunity to comment. Keira kept her arms at her sides, within easy reach of the gun. No sense in pushing. Even the best could be pushed too far.

Scott had placed his own weapon into the holster at his hip, but stood alert and ready, a respectable fifteen feet away.

"Have you two reconciled?" Jocelyn tossed a look past Keira's shoulder toward the bedroom. "Or is this just a little . . . for-old-time's-sake sex?"

"None of your business," Keira said.

"Maybe not personally, but professionally, it is. If you two are . . . connected . . ." Jocelyn wondered just how their powers strengthened. She knew what their powers were individually, but no one seemed to know exactly what happened once they were together.

Luke entered the room, looking young and handsome and virile in the gray flannel shirt he'd pulled on with his jeans.

Keira snapped her fingers twice near Jocelyn's face. "Here, *Jocelyn*. Focus."

She laughed. "I think I like you."

"I *don't* like you."

"I know." Jocelyn took no offense. "But we don't have to like each other to work together."

Keira's expression went combat-stiff. "We are not working together. We will *never* work together."

"Oh, never say never. You may change your mind when you hear what I have to say."

"What the hell is this about?" Luke stepped up beside Keira like a protective wolf.

"Doesn't involve you, handsome," Jocelyn said. "This is between us girls."

She pulled one of the photos from her pocket. Keira went very still. The anger in her face transitioned into apprehension.

"What the hell?" Luke reached for it. Davis grabbed Luke's arm and yanked him backward. Luke swore and shook off Davis's hold, but didn't advance again.

"I came to offer you a deal," Jocelyn said.

Keira crossed her arms. "You have nothing I want."

Oh, the naïveté. Jocelyn had once been that foolish. A lifetime ago.

"Not even your brother?"

It took two full seconds for the words to register. When they did, Keira's fresh face went slack.

"She doesn't have a brother," Luke said.

Jocelyn kept her eyes on Keira. "Cash O'Shay, thirty-nine years old. Birth date, April tenth. Mother, Lacey O'Shay. Father . . . the big *unknown*."

"My brother," Keira started slowly, "is dead. You should

get your information straight before you try to use it as leverage."

"Is he?" Jocelyn's eyes narrowed. "Did you ever see his body? Did they ever recover bones from the fire? Was a death certificate ever issued?"

"No amount of information you spit out regarding me, my brother, my mother, or my childhood would surprise me."

"I didn't figure you for a believer. That's why I brought this."

Jocelyn turned the photo to face Keira, displaying a picture of a man holding a *New York Times* newspaper dated the day before.

"That could be anyone." Keira pried her eyes away from the photo. "I've seen what a good computer artist can do. You could put the face of the pope on a penguin and make people believe it's real."

"Then hold it." She pushed the photo toward Keira. "That's your thing, isn't it? Your ability? Touch it."

Keira leaned back.

"What's wrong? Afraid it's real? Or are you afraid it's not? Or are you even sure? I know all about your many fears, Keira. I *understand* all your fears. The ones that have held you back all these years. It's a shame, really. A strong woman like you holding yourself hostage from the things that would make you happiest in life."

Keira narrowed her eyes on the image as if tuning in to it. "You're lying."

"Am I? Are you sure? Or are you just afraid? And are you going to let your fear keep you from the possibility of finding your only living family? Are you going to let it dictate your future? Your career? Your happiness? It's your life, Keira. *Live it,* for God's sake." She waved the photo. "And give your brother a chance to live his."

"Goddamn you." Keira snatched the photo from Jocelyn's fingers. She turned her back on everyone, took the photo with both hands, and bent her head.

Anticipation bubbled in Jocelyn's chest. Just how good was Keira? Jocelyn had heard stories, but she wanted to test her ability firsthand. She cut a look at Ransom to see if she could discern a connection between them, curious how their powers worked together, or if they actually did. But the blond hunk seemed distraught as he watched Keira wander a few feet away.

A low growl ebbed from Keira just before she whipped back and advanced on Jocelyn. Keira fisted both hands in Jocelyn's suit jacket, pushed her backward, and slammed her against the nearest wall. All so fast, Jocelyn didn't have time to react.

She cried out in surprise. Her instincts rolled beneath her skin, urging her to fight back, take Keira down. But her intelligence, her cunning, told her to hold back.

"Yes, I'm sure you're lying." Keira rasped the accusation an inch from Jocelyn's face. "This man is dead. And he has absolutely no connection to me whatsoever."

Scott and Davis raised their guns simultaneously. The metallic slide of a weapon sounded nearby. "Release her and step back," Scott ordered.

"Keira—" Luke's worried warning followed. "Keira, stop."

"I'm just getting started."

Keira jerked Jocelyn forward, then slammed her back again. A spike of pain traveled down Jocelyn's spine, but she let it flow, then ebb, determined to ride out this storm and see where it led. She'd learned the key to a person's character showed under the greatest pressures, and Jocelyn wanted to see if Keira lived up to her file.

"Who do you think you are, God? How dare you screw with our lives? I'm damn sick of it. Have you ever wondered what it would be like to have someone screw with *your* life? Follow *you*? Know every little detail of *your* existence?"

Keira's voice dropped to a tone that raised the hair on the back of Jocelyn's neck.

"I know where you work, what you drive, when you eat, sleep, and go to the gym. I know who does your hair, what medications you're taking, and which family members you're still on speaking terms with." Keira pushed a finger into Jocelyn's chest to punctuate her words. "But most importantly—I. Know. Where. You. Live."

"Let me go." Jocelyn forced her voice to remain cool.

The guard's meaty hand gripped Keira's bicep, and he pressed his weapon to her head. "Release her or I'll shoot."

"Keira," Luke pleaded. "Please."

She shoved Jocelyn away and jerked out of Scott's grip.

Jocelyn straightened. The combination of excitement, pain, and fear made her breathless. She searched Keira's dark blue eyes, wishing she could get inside the woman's head. She was even gutsier, more cunning than Jocelyn had expected. Never, in all her years in the military, in private industry, in intelligence, had Jocelyn met anyone quite like Keira O'Shay.

"You're right," she said. "He's not your brother. He's just an employee we used for the photograph. And yes, he died yesterday in a car accident on the way home from work. You're as good as they've all told me."

Hands on hips, Keira narrowed her eyes. "You were *testing* me? You fucking, coldhearted *bitch*. If you don't kill me right now you'd better sleep with these jerk-offs, because I'm gonna—"

"*This* is your brother." Jocelyn pulled another image from her pocket, ignoring Keira's rant. If she had a dime for every threat she'd ever received, Jocelyn could have retired five times over by now.

Here came the risk. The huge risk Owen had urged her

toward and one she still wasn't completely invested in. There was no telling what a woman like O'Shay would do with this information, but Jocelyn had to agree that having the kid with a team with paranormal powers of unknown limits was incredibly dangerous to their mission. It was also hazardous to many powerful political figures and ultimately for Jocelyn's career. She had to force Keira's hand, and Cash was her only current leverage.

And all thanks to Rostov and his whacked-out theory of how those chemicals would affect similar DNA patterns and children. The bastard's crazed attack on Cash's wife and son had almost exposed the entire system. If Jocelyn hadn't orchestrated the cover-up and ultimately imprisoned Cash when his personal investigation had touched too close to the truth, the whole mission would have collapsed in the biggest scandal since Watergate.

Now, she had to get the boy back and eliminate that possibility once again. This was really getting old.

She shrugged her shoulders and tugged at the hem of her jacket to get the garment back into place, smoothing her free hand over the wrinkles Keira had creased into the front. She'd just had it dry-cleaned, too.

"He *is* alive," she said, forcing her composure back into place. Refocusing on her goal now that her curiosity had been sated. "He's been working for us, but his usefulness is coming to an end. We can release him to you, or we can eliminate him. Your choice."

"Working for you?" Keira gave an absurd snort of laughter. "This is unbelievable."

Keira snapped the photo from her hand, a skeptical frown etching her forehead. But it didn't take long for her expression to shift. Anger to shock. Shock to torment. Keira pressed a hand to the center of her chest as if her heart ached.

Jocelyn had clearly won this battle. Maybe not the war—

yet. But this battle was over. "Getting a little more from this one, are you?"

Keira's hand closed around the photograph before dropping to her side. "I don't know what you think you'll gain—"

"The boy." Jocelyn went in for the kill. "We'll give you your brother if you give us the . . ." *Scamp, brat, pain in the ass* ". . . child. He has abilities that will be an invaluable asset to our military and ultimately our country. We want to help him grow and explore those abilities."

The only thing that enabled her to keep the grimace out of her voice was the knowledge the kid would be killed as soon as they gained custody. And his father would be eliminated as soon as he completed the experiment. Then all Jocelyn had left to get rid of was this damn team. That would be far trickier.

"I assure you, Cash is alive. Take some time with that photograph, and you'll know I'm telling you the truth. You'll have to be the one to make the final decision as to whether or not you're willing to sacrifice your only living relative for a little Greek orphan who means nothing to you."

Jocelyn strode to the door. Her loyal dogs followed. At the threshold, she paused with one hand on the doorframe and turned back toward Keira.

"You have forty-eight hours to decide. Then your brother's usefulness will have expired . . . and so will this deal."

"Dargan." Keira's voice brought her attention around one last time. The other woman's eyes drilled into Jocelyn with as much ice and determination as any enemy she'd ever faced. "I suggest you stay away from those picture windows in your living room."

SIXTEEN

Keira's gaze blurred on the bright, crisp early afternoon sunlight spilling through the windshield as she waited for Luke. She sat in the passenger's seat of Alyssa's crossover looking down the quiet street where the SUVs carrying Dargan and her two thugs had disappeared ten minutes before.

Damn spooks thought they could just walk into their lives, drop a bomb, issue ultimatums, and flounce out again. Screw them. Upside down and sideways. She'd get her brother back and she'd keep Mateo. She'd find a way.

Just holding the photo of her brother sent a smooth, molten heat flowing through her, filling all the gaps, easing all the loneliness. God, she'd idolized him.

But who was he now? Doubt edged in. Why would he go through life without contacting her? And was he truly working for her greatest enemy?

She lifted the picture and studied the man. He was sitting on a stool in some type of lab, looking over his shoulder at the camera as if someone had called to gain his attention. Unlike the other man Dargan had tried to pass off as her brother, this one looked back at her. Touched her. Spoke to her.

But it was her mother's voice that invaded Keira's mind.

*You good-for-nothing piece of shit. Look what you've done! You'll
pay for this, boy.*

A loud *gong* made Keira flinch. In her memory, she could
still see her mother, face creased with wrinkles from a lifetime of smoking, dyed-blond hair hanging in stringy
patches to her shoulders, grab the frying pan from the stove
and whip it against Cash's temple.

The splash of liquid. The roar of flames. The crackle of
wood.

And Cash's final scream. *Run, Keira! Get out!*

She forced her eyes open, her mind back to the present.

Luke trotted down the front steps, duffel bag in one
hand, phone pressed to his ear in the other. The sight of
him helped her refocus, and her heart squeezed.

She ran a hand over her thigh, the jeans rubbing coarse
against her fingers. Jeans of hers he still had in the depths of
his closet. Along with a few other odds and ends she had
forgotten when she'd packed for the academy.

What are you doing with these? she'd asked after Dargan had
left, and Luke had offered the pants for her to change into.
After all this time?

He'd shrugged. *I guess I was hoping you'd come back for them.*

She hadn't told him she still harbored a few of his shirts.
That she still slept in them every night. She would have, it
would have been the perfect moment, only she felt something shifting inside her. The news of her brother sent
doors in her psyche slamming shut. She didn't know why.
Didn't know how to stop it. Only felt herself splitting away
from the bond she'd forged with Luke.

It hurt. It frightened. And it was completely out of her
control.

Luke tossed his bag into the backseat, shut the door, and
slid behind the steering wheel. "Yes, Cash Evan O'Shay."

Keira flinched at the sound of her brother's full name. As
Luke continued to impart information to Mitch, a familiar

shell coated Keira's insides, a protective reaction she'd developed as a child, one that prepared her for the inevitable shit storm about to hit.

"I know he's supposed to be dead." Luke backed out of the driveway. "Check on that. We'll explain when we get there."

When he disconnected, Keira said, "Drive slow, Luke. I need to think."

"You should have been thinking *in there*." He tossed his phone on the dash and glared at her. "You just threatened a high-ranking federal employee. With witnesses who just happened to be federal law enforcement." He jerked the car into drive and pounded the steering wheel. "Christ. You're giving her exactly what she wants, Keira. Do you remember what happened the last time they had one of us on trial?"

That hadn't been the shit storm she'd been expecting.

"Well what *do* you expect," he said, "when you go and say things like 'stay away from those picture windows in your living room'? God. Sometimes, Keira, you just fucking floor me."

So much for blocking him from her thoughts.

She blew out a long breath and closed her eyes as Luke stopped at a light. Tears immediately stung the backs of her lids. The warmth and pressure of his hand on her knee gave her a fleeting taste of reassurance.

"Hey," he said, voice softer. She peeked at him from beneath her lashes. "Off the record, I'm damned impressed at the way you stood up to that bitch. Just don't do it again. I swear I feel older by the minute."

She pressed her lips together and nodded, then blurted the questions she couldn't hold back anymore. "Do you think Mateo really *is* my nephew?"

"Facts are leading in that direction, babe."

She huffed a humorless laugh and shook her head. A hell

of a lot more made sense now—her immediate feeling of connection to him, even before they met, that sense of familiarity when she looked into his face, the belief that Tony had been lying about Mateo's origin, the sense of deceit rolling off Dargan trying to spin the same story.

The responsibilities that went along with the very real possibility that Mateo was her own flesh and blood made her dizzy. She leaned her head against the seat. If they didn't find Cash, if they couldn't reunite Cash and Mateo, she was going to have to choke down her fears and take the boy in, because he was her family.

Yes, she'd considered the possibility, but now that possibility was almost a certainty. She had a freaking five-year-old *nephew* who didn't speak a word of English.

"*And* he's the cutest thing since Elmo. *And* he thinks you walk on water."

Her head lolled toward Luke as the light turned and he continued through the golden aspens and towering pines lining the roads. Either her barriers were shrinking or his clairaudient abilities were growing. "Elmo is not cute."

Luke grinned, his white teeth glimmering, his cheek creasing into a deep crescent beneath the morning's stubble. He hadn't shaved in the shower, leaving him scruffy and so sexy. That profile was to die for.

She had never loved anyone more. Never loved *him* more. And the split growing inside her was excruciating.

"Can I see the photo?" he asked.

She passed it across.

"Well, the resemblance is definitely there," Luke murmured, and set the photo in the middle console. He clenched his teeth until his jaw muscles rolled. "I think the best way to do this is to just spill it. Just start talking and don't stop until it's all out."

"There's a limit on confessions in a twenty-four-hour period. I'm over mine."

"Save the drama."

Jeez, she didn't know where to start.

"Start with the fire," Luke said.

"Stop reading my thoughts."

"You're *projecting*."

"Smartass."

Keira's mind was a jumble of events and emotions, of people and places and circumstance.

"The fire was my fault," she said. "My mom left me home while she went out to the bar. I was hungry, tried to cook something for myself. I don't even remember what, bacon and eggs I think, because whatever it was involved grease.

"The grease caught fire, and I was trying to put it out when Cash came home from his job. Some type of fast food place, I think. Right after that our mother showed up. She was drunk—as usual—and when she saw the fire, she lost it. Just freaked out. Cash took the blame and said that he'd started it. Our mom, God, I can still see it. She picked up the frying pan and hit Cash in the head. The grease must have spread, because a second later flames were everywhere, all across the kitchen, dotting Cash's jeans. All I remember after that was Cash screaming for me to run, get out of the house. So I ran. Didn't wait for him. Didn't look for my mother. I just ran."

She remembered the firefighters outside the house. How one had swept her up in his arms and jogged with her across the lawn, setting her on the step of his fire truck to check her over. She wouldn't recognize him now, but she'd never forget the depth of concern in his eyes, an emotion no one had ever shown for her but Cash, and one that had touched her deeply.

That one look had been the impetus for her quest into the fire service.

"The days after that are a blur. The police took me away.

I remember sitting in the corner of a dark room at some type of child services facility, and all I could think about was how they were going to take me to jail and I'd never see Cash again. And when they came the next morning, they did tell me I'd never see Cash again, only they told me it was because he'd died in the fire."

Keira numbed out. If she didn't, she'd short-circuit.

"Honestly, after they told me Cash was dead, my memory blacks out. I don't have anything more than spotty recollections about my life until a couple years later. And all that is just foster home after foster home until I landed with one couple who mined my value until I turned eighteen. None of which I want to talk about now."

Keira focused on the quaint shops lining Truckee's touristy downtown.

"You were five years old?" Luke said.

"Yes."

"And your mother left you alone? With nothing to eat?"

She rubbed her eyes. "Yes."

From the corner of her eye, she saw Luke's hand squeeze the steering wheel. "So, what Dargan said, about the death certificate, the proof . . . About Cash not actually dying in the fire . . . ?"

"It's true. I never had any proof. By the time I was old enough to understand that things hadn't been followed up, I didn't see a point in asking for proof. I believed he was dead. I couldn't imagine why anyone would lie. Why he would fake it. The possibility never entered my mind. All it would have done was force me to relive the terror. I just wanted to move on. To find purpose. To do something with my life that up until that point had seemed so pointless.

"Where has he been for twenty-five years? Why didn't he come find me? Why didn't he tell me he was alive?" She turned a burning gaze on Luke. "I've spent my whole damned life believing I was responsible for his death. Do you have any idea how much . . . how much . . . ?"

"Trauma . . . ?" Luke supplied.

The memory of his sister's suicide and the guilt he'd self-inflicted over not seeing her troubles took the heat out of Keira's anger. They'd both suffered in such similar ways over the course of their lives. How could she turn out so screwed up and he turn out so . . . damn perfect?

"Hardly perfect." He shot her a quirky grin. "I'm pretty sure you were screaming about that yesterday at the airport. And I had a complete *Leave It to Beaver* childhood. Don't keep beating yourself up over things you can't control."

"I was not screaming. I don't scream."

Luke laughed, low and throaty, rubbed a hand over his mouth, and slid a hot look her way. "Uh, yeah, baby. You do."

"Shut up." Heat infused her face. She smacked his arm. "And she said he worked for them. Does that mean he's involved in all this? That he knows what I—what we've—gone through, yet *allowed* it?"

"She also said his 'usefulness is coming to an end' and talked about 'releasing him' or 'terminating him.' Mateo told us his father was 'trying to get free.' That doesn't sound like employment to me. It sounds like incarceration. Consider the source." He pushed the photo toward her. "Wouldn't you rather trust your own information?"

She looked at the picture of her brother, alive and well. Pain swelled in her chest until she was sure she would crack. She needed a break before she tried to read that photo again.

"I need to call Angus." She reached for his phone on the dash. "Can I use your phone?"

He nodded and she dialed her boss's cell.

"Special Agent West," he answered.

His familiar voice lit off fireworks of emotion. She really

liked Angus. Enjoyed working with and for him. And the thought that he was one of *them* turned her inside out.

"Hey, Angus—" She cleared her throat, trying to sound . . . normal, although she didn't know what normal was anymore. "It's Keira."

An extended silence followed. Sickness rolled in her belly as she tried to hold on to denial.

"Well." His voice was tight. Curt. "You sure made a mess of things, didn't you?"

Ah, damn.

Disillusionment stung deep.

"Sir?" She'd play dumb as far as it would take her.

"That whole fiasco with Tony."

"I'm . . . not clear . . ."

"It really doesn't matter now. It's over." His voice lightened just enough to confuse Keira. "Call me an overprotective father figure, but you could do so much better."

"Um . . . thank you. I think."

"You can thank me by telling me you're not resigning."

"Re—? *What?*"

"Tony I was happy to get rid of, but you're going to have to come in and look me in the eye—"

"Tony *Esposito?*" she clarified.

"Do you know of another Tony in this office?"

She couldn't get her mind to fit the pieces together. "I'm sorry, sir, I'm confused. Are you saying Tony resigned? By letter? When?"

"It came by courier today. I thought you would know," he drawled, "considering one of the reasons he cited was a failed relationship with you, which he acknowledged was inappropriate behavior considering *it's against protocol.*"

The last words were nearly yelled across the line. Keira winced and pulled the phone from her ear. Interdepartmental relationships were a big no-no. But since she hadn't been in a relationship with Tony and since dead men couldn't write resignation letters, this had to be DARPA's attempt at undermining her position with the FBI. Which was, ironically, a huge relief, because it meant Angus *wasn't* one of them.

"Uh, sir. That . . . if I can be candid . . . is horse shit. Tony and I were never involved." She felt like a broken record. How many times would she have to deny this relationship? "And I don't have any intentions of . . ."

I'd be very happy with one. Boy or girl. Now or later.

Oh, shit.

Her two worlds collided. Again.

"Keira?"

"Yeah. So, I was calling to ask for a few days off." The faster she could get off this subject, the better. "I'm still pretty sore from the rescue."

"Sure." He sounded a little bewildered now. "But you're coming back, right?"

She hesitated. Struggled. Then finally answered, "Of course. I'll call you in a few days."

Luke held his tongue as he guided the SUV through the gates to Teague and Alyssa's property, pulled open by the same two fatigue-clad, subgun-toting men he'd jogged by that morning on his way out.

His stomach burned as images of Keira's childhood swirled in his head. Every time she opened her mouth to talk about her past, something shocking fell out. It was no wonder the hell she'd lived through—so much darker than he'd imagined—had instilled a fear of motherhood, tainted her view of family, left her untrusting and guarded.

Keira had gone quiet since she'd ended her conversation with West. Luckily, it didn't sound like he was in on the conspiracy, but that hadn't improved Keira's mood.

Over the last five minutes of their drive, she'd been concentrating on the photo. At least that's what she appeared to

be doing. His psychic connection to her must have intensified over the days they'd been together, because he could
sense the dark shield she'd erected. And if he asked her
whether she was okay one more time, she'd deck him.
She'd *projected* that very warning. After that, she'd stopped
projecting altogether. Put up a goddamned mental
wall. The sweet, warm woman he'd made love to such a
short time ago had been replaced with that stone-hard warrior.

Her hand pulled on the door handle before he'd even
stopped the car. He shoved the SUV into park and grabbed
her arm before she could bolt.

"Baby . . ." He waited until she looked at him, and the
hollow pain in her eyes sparked an anxiety he thought he'd
banished in the bedroom. *Patience. Curb the fear. Don't push.
Don't crowd.* "Can you talk to me?"

"Not . . . now." Her eyes darted away. She pulled away
from his touch. "I'm . . . I'm sorry. I need some space."

Keira climbed from the car and strode toward the front
door while Luke turned off the engine and sat there with a
knife in his ribs.

"Space?" he rasped in the empty car. *"Space?"*

The concept of space when they'd been as close as two
people could be just an hour ago struck him as absurd.
Then the nagging hurt that he'd been the only one to pro-
fess love in that bedroom returned. Yes, he knew, deep in
his heart, she loved him. Yes, he'd felt it. But it would have
been nice to hear the words from her mouth. As hot as it
was to hear her ask for more, deeper, harder, right now he'd
have preferred those *other* three little words. And this space
bullshit only reinforced his lingering insecurities.

Patience, he told himself as he stepped into the house. He
had to be patient and understanding and supportive. She
was at one of the hardest crossroads of her life, and he had
to be all the things he hadn't been when she'd needed him

at another crossroads. When he'd been blinded by what *he* had needed so desperately that he'd closed his fist too hard, and she'd slipped right from his grasp.

He wouldn't let this go bad again. He wouldn't.

As he crossed the threshold and shut the front door behind him, a familiar male voice sounded in the living area. Kai. "What the hell happened to you?"

"Crap," another voice followed. Nearly as familiar as his own. Seth. The man who'd shared custody of Kat while Teague had been in prison. "Why didn't you call us sooner?"

Alyssa already had both of them taming their normally far more colorful language.

"You didn't give us much of a chance," Teague said. "Everything's been happening so damn fast."

"That's the way they work," Seth said. "Faster than you can think. That's why they're still calling the fu—shots."

"I'm fine." Keira was in Kai's arms when Luke turned the corner.

"Whoa." Kai released Keira and stepped back, hands up, gaze flipping between her face and Luke's. "There is one hell of a lot of sexual tension cluttering up this room right now." He dropped his hands, pulled at the neck of his tee, and grinned at Luke. "Is it getting hot in here?"

"Shut the hell up, man." Luke joined the group and shook Kai's hand. "You have to run around in the shower to get wet? When are you gonna gain some weight?"

Their teammate hadn't aged a damn day since Luke had last seen him a year before when he'd come to visit, but his dark hair was still too long, his once muscular body still too thin. Kai was still struggling with the aftermath of the fire—as it seemed they all were in their own way.

Luke reached over to Seth and shook his hand. He had aged. But not in physical years. Since his wife, Tara, had been shoved off that psychological edge by the bastards at DARPA, had murdered Teague's girlfriend, and helped frame him for the crime, Seth had aged in years of the soul. It showed in his hollowed eyes.

"I've gained ten pounds." Kai flexed his bicep, which was pure muscle, since he didn't have an ounce of fat on him. "Can't you tell? Been working out. Drinking protein shakes." He pointed at Keira, who sported a dim smile listening to their conversation. "Now that little girl doesn't look so good."

She walked to the kitchen counter where Seth stood to hug him, then darted a look around the living room. "Where's Mateo?"

"In Kat's room," Alyssa said from where she'd curled into one corner of the sofa. "One of Mitch's guys is in there with them. They're fine."

One of Mitch's guys. Must have pulled in more Special Forces contacts. Which was not a good sign.

But Keira didn't listen. She headed toward the back of the house where the bedrooms were, with that nervous I-have-to-see-him-for-myself look. Luke cut her off and took her arm gently.

"Don't get him riled up," he said in an undertone he hoped only Keira heard. "He'll sense your nerves."

Luke tuned into the heat of her skin beneath his hand, the electric waves between them. But he heard nothing. Yep, she'd shut him out.

Patience. Curb the fear.

"I'm just going to peek." She deliberately stepped out of reach.

Luke clenched his teeth and waited.

Like an overprotective mother hen, she peered around the doorjamb and made a little finger wave. By the lack of Mateo's voice flowering in his typical *"Thia,"* Luke knew she'd gestured to whatever bodyguard hovered, unnoticed by the kids.

She backed away from the door and passed Luke with a

flick of her eyes and a brief press of her hand to his chest. Sweet. Thoughtful. Loving. A silent gesture of appreciation and acknowledgment. Apology.

Before she could pass, he grabbed her hand, closed his eyes, and pressed her palm to his mouth. She didn't pull away. As his lips lingered against her warm skin, the tips of her fingers brushed his cheek. And when he opened his eyes, he didn't have to read minds to translate the love and regret in her heart. The same look she'd given him the day she'd come to the house to say good-bye before she'd left for the academy.

He lowered her hand, but held on. *I can't lose you now.* "Please don't shut me out."

A film shadowed the blue of her eyes. "I'm trying."

He followed her into the living room, where everyone had gone quiet and every pair of eyes had been watching their interaction.

Teague's brows tugged in a frown, his eyes scanning Keira. "That's not what you were wearing—"

Keira stopped in her path and pointed at him. "Don't."

Teague smirked. "Is his head out of his ass?"

"His is," she muttered, and trudged across the room, looking about ready to punch a wall. "Mine's now screwed."

"Mitch," she said, turning on him as if she were about to close her hands around someone's neck and shake. "What about those things in Mateo's head? Are they going to hurt him? Can we get them out?"

"I turned the medical stuff over to Alyssa, but I did find out that these puppies"—he pointed to the coffee table, where the chip sat still wrapped in foil—"were produced at Millennium Manufacturing. They make big noise about being a private company—"

"But everyone knows they're a government contractor," Kai finished. "And I'll give you one guess who used to be their CEO before she went back into public service."

"Dargan," Luke said.

"Bingo." Kai made a gun with his fingers and shot at Luke. "Double or nothing if you can tell me who still owns big, big stock numbers in M & M. Here's a hint—it's not Dargan."

The room went silent. Eyes skipped around. Finally, Mitch said, "Our friend, Senator Schaeffer."

Luke scraped fingers across his scalp. "This is the kind of sh—stuff that makes people go postal."

"I'm still tracking down the developer," Mitch said.

"What about Mateo?" Keira asked, turning a sharp focus on Alyssa.

"I contacted a friend from medical school who went into neurology and now specializes in the treatment of spinal cord defects and injuries." Alyssa balanced a sheaf of papers on her curled-up legs. "He doesn't believe they can be manipulated without the control center. That chip we took out of his neck."

Keira's dark brows raised. "Believe? I can't trust Mateo's health on a belief. How can we get them out?"

Alyssa removed the reading glasses resting low on her nose. "We can't. Not without risking a lot more of his health than is at risk by leaving them in. The brain is an incredibly complex structure. As underdiscovered as the universe. There are areas that could be irreparably damaged.

"It would require extensive surgery, which always comes with incredibly high risks. It would require a specialist, which I don't even know exists beyond the person who put these in. All of Rostov's research has been confiscated or torched, so we'll never even know if that person is still alive. It's not at all feasible to take them out."

With each statement Keira's shoulders crawled closer to her ears. "We can't just leave them in there."

"Think of it as a bullet too near the spinal column for surgery. Didn't that happen to one of your colleagues?"

Keira rubbed her temple. "Yes, but—"

"And isn't he still fully functional? Healthy? Normal?"

"Yes, but—"

"But what?" Alyssa's doctor voice geared up. Firm, no-nonsense, I've-had-enough-of-your-bullshit. "Would you rather see Mateo as a vegetable, Keira, for your own peace of mind?"

"Of course not." She dropped her hands and started pacing. "That's a stupid thing to say."

"Seems like the only thing that gets your head back on straight."

Luke intervened before the two strongest women he'd ever known got into a blowout he knew neither of them wanted and both would regret. "We're pretty sure he's her nephew."

All eyes turned toward Luke. "Mateo," he clarified, waving a hand toward the room where the kids played. "Just like he told us. Her brother's son."

"We thought he might be." Alyssa uncurled from the sofa and sat up, her attention returning to Keira. "Mitch followed Cash's path until three years ago, when he seemed to disappear. And he *was* stationed in Greece for several years. We assumed he . . ."

"He's not dead." Keira slid Cash's photo from the back pocket of her jeans and walked it over to Alyssa, who cast a disapproving glance at Mitch as she took it.

"Hey—" Mitch held up both hands in a surrendering gesture. "I've had, what, fifteen minutes to look into his background? Give me a break."

Alyssa took the photo and pulled Keira onto the sofa next to her. "What's going on?"

Keira propped her elbows on her knees. "The brother I thought was dead is alive and either working for or imprisoned by the same spies who make us live looking over our shoulders. I've probably got a nephew I didn't know existed who has been used as a science experiment. And I can barely talk to him because he only speaks Greek." She pushed from the sofa to pace again. "I don't know what the hell is going on."

Alyssa looked at the photo in her hand with a frown. Her brows shot up. "Wow. You two look a lot alike."

Seth pushed off the kitchen island and held his hand out. "Let me see. Why aren't you reading it?"

"I've tried. I'm getting . . ." Keira cut an angry glance at Luke. "Interference."

Teague snorted a laugh.

Kai sent an assessing look between them. "You two . . . back together?"

"Yes," Luke said.

"No," Keira said at the same time.

What the . . . ?

"*Excuse* me?" He hooked his thumb toward the front door, which also happened to be the direction of his house. "After—"

"Maybe. God"—she pressed both hands to her temples and closed her eyes—"I don't know."

Damn. That hurt. "Sorry that topic is so miserable for you to contemplate."

"Luke." She sighed. "It's not. I'm sorry."

She had a headache coming on. He could see it in her eyes. And, yeah, he felt guilty for being petty and sensitive when she had such big things on her mind. But that didn't ease the pain of what felt like the beginnings of another change of her heart.

SEVENTEEN

Keira couldn't look at Luke. Her guts were already shredded. She'd gone from the most perfect morning to the most horrendous afternoon, and she knew she wasn't processing well.

She'd kept Luke's thoughts out for the most part, but hadn't lied about getting interference on the photo. Not exactly. She'd been tormented by ugly memories from her childhood—the emotional abuse, the drunken beatings, the fire, and hadn't been able to get anything directly from Cash.

The news about her brother and Mateo hit her like the explosion at the ranch. That, along with her memories from the past and Luke's angry reaction to them, had her seriously second-guessing this whole reunion.

Had she really thought she could give him that family he wanted?

She'd jumped the gun. Been so caught up in her love for him, his overwhelming confidence, she'd thought . . . *maybe.* That had been so unfair of her. To offer him hope of the one thing he wanted most only to yank it away. Worse than unfair, it had been cruel. Selfish. A perfect example of why she shouldn't be a mother. And the thought of someone hurting *their baby* the way Mateo had been hurt, the way her brother had been hurt . . .

Her throat closed with terror.

"Keira?" Alyssa was beside her, saying something, but she sounded like she was deep underground. "Keira, look at me. What's wrong?"

She opened her mouth, but couldn't speak. Because she couldn't breathe.

Luke clasped her face in both hands. She automatically dug her fingers into his forearms. He met her eyes and held them. His so deep blue, so confident, so focused.

"Breathe," he ordered, but in a voice filled with supreme calm. His hands tightened on her face. "You're okay. You're safe. Just *breathe.*"

He gave her head a little shake, cracking the wall of panic. Her throat opened, scraped in air.

"There you go." His hands loosened, but he didn't let go. "Everything's going to be okay. I'm here. You're safe."

As air fed her brain, the panic released its grip and her vision cleared. Adrenaline receded, leaving her shaky and sweating and cold.

"Okay." Luke slid both arms around her shoulders and pulled her close. "It's over. You're good now."

Keira curled into Luke's warmth. She pressed her face against the soft cotton of his shirt, the supple muscle beneath, and took a long deep breath of him. Instant relief.

"Since when does she have panic attacks?" Alyssa asked from nearby.

"The fire," Luke said, now stroking her hair. "Since that goddamned warehouse fire."

She squeezed her eyes tight. Gratitude washed over her. He was protecting her from the embarrassment of her childhood. Though this was new, there was no earthy scent nearby. God, she hoped this was a fluke. She didn't need another problematic issue.

Something touched her leg. Heat shot up her thigh, wound around her lower back, setting it on fire. Warmth pervaded her belly, her chest, suffused her limbs. Her chill abated.

"*Thia?*"

"Not now, baby." Alyssa pulled Mateo into her arms. "Where's Kitty-Cat? Kat?" she called down the hall.

"No." Keira turned out of Luke's arms and reached for Mateo. "No, I want him."

The grin that lit Mateo's face burned a bittersweet path through Keira's heart. He reached for her with both arms, and Keira dragged him close. As if he sensed her need, he held tight.

She exhaled, long and slow, and squeezed her eyes against the burn of tears. Her nephew. She had no doubt. This boy was her flesh and blood. Her *family*.

"He'd be in one of these locations." Mitch's voice cut into Keira's relief. She shifted Mateo to a seat in her arms and looked across the room where the men had gathered around the dining room table with a map spread across the surface.

Keira joined the group. A map of the United States had been marked with different-colored dot stickers.

"These are all the testing facilities in the U.S." Kai said. "Red are labs, green—headquarters, yellow—bunkers . . ."

"Freaking A." Seth fisted his hands against the tabletop and leaned into his knuckles. "There are dozens. How are we going to know —?"

"*Baba!*" Mateo leaned toward the table, almost falling out of Keira's arms as he pointed.

Keira set him on his knees, and he crawled across the bottom of the map to plant his finger on a red dot in the middle of the Nevada desert. He looked over his shoulder with excitement bouncing in his eyes and Greek pouring out of his mouth, but the only thing Keira could understand was, "*baba*" as he repeated it.

She darted a look at Mitch. "Get Panos on the phone."

Mitch dialed, spoke to Panos for a moment, then put his cell on speaker. After speaking with Mateo, Panos said, "This is where his father lives. *Baba* is what children call their fathers in Greece."

Keira crossed her arms, trying to repress all the crazy emotions coiling in her chest. "How does he know?"

"He says he can see him. He says"—Panos paused as Mateo spoke again—"He is almost done with his work and he will be leaving soon. He is coming home."

"Home? Where's home?" Keira tried to wrap her mind around Mateo's ability. "Greece? Here?"

"This kid is a remote viewer?" Seth asked, shocked.

Keira shrugged. "We don't know much about his skill or accuracy. Panos," she said, "can you ask him what his father is doing right now?"

Mateo pressed the palm of his hand over the red dot, closing his eyes. Then he spoke and Panos translated.

"He's looking at a map, too."

"A map of what?" Keira asked.

Panos asked the question, then said, "The Castle and the compound. Now, he's putting the map away and he's going to the door of his room and calling through the window with bars."

"This is like twenty freaking questions," Keira said. "Who is he talking to?"

"A guard," Panos said, "who takes him from his room to the lab where he works."

"He *is* a prisoner," Keira said, one part of her shocked, the other relieved. "Can't remote viewers hear, too? What are they saying?

"He doesn't know the language. He can't understand what they're saying." Panos said something to Mateo, then translated his response. "He doesn't understand the concept of prison. Only knows his father was taken there after his mother was killed and the boy sent to the ranch to live."

"But he couldn't have been more than two at that time," Keira said. "How could he know? How could he remember?"

"How can any of us do what we do?" Seth pointed out.

"Motherfucking—" Kai started, then cut himself off. "I can't believe this. We have to get him out of there."

Always the warrior, Kai spoke as if there were no doubt, no alternative.

"I'm going to use another phone." Mitch handed his cell to Keira.

"For what?" she asked.

"To get intel on this location."

"Keira," Luke said. "If he can see by touching that spot, maybe you can hear by touching it."

She handed the phone to Luke and stepped up to the table. Keira reached over the suspected location, closed her eyes, and lowered her hand to touch that spot on the map.

Silence.

She dragged in another breath through her nose, let it out slowly past her lips, moved her fingers over the red sticker, and listened.

With a shake of her head, she opened her eyes. "I'm getting nothing."

Before she pulled away, Mateo's palm covered the back of her hand. An eruption of sound burst in her head. So much at once, Keira jerked her hand back.

"Oh, my God." She curled her fingers into her palm. "That's . . ." *creepy.* "Oh, my God."

"What?" Luke asked, eyes darting between Keira and Mateo. "What happened?"

"When he touched me." She paused, swallowed. "I could hear."

"Then why'd you stop?" Seth asked.

"It just . . . scared me."

"Well, get over it," Kai barked, "and get your hand back on that map."

"Shut up," she snarled back. "You live with voices in your head, then try telling me to get over it."

But she returned her hand to the map, took Mateo's, and placed it on top of hers.

She didn't even need to concentrate. Sounds spilled through her head like water through an open faucet. And they kept coming.

"There's so much. I can't make anything out."

"Focus," Luke said. "Channel them into groups, then threads."

"Since when did you become an expert on clairaudience?" she said. "I couldn't even get you to talk about it for more than two minutes before I left."

"I studied up." His blue eyes pierced hers. "*Some* of us learn from our mistakes."

Ouch.

Channel. Fine, she'd channel him right out of her mind.

Keira closed her eyes and started separating like sounds into groups, then homing in on one group at a time. "Sounds echo, as if inside a large, industrial building. Concrete. Brick, maybe. The clop of boots on a hard, solid surface. A sliding or scraping sound, a loud click. Metal maybe."

"Cell door," Teague said, his voice somber. "He's in a cell. Concrete. Echoes. Boots. I would know."

"Panos," Keira said. "Can you ask Mateo about his father's location, his surroundings, without giving him the idea that it's a prison?"

Panos spoke to Mateo, who nodded and replied.

"The boy called it a jail on his own. I just asked what kind of building it was. A jail that looks like a castle."

Keira's body temperature heated and kept rising. "This is unbelievable. Whatever usefulness Cash had for them is over, so they just dump him and grab another. Nothing matters to them but the end result. They don't care how they get there, who they use, who they hurt, who they kill."

"We know why they want Mateo," Luke said, "but you and Mateo gained your abilities through chemical exposure. It's not like you were born with them. What would they want with Cash?"

"Chemistry." Mitch wandered out of the office, eyes on a handful of papers. "Just got another faxed report from my buddy at Langley."

Keira lifted her hand from the map. "You have a friend at Langley? Who is it?"

"Yeah, baby. Hate to tell you, but you're not the only Fed in my back pocket." His hazel eyes darted up, his mouth twisted in a sexy grin. "But I'd rather have you in my front pocket, so if you want to move, just say the word."

"Stop." She wasn't in the mood. "What about Cash?"

"He's a chem-head. When he went into the army, they saw a diamond in the rough, trained him in chemistry, then in covert ops, then put him in a lab where he did research. Biological weapons, nuclear fission. Way under-the-radar-classified shit." He turned a page and let out a low whistle from between his teeth. "Boy was a genius. IQ off the charts." One eyebrow dipped as he looked at Keira again. "What happened to you?"

"You're such an ass."

"But I'm a lovable ass."

"That's debatable." Keira refocused on the map. She darted a look at Mateo. "Ready to try again?"

She wasn't sure if he understood or if he was merely trying to please, but when Keira placed her hand on the map, he pressed his over the top.

Got the explosive putty out of the lab. Just told Mario I felt sick, was going to puke, and they didn't search me.

A man's voice. According to Mateo, her brother's voice. But it didn't sound familiar.

Study that map I gave you. I've marked off three different routes and numbered them. This was another voice. Deeper. Darker. Far more languid than the first man's. *It's simple, Sci-Fi, number one is your first choice. You hit a snag, move on to number two. Think you can handle it?*

"Someone's with him." Keira's eyes popped open and searched for the phone as if she were looking at a person. "Panos, ask Mateo who's with him."

"The boy says it's his father's neighbor," Panos said. "His name is Q."

"What kind of name is Q?" Seth mumbled.

"What can Mateo tell us about him?" Keira asked.

"Q is his father's friend." Panos and Mateo exchanged dialogue. "Q has always been there, since his father has been there. Sometimes he goes away and his father is very lonely."

"Is Q a prisoner or a guard?" Keira asked.

"A prisoner," Panos said.

"How many do they have?" Kai raged. "Mitch, what do you have on this place? Let's start planning the breach. I've got enough equipment and ammo in the plane to blow Norway into the Indian Ocean."

"Consulting, my ass." Seth crossed his arms. "Who the hell are you working for, Kai? A Colombian cartel?"

"The arms are mine. Call me a collector."

"Your boss know you're transporting guns and ammo in his jet?"

"Get off my ass. You won't be so judgmental when you've got Kevlar covering your chest."

"Guys," Alyssa murmured. "Be quiet. Let her work."

Panos and Mateo maintained a discussion separate from Kai and Seth. Panos said, "Those are the only two Mateo has seen, but the Castle is very big. He only sees the area where his father lives and the lab where he works."

Keira tuned into the voices again.

I want you to come with me, Cash said. *I'll come back after I blow the holding cell.*

I'm telling you, I can't make that run. I'll just bring you down. Now listen. Timing is everything. When you break tonight, you have to do it at the hour mark so you hit the change of the guard.

I got it. Cash again. *Come on, Q. I'll carry you if I have to. I can't just leave you in this hellhole.*

"They're planning an escape." Keira lifted her shaking hand from the map. "Tonight."

"Yeah?" Mitch looked up from his paperwork. "Good. 'Cause without help from the inside, this motherfucker would be nearly impossible to penetrate. Teague, grab me a pen. Keira, tell me everything you hear. Those two don't know it yet, but they're going to help us plot their rescue."

Jocelyn strode down the cement corridor, ceilings soaring above her like one of those cavernous museums Jason had dragged her to on their last trip to Rome.

"This is such bullshit," she muttered out loud only because she knew it would be drowned by the *clomp-clomp-clomp* of the boots worn by the five guards accompanying her to Cash's cell. "Why can't we control one damn man or one damn team of firefighters when we can annihilate entire Islamic paramilitary regimes?"

They turned another corner, faced another long, gray corridor. She was so damn over all this bullshit. She wanted all of them dead and gone.

The lead guard, Domino, paused at the cell door, wrapped one hand around the dull silver rungs of the window at eye level, beyond which everything was black, and pulled a key from his noisy key ring with the other.

"O'Shay," he called. "You've got company."

A tired groan sounded from the dark depths of the cell. "It's about time."

The click of the lock and scrape of metal bounced off the

walls, echoed into the heights. A shiver vibrated over Jocelyn's shoulders. She clenched her fists and entered the cell. With a flick of the wall switch, the five-star-hotel-worthy accommodations were flooded with fluorescence.

"Does it take all military ops this long to get their act together?" Cash rolled to a sitting position, covering his eyes with his hand. He wore a pair of khaki pants and a white button-down, even still had on his canvas cross-trainers. "Our country must be in a shit storm of trouble since I was last out there."

"Sleeping in your clothes is becoming a habit, I see." Jocelyn had no patience left to dance around this man. The *clip-clip-clip* of her heels was silenced as she traversed the thick, vibrant area rug in the sleeping area. She paused only feet away.

"I'm ready to go." When he uncovered his eyes, he tilted his head up, a strange expression on his face. "Been ready to go. Of course I'm dressed."

What was she missing? "And where would you be going, Cash?"

"Uh, somewhere the fuck out of here." He pushed to his feet, broadened his shoulders, creating a formidable front. "We had a deal. I create your material, you give me a new life. My son, my sister, included." His face hardened, teeth clenched as he pointed a rigid finger in her face. "If you are fucking with me, so help me God—"

"There is no material, because a key part of the lab report is missing. That's why I'm here. I want it back."

"What part?"

"The Method pages. You know damn well we can't do anything without those."

"Which is why I turned them in with the rest of my report. Have you talked to Abrute? I gave my report mere hours ago. Intact. If anything is missing, that's your problem. I held up my end of the bargain."

"Unfortunately, it *is* your problem. Because if those Method pages don't materialize, you'll have to repeat the experiment and rewrite the report."

"That will take weeks." He advanced, his eyes wide with an edge of insanity she'd seen on the battlefield. The guards stepped in and gripped both his arms, holding him back. "You fucking bitch. I knew you were full of shit. You never planned on coming through. Never planned on letting me out."

"Yes, Cash, I did. I still do. But I have to have a full report before that happens. So if you have that Method section in here somewhere, why don't you just tell me now and we can be done."

"I told you where it is. If it's missing, you should be tracking down Abrute. He's probably out selling it to the Iraqis right now."

"We have soldiers on their way to his house. In the meantime, I guess we'll have to do this the hard way. Domino," she said to the guard behind her. "Move Mr. O'Shay to holding and search this room. Top to bottom. Take all the time you need. If I find them in here, Cash, your kid and your sister are dead."

"And when you find Abrute is a mole, you'd better plan on doubling the money you're giving me to live on."

As the guards dragged Cash through the cell doorway, Jocelyn called, "Oh, and Cash. The last time I was here, you took my necklace when you attacked me. I want that back. Where is it?"

He stared back with those icy blue eyes rimmed in lashes as black as his hair. "I don't know what the hell you're talking about."

"If I find it in here, you won't get a dime to live on outside. Want to change your answer?"

"No."

Jocelyn fumed with a complete sense of impotence.

"When you're done in here, Domino," she said, watching for Cash's reaction, "secure Q and search his room, too. If you don't find anything there, go back to the lab and start again."

"Yes, ma'am."

"I'll be in the command center," she said. "Call me immediately if you find something."

"Yes, ma'am."

Just before they dragged Cash down the hall, his expression shifted. And though his mouth didn't curl in a smile, Jocelyn couldn't shake the sense that Cash was secretly laughing.

Luke stood off to the side of one of the pickups that had been left for them at the private airstrip just west of the Alamo Landing Field deep in the Nevada desert near Area 51. He watched Keira shiver in the night air as Kai rummaged through a huge plastic storage container holding a couple dozen Kevlar vests. The rest of their team, consisting of Teague, Seth, and Mitch, were already wearing desert fatigues, bulletproof vests, and helmets with night vision gear attached. Each carried an M14 and had a Glock strapped to their thigh.

"I don't know if I have one small enough to fit you," Kai grumbled.

"Find one," Luke ordered across the dark. "Make something work, or she stays here."

"Don't start, Ransom," Keira said. "You haven't been my boss for years now."

The other men chuckled. It didn't bother Luke. He was just relieved he'd gotten her to say more than two words to him. She'd been focused during the planning phase, sullen during their flight here. And while she stayed shut off from him psychically, he didn't need to read her mind to know she was as twisted as he'd ever seen her.

"Here, try this one." Kai pulled a vest from the very bottom of the pile and slipped it over her black, long-sleeve shirt, cinching the flank straps. "Yeah. That'll work."

Luke would be the judge of that. Keira slid her arms into her fatigue jacket and buttoned it against the desert cold. Plunked her helmet on, fastened and tugged the tab beneath her chin, and picked up her subgun. When she wandered over to the group, Mitch handed her a Bluetooth, which she positioned in her right ear, one that would patch them into the phone call with Alyssa shortly.

While the group studied the Castle floor plan, Luke pulled Keira aside under the pretext of checking her vest.

"Luke, it's fine."

"You whine as well as Kat." He tugged on the right strap, then the left.

"Don't. I can't breathe."

"You won't be able to breathe if a bullet gets past this Kevlar, either."

She indulged his need to fuss with the vest a moment longer.

He grabbed the curve just below her neck and held. "Talk to me."

"Luke." She sighed in exasperation.

"I think I've been plenty patient the last few hours."

Irritated blue eyes lifted to his. "This isn't the time—"

"Keira." He jerked on the vest, just enough to convey his seriousness. "You can't go into this distracted. I can't go into this worrying about what you're holding back. What happened in that head of yours between the time you left my bed and the time we got to Teague and Alyssa's house?"

Her gaze darted into the darkness over his shoulder. She huffed, shifted her stance, looked toward the team before meeting his eyes again with an apology that sent his stomach dropping toward rock bottom. "I realized I couldn't . . . I can't . . ."

"Just say it. Can't what?"

"I can't . . . do this. You, me. Us. The whole family thing. I mean, part of me wants to . . . with you. *For* you. But . . ." Pain and guilt sparked in her eyes. She waved an angry hand toward the Castle compound shining in the distance. "They're everywhere. Crawling into every crevice of our lives, trying to rip it apart.

"Every family I've ever had has been taken from me," she said. "Cash. Every foster home. The hazmat team. My life has been a pattern of failures. Time after time after time, ugliness has crept in, violence has followed, my family is crushed, and I'm left alone, more damaged than I was to begin with."

He searched her eyes, hoping for signs of a panic attack. Then he could tell himself she didn't mean what she was saying. But her gaze was clear, sharp, determined. Fierce.

"Keira . . . honey . . ." Jesus, how did he combat what she was saying? His mind wasn't functioning with the panic welling up inside him. All he knew was that she was closing him out. "I understand what you're saying. I know this seems overwhelming now, but you're getting ahead of yourself—"

"No. I'm not." She backed away with a look that he knew meant business. "I love you, Luke. More than anything or anyone. I've always loved you, *will* always love you. But what you haven't learned, what I've known my whole life, is that love isn't always enough. And I can't survive losing another family." She sniffled, wiped her nose with her sleeve. "I just *can't*."

She made the final jerk out of his grasp with tears shining on her cheeks. Luke stood frozen as she walked toward the team, swiping at the wetness.

"Come on," she yelled as she headed into the dark, tossing her M14 over her shoulder. "Let's get this damn thing over with. And there's obviously no cover here, boys, so no dragging your asses."

The team hesitated, their heads swinging from Keira's disappearing form to Luke. They quickly folded their maps and picked up their equipment packs.

"Too early to be sniping at us, boss—" Kai fell in behind her. "Bet your men love you when you're in a mood."

Seth followed.

"Come on, bud. Let's go." Teague hiked his pack higher on his back and gestured to Luke. "Give her some time. She's pretty freaked out right now."

No. She wasn't freaked out. He knew that look of conviction in her eyes.

I just can't.

He understood the conviction too well. For Keira, living with the fear of losing the family she loved would be more painful than living the rest of her life alone.

EIGHTEEN

Keira flipped the night vision goggles over her eyes, then set out at a good clip through the desert terrain. Shrubs scraped the tops of her boots as she tried to focus on what lay ahead instead of what she'd just left behind. Tried to block the pain rolling off Luke in rivulets. It was for the best. Maybe, in time, he could find someone else. Someone who could give him the family he craved, without all the risks Keira brought to the table, without all the problems, the drama, the headaches, the heartache.

She had to believe that. It was the only way she'd make it through the night.

She activated the microphone on her Bluetooth. "Alyssa? Are you there?"

A crackle came over her earpiece, then Alyssa's voice with the kids playing in the background. "I'm here. Are you at the ridge already? It's too early."

"No, we're on our way." Keira hated leaving her alone with the kids. Alyssa wasn't really alone, of course, but that didn't seem to do much for Keira's anxiety. "Everything okay?"

"My Lord, you're worse than Teague. Everything is as fine as it was when you checked eight minutes ago. And, yes, I have Panos on the other line. And yes, all *four* Special

Ops guys are still here, two inside and two outside. This is such overkill. Can you hear me, Teague? Overkill."

A click came over the line, then Teague's voice. "Nothing's too good for my baby."

"Be careful," she said. "And don't come on again until you're at the ridge. I've got kids to entertain."

The grade they trudged up helped train Keira's mind on the moment. Only it also drew attention to her body and all the aches Luke had left after an ambitious morning of amazing sex.

No, not sex. So much more than sex. Even more than making love. Their time together had been about mending damaged hearts, soothing pained souls. And whispered promises.

Promises she'd broken.

Again.

Already.

He deserved so much more.

She pushed harder. Moved faster. Wiped sweat off her temple.

"Hey, boss," Kai called from behind. Too far behind.

She stopped, swiveled, and squinted into the dark.

"You jogging this mountain or what?" He caught up with her, his chest heaving beneath his fatigue jacket. "You're going to kill Foster."

"Speak for yourself, Ryder." Mitch stopped and planted his hands on his knees. "But can we . . . save some energy for the . . . fucking rescue, please?"

Keira hadn't realized how hard she'd been pushing, and she had to admit, now that she'd stopped, she felt a little light-headed and nauseous herself.

Seth paused alongside Kai and hit his arm. "Remember her as a rookie? She could barely get up a ladder with just her turnouts on."

"Couldn't throw a ladder worth shit, either," Kai said. "Barely passed the freaking academy."

"Shut up." She stretched out the stitch in her side. "I beat your time on hose lays."

"Because I had a busted ankle."

"Right. Stick to that story."

Teague and Luke brought up the rear, and Keira scanned Luke's face, his gait, his body language, for any signs of physical distress. Couldn't detect any.

"Mitch is right," Teague said. "We're moving too fast. If we get there too soon, we're not going to mesh with their plans."

Keira nodded, let everyone take a swig of water, and rested another minute before heading toward the southwest ridge. She tried not to notice how unusually quiet Luke was. But it didn't work. Guilt gnawed. She rationalized it away as she forced her body to work.

Within ten yards something vibrated beneath her feet. Trembled up her legs. She stopped, hands out to balance. The guys stopped right behind her.

"Did anyone feel that?"

"Feel what?" Kai asked.

She canvassed the dark. Nothing but scraggly shrubs and a lone Joshua tree fifty yards away leaning into the side of the mountain they were climbing. "Maybe just an earthqu—"

Then she heard it. The sound vibrated in her head with an almost slow-motion echo.

"Chopper," she called. "Hit the dirt."

She fell, face-first, breaking her fall with her palms, and lay perfectly still. Within a second, the distant *whap-whap-whap* of a helicopter's blades sliced the air.

Keira turned her head just enough to see the bird, a blurred black spot in the midnight sky. Searchlights swept the ground. *Shit.* She held her breath as the flood passed right in front of her nose and seared her eyes.

"Comanche," Kai said in the wake of the chopper's pass. "Infrared comes standard. They might have already seen us. We'd better break for the ridge."

Keira was on her feet, digging into the sandy soil with the toes of her boots, forcing her quads to pump. She didn't slow until she'd hit the hard-packed wall of the ridge just below the Castle's boundary. She broke the momentum with her hands and swung around to search for her men. They all hit the wall, full speed, just as she had.

They crouched at the base of the wall. Silence filled the air. Everyone waiting for whatever surprise came next.

She turned a glare on Mitch. "Choppers? Why the fuck didn't we know about chopper surveillance?"

"So . . . ungrateful . . ." he panted. "I never . . . said my . . . sources were perfect."

She dropped her head. Wiped at the sweat again. How much of their other intel was bogus? How many other surprises would there be?

"Then I guess the faster we're in and out, the better." She glanced at the thirty-foot cliff they had to traverse to reach the entry point to the compound. "Last leg, guys. Ready for some mountain climbing?"

Keira searched the dark sky once more before scaling the cliffside. She used brush roots and rocks as leverage, testing each for stability before trusting it with her weight. Sand slipped beneath her fingers and the soles of her shoes, making the climb slow, and she worried about the men behind her, all significantly larger. And with her own ribs aching like stab wounds, she worried about Luke's trek up the wall as well.

At the top, she crouched with her weapon sweeping the terrain. Movement in the brush caught her eye. Her finger tensed on the trigger. A jackrabbit hopped around a clump of brush and disappeared. She didn't let herself relax until the scrape of boots and the spill of sand behind her ceased and all her men were at her side, including Luke, who continued to perform like a true hero.

Kai tapped into the phone. "Lys, we're here."

"Okay." Alyssa came on with a click. "We're all on the line."

"Panos," Keira said as she started toward the estimated five-hundred-foot mark along the chain link electrified fence surrounding the compound. "We're headed toward the hatch. Tell us when we hit it."

Silence filled the line as the six of them skirted shadows along the fence line where the field lights faded into night. The whoosh of their canvas fatigues and packs was nothing but a whisper in the night.

"Ekee pera."

Mateo's voice broke in her ear, followed by Panos's. "There. He says you're right there."

Teague swept a flashlight over the hard-packed dirt and brush that looked exactly like the rest of the desert floor. "They really don't know it's here. That's amazing."

Yes, it was amazing. Mateo's remote viewing had given the team information about the ancient facility that had been built at the original infamous Area 51 as a sister-site prison-slash-lab facility for aliens. Very *X-File*-like with a Habitrail of underground tunnels that hadn't been used in decades. According to Mateo, this entrance led to the southernmost tunnel system running beneath the wing housing his father's cell.

"Don't get excited, Creek," Mitch said. "It's nothing but dirt right now."

"Fucking pessimist," Teague said.

"Teague." Alyssa's familiar reprimand came over the line.

Mitch grinned. Teague shot his brother-in-law a *you-fucker* glare.

Keira barked an order before they killed each other. "Dig."

All the men dropped their packs, pulled out compact shovels, clicked handles into place, and started digging. Keira kept her weapon up, her gaze sweeping for movement, her senses open for choppers, voices, noises. All she got back was silence. But she did pick up on Luke's frustration, which she pushed into the background.

The deep *chunk* of metal on metal rent the air, followed by Teague's voice filled with a told-you-so air. "Not just dirt, Foster. *Pay* dirt."

A steady hum of adrenaline strummed through Keira's veins as she watched the men clear the heavy metal doors. Luke came in with bolt cutters and removed the ancient padlock.

Seth spread his arms. "Clear the area."

Everyone stepped back, and even though they each had their own powers, it was always amazing to watch another member work theirs. Seth, a strong telekinetic, sat back on his heels, laid his hands on his thighs, and closed his eyes.

His muscles strained. Sweat broke out on his face. The metal doors creaked and rumbled as if ghosts were trying to escape. Seth's hands came out, palms down. A glow started at his fingers, spread to his palms, slid halfway up his forearms.

Seth threw his arms overhead. The doors opened and flipped back, clanking to the ground in a puff of dust.

"Shit." Seth pushed to one foot, then the other. Wiped his face with the sleeve of his fatigue. "They're heavy as a truck."

The team gathered around the black cavern and peered in. Silently. But Keira could hear their thoughts. And every one was thinking the same thing.

Fuck me.

★ ★ ★

Cash curled his fingers around the bars on the small window built into the holding cell door and watched Domino hightail it back toward Cash's cell, where other guards were tearing the contents apart looking for something they'd never find.

He couldn't help the smile that spread across his face or the excitement burning his stomach, but he bit his bottom lip against the trill of laughter that wanted to roll from his chest.

No time for celebration. He had a long way to go.

He dug in his front pockets for the plastic explosive he'd created in the lab and smuggled out over the last week. He dropped to his knees and worked the clay hard in his palms, using the single stream of light spearing the small opening as illumination.

His body heat softened the clumps, and he thinned them, shaped them, and stuffed them around the hinges on one side of the door and around the lock on the other side.

He pulled the lighter he'd lifted off the janitor from his opposite pocket. His hand shook as he peered through the bars again, down the hall. But he relaxed when he found it empty. He turned his back to the door, flicked the lighter once. A spark flashed in the dark, followed by a steady flame.

Releasing the lever, he extinguished the flame and turned back toward the door. He pushed his wrist into the stream of light and checked the time. Soon. Very soon. But not soon enough.

He paced the cell, running over all the scenarios he and Q had lined out. He imagined Mateo closer with each tick of the second hand. Imagined seeing Keira again as a grown woman.

This was it. His last chance. He would make it or he would die trying.

★   ★   ★

Keira pulled the map from her front chest pocket. The other five men crowded around her shoulders as she unfolded it and thought over their plan one more time. She didn't like the idea of splitting up. At all. But she didn't see another option.

"Panos." She glanced at her watch. This was her last chance at communication with Mateo before they went underground. "Where is Cash right now?"

Mateo spoke, followed by Panos's translation. "In a cell, in an area away from his main room. The one you have marked on the map as C-three."

"And Dargan?" she asked.

"The last time Mateo saw her, she was in his father's room arguing with him. The guards had started tearing apart his things. He can't see her now; he can only see his father. He can only see one area at a time."

A dull growl sounded in Mitch's throat. "You people really have severe limitations with these so-called powers, don't you?"

"Lay off the kid," Teague said. "He's freaking five years old. You were probably still wetting the bed at five."

"Stop it," Keira said to the guys, then spoke to Panos again. "Are there guards around Cash now?"

"No," Panos answered. "Not that he can see."

"How far can he see?"

Panos had a short conversation with Mateo. "He's not good with distances. He says he can see to the end of the hallways leading in both directions, and there's no one."

"Not good with distances," Mitch muttered. "Beautiful."

"Shut up, Foster," Teague said.

"We'll stick with the original plan," Keira said. "I'll take Teague and Seth and we'll go for Cash, here." She tapped the map, then moved her finger to the route the others would take. "Kai will take Luke and Mitch to search for Q."

She met Kai's eyes, glowing green in her night vision.

"Don't dick around. If he resists, bail. If anything feels wrong, bail. We don't know anything about him. As far as we know, he could be a decoy, a plant, anything. If Cash tells us he's a legitimate prisoner, we can always come back for him."

"That's appealing," Mitch quipped.

Teague sighed, but it sounded more like a growl. "Foster—"

"I'm glad I put you two on opposite teams."

Keira folded and stuffed the map into her pocket and positioned herself over the tunnel. She let her gaze touch every member of the team—a silent message of connection.

Her eyes met Luke's last. Affection and support and lingering frustration trasversed the space between them. And intimacy. An intimacy from their firefighting days when they'd always connected just before having to separate at a fire scene. So many things said with one look—I love you, be careful, come back safe—she couldn't begin to name them all, but tonight "I'm sorry" was also foremost in her mind.

He looked away long before she was ready to let go.

The combination of her regret and the focus of her mission helped temper the anxiety growing in her chest as she tested the strength of the narrow metal rung leading into the shaft. Teague held both hands to steady her as she put her full weight on one, then another. When they held, she climbed down the ladder. Teague started down next.

The hole, lined with what looked like the same hewn rock as the tunnel at the safe house, was far deeper than she'd expected, and that creepy crawling sensation she'd been able to keep at bay started to slide over her skin. "I feel like I'm climbing into hell."

She used her arms to swing down to the last rung, hung off with one hand so she could tilt her head down and shine her night vision goggles below her, and found the ground.

Thank God.

"About a four-foot drop," she called to the men above.

Keira led the way down the narrow passage to where the stone walls split, creating two hallways. She turned right. Her team followed.

The blackened hallways were bright as daylight and shaded green in her goggles. Keira's gaze darted between the map in her hand and the tunnels ahead, which branched off in various directions every ten or twenty feet.

A left turn. Another left. A right. Straight.

"Crap," Mitch's voice whispered right behind her. "Every hall looks exactly the same."

Yes, it did. A freaking alien maze that tweaked her sense of direction the same way an ocean wave could turn a swimmer upside down. But they were close. She could feel it in an uneasy gnawing at that vulnerable space beneath her ribs.

With her heart throbbing, Keira paused at the next break in the stone wall and peered around the edge.

Clear.

She swung her weapon toward the opposite end of the corridor and scanned the length.

Five cell doorways lay recessed into the rock on the right. Wide slabs of metal with rivet-reinforced straps. A single two-by-two window centered in the top third with pudgy steel rods spaced three inches apart.

She held up her hand and pressed it into a fist, signaling the men to stop and hold position.

Teague and Seth remained behind her. Kai passed by with Mitch in his wake, then Luke. She willed Luke to reach out and squeeze her shoulder, touch her arm, even just slide her a glance. But he didn't. Which was only right. She didn't deserve the effort. Then he was gone, disappearing around another corner.

Keira forced her mind away from the parting by focusing

on Cash. On seeing her brother. On starting a new chapter in her life.

She glanced at her watch and let her eyes follow the second hand as it ticked down the last twenty seconds. When the black line reached the six-second mark, a distant sizzle met her ear and a matching fizz kicked off in her gut. They were in the right place at the right time.

She hoped.

NINETEEN

Luke hardened himself as he stepped in Kai's footprints, the hollow inside him growing in tandem with his distance from Keira.

Kai headed down the final passage toward the cell Mateo had indicated belonged to the mysterious Q. If there was such a man. One of the reasons Luke had wanted to be on this detail had been just that fear—that Q was a decoy. On the other hand, Luke knew Cash was real. He trusted Keira's abilities completely. But Q could be anything from a figment of a child's imagination to the government's idea of a sick manipulation. And he didn't want Keira anywhere near that game. She'd suffered enough.

Besides, having her on the opposite side of a pitch-black compound kept his eyes off her, which would keep his mind off the pain beneath his ribs. If he let himself dwell on the way her tortured look shattered his heart, he very well could end up dead. Which didn't seem like such a bad alternative at the moment.

They came to a corner, the connection of two hallways. Kai put up a fist, and Luke and Mitch stopped behind him. From studying the map, Luke knew the cell that belonged to Q was directly around the corner on the right. Cash's, one cell beyond. The Castle might be expansive, but from Mitch's intel, it seemed most of the space had been converted into labs, employee barracks, offices, and a control room. Only half a dozen cells filled this wing. And Mateo had said only two were occupied.

Kai held the M14 like the former soldier he'd been before becoming a firefighter. Mitch and Luke had chosen to hang their subguns over their backs and stalk with their Glocks.

Kai held up three fingers, two, one, and cocked his wrist in a semi-wave. Swift, sure steps thrust Kai around the corner. Luke followed. And came up short. Mitch stumbled up behind him.

"What the fuck?" Mitch whispered, then peered around Luke and Kai, who were blocking the open door.

Luke's gaze skipped across the mess, the cell's contents strewn all over the floor as if the tiny cement square had been the site of a home invasion.

"Time to bail." Kai took a step in retreat.

Luke let him pass and eased into the space, backing along the wall. A twin-size, wooden-frame bed had been overturned. The thin mattress gutted, the stuffing flat and gray against the charcoal cement floor. One sheet, one blanket lay in a heap. No pillow in sight.

"What happened here?" Luke whispered.

"Doesn't matter." Kai's gaze swept the hallway. "It's creeping me out. Let's go."

Luke tilted his head toward the neighboring cell. "Check the next room. It's supposed to be Cash's."

"But he's not—"

"Just check it," Luke ordered, swinging around to pin Kai with a look. He might be the lead, but that didn't make him the boss. Luke had a lot at stake here, as much as Kai. "See if he or *they* left anything behind." When Kai backed out and disappeared, Luke turned a fierce look on Mitch. "Watch the halls."

For once in his life, Mitch didn't argue.

Luke moved deeper into the cell, looking for clues. Anything to tell him more about Q. More about the guy's life in this hole. More about the people who'd held him here.

Books lay scattered on the concrete. Everything from Shakespeare to Clive Cussler. Toiletries were dispersed over a small tabletop—basic toothbrush, a single-blade shaving razor, a travel-size toothpaste, quarter-size ring of dental floss, bar of soap, and deodorant.

Luke stepped toward the overturned nightstand and kicked at the blankets. A book thudded from the mass. He crouched and picked it up. A Bible.

The book parted with something wedged in the pages. He cradled the spine of the Bible in his free palm and let the book fall open, tilting his night vision goggles to inspect the bookmark.

Shock tripped the regular beat of his heart. He leaned in, squinted at the silver dollar–size piece. One he'd seen before. One he had tucked away at home. One of only seven in existence. At least that he knew of.

"Kai!" The name flew from his mouth as soon as air whipped back into his lungs.

"I'm right here." His teammate appeared at Luke's side in what felt like an instant. "Man, that other cell could have been a room at a rustic Four Seasons. It's tossed, too." His head tilted down, goggles pointed at the book in Luke's hand. "What the . . . ?" The fear shimmering off Kai invaded Luke like a spirit and made him wonder if he'd picked up some of Keira's or Kai's empathic abilities. "How the fuck did that get in here?"

A moment of silence hung between them. Terrified silence.

"What's got you two whacked out?" Mitch came up, looked at the book, and reached for the coin.

Luke snapped the book closed. "Let's talk outside." He stuffed the Bible into the front pocket of his fatigue jacket. "I can't think right now."

Jocelyn had known they'd come, she just hadn't expected these tactics. When Keira hadn't contacted her within two hours of leaving Luke's house, she'd known their team had made other plans. She'd anticipated that, even hoped for it. Definitely planned for it.

The blinking red light on the digital floor plan display meant the facility had been breached, and the facility commander wanted to send his men into the bowels of this mausoleum as badly as Jocelyn did.

She pressed the intercom. "Hold tight, commander."

She leaned back, scanned the wall of security monitors in the Castle's control room, caught between frustration, fear, and excitement.

This was her chance. She almost couldn't believe it had happened the way she'd hoped. There had been so many other ways it could have panned out, but now, she had all the members of that damned team in one place. All except one. But she could deal with Jessica in a completely separate incident. And use those damned kids to get Alyssa Foster-Creek to give up all the dirt her brother had collected that had kept Jocelyn's hands tied for so long. Alyssa would be no problem. The real problems were in this facility right now. Within killing range. And since they had penetrated a highly classified government facility with obvious intentions of sabotage, she could spin this into a homegrown terrorist ring faster than the media could get it out to the public.

If any of Foster's documentation on corrupt political officials somehow leaked, it would be passed off as nothing more than the nonsensical hype of a mentally disturbed anti-American with ties to . . . well, whoever she wanted to give him ties to. Taliban sounded good.

The fact that it had all happened on the edge of Area 51 would only heighten the facility's mysterious reputation and bury the incident that much faster.

The only thing that would make this situation perfect would be finding those Method pages from Cash's successful experiment and getting the key to Jason's safe-deposit box back. But even the key wasn't that important. She had enough information on the bank it came from and enough clout with prestigious judges to get that box open other ways.

But she had to keep her cool and stay one step ahead of the enemy. If this went right, it could be the crowning moment of her career. If it went wrong, it could be the worst moment of her life.

"What's happening?" Jocelyn scanned the monitors, all black except for a few on the bottom row that were different from the others. "Why are most of these screens blank?"

The woman in charge, a burly Tongan by the name of Magna—first or last, Jocelyn didn't know or care—stood beside her, appropriately sober. "They've disabled them."

"How did they know about them?" She pointed a finger at the blinking light in an area of the facility she wasn't familiar with. "How did they know about that section of the compound?"

"I've heard . . . rumors. They have special abilities, don't they? Like Q is developing?"

"Yes, but none that—"

The boy. It must be the kid.

But he only spoke Greek. He couldn't have learned English in three days. Certainly not enough to convey this type of information. Had one of the others read his mind? Had

Keira heard his thoughts? Wouldn't he think in Greek? Or was there some universal language for thought?

Jocelyn pulled out her cell, walked to a private corner of the office, and dialed Owen. When he picked up, she said, "I need you to find out who Foster would use to translate Greek."

An extended moment of hesitation hung on the line. "Any other information you'd like to give me on that?"

"Someone military with Greek ancestry. Someone he's defended in the past. I think the kid is filtering information about the compound to them, but they have to have some way to translate it. When you find whoever it is, silence him."

"Okay," he said. "I'm on it."

"And, Owen?" She waited to make sure he hadn't hung up.

"Yeah?"

"I want to talk to you when this is all over. About what you said the other night. About wanting you. I do."

Another lengthy silence. "Music to my ears, Joce. I'll be waiting."

Jocelyn disconnected with another jumble of excited nerves squeezing her belly. As much as she wanted to send a swarm of guards into that maze of tunnels to hunt the team down, she didn't.

Take your time. Think this through.

"Where is Sergeant Decker?" she asked. "He left half an hour ago."

"The lab manager's home is on the outskirts of the base. He should return any time." Magna maintained a confident, unruffled air. She clasped her hands at her back. "Don't worry, ma'am, cameras or no cameras, we'll catch them. We're setting up a perimeter now, and we've activated all our surveillance choppers."

And look how well those had worked so far. One side of

Jocelyn's mouth crawled upward in a sneer. This woman had no idea who she was dealing with.

In one of the working monitors, a ghostly image grazed the screen, then disappeared. Jocelyn's eyes tracked for additional movement. "What was that?"

"What?" Magna asked, her body stiffening, gaze scanning.

Oh, yeah. Definitely the best.

"There was movement in that camera." Jocelyn pointed. "It's not a normal video; what is it?"

"Thermal sensor, ma'am. They're brand new. Installed last week."

Could there be an end in sight? "Get your commander in here."

The woman pressed a button on the panel. "Sir, Director Dargan would like to see you."

"On my way," a gruff, older male voice returned.

Within thirty seconds a door opened behind Jocelyn, but she didn't turn to look. She just pointed at the screens occasionally flashing rough rainbow-outlined clumps, unable to decipher whether they were the guards or the invaders.

"This," she said. "Where is this? Do you have men in that area of the facility?"

Jocelyn turned her head enough to evaluate the commander's expression. Perplexed. Overweight, uniform ill fitted, hair too long. Disgraceful. She wanted to suggest retirement. Would have, and not in a nice way, but worried by the way he was sweating and running a hand over his thick head of gray hair again and again. She didn't want to derail his thoughts.

"Ah, that's"—his eyes darted to the remaining screens, then back—"C sector and . . . ah, F sector. No ma'am. None of my men are in those areas."

Jocelyn's teeth ground. "Where the hell is Deck—"

The door opened and Sergeant Decker walked in grasping the arm of a man in pajamas, barefooted, hair askew, face terrified.

"Mario Abrute, ma'am," Decker said, clean-cut, serious, professional. Now this was more like it.

"Thank you, Sergeant Decker. I'll make sure your name is in my report."

He nodded, pivoted, and left the room. In the hallway, he set his back to the door, stance wide, at-ease position. That was a fine soldier. The kind of soldier Jocelyn had commanded.

She turned her attention back to the hand-wringing, eye-darting lab manager. "Mr. Abrute, we've had a serious breach of security today."

"Ma'am, I don't . . . know anything about . . . I didn't know . . ."

"I haven't asked you anything yet."

"Y-yes, ma'am."

"Key pieces of Cash O'Shay's successful experiment are missing. It's your job to see that his reports are completed and secured before he leaves the lab."

"I did." His hands flew up, palms out. "I scanned every page into the computer and locked the report in the file cabinet in the lab like I always do. Then I notified the commander that it appeared as if O'Shay's experiment had finally been successful so he could contact you."

"I'm not going to rehash all the details now." Jocelyn didn't give a shit what had happened or how, because all the employees here would be terminated—one way or another—once this mission had been completed. "All I want to know is, how much of his final experiment can you replicate?"

Abrute's mouth shut. His eyes went distant, then returned to Jocelyn with the spark of understanding. "Of course. I was very involved with Cash's experiments. I kept my own notes on his procedures and progress. We often discussed alternate strategies."

"And these notes are . . . where?"

"At home." Immediately understanding his misstep, he shook his head. "I know, I know, we aren't supposed to take anything from the facility, but I did it for just this purpose. The experiments were so important and I thought if the notes ever got . . . lost or . . . whatever . . . I keep them in a bulletproof, triple-locked briefcase, ma'am. No one knows they're in there but me. No one knows the combination but me."

"Speaking of combinations," Jocelyn said, settling her best interrogation stare on Abrute. "Cash has a very important key—a physical, metal key—and we haven't been able to find it."

"Oh . . ." His gaze dropped, skipped around as he thought, then shook his head. "I don't know anything about a key. I haven't seen it."

"Sergeant Decker," Jocelyn called.

"I'm sorry," Abrute's face flushed beneath his dark skin. "I—"

"Take Mr. Abrute back home to get his notes, please." Then she turned her attention to Abrute. "As long as that briefcase comes back to me tonight, notes intact, you will suffer no harm. Do you understand?"

Breathing hard now, eyes watery, Abrute exhaled a quick breath. "Oh, yes, ma'am. I understand, ma'am."

When the door closed behind a blabbering Abrute, she kept her gaze on the blobs of color progressing down the stone hallways in the adjacent building. Once this was over, she would research Abrute. If he'd had associations with anyone less than pristine, if Cash's accusation of Abrute smuggling secrets was true, the man was dead.

But, first things first.

"Commander."

"Yes, ma'am."

"It's time to get rid of this team." She could already feel the relief. "Get your men down there. Get every member of that team herded into one location and blow . . . them . . . up. And while you're at it, destroy the lab. Make sure there is nothing left of them or that facility when you're done."

A beat of silence passed.

"Everything, ma'am?" The tremor of disbelief in his voice didn't instill Jocelyn with confidence. "This is a state-of-the-art facility with—"

She gave him her do-it-or-else stare. "What part of *nothing left* didn't you understand, commander?"

Three.

Cash crouched into the corner of the holding cell.

Two.

Wrapped his arms over his head.

One.

Took a deep breath and held it.

The explosion washed Cash with fiery heat. Compressed his body against the concrete wall. Smashed his eardrums. His heart slammed against his ribs. A voice in his head urged him to *move out.*

When he lifted his head, Cash swore his brain slid sideways inside his skull. Smoke filled the cell and he had a moment of complete disorientation. He pressed his palms against the cold concrete, inched himself to his feet. Blinked away the bright white spots floating in his vision and shoved off the wall. Hands out in front of him, he groped through the now empty doorway and turned left.

"Freeze."

The female voice shocked the hell out of him. And he couldn't see a goddamned thing. With one hand on the wall to orient himself, he pushed his shoulders back and faced the voice. They didn't know how much he could or couldn't see.

"You may as well shoot me," he said, focusing to slow his breaths, " 'cause I'm not backing down."

His eyes adjusted slowly. He strained to make out the figures—their size, their number. He could take one down on his own, weapons or no weapons. Two, probably, since he already knew one was a woman. Three, maybe, if his adrenaline was running high and luck was on his side. More than that, forget it. But dying would be better than suffering in this shit hole a moment longer.

The lead pulled her head away from her scope. Cash barely detected the move, thought he was mistaken. Then she lowered her weapon. Just two inches. But it was the wrong move he'd been waiting for.

He ducked and charged. The crown of his head smashed against Kevlar. Pain tore through his skull. He grasped for the weapon, wrenched it out of her hands, and used it as leverage to spin her until her back was toward him, then brought the rifle down at her neck. With one yank, he dragged her against his body, the subgun across her trachea.

Something's wrong. That was too easy.

"I don't want to hurt anyone—" He spoke low in her ear. Not steady, but at least he didn't scream like he wanted to. "I just want *out.*"

"I know." Her voice was far too soft. Too understanding. Especially when she was trying to rake in air. "We're going . . . to get you . . . out."

Even if she'd been trying to trick him, he should have heard more fear. Then her hands released the weapon and covered his. Gently. When they should have been prying and clawing. She didn't struggle. Didn't attack.

Confusion set him off balance. He knew how to fight. He didn't know how to *not* fight.

"We're here . . ." She drew a raspy breath. "To take you . . . home. It's me, Cash. It's . . . Keira."

In the split second his mind stopped working, a gun found its way to his head. Then a male voice to his ears. "Drop the weapon."

"Teague," the woman said. "Turn on your flashlight."

The man holding some type of handgun at Cash's head flipped on a light, the beam pointed toward the floor. Cash assessed the scene quickly—two men, one woman, military camouflage, heavy-duty weaponry, night vision.

"Look at her." The man tipped the light toward the woman's chest, illuminating her face.

She flinched, turned her head to the side. "Teague," she snapped. "Get that out of my eyes."

Cash shifted to glance at her profile from his position behind her. The first thing he focused on was the freckles. A trail across her cheek, fading as they reached her cheekbone. Then that small nose. Those long black lashes.

A cold stream of shock trickled through his chest.

He ignored the weapon still pointed at him, lifted the rifle over her head, swiveled, and pushed her against the wall with the gun across her shoulders.

She lifted a hand to rub at her throat and cracked her lids, squinting against the light. Deep, smoky-blue irises peeked out.

"Oh, God," Cash murmured. "Oh, my God."

Keira. It really was Keira.

He released her, dropped the weapon, and stepped back, bumping into a hard body behind him.

"Wh-wh—?" What did he even want to ask? Where did he even start? "What—? When—? How—?"

Keira's grin glimmered and that lopsided dimple appeared. "That's a lot to answer at the moment. Can we get out of here first? I have the same questions for you."

A sound grumbled out of his chest. Emotions mingled

into an indescribable sensation. He swept her into his arms and held her as tight as the muscles in his arms allowed.

"Mateo," he whispered into her hair. "My . . . my son . . ."

"He's fine. And he's safe."

Gratitude swamped his throat. He swallowed hard and eased back. "There's another man, a prisoner—"

"Q," she said. "We know. The other half of our team is getting him."

"Thank you." He breathed a sigh of relief, turned, and pressed a kiss to her cheek. "I'm sorry for everything," he whispered. "I'm so, so sorry."

She hugged him back, a quick, fierce squeeze, before prying him away. "Don't you dare make me cry in front of all these guys. We have to move or we may not get out of here at—"

A *shhh-thump* sounded down the hall, coming toward them. Then a bouncing *clink-clink-clink* ending ten feet away. Then . . .

Ka-boom.

The grenade registered in Keira's mind a millisecond before it exploded. Everything slowed to quarter-time.

Cash swiveled, putting his body between hers and the threat and shoved her toward the floor, then came down over her. "Grenaaaaaade!"

She hit the concrete hard. Knees and palms first, followed by her chest and belly. Cash on top of her. Before the brain-shattering roar had ceased, Cash was on his feet, dragging her up.

He jogged backward, pulling her down the hallway in retreat; Teague and Seth were already ahead of them. With the weapon still in one hand, her arm in the other, Cash fired in the direction the grenade had come from.

Teague turned a corner and waited until they caught up. He pulled an extra pair of night goggles from his fatigue jacket pocket and handed them to Cash, who pulled them on and adjusted them like a pro.

"Which way out?" Teague's question sounded muffled to Keira's still-ringing ears. He had his map out, shining his mini-flashlight on the maze.

"This way." Cash took a step, but Keira pulled him back.

"No. We came in through tunnels that haven't been used in decades." She pulled out her own map and found her fingers numb and clumsy and handed it to Cash. "Here."

While the men looked at the map, Keira tuned into her senses, but if any voices sounded in her ears they were drowned by the continuing ring.

Cash's gaze skipped between the map and the hallways. "I thought these were a myth."

"Mateo told us about them," Keira said. "He's the reason we have this map. The reason we got in. But that's a story for the outside. Let's get out of here before they decide to throw another grenade."

"Uh . . ." Seth peered around the edge of the rock. "Too late."

Shhhhhhh-thump-thump. The device bounced off the cement floor, hit the rock wall, and ricocheted. *Clink-clink-clink-clink.* It rolled to a stop at Cash's feet.

A collective gasp seemed to draw the air from the passageway.

In a move worthy of a hockey pro, Cash smacked the explosive with the end of Keira's M14. It zigzagged back down the hallway. *Clink*—against one wall. *Click*—against the opposite wall. *Ka-boom.* Several terrorized shouts followed the fireball.

"Bull's-eye." Cash grinned, and Keira turned five years old again. Same five-year-old flippy stomach, same five-year-old fluttering heart. This was her big brother.

"That's a nice exiting remark," Teague said, leading the way through the corridors, map in hand.

Boots and shouts echoed somewhere behind them.

"Pick up the pace." Cash shoved Keira's shoulder.

She pulled her Glock and glanced over her shoulder as she ran. Left, veer right, hard right, left. After that, Keira lost track. Had they come this far? If it weren't Teague leading the way, she might question. But she'd walked through too many fires with this man. Trusted her life to him too many times to doubt now.

Footfalls came from the right as they approached another intersection. Teague ran through, but Seth didn't make it. A body T-boned him from the other corridor. Keira skidded to a halt, anticipating followers. Another guard passed right in front of her. Before she could make any offensive move, Teague swung his M14 and hit a home run against the man's neck. A loud snap, a grunt, and the guard pitched to the floor, face-first.

She followed the fight between Seth and the other guard. The men rolled on the cement, each with one arm extended overhead, battling for control of a handgun. Keira aimed at the pair. She was good with moving targets, but with this murky alien vision, both men in fatigues, both men wearing helmets with night vision, both men roughly the same size, she couldn't tell who was who.

She concentrated, scanned the men for the smallest telltale sign. Then she saw it, the thigh holster. One man had it, one man didn't. She aimed at the leg of the man without. Not as big a target as the chest, but she doubted her handgun would penetrate body armor.

"Drop it," she yelled. "Drop your weapon!"

In the second she gave the enemy to respond, instead of ceasing his struggle, his free hand grappled for the nine-millimeter at Seth's thigh and yanked it from its holster.

Keira fired. The man jerked, screamed, rolled off Seth. Lifted the handgun. Keira took aim at his head and squeezed her trigger. His head hit the cement. Arm fell to his side. Gun clattered against the concrete. Teague stepped in and swept up the weapon.

Peripherally, she registered Cash, standing off to the side, staring. Mixed emotions swirled from him like a hurricane. He wasn't quite sure about all of them. All of this. Keira understood. Neither was she.

Keira dropped to one knee at Seth's side. "Are you hit?"

"No." He was breathing hard, his eyes wide and shining demon green in her night vision, his face splattered with blood. "No, I'm . . . okay." He rolled to his feet. "Let's get the fuck out of here."

TWENTY

Luke's heart nearly leaped out of his chest when he rounded the corner where he'd heard the last gunshots.

With his subgun up and scanning, he took in the murky green scene. The bodies on the ground. His heart iced over. "Ours or theirs?"

Not Keira. Please not Keira.

"Theirs." Teague's voice.

A shallow breath puffed from his lungs. He didn't lower the gun but relaxed his grip and scanned faces and body structure more closely. Cash's civilian clothing registered, but Luke didn't relax until he'd located Keira. In one piece. On her own two feet. Breathing.

Relief rolled up his throat.

"There's more coming," Kai said from behind him. "Let's get out."

"Keira—" Cash took hold of her arm. "What about Q?"

"He wasn't in his cell," Luke said. "And it had been tossed, like someone was looking for something."

"Sonofabitch." Cash dropped Keira's arm; his gaze fell to the floor.

"Come on." Luke stood to the side of the corridor to allow the others to pass, waving his gun. "Out. Go." When Cash passed, Luke gripped his upper arm. "You, wait."

He popped open his fatigue jacket, slid his arms out, jerked at the straps of his vest, and pulled it over his head.

Keira turned. "What are you doing?"

"He needs this more than I do."

Her expression softened for an instant before solidifying again. She nodded once.

"I'm not taking his—" Cash started.

"Put it on, Cash." Her voice took on an impatient bite.

He followed orders, scowling with discontent. Luke didn't blame the guy. If the situation were reversed, he wouldn't want to take another soldier's vest, either.

Only ten yards away from the entrance to the tunnel, the familiar boot-beat sounded from both ahead and behind.

Trapped. Their only chance was to beat the guards to the entrance.

A group of four came into sight ahead of them, at equal distance to the exit as their team. Luke yelled, "Go, go, go!"

Fifty feet from the entrance, the enemy quad skidded to a stop. One of them counted, "One, two, three." All four drew their arms back.

The future fast-forwarded through Luke's mind—the toss, the explosion, the carnage.

His feet pushed, legs pumped. He opened his arms and slammed into Keira, Cash, and Seth. They, in turn, shoved Mitch, Teague, and Kai into the mouth of the final tunnel, and out of the direct line of fire.

Still, that wouldn't be enough. Not near enough.

Shhh-thump . . . shhh-thump . . . shhh-thump . . . shhh-thump sounded nearly simultaneously. Then a rain of *clink-clink-clink . . . clink-clink-clink . . .*

Luke's stomach went cold. "Run!"

He sprinted past the exit tunnel's opening, past his team, scrambling for traction on the cement floor. He dropped his weapon, set his stance wide, and stretched his arms overhead until he was a human X blocking the corridor.

The blast hit him with the force of a hurricane. Heat seared with the intensity of an inferno. He might not burn, but that didn't mean he didn't *feel* like his skin was being peeled off his bones. One inch at a time.

Luke turned his face from the brunt of the hit, gritted his teeth, and tensed every muscle to keep himself in place. White-hot fire flashed with each explosion, blinding him. The roar of combustion drove into his ears, spearing his brain like twin knives. Then he heard nothing but an incessant thunder rolling through his head. Every inch of his body screamed with pain. His blood boiled in every vessel, right down to the smallest capillary. He fisted his hands, let out a yowl that rumbled up from the soles of his feet.

The only thing keeping him holding on was the fact that not one spark made it past him. His team—his family, his friends, the love of his life—was safe.

When the explosion ebbed, the fire found nothing to gnaw but cement, and the flames quickly died. As quickly as Luke's energy evaporated.

His legs gave. He dropped to the ground, landed on the cement knees-first with a painful *crack*, then fell forward, turning his head just in time to avoid smashing every front tooth. His cheek hit the concrete instead, and a *snap* sounded near his ear. Pain radiated through the side of his face. A telltale signal of a cracked cheekbone, temple, or jaw. Which also verified what his body was already telling him—his powers had been drained.

"Luke!" Despite the urgency in Keira's voice, it seemed to be filtered through a pillow. "Pick up your weapon. Luke!"

Distantly, pops echoed in his ears. Gunshots? The cement vibrated beneath his cheek. Footsteps?

Luke! Please! Fight!

He couldn't tell if she was projecting, if he was reaching, or if he was just hallucinating. But it didn't matter.

Holding his breath against the pain, he pushed up on his hands, his eyes scanning for the M14. Six inches out of reach. Six inches that may as well have been six miles.

He gritted his teeth, made one final push, and lunged for the gun.

A kick to the chest knocked him back. The kick of a bullet. An explosion ripped through the left side of his body. Followed by fire. His breath stuck in his lungs. His teeth locked together. All he could do was writhe.

Keira's voice dragged his eyes open again. He didn't know how much later. Seconds? Minutes? Couldn't have been long, because the Castle's high ceiling blurred gray-green in his night vision goggles.

She was babbling. Yelling one minute. Coddling the next. Leaning over him with an expression of such agony he was sure he had to be dying.

"Breathe, you idiot." Keira tapped the side of his face as if trying to get him to wake up.

It worked. His lungs inflated, swamping him with a searing pain that forced a growl from the pit of his stomach.

"Come on, baby, fight. Do it for me. I need you." Keira's hands scraped through his hair, holding his head tight as she pressed her cheek to his. Whispering in his ear. Babbling again. ". . . we can be together . . ." ". . . we can be a family, have a family . . ." ". . . I can't lose you . . ." ". . . we'll find a way, Luke . . ."

He couldn't make sense of anything. His brain faded in and out. Pain shot nausea into his gut.

"Teague!" The nervous edge to her voice was not reassuring. She pressed her hand against the left side of his chest, and another stab of pain cinched his lungs.

Teague bent over him, face etched with worry. "We don't have time for this shit, Luke."

"He's bleeding bad." Her voice came out low, as if she were sharing a secret, but shaky with fear.

"I can hear you." Luke kept his teeth clenched against the pain. "I'm right here."

Teague took a deep, troubled breath. He curled and released the fingers of both hands several times. "Heat," he said. "You're going to feel lots of heat. I'm not going to heal you. No time, I'm just going to stop the bleeding."

"I'll . . . take what I . . . can get."

Teague replaced Keira's palm with his own. He rested on one knee at Luke's side, head bent in concentration. Keira stood, her weapon scanning one end of the hall, then swinging to the opposite side.

Luke's vision blurred with the onslaught of lava flowing through his chest. But instead of pain, the fiery sensation brought relief. Within twenty seconds, Luke was pushing Teague's hands away and struggling to sit up.

"Guess you're feeling better." Teague stood, put out a hand, and dragged Luke up by his good arm. "But getting you up that ladder without using that arm will be . . . entertaining."

He couldn't say he was feeling better, only that his mind had come back from a wasteland, but it was still working like garbage.

Shouts channeled down the corridor and pushed them into action. Teague pulled Luke's good arm around his shoulders, and Keira covered their backs as they headed for the ladder. Pain lanced Luke's shoulder, chest, ribs. His whole damn upper body.

By the time they reached the end of the tunnel, Luke had the strength of a rag doll and faded in and out of consciousness. Urgent orders drifted through his clouded mind, but he didn't understand them. Keira continued to touch him, whisper, but he couldn't process.

He gave his head a hard shake, hoping to clear it. Kai started up the shaft toward the exit. Then Seth. Then Mitch.

At the top, Kai lifted the door an inch and peered out,

then grunted as he pried the door up and groaned when he tried to flip it back.

"Get out of the way, lightweight," Seth said. "You're gonna get hurt."

Within seconds, the hatch laid wide open, stars glittering in the midnight-blue sky beyond, beckoning like a dream. Luke yearned to let go of all the physical and mental pain and just float into that tranquility.

But when Keira crossed the strap of her M14 over her chest, threw the weapon over her back, and looked at both Teague and himself with that stern warrior gaze, Luke knew there would be no tranquility in the near future. She curled her fingers around the first cold metal rung and said, "Hustle, guys."

"Easier said than done." Teague secured Luke against him with an arm at his waist, leaving one arm free to climb. "You're gonna have to help me out here, Luke. Push with your legs, or those guards are gonna be climbing up our asses in about sixty seconds."

Luke fisted his hand in the shoulder of Teague's fatigue jacket, kept his injured arm tight to his side, and pushed with all the strength he had left in his legs for the awkward, treacherous climb. How he would trek across the desert back to the vehicles after this, he couldn't imagine. But he'd worry about that when the time came, because by the sound of footsteps coming up behind them, they were about to go another round with those fucking guards.

They were halfway to the top when gunfire split the air. Bullets pinged off the metal, blew chunks of slate off the wall.

Teague turned into a rocket, jetting up the remaining steps, dragging Luke with him. Pain shot the length of his torso. Cut off his air.

Return shots from overhead burst in Luke's ears, followed by multiple grunts and the immediate cessation of enemy fire.

"Grab him," Teague called to the team above.

Oh, God, no. Don't.

A myriad of hands dove into the hole. Luke tried to brace for the pain, but it did no good. He felt as if his arms were being torn out of their sockets. As if his ribs were being peeled away one by one.

He tried not to scream. Kept the agony locked behind clenched teeth until that final show of force to drag his body over the lip of the entrance.

The pain swallowed him.

His brain went gray.

The last thing he heard before black washed over him was Mitch yelling, "Grenaaaaade!"

Keira dug her boots into the sandy dirt and pulled with all her strength alongside Cash, Seth, and Kai. The scream Luke finally let loose tore at her soul. By the time she had his head resting in her lap, he was unconscious and she was ready to puke from pure terror.

She'd watched those ferocious flames twine and curl around his body, trying to eat him alive. Seen his body jerk, twist, and flip when the bullet hit his chest. But the worst, the very bone-chilling, mind-altering worst, had been the spill of Luke's warm blood through her fingers as she'd tried to compress his wound.

Bile rolled toward her throat. She swallowed it back, concentrated on his warm skin under her fingers.

Teague's hands planted on the earth, and he hefted his body out of the hole in one muscled push-up. Seth and Mitch already had the doors halfway closed as he rolled out of the way.

The heavy *plunk-plunk-plunk* of metal on metal sounded

as the hatch shut. A plume of gritty dirt billowed when the men dropped the steel hatch, followed by an earth-muffled series of explosions.

The ground beneath them shook so hard, Keira feared it might cave and dump them right back into that wretched tunnel. But the shaking stopped and silence rushed in, the only sound their team's heavy breathing. Each tensed, prepared for the next crisis.

"Guess that maneuver backfired." Mitch broke the silence with his typical sarcasm. "Pun intended."

"Teague." Keira fought to keep her voice level. She slid her hand against Luke's neck, his pulse erratic under her fingers. "Can you do anything for him?"

Teague tore open Luke's jacket to expose his blood-soaked shirt. "You mean besides throwing him over my shoulder and carrying him to the truck?"

As Teague pressed his hand to the wound, Keira kept her fingers on Luke's pulse with one hand, stroked his whisker-roughened cheek with the other. He was willing to sacrifice so much for her. She would find a way to do the same for him. He just had to live.

"Mitch," Teague said. "Get Alyssa on the phone."

"I told you I shouldn't have taken the vest." The unfamiliar voice forced Keira to refocus. Cash had crawled up next to her, his expression filled with guilt and concern, and pressed his own fingers to Luke's neck.

Her guilt for allowing Luke to give the vest away nagged at her. One more thing to make up to him. They had to find a way to be together, because it would take the rest of her life to make things right.

"He's too fucking stubborn to die," Teague said. "He'll be fine. This will only slow him down and shut him up for a little while. We should enjoy it while we can."

"Hey—" Mitch called their attention and pointed to the Bluetooth in his ear. "Get on the line."

Everyone clicked on and Alyssa's controlled but stressed voice filled Keira's ear.

"We were making small talk about Panos's childhood in Greece," she said. "Someone came to his door, which he thought was odd because he wasn't expecting anyone. I heard the locks as he turned them, heard the hinges of the door squeak when he opened it. Then a pop. Just one. Then that crackle you get when someone drops the phone. I called his name, but he didn't answer. Then the line went dead."

"Did you try calling him back?" Mitch asked.

"Are your men still at the house?" Teague asked at the same time. "Do they know?"

"Yes and yes," Alyssa said, amazingly efficient. "I called back and got no answer. The men here know and they've called in reinforcements."

Fear pulled at Teague's features. "Hang tight, baby. We'll be home soon."

A tremor shook the ground. Small, barely there. But it sent a shiver up Keira's spine. She was just about to ask if anyone else felt it when the familiar *whap-whap-whap* invaded her head.

"Damn," she whispered, her gaze searching for cover. None. "Choppers coming."

"Choppers?" Kai asked. "As in more than one?"

"More than one." She couldn't tell how many. "Two for sure. Maybe three." She pushed at Luke's shoulders, lifting him toward Teague. "I'm going to take you up on that offer. You carry, I'll shoot."

"I don't hear any—" Cash's statement was interrupted by the swoosh of a chopper as it crested the Castle and dove toward them. He rolled to a crouch, M14 in hand.

"Do you speak Greek?" Keira asked him.

He sent her a distracted look. "What?"

"Greek. Your son speaks Greek. Do you?"

"It's rusty—"

"Better than nonexistent. Just translate what he says to you the best you can."

"I don't understand—"

"I'll explain later." Another chopper swung in from the north, panning its beam along the ground. "If you want to get out of this alive, talk to your son."

"That's not what I need to hear." Alyssa's voice floated into the black night. "It was disturbing enough to hear a man I didn't know get shot thousands of miles away."

A third chopper came in from the south. All three swept the area with floodlights. All three had artillery jutting from their flanks. All three had a man in fatigues hanging out the side door with a subgun in his hands.

"Sorry, Lys," Keira said. "Can you get Mateo talking to us? We need an escape route."

"He's right here, looking at the phone like it's a pastry." Alyssa clicked the phone to speaker. "Go ahead."

But Mateo was the first to speak. *"Baba! To'ksera oti tha erthis gia mena, baba!"*

Cash sucked in an audible breath. He opened his mouth, but nothing came out.

The choppers made another sweep, closing their search circles.

"Cash," Keira nudged.

He nodded and finally spoke, his Greek coming in fits and starts with lots of hesitation and 'ums' in between. But the two evidently communicated, because Cash turned and started into the desert at a forty-five-degree angle to where their vehicles were parked.

"Follow me," he said.

"The trucks are over there."

"But he says cover is over *there*." He lifted his chin in the direction he was headed. "Those choppers are going to close in fast. Let's go."

All Keira saw was rolling desert terrain in the distance. Then again, she hadn't known that hatch had been there, either. Mateo had a one hundred percent accuracy rate so far. No sense in doubting it now.

Teague hefted Luke over his shoulder and fell into line with the others. To keep her eyes off the sickening sight of Luke's limp body swaying with every step Teague took, Keira brought up the rear, watching the choppers turn in smaller and smaller circles, twisting her stomach in tighter and tighter knots.

"How much farther?" she called ahead.

"He's not sure," Cash said. "He says we might be halfway."

"Remember," Mitch said, "he's not good with distances."

Keira swore, cutting her eyes between the untraveled path beneath her feet and the threat above her head, already creating plans A, B, C, and D. "What kind of cover?"

"A bunker they used for training."

"Who used? What training?"

"The government, and who knows? We're on the edge of Area Fifty-one. Nobody but insiders knows what happens here."

"Seems to be a lot of that going around," she muttered.

Above, one of the choppers made a sharp turn, picked up speed, and swooped their way. Keira's stomach dropped.

"We've been spotted," she called. "Run!"

But as soon as the words were out of her mouth, she knew Teague would never make it anywhere near fast enough carrying Luke. The chopper was moving too fast.

Within seconds, the pop of rapid-fire weaponry tattered the air. The thud of bullets hitting the ground cascaded across the desert floor only a foot away. Her heartbeat spiked. An involuntary scream rose in her throat. She kept moving, kept pushing forward, as mini-plumes of dust created a temporary veil of concealment. When the next chopper swooped in the first's wake, his shots were more than five feet off-target.

The other five men were a good twenty yards ahead of Teague, Luke, and Keira now, weaving to make themselves difficult targets. The chopper's windstorm picked up grit and blew it into their eyes. Teague swore and spit. Keira's eyes burned like they were on fire.

Another round of shots startled her. She hadn't seen the third bird coming. Didn't know how close they'd hit. She stopped and turned, searching for the enemy. They were diving right at her, the artillery mounted on either side of the chopper sparking orange in the night.

She tripped over a clump of brush, fell backward. The chopper bore down on her. The panicked call of her name drowned in the bird's churning engine, the burst of gunfire.

In that instant she knew she was going to die. But, dammit, she was going to make sure those goddamned sons of bitches died with her.

She aimed her gun, focused the pilot in her crosshairs, and pulled the trigger. Held it down as she panned her weapon, tracking the chopper's trajectory.

Pang-pang-pang-pang . . . Her bullets continued to punch metal and glass. The dirt around her kicked up as a storm of gunfire from the chopper hit. She curled into the smallest target possible. The angry roar of the engine changed pitch. Angled downward. Then the ground convulsed. Followed by an ear-piercing crash of metal.

Stray shrieks and scrapes of metal continued to erupt from the downed chopper as Keira finally drew air. And promptly choked on sand. Still coughing, she repositioned her helmet and night vision and scanned the terrain. The helicopter lay in a smoking pit of sand, blades winding down like a broken windmill half a mile away. She scrambled to her feet and took off in the direction the others had gone. Luckily, none were in sight, which she had to assume meant they'd found the bunker. Now, if she could just find it before the other choppers—

Seth's earlier words rattled in her head. *Too late.*

An engine growled behind her, becoming a roar in her ear as it grew closer. Keira sprinted, pushing as far as she could before she turned, set her stance, and aimed.

This chopper started shooting sooner. So did Keira. She aimed at the gas tank, a larger target than the pilot. Her chest filled with adrenaline-laden vengeance. And it was intoxicating. She pulled the trigger and held it down with all her strength, letting the rifle kick her shoulder again and again as she trailed the chopper overhead and away, relishing that familiar, repeated *pang-pang-pang* of metal.

Droplets hit her face, as if it had started to rain. Then the pungent, unique scent of aircraft fuel reached her nose and satisfaction filled her chest. But not for long.

A burn in her right thigh dragged her attention to her fatigues and a dark stain growing there. "Dammit."

When she tried to take a step, her leg went out from under her and she landed in the dirt. Pain dug in, transformed into a deep, piercing throb that traveled like poison in the blood.

"Are you hit?" The voice startled her. She swung her weapon up and around with one hand, the other pressed against the wound on her thigh. "Whoa. It's only me."

Cash looked down at her. She dropped her weapon, her gaze turning back to the sky and the third chopper making a final, tight turn toward them. "Get back to the bunker."

"You're coming with me." He bent to pick her up, sliding one arm under her knees and one low on her back.

"No time." She pushed him away. The last helicopter came at them with all the fury of revenge for its lost comrades. "Cash . . . Shit." No time to run. "Get the fuck down."

Keira lifted her rifle. The gun fell from her hand, tumbling end over end, stopping five feet away. Her arm dropped to her side. When she looked down in panicked confusion, she saw another stain of blood spreading over her sleeve.

"Goddammit!"

She looked up at the chopper again. Red flashed on either side of the gun pods—missile ports ignited. Yep, they were officially pissed off and going to make sure there was nothing left of her to bury.

"Cash, run!"

He laughed, the sound an evil, vengeful chuckle. "And miss this fun? No way."

The helicopter angled in. Two missiles shot from the bird's tubes. *Pop-shhhhh-boom.* Cash covered Keira with his body. She curled into his protection as the world exploded around her. If she died, at least she wouldn't die alone. She'd found her family. But Luke . . . God, how she'd miss Luke.

Plumes of fire ebbed to smoke, then to sand and dirt.

Cash stood, drew his arm back, and bulleted something toward the chopper on its way out of the swoop, yelling, "Lousy aim, jerkoff!"

Another explosion. Midair. Huge. Violent. The chopper burst into a fireball, pieces flying off in every direction. Blades, gunpods, wheels, tail rocketing at the desert floor in a three-hundred-sixty-degree trajectory.

Cash covered Keira again and ducked his head. She watched from his protective hold as the chopper's momentum carried the remaining bulk of the bird toward the compound. Toward one of the buildings on the east side of the property. The fireball smashed into the building.

The crash initiated another explosion, one that seemed to come from within the building. A second later another explosion. And another. A chain reaction, ravaging the entire compound.

Keira's mind jumped back to the warehouse fire. The way those barrels had exploded with unexpected violence, taking out everything around them. "What the hell was in there?"

Cash pulled away from her and stood, hand to his forehead in distress. "Chemicals. A shitload of fucking chemicals. It hit the lab. God," he ground out with anguish. "I hope Q . . . I hope they took Q out before . . ."

As Keira watched the fire destroy building after building, portions of the flames shifted from neon orange to purple. At the center of some of the explosions, cobalt blue sparks jetted against the violet flames.

Yeah, there were chemicals in there, all right. The sense of satisfaction, of payback, of a certain justice rendered was there, but veiled by Cash's tormented concern for Q's fate.

Keira scooted toward her gun and studied the sky. What next? Would they send out the air force after them now?

But as the compound continued to burn and explosions continued to burst, she wondered if there would be anyone left alive in that facility to send anyone anywhere for any reason. Including Dargan.

As Cash leaned down to pick her up, three dark figures ran toward them from the bunker. Mitch, Kai, and Seth, coming to their aid.

"Just help me up," she said. "I can walk."

The three men crouched near them. Kai scanned the blood on her pants. "How bad?"

"I'll be okay," she said. "How's Luke?"

"You mean besides bitching at Teague to stop working on him and let him up to come out here to get you?"

Cash cast her a sidelong look. She couldn't tell if the suspicion in his familiar blue eyes came from the topic of Teague or Luke. Or both. "We have a lot to talk about."

TWENTY-ONE

"Shit, Teague." Luke squirmed beneath the press of his friend's hand. "I'm fine now. Keira needs—"

"Keira's got four big strong guys out there with her, none of whom she really *needs*. We need her more than she needs us."

I need you. Hadn't she said that to him in the tunnel? Along with *we can be a family, have a family.*

Now, with the pain ebbing, his wound healing, his brain came together, but everything she'd said to him while he'd been floating through different conscious states seemed to elude certainty.

Regardless of what she'd said or hadn't said, nothing would quell the urge to get to her. To see to her safety himself.

While Teague's healing powers poured into Luke's chest, he watched the bunker's entrance, willing Keira to appear. And with each lengthening moment that no silhouettes took shape, Luke's stomach dropped lower and his heart rate hiked higher.

All the moments in which he could have lost her over the last few days replayed in his mind, and the same question plagued him after each scenario—could he have lived without her? He kept coming back to the same answer—unequivocally, no.

And that very real fact put the fear of God into him now.

Luke used his good arm to grip Teague's wrist, pull his hand off the front of his throbbing chest, and push it away. "I can't just sit here."

As he stumbled to his feet, voices sounded from the bunker entrance. Luke moved that way, holding his arm to his side, grimacing against the pain. The group arrived, but all Luke could focus on was Keira, clinging to Cash as she hobbled forward.

Keira's gaze lifted and locked on his. The physical pain in her eyes mirrored what he felt in his body.

"Teague!" Luke yelled.

"I'm right here," he said from a step behind. "You don't have to scream."

Teague went directly to Keira and started unbuttoning her jacket.

"How bad is it?" Luke drew close, supporting her opposite Cash.

She shook her head, her beautiful face twisted with pain. "They're nothing. They just hurt like a sonofa*bitch*."

Luke almost laughed, but he choked on a sudden, gut-wrenching wave of gratitude. She was alive. He was alive. They had another chance to make things right between them.

"You can't be serious," she muttered.

Luke's chest tightened. Had she read his thoughts? Rejected them?

But her gaze had gone distant, the way it did when she was hearing something in her head. She used her good arm and swung her weapon toward the sky. "Another chopper."

Luke squinted into the night, strained his ears, but heard nothing beyond the sound of the distant fire. Then lights appeared, like stars against the dark, growing brighter. A second later, the familiar whap of blades.

Mitch put a restraining hand on her arm. "Don't shoot our rescue, babe. This one is friendly."

Mitch lifted his arms and waved them overhead, and the chopper lowered.

Grit kicked up in the blade's windstorm. A man jumped from the chopper and approached Mitch, shook his hand, slapped him on the shoulder. As he turned toward the group, Luke recognized the face—Joe Marquez. The pilot Mitch had sent to get Luke to the private landing strip in time to intercept Keira's kidnapping.

Marquez moved toward Keira. "Trouble. I knew it the first time I saw you." His smile shifted to a frown as his dark eyes lingered on her injuries. "I bet you came home with bruises and skinned knees every day as a kid."

"Every day." Cash grinned at her side. "Trouble with a capital T."

"Somehow that doesn't surprise me." Marquez glanced at Luke and shook his head. "You two were made for each other." He gestured to the chopper. "Come on. Let's get you both checked out. Load up, everyone. We're on the razor-thin edge of restricted air space here and I'd rather not play chicken with the young guns."

Inside the chopper, Keira sat with Cash's arm around her shoulders, their backs up against the cargo bay wall. The scenario reminded Luke of the way he and Keira had sat together on their ride to Mercy Medical Center just a couple of days ago and made him wonder what he could have done differently.

Trading one spiraling thought for another, Luke pulled out the Bible he'd taken from Q's room and opened it to where the coin separated the pages. He dog-eared the page so he could study the passages there later, hoping to find a clue. To what, he had no idea.

He held out the coin. Conversation in the cargo space ceased.

"What are you doing with that? Here?" Keira asked, her brow furrowed in confusion.

"I got it out of this." He held up the Bible. "In Q's cell."

Keira sucked in a breath and held it. "What am I missing?" Cash asked, his gaze darting from face to face.

"Each of us—I mean our team," Keira said, waving her hand in a collective gesture encompassing those in the cargo space, even though Mitch hadn't been part of their firefighting team at the time, "received that coin five years ago for our 'heroic' performance at a warehouse fire. The fire that caused all this." She swept a look over the other faces in the cargo area. "Do you guys all have your coins?"

Around the group, Seth, Kai, and Teague nodded.

"Well, I have mine, and Luke has his. That leaves Jessica."

"And Quaid." Luke paused. "Or . . . Q."

A heavy silence lingered in the cargo hold. "It's just a coin," Mitch said. "Couldn't they have been made and given to different groups?"

"They're not just coins." Cash narrowed his eyes on the metal piece. "We had them in the military, too. Some are minted specifically for a special team or event and are as unique as the number in the print run."

"Look what they've done so far: Teague, Cash, Mateo. And those are just the ones we know of. What would have kept them from taking others? There had to be others. Why not Quaid?"

"They closed the coffin," Keira said, gaze distant. "They said it was because of his"—she swallowed—"condition. Because he hadn't healed the way the rest of us had, but . . . now . . ."

"Think we should call Jessica?" Seth asked.

"And what?" Kai barked. "Tell her Quaid has been alive all this time, rotting in some jacked-up sci-fi prison? And, oh, by the way, he just died again?"

"That's what he calls me," Cash whispered.

"Who? What?" Luke asked.

"Q." Cash looked up. "He used to call me Sci-Fi because of my work in the lab."

"What can you tell us about him? What did he look like? What did he say about his past?"

"I never saw him." Cash shook his head. "They never let us meet. We talked through the heating vent between our cells. He could be one of you and I wouldn't know it. And we never talked about his past because he had no memory of it. They . . ." He hesitated, cast a look out of the corner of his eye at Keira, then dropped his gaze to the floor of the chopper. "He said they . . . in his words, fucked with his head."

Keira lifted a hand to cover her eyes. Kai swore a string of curses.

"In other words"—Luke's mind immediately centered on Mateo, the chips in his head, and what Cash would do when he found out just what those savages had done to his little boy—"they used him as a science experiment."

Cash lifted his eyes from the floor. Anger floated there, and determination; Luke had seen that look before—in Keira's eyes. "Q was—*is*—a good man. He kept me alive in there. I swore to him I'd make them pay. I'm on board, one hundred and ten percent. Whatever you need. Whatever I can do."

As Cash stared across the cargo space, Luke felt the connection as if they'd known each other for years. As if Cash had always been part of their team. "The reason they put me in that holding cell is because I have the key to a powerful experiment they've had me researching for years and thought I'd hidden in my room. They want that information bad. If we play it right, they'd sell, trade, give us anything, to get it.

"And speaking of keys . . ." He glanced at Keira. "Excuse me in advance."

Cash opened his mouth, stuffed his fingers inside. Luke cringed, fearing the man was going to make himself puke. Instead, he drew a thin, almost clear filament from his throat, the thread growing longer and longer, the way magicians drag never-ending scarves from their sleeves.

He covered his mouth and coughed something into his hand. Then held up a key.

"Good God," Keira said. "How'd you do that?"

"Tied the key to dental floss, floss to a molar, then swallowed it. I have no idea what it goes to, but it's important. It's Dargan's. She had it on a chain around her neck."

Keira tried not to keep checking on Luke from the corner of her eye, but she was growing more worried with each minute further into the flight.

After their short discussion on the coin and the key and Quaid, he'd gone quiet again. And while in the beginning, he'd been shooting off anger and frustration, now his vibes had shifted, resembling something closer to . . . extreme turmoil. But her abilities weren't working at full speed.

"Do you love him even half as much as he loves you?" Cash's voice brought her attention around again.

"What? Wh—?" She started to ask who, but her brother's gaze was locked on Luke across the cargo bay. Luke had his knees drawn up, his good arm curved around them, his chin propped on his forearm, and his gaze out the open door, as distant as the horizon brightening with the sunrise. Her heart filled until her entire chest felt tight from the pressure. "Probably twice that much."

"What's keeping you apart?"

In light of the last few days, her fears seemed so . . . insignificant.

"My life isn't exactly family-friendly," she finally said.

"What does that mean?" he chided. "You're going to throw Mateo and me to the wolves once we set down? We're on our own?"

"Of course not."

He glanced at Luke, back at her. Understanding dawned in his eyes. "Keira, if your life is friendly enough for us, it's friendly enough for a family of your own."

She looked at Luke again. Sighed.

"What's the problem?" he prodded.

"I'm not exactly mother material, Cash."

He barked a laugh. "This from the girl who had a hundred dolls? I swear I bought you a new one with every paycheck."

Keira smiled at the memory.

"Remember how you used to sleep with them? Took you hours to get them all ready, brush their hair, their teeth, change their clothes, sing to them, tuck them in. And then—"

"There was no room for me in the bed."

They laughed together. God, it felt so good.

"You always reminded me of that scene in *ET* where the alien is hiding in the stuffed animals."

The moment faded and melancholy drifted in. "I'm not that girl anymore."

"You're anyone you want to be." Cash set serious, knowing eyes on Keira. "Don't let others' mistakes dictate your future. What our mother did, what I did . . . God, there is so much to explain."

"Not now." She squeezed his hand. "We have lots of time."

"I was wrong. Our mother was just a sick bitch. Don't let our problems shape your life. You're so much better than that, Keira. You were born to shine. In any way you choose."

His words created a sweet burn beneath her ribs. Tears stung her eyes.

"I'm not in any position to give you advice, but let me just tell you this. When he looks at you, I see the way I felt about Zoya." His voice took on emotion; his eyes reflected deep pain and deeper love. "You've seen firsthand how fragile life can be. How the person you love most can be taken faster than you can say their name."

He closed his eyes as if the thought was too much for him to bear, pressed his cheek against her head, and squeezed the arm around her shoulder a little tighter. "If I could give you just one piece of advice, Keira, it would be family *is* life. You should be *making time* for everything else. Not the other way around. And I'll be here for you this time. Whatever you need. I'll never leave you again." He pressed a kiss against her temple. "Ever."

For the remaining ten minutes of the flight, Keira closed her eyes and leaned her head against her brother's shoulder, trying to figure out how she was going to fix the gigantic mess she'd made with Luke. Knowing she had Cash's solid support gave her a confidence she'd never had before, and for the first time, she thought she might have caught a glimpse of the underlying structure that kept Alyssa so damn strong—her relationship with Mitch.

The chopper slowed and angled. Keira opened her eyes and found Luke staring right at her. A zing of excitement burst deep in her chest—hot and sweet.

Cash and Jessica had both been robbed of that excitement. Never again would either of them open their eyes to see their true love, their best friend, the one person who knew what they were thinking before they even thought it—no powers necessary.

He looked away as the chopper eased to the ground. The air turbulence wafted through the open door and ruffled Luke's hair. The sunrise drifted over the horizon and lit his face with a healthy glow. Keira's heart burned with that same fiery luminosity.

She waited until Joe set the chopper's runners on the ground and the engine wound down before she sat up and slid from beneath Cash's arm.

"Luke?"

He lifted his eyes to hers for only a second before someone appeared at the open door. Alyssa. She ducked to avoid the hurricane-force winds, holding Mateo in one arm and Kat in the other, her huge belly poking out between them.

"What in the hell?" Teague jumped out the door and grabbed Kat from her arms, then Mateo. "Baby, you should not be carrying these two monsters."

Anticipation had Keira darting a look at Cash. His face had gone slack with what looked like a mixture of love and shock and pain. He seemed frozen against the side of the chopper.

"Oh, my God," he whispered without taking his eyes off Mateo. "My *God,* he's . . . *beautiful.*"

"*Baba?*" Mateo's voice took on a worried edge as his big brown eyes squinted to scour the faces in the dark cargo hold. *"Baba?"*

Keira elbowed Cash. "Hello." She put that *duh* tone in her voice. "That's you."

"Ye-ah." The word came out dry and broken as Cash emerged from his trance. He cleared his throat. "Yeah, buddy. Right here, I mean, um . . . *edw, gio.*"

"*Baba!*" Mateo shrieked, making Keira grimace as the sound pierced her eardrums. Sure of his destination, the boy released the fist he'd had in Teague's fatigue jacket and scrambled from his hold to lunge toward his father. *"Baba! Baba!"*

The moment Cash took hold of the boy, emotion exploded between them, radiating through the cargo space, so strong it nearly knocked Keira off her feet.

Love. Pure, absolute, infinite.

She had experienced milliseconds of the emotion during pristine moments with Kat. In that first touch of Mateo's hand. And she wanted it again. A lot more of it. Forever. She wanted a child to share that bond with. And there was only one man she'd ever want to have that child with.

She looked toward Luke, but he'd averted his gaze from the reunion, slowly scooting toward the open cargo door, his face twisted in pain. But the pain wasn't just physical. That turmoil she'd sensed earlier had grown dark.

"Luke . . ."

"*Tó'ksera óti tha erhósoon gia ména, babá.*" Mateo latched on to Cash with both arms, pushed his face into his father's shoulder, and started to cry.

Then Cash started to cry. He crooned to the boy in Greek, ran a hand over his hair, a thumb over his cheek, pressed a kiss to his forehead.

More tears burned Keira's eyes. "What does it mean?"

"He knew I'd come for him." Cash's handsome face filled with so many emotions it hurt Keira to watch.

"That's the first time he's ever cried." Mateo's whimper made her heart fold like origami. She put a hand against the boy's back and tried to ignore the tears Cash kept wiping away from his own cheeks. "He's been a brave little soldier."

"Speaking of brave little soldiers," Alyssa said, "Luke, get your butt out here. My doctor friend came in early this morning just to look at you." She extended a hand to Cash. "I'm Alyssa. Teague's wife. Welcome home. Keira is family, which makes you family, too." She grinned as Cash took her hand. "Like it or not."

Luke reached the edge of the cargo bay. Keira's attention refocused. The urgency to talk to him tightened her chest. "Wait, Luke?"

Alyssa took Luke's arm, helping him off the chopper.

"You can have him later. I'll take a look at you myself once Luke is settled. Anyone else who needs medical attention—cuts, bruises, bumps, pains, come now or forever keep your mouths shut."

Teague and Alyssa started for the SUVs. He dropped his free arm around her shoulder, and she wrapped an arm around his waist, tilted her face up, and kissed him. When she pulled back, a lightning-bug smile brightened her face. They kissed again. Spoke. Kissed a third time. So much love there. Such a perfect little family.

Luke kept his gaze on the ground as he veered toward the passenger's side of the first of a trio of black SUVs Keira didn't recognize. Alyssa broke from Teague with a pat on his ass and opened the door for Luke, then rounded the driver's side as Teague settled in the back with Kat, and took off.

For a reason Keira couldn't identify, the sight of Luke driving away caused a whip of panic to snap in her chest. "Whoever's coming with me, get in or get on the next bus."

"Uh-uh," Kai cut her off and slid into the driver's seat. "You're not driving with that arm."

"Thia," Mateo said. She turned and found his hand held out to her.

Her heart filled. She took his hand, kissed his palm. "Yes, baby. You and your daddy will always come with me."

With Kai driving, Keira followed the directions already programmed into the GPS system because the vehicle carrying Luke was already out of sight. This sense of panic was new and unwarranted. Illogical.

Keira parked in the lot alongside the same medical building where they'd taken Mateo to retrieve the chip in his neck. Mitch and Seth pulled up behind them. As they emerged from the vehicle, Kai directed each man to cover a different corner of the building.

Keira limped in through the side door and found Alyssa coming out of an exam room, the door closing behind her.

"Is Luke in there?" Keira started in that direction without waiting for an answer. "I want to hear what the doctor—"

"He's getting an X-ray." Alyssa put her fingers around Keira's upper arm and urged her across the hall, toward another room. "He's in good hands." She looked past Keira at Cash, still carrying Mateo. "Teague and Kat are in the waiting room with the toys. Cash, I'll check you out when I'm finished with Keira." She closed the door at her back, pointed to the exam table, and said, "Sit, honey. You don't look so good."

"You say that to me a lot." Keira obeyed but stared at the door. Luke's emotions had her unsettled. No, downright scared. Hadn't he heard anything she'd said to him in the tunnel? Or maybe it had been too little, too late. Maybe she'd broken his heart one too many times.

The rip of fabric drew her gaze down. Alyssa had donned gloves and now split her pants from the thigh down with rescue shears, exposing a very bloody leg. The cool office air licked at the wound, stinging deep into her muscle.

Alyssa sighed. "What a mess." With some gauze and saline, she cleaned the wound. "It's not deep, but I think it's too wide to stitch. Let's see your arm."

Keira shed her fatigue jacket, then let Alyssa cut her shirt sleeve.

"Now this one I can do something about," Alyssa murmured after looking at the wound on her upper arm. "I'm going to leave your leg to Teague. You're damned lucky, Keira."

She knew she was lucky. In more ways than she could count. And her mind was pinging in so many different directions, she couldn't keep them all straight.

Alyssa cleaned the wound on her arm. Her friend's belly rested against her thigh as she worked. The baby thumped. Keira startled and pulled away.

"He won't bite. Won't even get teeth for another six months." Alyssa lifted Keira's hand and pressed it to the belly bulging beneath her thin sweater. "You've never felt him, have you?"

"Uh, no." She watched Alyssa's stomach, mesmerized at the roll and thud beneath her hand. Something deep at her core clenched and ached. Brought tears to her eyes. Everything seemed to be twisting her emotions. "That's . . . wow. Amazing. Kind of . . . no offense to the little guy . . . weird. Like you have an alien in there." She pulled her hand away and pointed at Alyssa. "You can't ever tell him I said that."

Alyssa laughed. "As long as I get my belly button ring, my lips are sealed."

"How are you going to keep him safe?" The words drifted from her mouth, more a thought than a solid question. She met Alyssa's surprised eyes. "I mean, what if he's, you know, gifted?"

Alyssa turned to pull supplies from a cabinet, opened them, and started threading a needle.

"You mean how am I going to keep someone from kidnapping him and using him as a guinea pig?"

God, what a terrible thing to say to an expectant mother. Her friends must think she was so twisted. "I'm sorry, Lys. I'm just . . ."

"Worried," she said. "Get used to it if you're thinking about having kids. Starts as soon as you're pregnant and continues until the day you die. I can't ever envision a day I won't be worried about Kat or this baby."

"Great." Keira nodded. "That's reassuring."

Alyssa started stitching. "Maybe some statistics will reassure you. Your chances of dying in a car accident during your lifetime are about one in eighty-seven. Pretty high, right? Do you still drive? Yes. What do you do to keep yourself safe? Wear your seat belt, put your kid in a car seat, buy the safest vehicle, drive defensively, choose your roads carefully, et cetera. Right?"

Keira frowned. "Right."

"And did you know a woman's chance of getting cancer in her lifetime is two in three?"

"Shit, no. Ooops." She winced. "Sorry."

Lys waved away Keira's curse. "Not a lot of control over that, right? So you do what you can—eat healthy, exercise, don't smoke, get your yearly exams, listen to your body. And if something does happen, despite your diligence? You fight it. You get the best experts and fight it with all the modern technology and science you can find."

"I see where you're going," Keira said. "The Special Forces guys, the security system at the house, Teague teaching you how to shoot."

"You know Teague hates guns."

Keira chuckled, watching Alyssa's hands move, piercing her skin, tugging the string, moving on. "I remember. How times have changed. He's good with a rifle."

"He does what he has to do to stay safe and keep us safe." Alyssa grabbed a bandage from the tray and taped it over the stitches on Keira's arm, then gave her an extra squeeze. "The joy our family brings us every moment of every day is worth every second of worry and every extra effort for security."

That was what Keira and Luke would have to do. They'd just have to build safety into their lives like Alyssa and Teague. They'd have to join forces with their extended "family" and now her real family. Circle the wagons, wasn't that what they used to call it in the old days?

A fresh urgency pushed her from the edge of the table. She reached for the door.

"Wait—" Alyssa's voice was edged with surprise. "I need to have Teague—"

"Later."

She crossed the hall, put her hand on the knob, and for a split second thought about stopping to knock, then realized if she didn't keep her momentum up, she'd chicken out again, so she walked right into the exam room.

Luke sat on the end of an exam table, shirt off, fatigue-clad legs dangling over the edge. And, good God, he looked amazingly sexy. His head was bent inspecting some sort of three-fold brochure in his hands as a man in his mid-fifties stood next to him, taping a bandage across the wound high on his chest.

Complex emotions radiated off him in waves.

The doctor stopped midsentence and gave her a look somewhere between shock and annoyance. "Can I help you?"

Luke's gaze jerked toward her. He dropped the brochure he'd been looking at in his lap and sat up straight. The muscles of his chest and abdomen flexed. The sight shot heat from the center of her chest all the way to the soles of her feet.

"I-I-um . . ." She cleared her throat. "He's mine." *What?* "I mean, he's my . . . my . . ." *He's mine,* she wanted to repeat. She made a motion between herself and Luke, growing more self-conscious and frustrated by the moment. "I'm . . . with him."

Luke's eyes sparked, but she couldn't tell if that was a good thing or a bad thing.

Alyssa came in behind her, her hand resting on the knob. "I'm so sorry, Adam. Keira"—her voice held that doctor tone, the one that always made Keira want to say 'yes, ma'am'—"get your butt—"

"It's all right, Lys." Luke brought their heads back around. "She can stay. For now."

For now? Keira clamped her mouth shut and started to cross her arms, then her stitches pulled and she dropped them at her sides again. Alyssa shot her a you'll-pay-for-this-later look and backed out of the room, closing the door behind her.

A moment stood still while both men simply stared at her. The older man finally turned back to taping. Luke continued to look at her as if she'd finally gone and lost her last screw.

"I'm, um, sorry to interrupt, doctor." She shifted her feet, threaded her fingers. "I'm just . . . I've been, you know, worried about him."

Luke's mouth curved. Just one corner. Hardly noticeable. It was the spark of affection in his eyes that clued her in to the grin. Then, as quick as it had come, the warmth vanished and he dropped his gaze to his hands and the paper there.

The dark turmoil within him eased, and Keira's stomach loosened in response.

"So, doc." He lifted a freshly intense look to the doctor, threaded the brochure through his fingers. "When can I do this?"

The other man pressed the last bit of tape to the bandage. "Any time. Just make an appointment with my nurse on the way out."

"For what?" Keira's gaze darted to the paper, now rolled into a tube in Luke's hand. "Do you need a follow-up visit?"

Luke's blue eyes skipped to her again. The remaining anxiety ebbed. A soothing balance and sense of well-being filled its placed. Keira felt it settle on her like a warm light.

He held her gaze a second longer, then refocused on the doctor. "I'd like to do it now."

"Do *what* now?" She stepped toward Luke. "What are you talking about?"

"Don't you want to . . . ?" The doctor's eyes cut to

Keira, then back to Luke. "Take some time to think about it, Luke. You're so young—"

"I've had three years to think about it. I know I don't have an appointment, but I'll pay you in full, in cash, if you do it right here, right now."

Luke's jaw set. She knew that look. Panic leaked into her chest. She jerked the paper out of his hand and scanned the front.

"Vasectomy?" She crunched the brochure in her hand and glowered at Luke. "A *vasectomy*? What the hell, Luke?"

The doctor took off his gloves and rubbed his hands together. "It's really a simple procedure." He directed his reassuring tone toward Keira. "If you're worried about how his chest wound would affect this, it was a through and through. The bullet went in clean and came out clean. I stitched him up, gave him a prescription for antibiotics. He'll need follow-up care, physical therapy, but considering how young and healthy he is, he should be fine."

Sweat broke out on Keira's forehead. For half a second, she allowed herself to imagine a future in which Luke had gone through with the vasectomy. This was an opportunity she would have jumped at a few days ago. All Luke—no kids. Which also meant no facing her past, no fighting her demons, no risk.

It took less than a quarter of a second for a hollow sensation to invade her chest right where her heart lived. And for the first time, she realized that was the fear Luke lived with when he thought of going through life without children of his own, without making a family with her.

"The procedure is done right here in the office," the doctor continued, "with a simple local anesthetic. We have all the latest equipment. Recovery is usually very smooth and quite fast with few side effects—"

"Can you . . ." Keira closed her eyes. "I'm sorry. Can you just give us a minute?"

"Absolutely." He looked at his watch, then with another cautious glance at Keira, turned his gray eyes on Luke. "If you decide you want to do it now, I'll need to know pretty quick."

Luke nodded. "Okay."

As soon as the door closed, words burst from Keira's mouth. "That explosion fried your last brain cell."

A dry laugh scraped out of Luke's throat, but he said nothing. Just pressed one hand to his thigh and stared at her from beneath those golden brows.

Anger, frustration, and a truckload of fear built again. "Stop looking at me like you're waiting for my head to spin around."

"Then stop acting like you're possessed."

"*I'm* not the one asking for a vasectomy on the spur of the moment."

"*You're* not the one with the dick that's keeping us apart."

Her mouth opened, ready to shoot back with another dart, but nothing came out. In fact, nothing even came to mind. Because her mind was in as many knots as her heart.

She blew out a breath. "Didn't you hear me in the tunnel? I told you I wanted to have a family with you."

"You told me that because you wanted me to fight to stay alive."

She swallowed back tears. But there were too many. Remembering the fear of him slipping away from her was too strong. "No." She held out her hands, still tinged red, as wetness slid down her cheeks. "I said that because your blood was seeping through my fingers and I was scared to death I was going to lose you and never have a chance to fix my royal fuck-up."

Luke's warm fingers closed around her wrist and pulled her toward him. He dragged her between his knees and clasped his hands at the small of her back, securing her there.

She ran her fingers over the skin of his chest, grateful for the beat of his blood at the base of his throat. "I'm sorry I'm so messed up. But I love you. And after finding Cash and seeing him reunited with Mateo"—she pressed her forehead to his—"I know that's what I want. A family. With you."

"Baby—" His voice shook. "You are not messed up. Look at me."

She heaved a breath and lifted her eyes to his. And she knew. There was no going back.

"You are *not* messed up. You are perfect. As is. I want you. As is. Only you. Do you hear me? *Only you. As is.*" He brought one hand around to lift her chin up when her eyes dropped away. "Keira, I can live without kids. But I was wrong when I thought I could live without you. You already *are* my family. The only family I need. I'm trying to make a permanent statement here."

Her breath stuttered on every inhale, every exhale. But it wasn't nerves. It was excitement.

She trailed her hands up his chest and let her fingers slide through his hair, wrapped them around the nape of his neck.

"I have a different kind of permanent statement in mind. What do you think of honeymooning somewhere . . . tropical? Lots of water—waterfalls, ocean, beaches, lakes. Not a desert in sight. Somewhere we could have lots of privacy to start working on that family?"

Excitement flashed in his eyes. That luscious mouth lifted in a smile she could look at forever. "Are you asking me to marry you, O'Shay?"

She narrowed her eyes, but smiled back. "Are you in my head again, Ransom?"

"No, baby. You were *projecting*. Loudly."

He brought his hands up to cradle her face between big,

warm, steady palms, and everything inside her calmed. This was exactly where she belonged.

He bent his head and brought their faces close. "And here's my answer."

His mouth covered hers, and a single word resonated in her mind.

Yes.